WHAT DO
WOMEN
WANT?

a novel by

DAN GREENBURG

WYNDHAM BOOKS

NEW YORK

Published by Wyndham Books
A Simon & Schuster Division of Gulf & Western Corporation
Simon & Schuster Building
Rockefeller Center
1230 Avenue of the Americas
New York, New York 10020

WYNDHAM and colophon are trademarks of Simon & Schuster
Designed by Eve Kirch
Manufactured in the United States of America

10   9   8   7   6   5   4   3   2   1

Library of Congress Cataloging in Publication Data

Greenburg, Dan.
  What do women want?
  I. Title.
PS3557.R379W5   813'.54   81-23118
ISBN 0-671-43793-3   AACR2

For technical information on airline safety the author is indebted to Laurence
Gonzales—journalist, author and pilot.

To the memory of Sam Greenburg, my father and teacher

"What do women want?"
                                    —Sigmund Freud

"There aren't any hard women, only soft men."
                                    —Raquel Welch

1

On the last day of May, precisely three weeks before his fortieth birthday, Lance Lerner realized with suffocating clarity that his wife was having an affair with his best friend.

He had once too often walked into a room where the two of them, chatting together *sotto voce*, had abruptly and awkwardly fallen silent at his appearance. He didn't need a house to fall on him.

His first reaction was disbelief—it wasn't possible. His second reaction was belief—it was possible. His third reaction was rage, his fourth was a profound sense of having been betrayed, his fifth a horrid feeling of having been abandoned, his sixth a brief but overwhelming attack of nausea.

His seventh and most enduring reaction was something approaching calmness and acceptance. It was, he reasoned, after all not really so odd that his two favorite people in the world should be attracted to each other. He did not think that Cathy would want to leave him—he'd given her everything, what more could she want? He did not, he was sure, want her to leave him. And yet . . .

And yet this knowledge of his cuckolding—for, everything else aside, that is what it was—had made his marriage disconcertingly lopsided. For a man as compulsive, as *fanatical* about order and balance as was Lance Lerner, this lopsidedness could not be tolerated. It would have to be corrected. Balance would somehow have to be restored if the marriage was going to continue, but what was necessary to tip the scales back to flatness? Some kind of equal and opposite reaction was clearly called for, but what?

And then he knew. It was so simple, really. Even a child could appreciate its simplicity and its appropriateness: to redress the balance of their relationship (a term he hated), he would simply have a brief affair with his *wife's* best friend. The only problem, really, was in determining which of two quite different women that person might be.

Cathy Lerner was, at age thirty, what they called a beauty. Tall, long-boned, both big-breasted and delicately featured—an unlikely combination. Her straight shoulder-length hair was described as either light brown or dishwater blond, but in summer it was always streaked with sunshine. Her eyes varied between gray, blue, green and violet, depending on the weather and her mood—a sort of corneal litmus paper.

Like many beautiful women, she was ambivalent about her physical attributes—women as well as men focused on her looks and blurred her intellect and spirit. In self-defense she frequently hid behind high-necked blouses, baggy suits and trousers, even outsized horn-rimmed glasses.

The night that Lance met Cathy he thought she might be a little bookish for his taste. She was wearing the glasses and the baggy suit and she had told him she was an editor at the *New York Times Book Review.* To be honest about it, Lance, a prolific novelist, had at first considered her less a romantic partner than a good professional contact. The first time he saw her undressed he forgot about his professional life for sixteen consecutive hours —for him, a record.

Cathy was what Lance had always wanted—the male dream, the virgin whore. But she was more selves than two, she was a dozen at least, and she loved playing whichever one came up: smoldering temptress, petulant child, regal hostess, wide-eyed maiden, flaming bitch. Just which Cathy would come home to him at the end of the day he never could be sure. He almost never tired of the variety—it was like dating a dozen different women at once.

Sometimes Lance wondered what it was that Cathy saw in *him*. He guessed it was his ability to adapt to and take joy in whichever self she chose to be at the moment. Cathy could have been a fine photographer, an excellent model, a passable painter, a moderately good writer. Threatened equally by failure and success, she chose to do none of these. She became an editor, not out of any love she had for guiding or shaping a piece of writing but out of an ambivalence she had about being in the spotlight herself. Having come to it for the wrong reasons, she blamed editing for its limitations.

Lance found Cathy brilliant yet surprisingly naive—persistently new, like a child hearing something for the first time. That she had come to New York from Oklahoma didn't explain it. One of his terms of endearment for her was Cute Bunny. Once Lance had made reference to the old joke about Cecil B. De Mille—the one where De Mille laboriously stages the costliest shot in his biblical epic with thousands of extras and special effects, how he has the action covered by three different camera crews in various locations to ensure getting the coverage he needs, how as soon as the scene is over the first two camera crews shamefacedly radio in technical problems, and how he radios the third cameraman, who replies: "Ready when *you* are, C.B." Lance and Cathy were about to leave the apartment to go to dinner and Cathy had asked if Lance was ready. He'd replied, "Ready when *you* are, C.B.," then asked if she knew what the reference was. She said yes, but he sensed she was bluffing. "OK," he said, "what does C.B. stand for?" "Cute Bunny," she said, as if it were obvious.

At times Cathy told him extravagant stories about her adventures during the day, which trailed off into wistful resolutions. If Lance pressed her for details, she sometimes cocked her head and thought a moment, then replied, "I may have made that part up."

Lance wasn't sure Cathy always knew who she was. At times there seemed to be little connection between her intellectual and physical selves. It was as if she found her body a nice place to visit but didn't really live there. Once he found her brushing her hair in a distracted manner in front of the full-length mirror in the bathroom. Her robe accidentally fell open, revealing her amazing body, and she let out an audible gasp of surprised pleasure. "Sometimes I take my breath away," she explained, reddening, as if she'd been caught in an act of voyeurism.

When they had foolish spats about nothing at all and Lance

was too stubborn to suggest making up, Cathy would hold out her arms to him and he would gratefully rush into them. At least at first.

Shortly after the first novel he'd written had become the best-selling book of 1973, Cathy had presented herself to Lance. Presented herself as a person with no needs, a person who lived only to serve him, his greatest fan. It was a promise she was later to retract—Cathy was to become the last woman in Manhattan to embrace the feminist movement—but Lance found no difficulty in accepting it. Spoiled all his life by an adoring Jewish mother, he was not in the least surprised that another woman wished to take over his mother's duties. That the woman was considerably younger than his mother and not remotely Jewish made it possible for sex to be part of the deal as well.

Cathy went to bed with Lance on their second date, stayed the night and never left. Her two roommates warned her not to sever ties with other men too quickly, but she paid them no attention. They had, she suspected, their own too personal reasons for being wary of the love that had sprung up so rapidly between her and Lance:

Cheryl, the blonde TWA stewardess, distrusted all men because of the ease with which she drew them to her side. Like Groucho Marx, she scorned membership in any club that would have her as a member.

Margaret, the junior CPA, was already spinsterly at twenty-three, distrusted all men because of the *difficulty* with which she drew them to her side, but used the guise of sexless frump to hide her true identity—a closet sensualist who secretly believed no man was good enough for her.

A year after Cathy moved in with Lance, she announced to Cheryl and Margaret that she was getting married. Both women shrieked with glee, danced around like dervishes, and were secretly appalled. The marriage, they knew, would never work. Although they were right, it was for the wrong reasons.

In any case, Cathy's marriage produced such profound depression in her former roommates that Cheryl moved in with a male flight attendant whom she outranked, and Margaret seduced a young securities analyst, was married three weeks after Cathy and Lance, and filed for divorce the day her processed marriage license arrived in the mail.

Lance and Cathy. Cathy and Lance. For seven years they had seemed the ideal couple. For seven years they had been the marriage against which their friends measured their own. Cathy was the perfect antidote for Lance's writerly neurosis, calming him during fits of depression, flattening out his lows and nimbly avoiding flattening his highs, planning and executing lavish dinner parties and casting them with influential people in both publishing and show business.

Lance took marvelous care of Cathy too, shoring her up when her self-confidence slipped, encouraging her short-lived projects in writing, painting or photography with hours of sober counseling, and being commendably patient about the half dozen or so men who always seemed to be hovering around her like mosquitoes looking for a place to light.

Lance had always found the sight of a woman in garter belt and stockings very exciting, but Cathy refused to wear them. Garter belts, she said, were binding, cumbersome, old-fashioned and dumb. Once when Lance was out of town on business, though, Cathy went to her first porno film with a friend, saw women wearing garter belts, and decided they were sexy after all. The night Lance came back he and Cathy went to a formal dinner party. Shortly after they were seated Cathy took Lance's hand under the table, placed it on her knee and led him to discover she was wearing the much-longed-for lingerie. They went into the bathroom together between courses and managed a quickie standing up.

When they were first married Cathy took great delight in seducing Lance into making love out of doors. Once they had sex under a blanket at the beach and Lance got a severely chafed penis from a few grains of sand. Once they did it in the woods and Lance got a poison ivy rash on his butt. Thereafter, Lance balked at love in the great outdoors, but Cathy persuaded him to do it in the city on their terrace, certain they couldn't be seen. A crazed neighbor on an upper floor of an adjoining building lobbed rocks at them, however, and so, much to Cathy's disappointment, Lance moved his amatory activities permanently indoors.

Without realizing it, Lance was making Cathy into what he needed in a mate, although not what he wanted. He was nipping the peaks of her sexual passion because they made him uncomfortable. They made him feel he was losing control, and he was terrified of losing control.

Their sex together grew less passionate. Every single night became three nights a week, then twice a week, then mostly Sunday mornings—and not every Sunday, at that. Two- and three-hour sessions utilizing eight positions sifted down to twenty-minute sessions of your basic missionary position. They reassured each other and themselves that this didn't mean they were any less in love, only that their love was going into a different gear. A higher one, to be sure.

Several times Lance was tempted to play hide-the-salami with one or another of the women who meandered through his mostly happy marriage. Women who were turned on by his growing success and fame. Women who were turned on by his slim and well-tuned body, his dry wit, his droll and mildly self-mocking manner. Women who were turned on by his wife's considerable sexuality and didn't know how else to deal with it. Women who were turned on by the mere fact of Lance's being married and therefore inaccessible and safe.

Lance had always been willing to flirt with them, but never more. He was afraid of wounding Cathy, of being caught and damaging his marriage, although the prospect of exploring an unfamiliar female body was so exciting to him he sometimes found it hard to breathe, and although the prospect of conceiving and executing a secret plot to bring it off was possibly even more exciting to him than that of the adulterous act itself.

Lance was always able to sabotage his own best efforts at married flirting. If he and Cathy had gone to dinner at a friend's house and he had flirted with an attractive woman there, he tried to disguise his interest in her either by going on at some length about the woman's unattractive qualities, or else by doing the reverse—frankly stating how delicious he thought she was—on the theory that any pronouncement so blatant couldn't be anything but innocent. The only problem was that Lance often forgot which tack he had started out on, and consequently found himself saying wildly contradictory things about the woman in question.

Lance had never gone farther with these casual crushes than occasionally taking them to lunch, having a few too many vodka-tonics with them, and trading suggestive remarks. He consummated these crushes in fantasy while making love to Cathy, and he sublimated his growing horniness in his writing and in his vicarious joy in the sexual exploits of his best friend, Les.

Les French was dark, curly-headed, bearded, and full of the old piss-and-vinegar. Les was nearly fifteen years Lance's junior, yet Lance felt more comfortable sharing his daily frustrations and fantasies with Les than anyone he knew except for Cathy. Les was either quite a bit more mature than your average twenty-five-year-old, or else Lance was quite a bit less mature than your average forty-year-old. Recounting to Les in elaborate detail the circumstances of his latest unconsummated flirtation had always been enough for Lance. At least till now.

Lance resented the loss of Les as a confidante almost as much as he resented the fact that Les was slipping it to his wife. God, what kind of a man would slip it to his best friend's wife? After all he'd done for Les! Why, Les was not only his best friend, he was his goddamn protégé! What kind of a protégé slips it to his mentor's wife? The ungrateful little creep!

He wondered what Les and Cathy said about him when they discussed him. Did they make fun of him? Was Cathy telling Les the secret things about Lance that only Cathy knew? Like what they did in bed together? Like talking in bunny voices? He prayed that Cathy had more restraint than to tell Les about stuff like that. Perhaps Cathy had been the aggressor. Perhaps she had actively seduced him, and Les had mainly gone along with it so as not to seem impolite. If that were the case, perhaps it was not quite fair to blame Les for what had happened. It was something that, one day, they would have to work out if the friendship were to continue. For now, though, what he had to do was determine who was Cathy's closer friend, Margaret or Cheryl, and then steer that person into the sack at the earliest possible opportunity. That was the only course of action that seemed likely to bring peace to his fanatical, compulsive mind.

Lance was compulsive in all things. Compulsive in his work—about the way he had to have everything in his office lined up in neat stacks, parallel or perpendicular to everything else. Compulsive in his eating—about the way he always ate each thing on his plate separately, never mixing them together, always saving the best for last (early training in deferred gratification), always finishing everything on his plate, even if he hated it. Compulsive in his driving—he owned an old Porsche, and if he failed to respond to a passing Porsche owner's wave or toot or flash of headlights, he felt horrible about it, once even making a U-turn in the middle of the road and taking off after the startled motorist, madly waving and tooting and flashing his lights at him.

If Lance had been less of a compulsive, less of an extremist, less of a fanatic, the choice would have been easy: he would simply have begun plotting the seduction of the blond TWA stewardess. But because of his fanaticism—his conscientiousness, as he chose to view it—he suspected that Margaret was actually the closer friend and therefore the more appropriate target of his retaliatory mission.

To settle the issue, there was one way to find out whom he would pursue.

2

"Hey, Cathy?"

"Hmmm?"

"How's your old friend Cheryl these days?"

"Cheryl? I don't know. OK, I guess."

"She still living with that male stewardess of hers?"

"I think so. Why?"

"Oh, no reason, no reason. I was just thinking. Cheryl is a pretty good friend of yours, isn't she?"

"Sure. Why?"

"She's probably your *best* friend, wouldn't you say?"

"My *best* friend? Oh, I don't know. Certainly one of my *two* best. Her and Margaret, I mean."

"Mmmm. You know, I always thought you liked her just a tiny bit more than Margaret, somehow."

"Really? I don't know what would have given you *that* idea."

"I don't know. Maybe it's just that I sense that you *admire* her more than Margaret or something."

"Admire? Cheryl? No, I really admire Margaret a lot more than Cheryl. What's this about?"

"Wouldn't you say, though, that it's pretty much of a toss-up? That Cheryl and Margaret are about equally close to you?"

"Not really, no. I'm really closer to Margaret. What's this about, Lance?"

"Nothing, really. It just happened to cross my mind that you were pretty tight with both Cheryl and Margaret, and I started wondering who you liked more, that's all."

"I see."

"Funny how I always thought you liked Cheryl better."

"Yes, it is. I don't know why you would have thought that."

"Mmmm. Let me ask you this: Did you *ever* like Cheryl better than Margaret?"

Cathy burst out laughing.

"Lance, will you tell me what this is all about?"

"Nothing, honey. I was just wondering, that's all. Can't a person wonder about his wife's best friends and not have it be *about* something?"

"Sure, but it's sort of weird, that's all. Spending that much time thinking who I like better, Cheryl or Margaret. It just seems kind of weird, you know?"

"I don't see what's weird about it. Why do you think it's weird?"

Cathy looked at him strangely.

"If I didn't know better," she said, "I'd say you were deliberately trying to get me to say that I liked Cheryl better than Margaret."

He had gone too far.

"Why would I ever want you to say a thing like that?"

"I don't know, Lance. *You* tell *me*."

"Forget it," he said.

The choice, willy-nilly, had been made. In order to save his marriage, he was now *forced* to sleep with Margaret.

3

He had planned to call Margaret for a lunch date as soon as Cathy left the apartment, but Cathy was working at home while her office was being redecorated and seemed to be around whenever he managed to summon the courage to make the call.

Eventually, one particularly balmy day in early June, Lance decided to call from a pay phone in the street. At the first phone he tried an elderly man with a two-day growth of beard was permanently affixed to the receiver. The next two phones were out of order, and when he finally found one that worked it happened to be on one of the noisiest corners in midtown Manhattan.

He dialed the number and, as it started to ring, his pulse suddenly started pounding in his throat. He realized he was seven years removed from the practice of calling women for dates and he had forgotten what the rhythms sounded like. When he was in college he often wrote out entire scripts before phoning girls for dates, usually reading his lines right off the paper. Happily, he'd outgrown the practice when he graduated.

On the fifth ring somebody answered, but the voice didn't sound familiar.

"Is, uh, Margaret there?" said Lance.

"This is Margaret," said the unfamiliar voice. Was it really Margaret or was it somebody masquerading as Margaret?

"Margaret?" said Lance.

"Yes?" said the voice.

"Oh," said Lance. "Hi, Margaret, it didn't sound like you."

"Who is this?" said the voice.

Sweat suddenly prickled his forehead and the space between his shoulder blades.

"I'm sorry," said Lance, "This is—"

At that moment the driver of a passing cab gave in to the accumulated frustrations of having been able to move only three blocks in the past half hour and leaned on his horn for approximately sixty seconds.

"What did you say?" said Margaret.

"I *said* this is—"

The cabdriver, clearly an emissary from a God who did not approve of adulterous affairs, no matter how justifiable, gave the horn another thirty seconds.

"I can't *hear* you!" yelled Margaret.

"I'm sorry. This is . . ." Lance eyed the cabdriver warily, then screamed: "LANCE!"

"Jesus Christ," said Margaret, "I think you punctured my eardrum."

"I'm sorry," said Lance. "I thought he was going to honk again."

"Where are you calling from, Lance, the Holland Tunnel?"

"Ha ha. No, from the street, actually. I just happened to be walking along Madison Avenue and I thought I would call you up and say hello."

Now *there's* an assholic way to start a conversation, he thought. Maybe I should go back to writing out scripts.

"I see," said Margaret. "Well then, hello, Lance. How's Cathy?"

"Cathy?" he said. The sweat began flowing out of glands he didn't know he had, drenching his clothing.

"Your wife?" said Margaret helpfully. "Tall, good-looking woman with large breasts and dishwater blond hair?"

"Ha ha. Yes, I know the one you mean," said Lance, trying to get into the spirit of banter. "Cathy is fine. Saw her only this morning, as a matter of fact."

"Tell her I couldn't find the Ralph Lauren blouse she wanted," said Margaret. "Bloomingdale's had it in beige, but not in mauve. Ask her to call me if she wants it in beige."

"I, uh . . . don't know if I'll be able to do that," said Lance. What was he supposed to say: "Oh, Cathy, when I was phoning Margaret to see if I could get into her pants, she gave me a message about a blouse . . ."

"You what?" said Margaret.

"I mean I . . . might forget," said Lance. Then it occurred to him that Margaret would now phone Cathy and repeat their conversation, and Cathy would ask Lance why he was calling Margaret, and . . .

"On second thought," said Lance hurriedly, "I'm writing it down. Here . . ." He pretended to write on a piece of paper. "Bloomie's had . . . blouse in beige . . . not in mauve . . . call Margaret if . . . want in beige."

"Good boy," said Margaret.

"Listen, Margaret, the reason I'm calling—how's about lunch tomorrow?" Lance blurted.

"Tomorrow? Tomorrow's OK, I guess," said Margaret. "Just you and me and Cathy, you mean?"

"No no no," said Lance nervously, "not Cathy. You and me and . . . nobody."

There was a puzzled silence on the other end.

"Is this a surprise for Cathy?" said Margaret.

"In a way," said Lance.

"Well, sure," said Margaret. "Why not? Where do you want to eat?"

Lance was almost overcome with gratitude.

"How's about Maxwell's Plum? Sixty-fourth and First. About twelve-thirty?"

"Fine," said Margaret.

"Oh, and don't mention this to Cathy," he said. "I mean it would spoil the surprise."

When he hung up the phone, Lance was so drained of energy he could scarcely walk.

"Hi honey," said Cathy, as Lance let himself back into the apartment. "Where've you been?"

"Where've I been?" said Lance. "Out."

"I *know* you were *out,* silly," said Cathy. "I mean where?"

"Oh, I went to the store. To buy some yogurt."

"We have about twenty containers in the fridge," she said.

"I know," he said. "I mean, uh, I realized that once I got to the store."

"I see," she said, looking him over with interest. "Have you been running?"

"Running?" he said. "Why no. I mean why do you ask?"

"Well, you're all sweated up and you're out of breath."

"Oh, that," he said. "Well, I did do a little running, as a matter of fact. I was suddenly feeling kind of sleepy, so I ran around the block a couple of times to kind of get my heart going."

"You ran around the block a couple of times to get your *heart* going?" she said.

"Yeah."

What *is* this, he thought. *She's* the one who's sleeping around —why am *I* feeling so guilty?

Cathy shrugged and went into the bathroom to shower. Lance collapsed into a chair.

He thought he ought to prepare for the lunch better than he'd prepared for the phone call. It was a more difficult script, and he wouldn't have the luxury of reading it off a piece of paper either.

He wondered what Margaret's reaction would be. He wondered if she'd be shocked and disgusted at what he was going to propose to her. He wondered if she'd go straight to Cathy with the whole thing.

If he'd had any idea of what he was about to get into, he'd have thrown Margaret's phone number right into the toilet.

4

Maxwell's Plum was ornate and cheery. A million dollars' worth of Tiffany lamps, art deco figurines of naked ladies, and sculptures of animals hanging from the ceiling looked down on Lance Lerner as he waited in the darkest corner of the restaurant for the appearance of his wife's best friend, who was now twenty minutes late.

Had she misunderstood the arrangement? Hadn't he told her "Maxwell's Plum . . . Sixty-fourth and First . . . about twelve-thirty?" And hadn't she said "Fine"?

Maybe she'd got the day wrong, No, he'd definitely said "Tomorrow," meaning today. Maybe she knew what he had in mind and had called Cathy. Would she do that? No. If she were going to do that, she would have done it immediately, and he would have heard about it immediately too. The fact that she hadn't called Cathy suggested that she was planning to come. Regardless of whether she knew what he had on his mind.

A waiter appeared once more at his elbow.

"You wish to order another drink, sir? While you're waiting?" he said in an amused, patronizing voice. Clearly, the fucking waiter was enjoying the sight of a guy nervously waiting for somebody who appeared to be standing him up. Clearly the sonofabitch had never been stood up himself, the faggot bastard.

"Why, yes," said Lance, with a tone he hoped conveyed just the right mixture of disdain and boredom, "Another vodka-tonic will be fine."

"Very good, sir," said the waiter, and minced off to the bar to regale his colleagues with accounts of Lance's stoodupness.

Lance looked at his watch for the fortieth time. It was now one o'clock. She was a half hour late! How long could he be expected to wait for her, the miserable twat? He had half a mind to simply get up and leave.

He looked around for the waiter. He could just cancel the drink, pay the bill and leave. She clearly wasn't coming now, but how was he supposed to act toward her when he saw her again with Cathy? Would he be able to contain his anger?

Unless. Unless she had arrived punctually at twelve-thirty, maybe even a little before that, waited five or ten minutes, figured he'd changed his mind and left—he had, after all, been about five minutes late himself . . .

And then it hit him: she'd been struck by a cab on the way to the restaurant. She was so preoccupied with her own ambivalence, lust and guilt over the prospect of an illicit meeting with her best friend's husband that she didn't look where she was going, and a cab going much too fast ran a red light, swerved to avoid her at the last instant, but not quickly enough. Margaret's body was tossed into the air by the cab's fender like a hapless matador on the horns of a bull. She lay, even now, on a stretcher in a city ambulance, her life's blood drenching the pretty clothes she had worn especially to please him.

Poor Margaret! What a horrid way to die! He would have her death on his conscience for the rest of his life, and he'd never be able to tell Cathy about it either.

That must have been what happened. That *better* be what had happened, he thought—for *her* sake.

"Hi, Lance. Sorry I'm late."

He looked up. It was Margaret, alive and intact. She looked like she'd been running.

"Well, hi," he said coolly. "I didn't think you were coming."

"I'm sorry," she said, sliding down into the banquette, "I . . . got detained."

Was that it? Was that all he got after almost forty minutes of waiting and having to be humiliated in front of an entire corps of waiters—*I got detained?* He was fast becoming so furious he was not going to be able to speak at all.

"Monsieur?"

The waiter appeared with Lance's vodka-tonic and nodded to Margaret.

"I'll have a Tanqueray martini," she said. "Straight up."

"Very good, madam," said the waiter and withdrew.

Margaret smiled at Lance. He did not return the smile. She was wearing a tan blazer, tan skirt, and a beige silk blouse. She had a dutchboy haircut with medium brown hair, flat brown eyes and horn-rimmed glasses. She wore practically no makeup, no lipstick or rouge, and no perceptible eyeliner. He did not find her the least bit attractive. For the first time he thought she might be a lesbian.

"I'm really sorry I was so late, Lance," she said in a quiet, feminine voice he had never heard her use before. "I'll tell you the reason, but first . . ." Her voice trailed off, and he thought she might be blushing.

"Yes . . . ?" he said.

"Well, first I want to hear why you wanted to see me."

"Why I wanted to see you?" he said stupidly.

He took his second drink and poured it down his throat.

"Yes," she said. She was looking at him very directly—almost sensuously, a slight smile on her face. And she was very definitely blushing. She *does* know why I wanted to see her, he thought. That makes it easier. And harder.

"Well," he said, beginning slowly, stalling for time, using the trick that all schoolboys learn when they don't know the answer to what the teacher has asked them, beginning the answer by restating the question, "why I wanted to see you was . . . I wanted to talk to you."

"About what?"

"About what? About a lot of things, actually. First of all, I wanted to talk to you about, uh, something that has been on my mind for quite a long . . . You see, Margaret, although you and I have known each other for several years, for almost eight years now, as a matter of fact, I don't think we have ever talked—really *talked,* you know?—about things like, uh, well, like the kinds of things that, perhaps, you and I would have talked about, assuming that we had had the opportunity to talk about them. To really *talk* about them, I mean, you know?"

He was awash in perspiration. She was looking at him closely. The slight smile was still on her face.

"Lance, do you want to fuck me? Is that it?"

He exhaled sharply. Blood surged into his cheeks and forehead.

"Well, yes," he said, finding his voice now slipping into an odd, quiet and slightly manic tone. "The fact is, Margaret, I've always found you incredibly attractive, incredibly sexual. I quite frankly didn't think it was appropriate to even *have* such thoughts, much less to voice them, and I swear I never intended to, but every time you've been in our house and we've been physically close to each other, it's been all I could do to restrain myself from taking you in my arms."

"I know," she said quietly.

"What?" he said.

"I could tell how you felt about me," she said softly. "I'm afraid you weren't as discreet as you thought you were."

He fought the impulse to burst out laughing, deciding it would be a tactical error.

"You don't think that *Cathy* . . . ?" he began.

"Oh no. No no, I don't think Cathy noticed," she said. "I don't think Cathy would even *dream* that you—or *any* man of hers, for that matter—would so much as *look* at me, but I could certainly tell that you were interested."

"I see. And . . . how do you feel about that?" he asked cautiously.

She shrugged.

"You're not the *first* of Cathy's men who's wanted to sleep with me," she said.

"I'm not?"

She shook her head.

"Naturally, I feel some ambivalence about it," she said. "Cathy is, after all, one of my three closest friends. I wouldn't do anything to hurt her. And yet . . ."

"Yes . . . ?"

"Well, I knew what you were going to say to me today. And I guess I *was* pretty ambivalent about it—that's why I was so late. I left the office three times. I almost didn't come at all. I was going to telephone you at the restaurant and tell you I wasn't coming, that I didn't think it was right. But then I thought, what if that wasn't what you wanted to talk to me about, you know? I would have looked like an ass. Tell me, why did you finally call me *now*? After all these years of lusting for me in silence?"

"Um, well, because of a couple of things, I guess. First of all, I've discovered that Cathy is . . . I've discovered that Cathy is having a little . . . fling herself."

Margaret's eyes widened.

"With whom?" she said.

"What does it matter?" he said.

"It doesn't," she said. "I'd just like to know."

"I'd rather not say," he said. "I mean, if she had wanted you to know, I guess she would have told you herself."

"I suppose you're right," she said. "You know, I *thought* she was having an affair. Only I was afraid to ask. I'll bet I know who it is."

"Who?" he said.

"That cute guy at the health club. Sven. The one who teaches yoga. She's always kidding around with him. Is that it?"

Sven? The guy at the health club who teaches yoga? Was she having *two* affairs?

"It's not Sven," he said.

"It doesn't matter," she said. "If she'd wanted me to know, she'd have told me herself. So. What is this, an eye for an eye?"

"Pardon me?"

"What is this—evening the score? *She's* sleeping around, so you're going to do it too, to retaliate?"

"No no no, nothing like that. Of course not. No no. It's just that . . ."

"It wouldn't be so hard to understand if that were it," she said.

"It wouldn't?" he said. "Oh, well, I mean, I suppose there must be an *element* of that in this, you know, but it's certainly not the most important one."

"It isn't?"

"No. Of course not."

"Then what is?"

"The most important one is how I feel about *you*. This incredible attraction that I feel for you, that I've felt for some time now. That's the most important one. Of course, the fact that I've found out that Cathy herself is, uh, you know, having a fling sort of makes it easier. To tell you how I feel about you. How I've felt for some time. You know something? You haven't said yet how *you* feel about *me*."

She smiled again.

"I find you a . . . reasonably attractive man," she said.

He snorted with laughter.

"Jesus Christ," he said. "After all that, the most you can say is, 'I find you a reasonably attractive man'?"

Color came into her cheeks.

"All right," she said, "I fantasize about you a lot."

"You do? That's better. Tell me what you fantasize."

"Oh, I fantasize about a lot of things."

"C'mon," he said. "You can do better than that. What are you fantasizing right now? Right this second?"

Her face got redder. She started to say something so quietly that he could hardly hear her.

"What's that?" he said. "I can't hear you."

"I *said*," she said, "I am fantasizing that you are going to slide under the table right now as we're talking, pull down my panties, bury your face in my pussy, and lick me till I scream."

There was an immediate crash behind them. Lance looked around to see the waiter retrieving a tray that had once held several drinks. Lance was aware that the people at the tables on all sides of him had stopped talking and were pretending relentless interest in their silverware and ashtrays. He felt his penis begin to get hard.

"I'm sorry," she said, flustered. "I guess I shouldn't have been quite that honest."

"No no," he said, "I really admire an honest answer."

The waiter was still picking up pieces of glass and ice cubes, hoping that there would be more.

"You haven't said how you feel about what I just told you," she said.

He checked the people at the adjacent tables and waited till his gaze forced them to resume their conversations. Then he turned back to the waiter, who was mopping up liquid as slowly as possible.

"How's about I just mail you a transcript of our conversation?" Lance said pleasantly. The waiter got very huffy and stood up.

"I'm sure I have better things to do than to eavesdrop on your asinine sexual conversations," he said and flounced away.

Lance leaned across the table toward Margaret. He was aware of her perfume. She had never before, to his knowledge, used perfume.

"Can we go back to your apartment right now so I can do what you were fantasizing?" he said hoarsely.

Margaret looked away. Her breathing was beginning to be labored. She hadn't needed rouge after all.

"I don't know what I want to do," she whispered.

"You don't?" He was incredulous.

"I mean I *do* know what I want to do. I just don't know if I *can.*"

"Because of Cathy?"

"Because of Cathy. I don't know if I can do this to her. I *love* Cathy."

"*You* love Cathy? How about *me?* I don't love Cathy? I *worship* Cathy, for God's sake. Cathy's a goddam *saint,* that's what she is."

"You're telling me? Cathy was my *roommate,* Lance."

"Your *roommate?* She's my *wife,* for Christ's sake!"

"Well, I know that. And that's why I don't know if I can do such a thing to her."

"You don't know? What do you need to make up your mind?" he hissed, sliding his hand underneath the table and grabbing her knee.

"Don't," she said softly.

"Don't what?" he said, leaning farther forward, sliding his hand under the hem of her skirt, up the inside of her thigh.

"Please don't," she said even more softly.

"Why not?" he said, sliding his hand up to the flesh of her upper thigh adjoining her pudendum.

"Because," she whispered.

"Because what?" he whispered, leaning even farther forward and slipping his hand over the silky crotch of her panties. The position he was forced to take to reach his hand that far under the table was giving him a pronounced pain in his right shoulder.

"Because it isn't fair," she whispered.

"Why isn't it?" he whispered, and just then a muscle in his shoulder began to spasm and he emitted a sharp cry.

"What's wrong?" she said, alarmed.

"Nothing," he said, withdrawing his arm from under the table and wincing in pain. "Just a little muscle spasm, that's all. Margaret, I think we should leave here. I think we should go back to your apartment."

"I don't know if I can do that, Lance. I need time to think."

"O.K., we'll walk there—you can think on the way."

"I need more time than that."

"How much more?"

"I don't know. A few days. Maybe a week or so."

"Can't you think any faster than that?"

"Please, Lance. You have to let me get accustomed to the idea. It's going to take time. I'll let you know as soon as I've thought it through."

She got up.

"Where are you going?" he said.

"I'm very conflicted. I have to leave."

"But we haven't even ordered yet."

"I couldn't eat anything now anyway. I'm too upset."

He got up and followed her to the door of the restaurant. Every head in the place charted their progress from table to door.

"Will you call me when you decide?" he said.

"How can I call you?" she said. "How do I know Cathy won't answer the phone?"

"I'll answer all calls for the next few days," he said.

"What if you have to go to the bathroom?" she said.

"It's a long cord," he said, "I'll take the phone in with me."

"You'd better call *me*," she said, opening the door to the restaurant.

"When shall I call you? Is tonight too soon?"

"Yes. Don't call for several days. Don't call me for a week."

"A week? I can't wait a whole week."

"Please, Lance. Wait a week. Promise me you'll wait a week."

The waiter, suddenly afraid that Lance was attempting to leave without paying, raced up to the door, waving the check.

"Just a moment!" he yelled. "Just a moment there, fellow!"

"A week, then," said Lance. "June 14th. But no later."

"Aren't you forgetting something?" said the waiter unpleasantly, reaching the door and barring Lance's passage with his outstretched arm. Lance turned to face him, incredulous.

"If you don't drop your arm this instant," said Lance, "I'm going to stick my fingers up your nose and rip it off your face."

5

By the time Lance reached home he had almost recovered from the drinks at Maxwell's Plum. He let himself into the apartment and went to the bathroom to change.

"Honey, that you?" called Cathy from another room.

"No, it's the cat burglar," he said, swiftly removing his tie and jacket to avoid answering questions about where he'd been. Cathy came into the bathroom just as he was slipping into a denim work shirt. She grabbed him from behind and kissed the back of his neck.

"You're pretty cute for a cat burglar," she said, hugging him hard. "You want to fool around a little before my husband gets home?"

Lance winced, was about to make a bitter retort, and stopped in the nick of time. Cathy turned him around and kissed him on the mouth.

"Hey," she said. "Where've *you* been?"

"Out shopping," he said. "I had to get a couple things from the hardware store."

"Then why is there vodka on your breath?" she said.

"Vodka? On my breath?" he said. "What do you mean?"

"I mean I smell vodka on your breath," she said.

He realized that Wolfschmidt had sold him out.

"Vodka," he said inanely, "has no taste. You can't smell it on somebody's breath."

There may have been one or two acceptable replies to the question she'd posed. This had not been one of them. The smile and the playfulness slowly dissolved.

"Where have you been?" she said.

"To the hardware store," he said. "I told you."

"They serve vodka now at the hardware store?"

"As a matter of fact, smart-ass, today they did. It just so happens that today was Midtown Hardware Store's twenty-fifth anniversary in business, and they were serving vodka and white wine and little canapes with red caviar and sour cream. I thought you'd be pissed at me for drinking on a day when I had work to do, but I may as well confess, since you've got the nose of a bloodhound. I admit it, Officer Lerner—I've been drinking."

He chuckled and tried to hug her, but she couldn't be jollied back into her playful mood. He knew he had made a big mistake.

Soon he would make one about eighty times worse.

6

Cathy and Margaret walked into the locker room of the New York Health and Racquet Club. The buxom Puerto Rican attendant opened two lockers for them and gave them two towels. Both women began undressing. Both seemed preoccupied.

"You know what I think, Margaret?" said Cathy, pulling her sweater over her head, "I think Lance might be having an affair."

Margaret counted slowly to ten before she trusted her voice to reply.

"What do you mean?" she said.

"I don't know," said Cathy, stepping out of her skirt. "He's acting very weird. He came home a few days ago with vodka on his breath and tried to sell me some cockamamy story about the hardware store having an anniversary and serving liquor."

"Oh, I've heard of things like that," said Margaret. "The hardware store around my house did that about a month ago, in fact. They served liquor and champagne. That's quite a common practice for hardware stores these days."

Cathy hung her skirt and sweater inside the locker and turned to her friend. The familiar sight of Cathy's briefly-attired body always made Margaret vaguely uncomfortable.

"You don't think Lance is having an affair then?" said Cathy hopefully.

"Oh no," said Margaret, shaking her head vigorously, "absolutely not. I mean I'd know if he was, and he isn't." She couldn't believe the words which had just walked out of her mouth.

Cathy frowned.

"What do you mean you'd know if he was?"

Margaret's mind raced for an explanation.

"I mean," she said, "that if Lance was having an affair, there wouldn't be any doubt in *your* mind. And if there wouldn't be any doubt in *your* mind, then there wouldn't be any doubt in *mine*. After looking at you, I mean. I mean you couldn't hide it. From your friend, I mean."

Cathy sighed and regarded her reflection in the mirror on the wall.

"I guess you're right," she said. She unhooked her bra, paused, flashed first one breast and then the other at the mirror, stripper style, then hung her bra in the locker. "I guess I *would* know if Lance was having an affair. I guess he probably isn't," she said.

"I'm sure *he* isn't," said Margaret. "Are *you*?"

"Me?" Cathy burst into laughter. "Hell no. Why did you ask me that?"

"I don't know."

"Well, I'm not," said Cathy.

7

True to his word, Lance waited an entire week, till June 14th, before seeking out another pay phone and calling Margaret. In the intervening seven days his apathy toward Margaret had reversed itself and hardened into a fine obsession. He replayed the fantasy she had described in the restaurant with endless variations. It was all he could think about.

He made love to Cathy and imagined it was her plain-looking friend. He had endless visions of Margaret—of her pulling down her panties under the table in the restaurant and his going down on her, of her slipping under the table to go down on *him*, and so on. The concept of making love to someone as beautiful as Cathy and having fantasies about someone as plain-looking as Margaret was ludicrous, though not, he suspected, at all unusual. Wasn't it George Burns who said even if you were married to Marilyn Monroe you would still be out trying to pick up pigs?

By the seventh day following Lance's lunch with Margaret he could stand it no more. He went out into the street and, after losing six dimes in the first two pay phones, finally reached her.

"Have you decided?" he said.

"Who is this?" said Margaret.

"Oh, I'm sorry. It's Lance."

"Oh, Lance. I didn't recognize your voice. You're back in the Holland Tunnel, I see."

"Ha ha. Look, you've had a week now. What did you decide?"

"Well, I don't know yet. I need a little more time."

"More time? How much more time?"

"Another week."

"Another *week!* I can't wait another week. Why can't you decide now? Why don't you know what you want?"

"Lance, Cathy thinks you're having an affair."

"What?"

"She said you came home with vodka on your breath. She said you told her you got it at an anniversary celebration for a *hardware* store."

"It was all I could think of on the spur of the moment," he said sheepishly.

"I told her hardware stores in my neighborhood had anniversary celebrations with liquor all the time."

"Oh God. Look, when can I see you?"

"I need more time."

"When can I see you?"

"I don't know, I don't know. O.K., a week from today. Next Thursday."

"Thursday? The twenty-first? That's my birthday."

"So? How are you planning to celebrate it?" she said. "Is Cathy taking you to dinner or what?"

"I guess so. I don't know. It's my fortieth birthday. Cathy hasn't mentioned it, though. Frankly, I think she's forgotten. I'm not exactly uppermost in her mind these days."

"I'm sure you're wrong."

"No I'm not. Well, what the hell. If she doesn't remember, I'll tell her myself. But I guess I can meet you before dinner for a drink. A drink and . . . whatever else you decide to do. O.K. then, Thursday it is. What time Thursday?"

"Five-thirty. At my place."

He chuckled.

"At *your* place, eh? Then I won't *ask* what you're planning to give me for my birthday."

8

Thursday. June 21st. The first day of summer. Lance's fortieth birthday. He studies his barely noticeable bald spot in two strategically placed mirrors in the bathroom and makes a mental note to consult a dermatologist about it—right after he consults a nutritionist about a more healthful diet and a program of vitamins, and right after he renews his lapsed membership in the health club where he used to swim laps.

On the morning of his fortieth birthday he actually breaks down and reminds Cathy it's his birthday. Actually has to *remind* her. He inquires what she would like to do for dinner. She says it's up to him. Up to *him. On his fortieth birthday.*

He is now doubly justified in fucking her best friend. It is only fitting that he will be doing it today. It is now four-thirty. Feeling sorry for himself, he pours two quickie drinks and downs them before he leaves the house. He tells Cathy he is going to Bloomingdale's and Hammacher-Schlemmer to buy himself some birthday presents and will be back at eight to take her to dinner.

He leaves the apartment and walks slowly uptown to Margaret's. He stops in a bar and has another drink. He tries to picture what he will be doing with Margaret only an hour from now. He tries to picture Margaret naked. The no-nonsense Margaret without her clothes. Without her horn-rimmed glasses. Without her dry accountant's manner. What will she feel like naked? What will she smell like? What will her dry accountant's body taste like when he begins to devour it with tongue and teeth? What noises will she make, if any, in the throes of orgasm?

He arrives at her apartment building. He looks at his watch: 5:25. He is five minutes early. He goes on in anyway. Heart hammering in his chest. Pulse pounding in his pants. This will be his first woman other than Cathy in more than seven years. Will it be heaven? Will he even be able to get it up?

He rings the doorbell. She buzzes him in. He takes the elevator up. He pauses briefly before her closed door. Is this really what he wants to do? Fuck his wife's best friend on his fortieth birthday? It is. His wife has given him no choice. He knocks.

It takes at least three minutes for her to come to the door.

"Who is it?" she says.

"Who do you think?" he says.

The door is unlocked. It swings inward. It is dark inside. She has drawn the blinds and drapes. He slips into her apartment. He reaches out for her, touches her shoulder. She pulls away, giggling. He thinks he smells bourbon on her breath—so she has had to sneak a couple of drinks for courage too!

"Come here," he whispers.

"Not yet," she says, her voice retreating.

"Where are you going?" he says.

"To get something. Make yourself comfortable."

A door at the other end of the room opens, then clicks shut.

He sighs, sits down. He imagines her in her bedroom, pulling her dress over her head, stripping down to bra and panties or a flimsy negligee. The image is too much for him. He feels his penis begin to stiffen. The room is warm. He slips out of his jacket. Takes off his tie. He carefully removes his boots and socks and tiptoes across the living room to her bedroom door. He starts to knock, stops, has a better idea. He slips out of his shirt, slacks and undershorts. Stark naked, his now-hard-as-a-rock penis preceding him, he raps at her bedroom door.

"Here I come, ready or not!" he calls.

"Come on in," says Margaret in a strange, high, possibly ambivalent voice.

He turns the knob and walks into the darkened bedroom.

Blinding lights. And forty people yell: "SURPRISE!"

9

In a perfect world it would never have happened. In a perfect world Margaret would not have perversely neglected to warn Lance in case he might at the last moment decide to do something spontaneous like this. In a perfect world he would have entered the bedroom *before* taking off all his clothing.

In a perfect world he might have realized somewhat before the lights were switched on that what he had mistaken for the evidence of an affair between Cathy and Les had been merely the clandestine arrangements for a mammoth surprise party.

Now time has stopped dead and he stands staring into the faces of his wife and his best friend, who are holding a long rectangular mocha cake with forty lit candles on it, flanked by Margaret and Cheryl and thirty-six other utterly paralyzed people who are all desperately wishing to be somewhere else.

There is total silence. No one so much as draws a breath. Forty mouths are open, frozen in position. Eighty eyes bulge forward, staring at his nakedness, at his rapidly deflating erection. Eighty lungs are holding in their already used-up oxygen, pending potential deliverance by means of the next words from Lance's lips.

"I can explain this," he begins, wildly ransacking his mind for anything—anything at all in the memory core—that will get him out of this. "This isn't what it seems," he babbles, but by now those in the room have already sensed disaster—like fans whose team is losing the championship game by a single point and who watch the basketball leave the hands of the team's star center and hear the final gun go off and know even though it has not even reached the zenith of its trajectory through the air that the ball will never in a million billion trillion years go through that hoop but will bounce impotently off the rim and the game and the championship if not their very lives are lost lost lost and their prayers have once more gone unanswered by an indifferent God.

The next five minutes would be among the worst ever experienced by any person in the room who had not been in a major war. If a passing vendor had suddenly appeared with a tray of cyanide pellets and single-edged razor blades he would have sold out his entire stock in twenty seconds.

"As you may or may not be aware," Lance continued, "Margaret's apartment happens to have a fairly heavy infestation of cockroaches. The instant I entered the living room, a roach dropped off the ceiling and fell into the space between my shirt collar and the back of my neck . . ."

Both Cathy and Margaret had burst into tears. Everybody else, faces averted and mumbling unintelligible phrases, was pleading pressing engagements upstate and making for the door.

". . . As I happen to have an almost pathological aversion to cockroaches," Lance continued, his tone now approaching hysteria, "I immediately began pulling off articles of my clothing in a vain attempt to . . ."

It was hopeless. Nobody was even listening to him anymore.

10

At home Cathy was surprisingly adult about the whole thing. All right, so she broke a few dishes and screamed a little. But then she stopped. She dried her tears. She composed herself. She packed a small canvas bag and went to stay with Cheryl and her male stewardess.

Lance wondered whether the neighbors had been able to hear her screaming, and then berated himself for caring about such insignificant things in the midst of something as serious as having your wife leave you.

Lance was miserable, but he knew she'd be back in the morning.

She was not back in the morning. He called Cheryl and asked to speak to Cathy.

"I don't think she wants to speak to you," said Cheryl.

"What makes you think that?" he asked.

"Because every time the phone rings she says, 'If that's Lance I don't want to speak to him.' "

"Ask her."

"It won't help, Lance."

"Ask her anyway."

A sigh.

"OK, but it won't help."

He heard her put the phone down. He heard voices in the background. He heard the phone being picked up.

"Cath?" he said gently.

"No," said Cheryl, "it's Cheryl. She won't speak to you, Lance. I told you."

"How about if I come over there and try to speak to her in person?"

"I wouldn't advise it."

"Why not?"

"I don't think it would help."

"Why not?"

"I think it would just make her angrier. I don't think you want to make her any angrier now than you have already. I'd just give her a while to cool off."

"How long?"

"I don't know. Couple of months, maybe."

"Ha ha. How long, Cheryl?"

"I don't know, Lance. But I don't think she plans on coming back to you for a while."

"What do you mean? How do you know that?"

"Because. Since she's been here she's been going through the real estate section of the *Times,* circling ads for apartment rentals."

"Oh my God. Are you serious?"

"Absolutely."

"What should I do, Cheryl?"

"Like I said. Just give her some time to cool off."

"OK. Will you let me know if there's anything I can do?"

"Of course."

"Thanks, Cheryl."

11

There being no longer any need to use a pay phone on the street, Lance telephoned Margaret from the apartment. She hung up the moment she heard his voice. He called back and began shouting before she could disconnect:

"*You* hang up on *me*? After cockteasing me into dropping my pants in front of my wife and forty of my closest friends, *you* hang up on *me*?"

"Did you wish to speak to Margaret Pusser?" said a fey male secretary.

"Uh, oh, excuse me," said Lance pitching his voice several octaves lower, "yes, may I please?"

"I'll see if she's in."

"Don't see if she's in," said Lance, getting heated up again, "I just *talked* to her. Tell her she has a choice—either come to the phone to hear what I have to say now, or else read it tomorrow in a full-page ad in the *New York Post*."

"I'll see if Miss Pusser can come to the phone," said the voice.

The line was put on hold. Easy Listening Muzak was piped into Lance's ear, getting him hotter. If he'd wanted to hear Easy Listening Muzak he'd have taken an elevator ride. Somebody came back on the line.

"Margaret?" said Lance tentatively.

"Yes?"

"*You* hang up on *me*?" he shouted. "After cockteasing me into dropping my pants in front of my wife and forty of my closest friends, *you* hang up on *me?*"

"What do you mean *cockteasing?*" she said. "*I* didn't tell you to take off your pants in front of all those people."

"What do I mean by cockteasing? Were you or were you not the person who invited me up to her apartment to have sex?"

"I didn't invite you up to my apartment to have sex, I invited you up to my apartment to have a surprise birthday party. Cathy and Les and I had been planning that party for weeks."

"Is that so? And what did you tell Cathy you were going to say to get me up there?"

"I told her I was going to be very mysterious and even a little flirtatious and say I had something very important to discuss with you."

" 'A little flirtatious,' is that it? Did you tell her being 'a little flirtatious' included an invitation to bury my face in your pussy and lick it till you scream?"

"I don't recall saying anything that specific to you."

"No? What *do* you recall saying, *specifically?*"

"I recall saying that I had had some . . . romantic notions about you and that I—"

" 'Romantic notions'? Those are the words you recall? Nothing about burying faces in pussies or licking anybody till they screamed?"

"I'm afraid not. I *did* want to be enticing enough to lure you to my apartment in time for the party, but I certainly wouldn't have said anything that vulgar to the husband of one of my best friends."

"I see. Did being 'enticing enough' include allowing me to slide my hand up your thigh and stroke your pudenda, or don't you recall that either?"

"I recall your grabbing my knee and my pulling away from you, and that is all I recall," said Margaret. "And now, if you don't mind, I really do have to get back to work."

"Listen to me, Margaret—please," said Lance, softening his tone. "Do you at least admit that you had sexual feelings for me at Maxwell's Plum and that you were seriously considering going to bed with me? Will you at least admit to that? It's important that you be completely honest with me."

"Lance, I'll be completely honest with you. I think you're a very interesting man, and I'm very fond of both you and Cathy, and I'm sorry you two are having this trouble now, but I'd be less than fair unless I told you the absolute honest-to-God truth. And the absolute honest-to-God truth, Lance, is that I do *not* find you physically attractive. I know you've always had the hots for me and it must be painful to hear that the feeling is not reciprocated. As I told you in the restaurant, you're not the first of Cathy's men who's wanted to sleep with me. You *did* ask me to be completely honest with you."

"Yes," said Lance, "I guess I did. Well, that's about it, then, Margaret. Thanks for being honest."

Margaret put down the receiver and stared into the middle distance for several minutes. Most of what she'd told Lance was the truth. She really *had* invited him up to her apartment for a surprise birthday party rather than sex. She really *had* told Cathy and Les she was going to be mysterious and a little flirtatious and say she had something important to discuss with Lance in her apartment. It was ironic that Lance had invited her to lunch at Maxwell's Plum the very week that she and Les and Cathy were trying to figure out where to have the party and how to get him there. When he called, she realized she could use the vague promise of sex to accomplish their goal, and she immediately told Cathy and Les her plan.

All right, maybe not immediately. There *had* been a short period of time in which she considered slipping into bed with Lance. So she'd told him a tiny fib. Not that Cathy would ever have suspected. Not that Cathy would ever think for one single second that any husband of hers would find Margaret even the slightest bit attractive. Cathy, as much as Margaret loved her, had a somewhat inflated opinion of her fatal attractiveness to men. Cathy would have been amazed at how many of her old boyfriends had made flagrant passes at Margaret. Not just Lance. There was also Randy.

Randy had pursued Margaret and pursued her, the whole time he was dating Cathy. Finally Margaret gave in and slept with him. Randy was amazed at how hot Margaret was in bed—that was exactly how he put it—but he never wanted to sleep with her a second time. Which was just as well, because Margaret didn't really like Randy all that much, for one thing, and for another thing she felt a little guilty about Cathy. Which was probably one of the main reasons she finally decided not to sleep with Lance and to turn his sexual invitation into merely a means to get him to the party. If there hadn't been a Randy, Margaret might have slept with Lance. But there *had* been a Randy, and Margaret didn't think she could handle another one.

Too bad she had to tell Lance she found him unattractive. However, she suspected the main reason he wanted to sleep with her was to get even with Cathy for allegedly sleeping with Les, so it probably served the bastard right after all.

Lance thought of calling Les for advice, but then he decided not to. He had been so upset by the notion that Les was slipping it to Cathy that, even now that he knew it wasn't true, he could only forgive him about eighty-five percent. There was still resentment. It made no sense, but there it was.

He impulsively called Cathy at the *Times Book Review* to tell her that he loved her. It rang about forty times and then a secretary answered and put him on hold before he could ask for Cathy, and then they were disconnected. He dialed again and the line was busy, but he finally got through and asked for Cathy. She said that Cathy was in a meeting and was there any message.

"Yes," he said, "just tell her that Lance called to say he loves her."

"Will she know what this is in reference to?" said the secretary.

He finally called up his old psychotherapist and made an appointment to talk it over with her. His therapist was a marvelous middle-aged woman named Helen Olden. Helen was a former Freudian and a high-cheekboned former beauty who was now silver-haired and distinguished-looking instead of a beauty, and who no longer felt limited in her replies to patients' questions by the two official Freudian responses of "Well, what do *you* think?" and "What comes to mind about that?" It was partly that Helen had discovered that the Freudian approach wasn't doing much for patients like Lance who tended to overintellectualize everything at the expense of their feelings, and it was perhaps even more that she had been repressing her natural chattiness over the years and it had finally welled up and spilled over the top.

Lance had gone to Helen for a couple of years before he married Cathy. He'd seen psychotherapy as being a bit like surgery —like taking apart a living being to remove an organ which had once been necessary for survival but now interfered with it. He and Helen thought they'd removed all the unnecessary organs and decided to sew him up shortly after he was married. Now he had returned to her, badly shaken, mystified at the sudden turn of events in his life, and ready for more exploratory surgery.

They began the session with Lance allowing Helen to tell him all about the new book she was writing and, even though it was technically on his time, he gave her what advice he could about book promotion and distribution, trying hard not to feel envious at hearing that the advance she was getting for her first book was more than his last three advances combined.

Then Lance told her about his false perception of an affair between Cathy and Les, and of his attempts to balance the scales, of the lights coming on and forty people yelling "Surprise!"

Helen—she encouraged her patients to call her Helen instead of Dr. Olden, now that she was no longer a Freudian—took a long drag on her Gauloise, let out the smoke and said:

"What made you think that fucking your wife's best friend was going to solve your problem?"

Helen used words like "fucking" a lot since she had quit being a Freudian. She was the only person Lance knew who could use vulgar language and still sound classy.

"I don't know," he said. "I guess I was trying to even the score."

Helen made no reply but looked at him in the infuriating way he remembered from when he had been in therapy years before, a vague I-know-something-but-I'm-not-telling half-smile on her face.

"You don't think I was trying to even the score?" said Lance.
She shook her head.

"OK," he said, "what *was* I trying to do?"

"I'd rather have you tell me what *you* think," she said.

"C'mon, Helen. Don't give me that neo-Freudian bit of answer-

ing a question with another question. I asked you what you think
I was trying to do."

"If I told you now it wouldn't mean very much to you."

"Try me. What was I attempting to do?"

"You were attempting to get out of the marriage."

"You're crazy," he said. "Get out of the marriage? Why would
I want to do *that*? I *love* Cathy. Why would I want to get out of
the marriage?"

"I *told* you it wouldn't have much meaning for you now."

"C'mon, Helen, for Christ's sake—why would I be attempting
to get out of the marriage?"

"Because it threatened you."

"How did it threaten me? What threatened me?"

"The closeness. The intimacy. Separation, like underarm de-
odorant, takes the worry out of being close."

"Why would closeness worry or threaten me?"

"Why do *you* think?"

"Oh Christ, we're not back to that old Oedipal crap, are we?"

"I don't know, are we?"

He sighed.

"Great," he said, then declaimed in a singsong voice: "I'm
threatened because I think my wife is my Mommy, and if I'm
fucking my Mommy, then Daddy will kill me. Is that it?"

"Let's put it another way. Let's put it in terms of the incest
taboo. We grow up being taught it's not nice to have lustful feelings about anybody we live with—Mommy, Daddy, sister,
brother, and so on. Then we grow up and move in with a wife or
husband, and suddenly it's supposed to be OK for us to have
lustful feelings about them. But deep down inside, our early
training is telling us that it's still wrong, that the old rules still
apply. That it's wrong to be sexual toward anybody we live with."

"So?"

"So we lose interest in having sex with the person we live with.
We feel anxious, depressed, suffocated, guilty. We find ways of
putting distance between our mates and ourselves. We convince
ourselves we're not feeling well enough to make love. We pick
fights over nothing at all. We get sexually interested in people
with whom we could have only distant relationships and we have

affairs. Or we imagine that our *mates* are having affairs with others and are cuckolding *us*. The means hardly matters. The end is the point: to create distance. To push away the threat of having taboo sex with somebody you live with."

Lance thought it over.

"Look, he said, "maybe there's something in what you say. But that's not my problem right now. My problem is that I acted like an asshole and my wife has left me and she's now circling rental ads in the *Times*. My problem is how do I get her to come back to me?"

"As long as you think that's what your problem is, you're not going to be able to solve it," said Helen flatly. She looked at her watch and stood up. "I'm afraid our hour is up, Lance."

"Hey, look," he said, "I need help. Are you saying you won't help me?"

"I'm saying that if all you want me to do for you is help you get Cathy back, then it's going to be a waste of my time and your money. You may get her back for a while, but you'll just drive her away again. Or you'll fall in love with someone else and just repeat the same pattern. I'm not interested in helping you continue self-destructive patterns, Lance. If you want to work on the larger problems, I'll be glad to help you."

"I've had so much therapy already," said Lance. "Do you really think there's any point in starting the whole thing over again?"

"I think it would be very helpful for you to get into a group," she said.

"A group?"

He made a face.

"I think it would be very helpful to you," she said, walking to the door. "But right now we really do have to stop."

She opened the door and smiled a professional smile.

"I'll think about it," he said.

He noted with some satisfaction that he had managed to squeeze an additional five minutes out of her that he wasn't paying for.

12

Cathy came back to the apartment the following day. He was overjoyed to see her and went to hug her, but she eluded his arms.

"I've been doing a lot of thinking," she said.

"I know," said Lance, "so have I. I realize how upset you are with me and I just want you to know that if you—"

"I'm not upset anymore," she said.

"Good," he said.

"I was very upset the other night, I admit it," she said, "but I'm not upset now."

"Wonderful," he said.

"I've thought everything out very carefully," she said. "I found a nice little place in the West Eighties. One small bedroom, a tiny living room, a kitchenette. It's not gorgeous, but it's clean, and it's only $875 a month. You can have this place. All I want is the furniture."

He chuckled tentatively, suspecting that she was kidding. She left, knowing that she was not. She had said she wasn't upset anymore, but he could tell from how she had eluded his arms and slammed the door on her way out that this was not quite accurate. He knew it was useless to try to talk to her until she calmed down. He spent a horrid, sleepless night, managing finally to drop off to sleep at six in the morning.

Promptly at seven the doorbell rang.

He lurched out of bed, his lips and eyelids glued together, his hair pasted to his forehead. He pulled on jeans and a T-shirt and staggered to the door. He pressed the intercom.

"Who's there?" he said.

"The Motherloaders," said the voice of an android.

"The *what?*" he said.

There was no further response from the intercom. Instead, the door was unlocked and opened. In walked Cathy, followed by four females in work shoes and coveralls on which was stenciled the word "Motherloaders." They were built like stevedores, uniformly short and stocky and very broad in the chest and shoulders. Their necks looked about a size 18. The four women trooped into the living room, followed by their leader.

"What's going on?" said Lance.

"I told you yesterday," said Cathy. "You're keeping the apartment, I'm taking the furniture."

"But this is so abrupt," said Lance. "Can't we talk about it?"

"We talked yesterday," she said, turning toward the four androids. "Start with the living room and work your way to the door. Everything goes."

As Lance watched helplessly, the four mannish movers, smirking faintly, carted out all their furniture—their expensive chrome and leather chairs and modular seating sections, their glass and stainless-steel coffee tables, cartons hastily piled with pots and pans and dishes and glassware and stainless-steel flatware they had got for their wedding, boxes packed haphazardly with books, including some he had bought long before he'd even met her.

He said nothing, partly because he felt so guilty over what had precipitated this action that he thought he had no right to object to anything she did to him, partly because he figured she was simply overdramatizing and would be back with all their stuff in a week or so—the moment she calmed down and came to her senses—and partly because he sensed that, were he to hurl himself in the path of the quartet of muscular Motherloaders they would simply trample him into the parquet floor.

He looked at the four Motherloaders and was unable to differentiate between them; they were all short, squat, muscular and unattractive. He recalled Cathy recently saying he viewed women

as sexist stereotypes, that he never bothered to differentiate between them, that he couldn't bring himself to make one-to-one
contact with women and therefore dehumanized them. Here he
was, doing the very thing she had accused him of.

The toughest of the four Motherloaders galumphed by him,
carrying a heavy armchair over her head. He sprang in front of
her and opened the door for her. He heard her grunt something.
He decided to behave as though she'd said thank you.

"You're welcome," he said.

She grunted something else and moved through the doorway
with the chair. He followed after her, suddenly determined to
make one-to-one contact with her.

"That must be pretty heavy," he said, trailing her down the
stairs.

"Yep."

There seemed to be nothing else to say to her. He raced ahead
of her to open the downstairs door and nearly tripped her in the
process.

"Sorry," he said. "I was just trying to help."

She grunted something.

"My name's Lance," he said. "What's yours?"

"June," she said, and left him standing stupidly on the curb.

Well, he thought, so much for one-to-one contact.

In less than two hours they were gone.

He was alone in an empty apartment. She had left him only
their bed, his clothes, the liquor in the liquor cabinet, his manuscripts and electric typewriter. He sat down in the middle of the
dusty floor and cried like an infant.

For the next several days Lance was immobilized. He had no
desire to receive visitors, shower, shave, dress, look at the mound
of unopened mail that was beginning to collect under the mail
slot in the front door, answer his constantly ringing telephone, or
call up his answering service to find out why they waited till the
thirty-seventh ring to answer, or to have them dictate a long list
of cryptically encoded callers' names and numbers and then have
to try to decipher them. A message from "Canoes Arts" had once
proved to be from the Cuisinart company, one from "Pastor Galley" turned out to be from the Poster Gallery, and one from a

"Miss Terry Gardes" was revealed to be from his old friend in Hollywood, Harry Gittes.

Les came to the door twice and asked if he could do anything, but Lance, fresh from his noncuckolding trauma with Les, sent his friend away.

Lance drank unknown quantities of vodka, and ate canned ravioli at erratic intervals during the day and night, after removing the tops of the cans with a hacksaw because, along with everything else, Cathy had taken all the can openers.

Lance awoke most mornings at four a.m. with a throbbing, skull-pounding, eyeball-squeezing, forehead-shattering headache, stumbled into the bathroom and then struggled for ten minutes, trying to get the child-proof cap off the Bufferin bottle. There were no children in his household, and yet he seemed incapable of buying any kind of medicine that had a cover on it he could remove without getting contusions of the fingertips. If these bottlecaps gave *him,* a comparatively grown man, that much trouble, then what the hell did they expect a *child* with a roaring hangover to do at four a.m.?

Lance alternately watched TV and slept, fully clothed, lying face down across the bed. There was no program, however mindless, that he did not watch—game shows, kiddie cartoon shows, inspirational religious programs—he devoured them all hungrily and without judgment because they permitted him to not think about what had happened.

Lance felt pain, sorrow, fear, anger, depression, and wondered whether he was losing his mind. All the assumptions he had ever made about living with a woman no longer seemed to be valid. He was dimly aware that it was July 4th, Independence Day. He did not feel at all independent. He found himself unable to do any of the things he used to be able to do before Cathy had left him. Although he had been a passable cook, he could no longer quite recall how to turn on the stove. In some preconscious section of his mind he felt that, were he to starve, Cathy would somehow hear about it and come back and feed him.

What little food remained in the apartment went moldy in the refrigerator or furry on the shelves, but he was reluctant to throw it out, seeing it as the last nostalgic remnants of a happier life with Cathy. Indeed, foodstuffs were only the first of a series of things that lurked in cupboards, waiting to be discovered by him and—like emotional land mines—inflict tremendous damage, recalling memories of happier times with his loving wife.

There was another reason he was reluctant to throw out the spoiled food. When he was very small he was a skinny, sickly child. His parents tried to fatten him up, having been told that he wouldn't survive if he remained so thin. They force-fed him like a Strasbourg goose, cajoled and shamed him into eating every last bit of food on his plate, alluding to starving children in Poland who lusted after his soggy mashed potatoes and cold spinach, even anthropomorphizing the food in their desperation to prevent him from rejecting it: "If you don't eat your nice spinach, you'll hurt its *feelings*," they'd whimper when he disdained the proffered spoonful.

Oh-oh. Now that was something he could get into, the notion that spinach had feelings and could be offended. He had a very weird imagination—all little kids do, particularly those who grow up to be fiction writers—and the idea that he would be hurting tender spinach sensibilities if he didn't eat it was unbearable. He was already carrying around a fairly heavy load of nonspecific guilt as it was, and he didn't need wounded spinach feelings on top of it. So that was what they used on him the most: "You don't want that lovely cauliflower? The little cauliflower is *crying*." Oh God, crying cauliflower—he couldn't stand it! "You don't want that lovely glass of warm milk? The poor little milk is *crying*."

No, *stop*, he thought, I'll eat *anything, anything*, only don't tell me it's crying. If he had been a little sharper he might have noticed that it was only certain foods that cried when you didn't eat them. Ice cream he never remembered crying, for example. Not one piece of chocolate cake shed a single tear during his entire childhood. It was only the unpopular foods that always seemed on the edge of despair.

His parents were delighted they'd found a way to make little Lance eat. He eventually gained enough weight to make it into adulthood, but he had paid a terrible price: compulsiveness in all things and a continuing tendency to anthropomorphize everything. Not only was he unable to throw away cauliflower, warm milk, mashed potatoes and spinach, he got teary when he had to part with chicken bones, squeezed oranges, old coffee grounds, and used Kleenexes. His parents literally had to sneak the garbage out of the house while he slept.

The important thing, of course, was that it had got him to eat. He grew up healthy. Only the other day his internist had told him he was the ideal weight for his height. And whenever he went to a restaurant, the waiter always remarked what a good eater he was. The only irony was that the woman he married had never even *heard* of the Clean Plate Club. And whenever Lance had chided her by saying that the poor little breadcrusts were crying, she only laughed. Lance would get so upset he'd end up eating them himself.

Till now, that is. Now the only breadcrusts he had to worry about were his own. And the idea of throwing out any of the rotting food they'd owned together was unthinkable.

He began making late-night forays to an all-night supermarket, looking unshaven and seedy, and realized that there was very little in the way of footstuffs that he could buy whose preparation did not now totally befuddle him. He loaded up on frozen TV dinners, canned ravioli, tortilla chips, beer and Mallomars.

He made a few abortive attempts at cooking, with awful results —his unwatched pot bubbled over, charred and burnt out, with thick gooey stuff forever doomed to be encrusted in the innermost recesses of stove and sink and countertop.

He ran out of socks and underwear. He tried washing the dirty ones in the sink, but managed to get them neither clean nor totally dry. Wearing a bathing suit instead of undershorts, and no socks inside his boots, he took a pile of his dirty laundry in a pillowcase to the laundromat.

He did not know how to operate the washers and driers. When he attempted to ask the women there the most rudimentary questions about how the machines worked, they shied away from his wild-eyed unkemptness as if he were a leper, a child molester or worse. He managed at last to do his laundry without their help, although his whites were permanently stained from running colors, and several of his garments shrank down to toddler size.

On July 14th, Bastille Day, he showered and shaved and went to the housewares section at Bloomingdale's to buy pots and pans and a guide to basic cooking information. Once more he was at a loss about how to proceed, but a matronly saleswoman took pity on him and showed him what to buy to stock a basic kitchen. He was childishly grateful and repressed a powerful urge to hug her to him and rest his head on her bosom and sob.

One day he was having a dream that Cathy had come back to him and was giving him a bath in the bathtub and he was happily showing her his rubber ducky when the rubber ducky rang like a telephone and he knew it was Cathy calling to say she was coming back. He reached out for the phone by the bed, knocked the receiver off the hook and finally managed to pick it up and croak: "Cathy, is that you?"

There was a puzzled pause on the other end of the line.

"Mr. Lerner, please," said a shy teenaged voice.

"Who is this?" he said warily.

"Is this Mr. Lerner?" she said.

"It depends," he said. "Who's *this?*"

His caller giggled.

"This is Dorothy Chu," she said, as if he would instantly recognize the name.

"I'm sorry," he said, "am I supposed to know you?"

"I . . . thought you would," she said. "I guess I was presumptuous. It sounds like I caught you at a bad time. I'll let you go back to whatever you were doing."

"OK," he said.

"It's just that I did something I'm ashamed of and I wanted to apologize."

"Apologize?" he said. "For what?"

"You really don't know?" she said.

"I really don't know," he said.

There was a short pause.

"Mr. Lerner, I'm a senior at the High School of Music and Art and, well, I'm a writer myself, you know? I sent you a fan letter a few months ago. I asked you for advice on writing, and you were kind enough to tell me a lot of stuff—formulas for fiction and nonfiction and stuff. Do you remember now?"

"I'm . . . afraid not," he said. "I get a lot of mail like that, frankly, and I try to answer all of it. It's hard to remember what

I say or whom I say it to, though. What was it you wanted to apologize for?"

"Well," she said, "my friend Janie and I—she's a writer too, sort of—we were going over your letter about a week ago with all the stuff you told me about how to write fiction and nonfiction and everything? And we were both pretty stoned, and I said I thought you were very sexy for an older man, and, well, that's why we took those Polaroids and sent them to you. We're both author groupies, you might say."

"You say you sent me Polaroids?" he said.

"You mean you didn't get any letter with Polaroids? Of a semi-nude Chinese girl? I mailed it about a week ago."

"Oh, *those* Polaroids," he said, thinking fast. "Just a minute. I'll see if I still have them."

He scrambled out of bed and out into the hall and began feverishly digging into the several pounds of mail by the mail slot. He found and tore open three letters addressed to him in fairly childish handwriting before he found the right one. Out tumbled five Polaroid pictures. Three of them featured a girl of about seventeen or eighteen with long black hair to her waist, Oriental features, and a very pretty face. She was wearing white panties and no bra. Her breasts were small but they stirred something in him immediately. The other two pictures featured the same girl with another slightly older-looking Oriental girl behind her, also seminude, with her arms around the first girl's waist. Both girls were grinning idiotically.

Lance raced back to the phone, tripped on the cord and sent the phone crashing into the wall. When he picked up the receiver, the line was dead.

13

He couldn't believe it. The line was absolutely dead.

"Dorothy!" he shouted into the dial tone. "Dorothy, come back!"

He could hear nothing but the dial tone. He slammed down the receiver, cursing. He went to get the letter with the Polaroids again, desperately hoping there would be a phone number, and found a note written on lined yellow notepaper:

> Dear Mr. Lerner,
>
> Or may I call you Lance? I thought it was really sweet of you to write to me and answer all my questions at such length. If you can drag your fingers off the typewriter long enough to dial a phone number, please give me a call. I am hoping the enclosed pictures will be an inducement to call.
>
> Love,
> Dorothy

There was no telephone number anywhere on the letter, front or back. He picked up the envelope. On the back of it she had scrawled: "Chu/16 Mott St./NYC."

He picked up the phone and dialed Information, but the operator could find no listing at that address. He hung up and was just considering taking a subway to Chinatown to hunt her down when the phone rang again. He snatched the receiver out of its cradle on the first ring.

"Dorothy?" he said.

There was silence at the other end. Then:

"Lance?"

The voice sent shivers through him.

"Cathy?"

"That's right," she said coolly. "Perhaps I should hang up so that you can talk to Dorothy."

"No! Cathy, my God—how are you, darling?"

"All right, I suppose. I was just calling to see how *you* were, but I suppose you've already told me. I must say, you certainly don't let the grass grow under your feet. Where did you meet Dorothy?"

"Dorothy is nobody," he said. "When can I see you?"

"Well, I don't know," she said. "How about lunch this afternoon? Or is that too short notice?"

"Come on, Cathy, give me a break. This afternoon is fine. Where and when?"

How about Maxwell's Plum at one o'clock?"

"I'd . . . prefer another place, if it's all the same to you."

"OK. How about the Russian Tea Room? At one?"

"The Russian Tea Room at one. You got it."

He arrived at the Russian Tea Room twenty minutes early, got a booth near the front door and ordered a double White Russian from the Puerto Rican waiter in the high-necked Slavic peasant costume. Lance was clean-shaven and showered and shampooed and as nervous as a high-school kid on his first date. He had totally forgotten Dorothy Chu and whatever it was she needed to apologize for and was rehearsing his own set of apologies when Cathy walked into the restaurant.

She looked sensational. She was wearing a pair of tight chocolate-brown slacks, a brown tweed jacket and a café-au-lait cotton shirt with the buttons open almost to her navel. Was it a good sign or a bad one that she looked so terrific? Had she dressed this spiffily to entice him into a reconciliation, or did she do it because she was now free of him and on the prowl for men?

She offered him her cheek for a perfunctory kiss, and sat down in the booth. She looked at once happier and sadder than he'd ever seen her before. It was impossible to tell what she was feeling.

"What are you drinking?" she said. "It matches my outfit."

"Oh, this? It's called a White Russian. It's Kahlua and cream and vodka, I think. You want one?"

"Sure."

He tried to signal the waiter but couldn't manage to make himself sufficiently visible. He and Cathy looked at each other and smiled. It was going to all be OK, he thought. Thank God, it was all going to be OK. He wanted to take her in his arms and tell her how happy he was. He got a flash of the depth of love he felt for her and his eyes filled up.

"I love you," he said.

"I love you too," she said, and took a breath. "But I want a legal separation."

He couldn't believe he'd heard what he'd just heard. She couldn't have said what he thought she'd said.

"What are you saying?" he said.

Tears sprang to her eyes and spilled down her cheeks.

"I've thought about it a lot, Lance. I've talked to about a thousand women I know over the past month—I even had two sessions with a shrink—and I've decided that that is what I want."

He felt sick to his stomach. His vision was strangely blurred, like looking through a movie camera lens that had been covered with Vaseline. He thought he might vomit up White Russians all over the perky little red leatherette and brass booth.

"I don't understand," he said. "You want a legal separation just because I made a fool of myself in front of all our friends? Just because I wanted to have sex with Margaret to punish you for the affair I thought you were having with Les? I admit what I did was moronic and thoughtless and demeaning, but is it a reason to end a happy seven-year marriage?"

"No, of course not. What you did *was* moronic and thoughtless and demeaning, but that's not the reason I want to end our marriage."

"What then?"

"You said we had a *happy* seven-year marriage. Is that what you really think we had, Lance?"

"Sure. Don't you?"

"No, not really. Oh, I admit I was pretty happy at first. I didn't know any better."

"What do you mean you didn't know any better?"

"I mean that I didn't know what I needed. I though it was enough to be your servant. Your slave. I thought it was enough merely to live in your shadow, merely to be the wife of Lance Lerner, best-selling author and charming talk-show guest. I thought I had no needs of my own. I was wrong, Lance. I'm sorry. I misled you."

"Cathy, listen to me. I *know* you have needs. Honest to *God* I do."

"You do?"

"Yes. Do you really think you were my slave, though? I mean is that what you really think or is that just feminist rhetoric?"

Her eyes narrowed.

"You weren't thinking of attacking feminists now, by any chance, were you?"

"No, of course not. I have nothing but admiration for the movement."

"Good."

"And I'm sure that splinter groups like MATE don't, as they say, necessarily reflect the views of the management."

"*Mate?*" she said.

"You don't know about MATE? M–A–T–E? Men Are The Enemy? Don't tell me you haven't heard of them."

She shook her head.

"It was on *Eyewitness News* only last night. Men Are The Enemy. They abduct a man, they tear his clothes off, abuse him sexually, then write slogans all over his body in spray enamel, like 'Rape is a political crime.' I can't believe you haven't heard about MATE."

Her manner turned chilly.

"I'm sure that's a very amusing concept you made up. You ought to use it in your next novel. I'm glad you have such a sense of humor about the movement."

"Cathy, I'm not making it up—it was on the goddamn *news* last night—goddamn *Eyewitness News*."

"I'm sure you're right," she said. "And I'm sure you've never made cruel and satiric remarks about the women's movement before, either."

"I think the women's movement has accomplished some marvelous things, I really do. I'm behind them one hundred percent.

But nobody has ever accused the movement of having a sense of humor about itself, either."

"I did not," she said icily, "come here to talk about the women's movement. I *did* come here to talk about us."

"Good," he said. "So did I. Let's talk about us."

"Fine," she said. "Now then. As I said before, I have done a lot of thinking, and what I have decided would be best for both of us would be to have a legal separation. I'm not saying a divorce —not at this point, at least—and even if it came to that, I wouldn't want any alimony. I don't even think we need to have a lawyer, if you're willing to—"

"Cathy. Stop. Listen to me. How can you do this? Doesn't our relationship mean *anything* to you?"

"It means a great deal to me. But so does my relationship with myself. So far I've been giving that one the short end of the stick."

"But we're so good together, Cathy. We take care of each other. We have good times. Don't we have good times?"

She shrugged.

"Sometimes they're good," she said. "Sometimes they're not. Do you know how much I hate the process you go through every time you write a novel?"

"God, no," he said. "What part of the process is it that you hate?"

"Every goddamned part," she said. "When you're writing it and it isn't going well, you're depressed and cranky and a pain in the ass to be with. When you're writing it and it *is* going well, you're at your desk sixteen or seventeen hours a day, and it's like you don't even know I exist. When you've finished a draft and you ask me to read it, you *watch* me, for God's sake—you watch me while I read it. And then if I say anything that's the least bit critical about it, you jump on me and practically tear my *throat* out."

"I do not," he said in a wounded voice. "I happen to take criticism very well for a novelist."

"The hell you do," she said. "The slightest thing I point out that I think needs changing and you go and sulk for about three days. So then you turn it in to your editor, and you're so nervous till you get a reaction from him that you're practically jumping right out of your skin."

"But then I get better, right?" he said hopefully.

"The hell you do," she said. "When you've finished all your revisions and your editor thinks it's perfect, *then* is the time you start worrying about how the publisher is going to screw you by not advertising it or promoting it properly, and you become absolutely obsessed with various stratagems to get the book into the media and to get the publisher to send you out on a promotional tour."

"Cathy, you *have* to do that. If you don't—"

"I *know* you think you have to do that. So then you finally persuade them to send you out on tour, and I get to see you about twice in the next six weeks. And when it's over you come home exhausted, you have laryngitis from doing eight talk shows a day, you're usually running a fever of about a hundred and three, and I not only get to be your Mommy and take care of you, I also have to hear all the usual atrocity stories of how the books weren't in any of the stores, and how some of the shows you were supposed to be on didn't even know you were coming, and how others were so ineptly run that you—"

"But it's all *true*—"

"I'm sure it is—and that doesn't make it any more fun to listen to, either. So then, after a couple of weeks you've recuperated, but you've managed to think of an idea for a new novel, and the whole goddamned process begins all over again."

"Jesus," he said. "That's what you've been feeling all these years?"

"That's what I've been feeling," she said.

"I don't know what to say," he said. "I mean, you've just described my life. That's what I do for a living. I write and sell novels. I had no idea it was so painful for you. How come you never told me this before?"

"I did," she said quietly. "You just never listened to me."

"Is it really so terrible for you during the writing phase?" he said gently.

"No," she said. "The other phases are the terrible ones. The writing phase is like living alone. And that's what I'm doing now."

"God," he said, "I had no idea. I mean I feel I ought to apologize to you and promise to change, but I don't really think I could do my work any other way, you know? If I didn't throw myself into my writing when it was going well and work sixteen hours a day, I'd never be able to finish anything. And if I didn't agonize about each book's promotion and then go out on tour with it, the public would never hear about it."

She shook her head sadly.

"You're just a workaholic, Lance—why don't you admit it?"

"Maybe I am," he said. "Workaholics are people who have to overcompensate for their own laziness and their urge to procrastinate, for their inner voices telling them that however much they're doing it's not enough, it's *never* enough, they're still not a good boy. But I also happen to love my work. I hate it when I'm not working. It's more than hate—I'm terrified when I'm not working. I'm like a shark—if I stopped moving I'm sure I'd die."

"I know that's what you think," she said.

"It happens to be true," he said. "But look, forget the work for a moment, because I don't even know what to suggest in that area. At least there are other areas that are good in our marriage, right? I mean, we still have a good sex life, for example, don't we?"

"Is that what you think?" she said.

Lance was badly shaken. He looked around quickly to see if any waiters or other diners had heard this.

"You don't think we have a good sex life?"

"How often do we make love now, Lance? Will you tell me that?"

"I don't know. I mean, I don't keep score on the headboard, I—"

"When we first started living together we made love every day. More than once a day at times. How often do we do it now—once every Sunday? Once every other Sunday?"

"Sssssshhhhhh," he said. He glanced around again. The people at the other tables weren't looking at them, but they weren't talking, either. He leaned across the table to her and continued the conversation in whispers.

"The last week we were together," he whispered, "we did it twice."

"Sunday and when else?" she said.

"Sunday and Wednesday," he whispered.

"And the previous two weeks not once," she said.

"There was a reason for that," he said. "First I was sick, and then we had all those late evenings and we were both too tired—you said so yourself."

"*You* were too tired," she said. "*I* wasn't too tired. I am *never* too tired."

"You are *so,* he said.

"Are not," she said.

"Are so."

"Are not."

"Well, maybe you're right," he said. "After all, why should you be tired? What's tiring about lying there like a lox while I do all the work?"

Her eyes widened and her nostrils got very big.

"Is that what you think I do?" she said. "Lie there like a lox?"

"Do you deny that you don't respond right away when I stroke you? Do you deny that you don't let me do anything but massage your legs for about forty minutes before you even *begin* to let me touch your—"

"Do *you* deny that you would go straight for the old crotch every single time if I didn't stop you?" she said. "Whatever happened to foreplay? Whatever happened to afterplay? Whatever happened to experimentation?"

"What are you *talking* about?" he said. "I ask you all the *time* about all *kinds* of experimentation."

"What you ask me about all the time is not experimentation, it's perversion! You honestly think that having me dress up in a nurse's uniform or wanting to do it with me and another woman or wanting to tie me to the bed is *healthy?*"

"Why isn't it healthy?" he said, but just then the Puerto Rican waiter in the peasant's costume returned to their table with luncheon menus and Lance ordered White Russians for both of them.

"You're so damned predictable," she said even before the waiter was entirely out of earshot. "Whatever happened to spontaneity? You used to be so spontaneous. We used to make love in the bathtub, on the living-room floor, in the car, under a blanket on the beach, in swimming pools . . . Nowadays it's only in bed and we never do anything but the straight missionary position."

"Who the hell's fault is that?" he hissed. "You told me that's the only one you can have an orgasm in."

"Sssssshhhh!" she said.

"Did you or did you not tell me that the missionary position was the only one you could come in?" he whispered.

"I might have told you that," she admitted, "but who says I have to come every time we make love?"

"Who says?" he said. "*You* say, that's who says."

"I told you I have to come every time we make love?" she said.

"Maybe not in so many words," he said. "But if you *don't* come, you keep guiding me back there till I get a chafed penis or a spasm in my finger or lockjaw."

She glared at him.

"*God,* you're horrible," she said. "I never realized how horrible you really are. I'm seeing you now for the first time."

It was not, he decided, going as well as he had hoped.

14

"Women waste their whole *lives* on men," said Cathy heatedly, sitting, not lying, on the therapist's couch. "You meet a man, you fall in love with him, and then you do whatever it takes to land him and keep him happy—no matter how humiliating—because you've been taught that that is woman's *role*. To wait on a man and to compromise yourself for him."

"Mrs. Lerner . . . ?"

"The man, of course, just accepts it as his *due*, because most men have gotten away with such spoiled treatment all their *lives*

—first from their mothers, and then from their mates. Women are—"

"Mrs. Lerner, I wonder if we might—"

"Women are in endless pursuit of the man they love," Cathy continued. "Men are in endless pursuit of *all* women. The only time a man will pursue a woman is when she stops waiting on him. Then he'll do anything—*anything*—to get her back again and restore the status quo."

"Mrs. Lerner, can we—?"

"If he can just get her back, then he can pretend that things are still the way he imagined them to be—that he's still the prince, that he will still be waited on, that she will always be devoted to him no matter what he does, and that he wasn't wrong about how he perceived the world before she left him. That's why it's so important to get her back, to—"

"Mrs. Lerner, I—"

"*Please,* Dr. Freundlich," said Cathy, "it's important that you understand this. Now then, the woman's level of rage gets to a certain point—she realizes the dream isn't going to work, and suddenly it's over for her. She's through with him. Finished. The man is *astounded.* From his point of view, nothing's changed—he's done nothing different, she's done nothing different, nothing's changed—so what could be wrong? Then, if the woman continues to ignore the man's *earnest* entreaties to return, he says, 'Well, that's women for you—you can't live *with* 'em, and you can't live *without* 'em.' He forgets the whole thing. He pretends it never happened. And then he meets a new woman and he does the same thing all over again, having learned absolutely nothing from the entire experience. And that's why men are assholes."

The doctor smiled at her.

"Am *I* an asshole?" he said.

"You're a man," said Cathy, "so you're an asshole."

"And yet you chose to come to me—a man—for counseling, instead of a woman."

"I'm an asshole too," said Cathy.

The doctor gave her a bland, professional smile.

"You say that women are in endless pursuit of the man they love," said the doctor. "But most of them *want* endless pursuit, because victory is too threatening to them."

"Are you saying that I waited on Lance and compromised myself for him for almost eight years because I *wanted* him to act as though I wasn't there?" said Cathy. "Because I would've been threatened if he'd acted like I *was* there?"

"Since I still don't know you very well," said the doctor, "I'd be foolish to say such a thing. What I can tell you, though, is this: Very often in intimate relationships, one of the partners will be very generous and very giving and very self-sacrificing, hoping that the message that's being conveyed is, 'This is how I want *you* to take care of *me*—with the same unselfish, unstinting, nothing-held-back attitude,' but—"

"But the other partner is a Jewish Prince and he just accepts it as his due because he's spoiled rotten," Cathy snapped. "He's so spoiled he'll always ask his mate where something is, rather than look for it himself. He's so spoiled he'll—"

"What I was going to *say*," said the doctor carefully, "was that this sort of behavior is very seductive. It seduces the partner into thinking you don't need anything at all from him in return, that you're just one great big giver—a walking human cornucopia. So then you become resentful that you're giving too much, that you're not getting anything in return, and then you feel justified in leaving him. But if you had merely communicated your true feelings to him in the first place, and not given him this seductive and untrue picture of yourself as a human cornucopia, then he might have reciprocated, and you wouldn't have had any justification for getting mad and leaving."

"Are you saying I set it up?" said Cathy.

The doctor shook his head and sighed.

"I'm saying," he said, "that the situation you describe is not something that was *done* to you, it's a situation that you helped create. You are not its victim."

"You think I'm portraying myself as a victim?"

"Don't *you?*"

"I asked you first."

"I think that many people try to show how impotent and victimized they are in order to preserve their sense of innocence. There's a word that always comes with 'victim' and that's 'innocent.' Innocent victim. The victim is innocent by definition. Unfortunately, what you do when you become a victim is forfeit any possibility of helping yourself—as if to be able to help yourself is to admit not only your strength but your guilt."

Cathy pondered this for several moments before she spoke again.

"Do you think I have any strength?" she asked.

"I think it took *enormous* strength to leave Lance," he said. "And I think it took enormous strength to come here."

Cathy nodded her head slowly, apparently satisfied with both answers.

15

"I can't believe the things she said to me," said Lance.

"What did she say to you?" said Helen, taking a drag on her Gauloise.

"That we don't make love long enough, that I don't give her enough foreplay, that I'm not spontaneous enough, that I'm not imaginative enough, that I'm kinky—things like that."

"Are they true?"

"Some are, some aren't."

"Which are?"

A long sigh.

"When Freud said 'What do women want?,' I could have told him. You know what they want? Three hours of goddamn foreplay, that's what."

"How long do you generally spend on foreplay with Cathy?"

"I don't know, Helen, I never timed it with a cake timer."

"Less than three hours?"

"Yeah, less than three hours."

"Less than half an hour?"

"I don't know. Maybe less than half an hour."

"Less than three minutes?"

"Hey, Helen, give me a break, will you? I said it was maybe less than half an *hour,* I didn't say it was less than three *minutes,* for God's sake."

"I'm sorry. So after you've spent less than half an hour on foreplay, then what?"

"Then we make love."

"For how long?"

"I don't know. More than half an hour. Sometimes an hour, sometimes an hour and a half. Sometimes two hours. Sometimes longer than that."

"It sounds to me like you have a fairly active sex life."

"It's active all right. It's so active I can hardly *move* afterwards. I work as hard at sex with my wife as I do working twelve hours at the typewriter."

"Does it take you that long to achieve an orgasm?"

"Hell no. I can do that in about three minutes. But if I do, she doesn't have time to have one herself. So I hold it back, and I hold it back, and when I hold it back long enough I lose my erection. I feel like I have to stay hard long enough to make her come."

"You resent that, don't you?"

"You're damn right."

"And that's why you lose your erection—out of resentment?"

"I guess. I feel I have to be ready for her anytime she wants it. Sometimes I'll come to bed after working very late in my study, when I think she's asleep, and just as I'm dozing off she'll reach over to my groin and start caressing me. I feel guilty if I can't get hard immediately. Even if I'm half asleep, or if I'm just not in the mood."

"And how does that make you feel—angry?"

"Sort of. And less than manly, too."

"Why do you feel that to be a man you have to be able to produce hard-ons on demand?"

"I don't know, Helen. Men have been getting really bad press for the last few years, you know? They say we're selfish lovers, they say we're insensitive to women's needs. Some say a *woman* can satisfy a woman better than a man. Well, probably all of that is true. I've become a selfish and insensitive and unimaginative lover, and I didn't use to be. I used to be fucking dynamite in bed, Helen, and now I'm a lousy lay."

"Why do you say that?"

"It's true. I used to be spontaneous and imaginative. We made love everywhere—on the beach, in the car, in swimming pools, in the ocean, in revolving doors—everywhere. And then I was married awhile and I became a lousy lay. I've lost interest in sex, unless I've had a lot to drink or unless I'm looking at another woman and fantasizing, and I think part of the reason is that it's just not that much fun anymore. It's a job. It's mostly give and very little get. I don't get that much out of it anymore."

"Then why do you do it at all?"

"I want to do what's right. I think my wife is entitled to be satisfied sexually, so I do it. I know that sounds horrible, but that's what I feel."

"It sounds horrible all right."

"It's so horrible I try to forget about it most of the time. I pretend it isn't happening. I pretend that things are still really great between us, that we're still the perfect couple, you know? And sometimes I try to do something to improve our sex life, but I always find some way to sabotage it. Like sometimes I ask her what I can do that particularly turns her on, but then when she tells me, I feel controlled and resentful, even though I asked her to tell me—isn't that crazy?"

"Yep."

"Sometimes when I get into bed at night after I've been working late I'm thankful it's a king-size bed because I can get into it without touching her and risking waking her up and starting something, and I think, 'Jesus Christ, what kind of a man are you to be feeling like that?' I mean, I'm still horny, I still have constant fantasies about sex, but I don't have much desire to have sex with her, you know?"

"Do you masturbate?"

"Yeah. I go into the john and do it and hope she won't find out, feeling like I'm about fifteen years old. And then when I come out, usually she wants to make love and I have to think of an excuse. What the hell is wrong with me, Helen—am I turning into a fag or what?"

"I don't think you're turning into a fag. I do think you're very resentful and very angry about the sexual demands you feel are being made of you, whether they are or not. I also think it's as hostile and controlling for a man to become impotent with a woman as it is for a woman to be unable to have an orgasm with a man. We're going through a difficult transitional period now, from a culture that looked reproachfully on sex to one that suddenly places a lot of emphasis on frequent and varied sexual activity and on performance . . ."

"Yeah . . ."

"But part of it is that women have *always* known they had the right to refuse to have sex. Men haven't had as much practice as women in saying no, so they aren't too sure how to handle a woman's advances without feeling guilty. You have to remember that nobody is *always* in the mood for love, no matter what the songs say. And you have to be able to say *no* if you're ever going to want to say *yes*."

16

It was not a call he looked forward to making, but it was a month since he and Cathy had separated and the longer he delayed making it the worse it was going to be. They would have to be told eventually. He dreaded their reaction. He heard the line ring about five times and then it was picked up.

"Hello?" said the voice of his mother, certain that whoever it was couldn't possibly be calling with news of anything good.

"Hi, Mom," said Lance, then added needlessly for an only child, "it's Lance."

"Lance!" shrieked his mother. "It's Lance!" she called to his father. It was as if he didn't talk to them once a week. Why was a call from him such a big deal? And if it was, why didn't he dole out more of them?

"How are you doing?" said Lance, trying to offset his mother's relentless premonitions of disaster. Lawyers and mothers, he mused, always know the worst that could happen in any given situation.

"Lance, what's wrong, dear?" said his mother, then yelled again to his father: "It's Lance!"

"Lance is in town?" he heard his father call out from somewhere in the background.

"No, Harry, on the *phone*—Lance is on the *phone!*"

"Oh," said his father, "on the *phone.* Why didn't you *say* so!"

"Lance," said his mother, "what's the trouble, darling?"

"Trouble?" said Lance. "Why do you always assume when I call you that there's trouble?" It irritated him that she did that, the more so because she was usually right.

"Hello, Lance?" said his father, getting on the extension. "How are you, son? What's new in the Big Apple?"

"Hi, Dad. Nothing much. How are you?" said Lance. His technique of breaking bad news to them was to start off slowly and then sort of quickly pop it in there like a surprise lay-up.

"Can't complain," said his Dad. "How's the writing?"

"The writing?" said Lance.

"What?" said his father. Neither of his folks was hard of hearing, but both were absentminded and tended not to listen very closely.

"How's the *writing?*" said Lance.

"*You're* the writer," said his father, "what're you asking *me* about the writing?"

"No, no," said Lance, wondering if his family might have blood ties to Abbott and Costello, "you asked me about the writing, you see, and I . . . The writing is fine, Dad. Although I've been doing less writing of late than reading."

"Than what?" said his mother, "*bleeding?*"

"*Bleeding? Who's* bleeding?" shouted his father.

"*Nobody's* bleeding," said Lance. "I didn't say 'bleeding,' I said 'reading.' I said I've been doing less writing than *reading.*"

"Oh, *reading,*" said his father. "Reading is perfectly fine. I thought he said *bleeding.*"

"So did I," said his mother. "I almost had a coronary."

Lance winced. Any talk of coronaries from his parents triggered ancient fears of their dying, of him being left to fend unsuccessfully for himself.

"So," said his father, "then nobody is hemorrhaging there in New York after all. I'm relieved to hear that. And things are going well?"

"Yeah," said Lance. "Pretty well."

"So how is Cathy?" said his mother.

"Cathy?" said Lance. "Cathy is . . . fine. I mean we just got separated, but she's fine."

"Oh, God!" cried his mother, "I *knew* it was bad news. Didn't I tell you it was bad news, Harry?"

"You got what, *separated?*" said his father.

"Yeah," said Lance, "but it's no big deal. She'll probably come waltzing back in here tomorrow or the next day just like nothing happened."

It was a lie so blatant that nobody could possibly mistake it for the truth, even people who heard "bleeding" for "reading." Why, then, did he say it—to convince the operator?

"What happened?" said his mother. "You both seemed so happy when we saw you last."

"I know it," said Lance. "It was just one of those things, you know?"

"Is it another fella?" said his father, quietly, so the neighbors shouldn't hear. It was no mystery to Lance where he'd learned his anxiety about eavesdropping strangers.

"No, no, it's not another man, nothing like that," said Lance.

"Then what is it?" said his mother.

"A misunderstanding," said Lance. "Nothing more than that. We'll get it patched up again, don't worry."

"Worry?" said his mother. "Why should I worry? You're a

grown man, forty years of age. You think I'm worried you can't take care of yourself?"

"No, Mom, I don't think that . . ."

"Don't you think I know you can cook and wash your own clothes and clean up a little around the house whenever the dust gets so thick you can't see the furniture?"

"Yes, Mom, I know you know that."

There was a pause.

"Honey, do you want your Mom to come to New York to take care of you for a little while?" said his mother softly, as if she wanted to speak quietly enough so that he himself wouldn't have to hear the question and be embarrassed by it. Her query and the enormous love which had obviously prompted it momentarily connected with the terrible feelings of abandonment and help-lessness he thought he had successfully repressed, and he had to bite back a sob. Tears filled his eyes, but he managed to make his voice absolutely calm again in seconds.

"I'm fine, Mom," he said, "honest to God. I appreciate the offer, and I may even take you up on it sometime, but for now I'm OK, and I think it would be better if I worked this all out by myself."

"All right, dear," she said.

"Do you need some money, son?" said his father softly. Lance had at least ten times as much money as his Dad, but whenever he was in trouble his father always offered him money.

"No thanks, Dad," said Lance. "I have enough money."

"Do you want to tell us what the fight was about?" said his mother. "After all, your father and I have been married fifty years—about fighting we happen to know a little something."

"I don't think I really want to talk about it just now," said Lance, shuddering at the prospect of describing the moment when the lights came on and forty people stood staring at a naked Lance with a hard-on and the word 'Surprise' came halfway out of their throats and froze there.

"Well," said his father, "whatever it is, I'm sure you'll be able to work it out. We both have a lot of faith in you, kid."

"Thanks, Dad," said Lance. "That means a lot to me."

17

"My *God*, Lance," said Howard Leventhal, ushering him into his neatly cluttered office, "you look absolutely *awful!*"

"It's good to see you, too, Howard," said Lance, pushing a pile of perfectly squared-off manuscripts aside and sitting down on the brown velvet couch opposite his editor's desk, a study in controlled chaos.

Howard, a prissy, paunchy man with thinning sandy hair, an unexpectedly handsome face and Ben Franklin glasses, was actually eight years younger than Lance and leapt upon any apparent flaw in Lance's generally superior appearance with thinly disguised relish. Since Lance knew where it came from, he found it more flattering than insulting.

"Really," said Howard, "you look *ghastly*—is anything *wrong?*"

"Well no, not really," said Lance with elaborate casualness. "I have a mild headache and a slight upset stomach, and Cathy has left me, but other than that, everything is perfect."

"Cathy's *left* you?" Howard slapped his forehead. "Oh, my *God*. When did this *happen?* Where did she *go?* How are you *surviving?*"

Howard tended to speak in the italicized cadences generally employed by homosexual men, though Lance doubted Howard was a fag. Howard, in fact, appeared to have quite a crush on Cathy.

"Get a grip on yourself, Howard," said Lance. "*I'm* handling it nicely, there's no reason why *you* shouldn't."

People like Howard were always trying to co-opt your troubles and get more pain out of them than you did yourself. Lance resented such behavior. He had worked hard to get himself into the mess with Cathy, and he was damned if he was going to share his pain with anybody.

"Do you want to *talk* about it?" Howard asked, adopting a confidential and solicitous tone.

"Sure," said Lance, "but not now. Now I'd rather talk about the promotion of *Gallivanting*."

"I understand, I understand," said Howard, grabbing Lance's hand and squeezing it. "Is there another *man* or what?"

"Not exactly," said Lance. "But we can discuss it at greater length some other time."

"Good," said Howard. "I don't *blame* you for not wanting to talk about it. We'll just go on into Mike Fieldston's office—Mike is our head of promotion and advertising, I don't believe you've met him yet—and we can talk about personal matters later. It's *not* another man, you say?"

His father, Lance decided, was allowed to ask about other men. His editor was not.

"*No,* Howard," said Lance, "it's not another man."

"Good," said Howard. "Say, it's not another *woman,* is it?"

"*No,* Howard," said Lance, beginning to get annoyed, "it's not another woman, either. Five down, and over to you, Arlene Francis."

Howard flashed Lance a forced smile and took him on into Mike Fieldston's office. Mike Fieldston was tall, Waspy, blond, and, like Howard, had a paunch, thinning hair and somewhat Benfranklinesque glasses. Maybe those were prerequisites for working at Firestone.

Mike stood up and shook hands with Lance as he and Howard entered. Then he introduced Lance to three other people who were already there for the meeting: a mousy woman of twenty-five named Charlene who worked in publicity, an acne-scarred but otherwise attractive brunette named Judy or Julie who was also about twenty-five and also worked in publicity and who was either slightly below or slightly above Charlene in rank, and a pipe-smoking blond chap of about thirty by the name of Brad who worked in advertising and was merely teetering on the *brink* of paunchiness and thin-hairedness.

Everybody found seats. Mike cleared his throat. Lance wondered idly how Judy-or-Julie's acne scars had affected her love life. He wondered what he'd do if someone offered to return Cathy to him with the provision that serious acne scars came with the deal. He'd take the deal even if it were leprosy.

"Lance," said Mike, "Judy, Charlene, Brad and I have been kicking around some ideas for the promotion of your book, and, well, frankly, I think we've come up with a helluva campaign."

"Great," said Lance. "What's our budget, by the way?"

"What's our what, Lance?" said Mike, frowning as though the word might be new to him.

"Our budget. How much is Firestone allocating for the promotion and advertising campaigns of my book?"

Mike looked quickly at Howard and then back to Lance and cleared his throat. Lance began to get uncomfortable. It made him uncomfortable any time others in a room knew something he didn't.

"The budget," said Mike, "has not as yet been finalized."

"I see," said Lance, waiting for the rest of it.

"We do not, quite frankly, have a whole carload of money to play around with," said Mike, flashing Lance a smile to let him know he knew that "a whole carload of money" was a helluva charming metaphor. "I think I'd better say that right off the bat."

Lance's discomfort began edging smoothly into anxiety. From experiences with his previous six novels he knew that the act of publishing a book was largely a self-fulfilling prophecy. Three of his previous books had been dubbed bestsellers by their respective publishers before they had even been set in type. They were advertised and promoted like bestsellers, and bestsellers is what they became. His other three novels had been dubbed dogs by their publishers at about the same point. They were scarcely advertised or promoted, and dogs they surely became. This of course caused Lance to take a loss on the years invested in the books, but it also made it hard to find a publisher for his next novel after each failure, since it is authors who get blamed for lack of sales and not their negligent publishers.

When Lance had made his deal with Firestone on *Gallivanting*, his latest, they seemed to feel it would be a blockbuster. They promised him a promotion and advertising budget in excess of a hundred thousand dollars, just for starters, and a twenty-four city promotional tour.

"Is the budget less than a hundred thousand dollars?" said Lance.

"Oh yes," said Mike. "Quite a bit less than that, I'm afraid."

"I see," said Lance. "Is it less than fifty thousand?"

"Oh yes," said Mike. "Quite a bit less than that."

"Is it less than twenty-five?" said Lance.

Mike looked at Howard again. Howard shrugged.

"I'm going to be honest with you, Lance," said Mike. "The budget is five thousand dollars."

Lance turned to Howard. He was stunned. He felt slightly dizzy.

"Is this true, Howard?" said Lance.

"Lance," said Howard, "there's a *hell* of a lot you can do with even *that* amount of—"

"I want my book back," said Lance, feeling like a five-year-old. "If you're spending that little, you're throwing it right into the toilet. I'd rather publish it *myself* than—"

"Now hold *on* there, Lance," said Mike, "let's not be childish."

"No, let's not be childish," said Lance, getting more and more excited and childish. "Let's be really grown up and professional and pretend that five thousand dollars is going to be able to do anything at all to let the reading public know my book even *exists*."

"Lance," said Howard, "it's not *our* decision to limit the budget to five thousand—"

"Whose decision is it?" said Lance.

"The head of *sales*. And old man Firestone *himself*," said Howard.

"I thought you were going to give me a big send-off," said Lance, hating the five-year-old tone that clung to his voice, but unable to mature it. "That's the only reason I signed with Firestone in the first place. You promised me a twenty-four city promotional tour and a hundred-thousand-dollar budget, do you remember that?"

"I remember . . . that we were *hoping* it would be a bigger book than the men now feel it's going to *be*," said Howard carefully.

"The *men*?" said Lance. "You're telling me that the sales force has already decided—before the book has even been *printed*—that it's a dog?"

"That's their feeling, Lance," said Howard. "The men are usually *right* about these things, too."

"On what are they basing their feelings?" said Lance. "Have they all read the manuscript?"

"Lance," said Howard patronizingly, "we publish three hundred and sixty-five books a *year*. That's a book a *day*. Do you honestly expect the men to read every *one* of them?"

"No," said Lance, "just mine."

Mike, Brad, Judy and Charlene chuckled, anxious for the opportunity to lighten up the mood.

"If they haven't read my book," said Lance, "then on what did they base their feeling it's not going to sell?"

"On what I told them about it at *Sales* Conference," said Howard.

"How long did you talk to them about it at Sales Conference?" said Lance.

"Well, they only gave me a couple minutes for each book on my *list*," said Howard, "but don't worry, I gave yours quite a build-up."

"I'll just *bet* you did," said Lance. "What did you say about it?"

"I read them the paragraph I wrote about it for the spring *catalogue*," said Howard.

Lance took a deep breath. He felt he was in quicksand, and someone had thrown him a breath mint.

"Howard, how can they tell anything about whether my book is going to sell from merely hearing a paragraph that you wrote about it?"

Howard looked at Mike. Brad looked at Judy and Charlene. They wondered why every single author they handled had to be certifiable.

"Lance, they didn't think your book was very well *written*," said Howard in a vaguely accusatory tone.

"They didn't *read* my book," said Lance. "They listened to you read them a paragraph *you* wrote. Was the paragraph *you* wrote well written?"

"It . . . frankly needed work, Lance," said Howard, "I'm not going to deny that. Look, *you're* the writer, not *me*."

"Yeah, I'm the writer. And my writing is being judged by what a self-confessed *non*writer wrote about it."

Lance looked from face to face. They showed him tight, fakey little smiles. It wasn't fair. Their logic made no sense at all, yet they were acting as though *he* were the crazy one.

"Lance," said Howard patiently. "The initial orders from the *stores* have borne out the men's pessimism—the orders aren't, frankly, very *good*, Lance."

"How *could* they be good?" said Lance. "The men didn't like what you told them at Sales Conference. How do you think that made them sell my book?"

It was futile to continue this, but he couldn't seem to stop.

"Look, Lance," said Howard, "if the word-of-mouth on the book is *good* among the public and it really takes *off*, then I'm sure the house will really get behind it."

"If the word-of-mouth on the book is good and the book takes off," said Lance, "who the hell *needs* the house to get behind it?"

"Look, Lance," said Mike, "there's still a helluva lot of mileage we can get out of that five thousand dollars."

"Like what?" said Lance.

"Well," he said, "first of all, we'll get you a lot of interviews in the New York area, then we'll take a couple small space ads and, uh . . ."

Lance turned to Judy and Charlene.

"What kind of interviews are you working on for me in the New York area so far?" he said.

"Well," said Judy, "we've got a few interviews tentatively lined up . . ."

"Anything on network TV?" said Lance. Network TV could make a book a bestseller.

"Not really," said Judy, "but . . ."

"Anything on *local* TV?" said Lance. Local TV could be very effective in certain cities.

"Not really," said Judy. "Pub date isn't till September 15th, but we do have tentative interviews set up on a couple of FM radio shows in New Jersey, and I'm working on a press interview in the Moonie newspaper . . ."

"The Moonie newspaper?" said Lance incredulously. He

thought she might be joking, then realized she had no sense of humor.

"The Moonie newspaper has quite a circulation," said Charlene defensively, "you'd be surprised."

"So that's it, eh?" said Lance, vaguely nauseated, turning to Howard, "That is what you're giving me to bring my book before the public—FM radio in New Jersey and Moonie newspapers?"

"It's not a bad start," said Mike.

"It's better than *nothing*," said Howard.

"No, it isn't," said Lance. "It is *not* better than nothing, Howard. That's where you're wrong."

Howard sighed.

"You know, Lance," said Mike, "half the problem is that it's just a bitch to promote fiction."

"It's also hard as hell to sell anything with sex in it," said Judy.

"The one thing they absolutely won't *touch* on most of your TV talk shows today," said Charlene, "is sex."

"Sex," said Judy, "or humor."

"Sex, humor, or politics," said Mike. "And I'm afraid you've got a helluva lot of all three in this book."

"What the hell's the difference?" said Lance. "If I took all the sex, humor and politics out of my book and turned it into a piece of straight reportage, you still don't have any budget to promote it with."

"Lance, why don't you contact old man Firestone and see if *he'd* be willing to increase our budget?" said Howard wearily.

"I may just do that," said Lance.

To the absolute surprise of nobody, Firestone never responded to Lance's phone call nor to the three messages he left on subsequent calls. He was assured every time that Firestone had received his messages and was trying to find time to return his calls.

It was clear how much Firestone valued his authors. Someone ought to teach the sonofabitch a lesson. If only authors weren't such independent bastards. If only they'd band together and force some basic issues. Like guaranteeing, when you were on a tour to promote a book, that there would be copies of it available for sale in bookstores. It didn't seem a lot to ask, and yet finding your book in stores when you were on tour was the exception rather than the rule.

In all fairness, Lance knew, it was not possible for any author to be satisfied with the way his book is published. To use a metaphor common among authors, it was like carrying a baby through nine months of pregnancy and then surrendering it to someone else to bring up while you hung around and watched. Even if the person were doing the best job she could, you still wouldn't be satisfied with the way she was raising your kid. But what usually happens is that the person decides that she can't afford to buy your baby clothes, so the child runs naked; the person often forgets to feed it, and so the child grows sickly. Eventually the person forgets the child exists altogether and one day sits down on it by mistake and crushes it to death. And then this person has the gall to tell you that your child was never really healthy to begin with and that what happened simply put it out of its misery.

Even if publishers did the best jobs they could, most authors would still find something to be bitter about, Lance knew. But why did publishers give authors so *much* to be bitter about? Why, for example, was it the exception rather than the rule when a book appeared without major typographical or production errors, or when it was actually to be found in the bookstores on publication day? Why, he wondered, was it the exception rather than the rule when a book was advertised or promoted enough to even come to the attention of potential readers, or when it was actually available to be bought when people came to buy it? If they sold bread the way they sold books, Lance mused, the bakers wouldn't stand for it. Why did the authors?

The first time Lance had ever gone into Brooks Brothers and had seen the suit coats turned inside out and stacked on tables instead of hanging on a rack, he was greatly intrigued. He approached a salesman and asked him why they stacked their jackets this way. "We've *always* done it this way," said the salesman haughtily.

"Because you found out that a jacket keeps its shape better this way or what?" said Lance.

"No," said the salesman, bored with Lance's obtuseness, "because we've always *done* it this way."

Although conglomerates had bought most of the publishing houses and forced them to update their sales and distribution methods, publishing was still a lot like Brooks Brothers, Lance felt.

Charlene in publicity called him on the phone.

"Well, I finally heard from the *Tonight Show*," she said. "It's a no."

"What talent coordinator did you talk to?" said Lance.

"Sheldon Aronson," she said.

"Well, I don't know that name," said Lance, "but I've been on the *Tonight Show* a couple of times before, and my talent coordinators were Jamie Severeid and Bob Shirley. Why don't you try one of them?"

"I'm sorry," she said, "I only deal with Sheldon Aronson."

"How come?" said Lance. "Do you have such a good batting average with him you're afraid to jeopardize it or what?"

There was a short silence at the other end of the line.

"I have never managed to get anyone on the *Tonight Show*," she said.

"I can see why you wouldn't want to jeopardize that record," said Lance.

18

Cathy was exhilarated. Exhilarated and frightened. She had rented the first apartment she'd looked at, a tiny three-room job in an old building on the far West Side. It wasn't anything to look at, but it was available, it was $875 a month, which was relatively cheap, and mainly it was *hers*.

Hers. Hers to do with whatever she wished. Hers to fix up beautifully and keep looking immaculate or hers to throw soiled laundry around and pick it up only when or if she pleased and not when one's obsessive, anal-compulsive husband thought one ought to. Hers to listen to loud rock music in, even though one's husband hated it and only liked classical—she had never listened to rock music when she lived with Lance, even when he wasn't home! OK, so it wasn't as fancy as the place she'd lived in with Lance. That was all right—she'd always felt something of a fraud living in a swell apartment that was strictly a reflection of *his* income, not hers.

She had a phone installed immediately and fell in love with its whiteness and its newness and its absolute *hersness*. She had never owned her very own phone before, never had a number at which only *she* could be reached. In her apartment with Lance, people who called were calling for either of them, but mostly for Lance. In the apartment she had shared with Margaret and Cheryl, people were calling for any of them, but mostly for Cheryl. Before that she had lived in a college dorm and before that with her parents, and neither of those phones were hers by a long shot. But with this phone, anybody who called would be calling only for *her*. Except for wrong numbers, of course.

Cathy spent the first Saturday in her new apartment painting it white—virginal white. She chose a glossy enamel so that the walls and ceilings would look exceptionally clean. She didn't have to buy any furniture but a bed—the stuff she had brought from Lance's apartment filled the tiny rooms so tightly she could scarcely squeeze between the pieces. Perhaps she should have left a few pieces for Lance. Perhaps not. If he needed furniture, let him *buy* it. Fuck him.

Her rage at Lance, she realized, was a little stronger than it needed to be. His moronic attempt at seducing Margaret at his fortieth birthday party was too pathetic to inspire the kind of fury she was now feeling. Perhaps it went deeper than Lance. Perhaps it didn't. The incident at the surprise party elicited less anger from her than the mere image of Lance sitting at his desk, typing away at his novels, totally oblivious to her existence.

Her father, whom she loved very much—too much to even talk to more than twice a year—had had a similar ability to lose himself in his work and disappear totally from his family in every sense but the physical. Cathy's father wrote insurance policies instead of novels, but the effect was the same. Cathy didn't believe in the existence of such mystical phenomena as out-of-body travel, but she supposed that if such a thing were possible, the bodies which out-of-body travelers left behind would appear to their families the way that Lance's had to Cathy during their marriage and the way that Cathy's father's had to her and her mother while her mother was still alive.

It had been Lance's idea that Cathy's mother's cancer was psychogenically induced, which Cathy felt was as disrespectful as it was absurd. Cancer was cancer, as far as Cathy was concerned, and she worried constantly that it was hereditary and that sooner or later it would show up in her own breasts or her cervix or her ovaries or something. She was always discovering lumps in her breasts, which lasted long enough to produce fantasies of mastectomies and of being abandoned by Lance before she made appointments to have the lumps inspected by a doctor, following which they generally went away.

Lance maintained that Cathy's mother was never able to get her father's attention except when she was ill, which was simply not fair, although probably true to some extent. Every time her mother got sick, Cathy's father had dropped his work and waited on her hand and foot. And every time she got well he withdrew his attention and returned to his insurance policies. That much was certainly true.

And what was also true was that every time Cathy's mother got sick her father was just a little less attentive to her with each successive illness. Until Cathy's mother got lumps in her breasts and it looked as though she might have cancer. Then her father was as attentive to her as he had ever been since they'd gotten married. And when it turned out that the lumps were benign, Cathy's father was immensely relieved, but after a while he returned to his work and it seemed to Cathy and her mother that he had never left it.

Cathy's mother had two more cancer scares before they finally discovered a malignancy. Lance said—unfairly and cruelly—that Cathy's mother had finally, through trial and error, figured out how to do it right. Why would Lance *say* such a thing? Why would anybody deliberately give themselves cancer, assuming that such a thing were physiologically possible? Never mind what Lance thought. One of Lance's favorite things to argue about at dinner parties was that all illness was psychogenically induced, even his own.

Well, if Cathy—God forbid—ever got cancer, it wouldn't be because she'd wished it on herself, and that was for sure, and the fact that she occasionally got sick when she was living with Lance and enjoyed the fabulously attentive care he gave her did not at all prove he was right. She did not need his care, she rejected absolutely his support: "So long, succor!" she yelled out suddenly and giggled.

She wondered who would take care of her now if she did get sick. She supposed that whichever man she was dating at the time would do as much for her as Lance had. Well, almost as much. The thing was to hold off getting sick until she was involved with another man seriously enough to have him take care of her if she were ill.

Another man. The prospect of becoming involved with another man was wildly exciting and delicious. Who would she become involved with? Which of the dozen or more men who had constantly buzzed around her while she was with Lance would now become her lover? The thought of taking other lovers made her feel guilty. Well, there was ample time for that. Right now she was more interested in getting her new life together than in having lovers. She was on her own now for the first time in her life and she liked it. "I *like* myself, I *like* myself!" she chanted, prancing through her new apartment. She went into the tiny white bathroom and took a long, luxurious bubblebath. She got out and sat on the bed, rubbing scented creamy lotion lovingly on her body. She absentmindedly kissed her right knee and giggled at what she'd done.

She didn't need Lance. She didn't need other men. She didn't need anyone at all—she had *herself* now. She would take more bubblebaths. She would masturbate. She had surprisingly little guilt about masturbation, probably because of the matter-of-fact way her mother had dealt with the subject. Cathy thought that female masturbation was normal and healthy and even beautiful, unlike male masturbation, which was gross and tacky and perverted.

She might even start using the Ben Wa balls that Lance had given her a couple of years ago. She hadn't at first known what the two little gold balls in their purple velvet jewelry box were when Lance gave them to her. She thought he was kidding when he said that women wore them inside their vaginas, especially in the Orient, for the pleasant sexual sensations they produced. But she had dutifully tried them, and if they hadn't exactly driven her mad with pleasure, they were, as Lance put it, better than a poke in the eye with a sharp stick.

She went over to the top dresser drawer where she kept the Ben Wa balls and was surprised not to find them there. She looked through her other drawers as well. She searched every drawer in every piece of furniture she'd brought with her, but she couldn't find them. Where the hell could they have gone? She was positive she had taken everything with her when she'd moved. She was positive they weren't still in Lance's apartment. So where could they be? It wasn't even that important to find them, but the idea that they were lost and she couldn't have them when she wanted them was causing her to get unduly upset.

19

Lance was finally able to speak to Les, and to forgive Les for seeming to have been humping his wife. Les urged Lance to begin dating other women.

Lance told Les he didn't think he was ready yet. It had been years since Lance had had to think about the business of picking up and seducing women, and he didn't know if he was up to it. Not that it was so hard to do. Not that he hadn't flirted with lots of women in the eight years he had lived with Cathy, because he had—Margaret was the latest example of that, of course. But married flirting was different, somehow, from singles pickups. Married flirting was sneakier, naughtier, less serious. There seemed little likelihood that it would ever lead to anything hard-core.

He wondered what sex would be like with someone other than Cathy. He wondered if he'd even be able to get it up.

A publishing party in a cavernous nine-room West Side apart-ment. Three people who could afford separate but smaller apart-ments on the more fashionable East Side of Manhattan shared the apartment—a handsome and well-connected city editor of a large metropolitan newspaper, a bespectacled, relentlessly polite chap who wrote caustic reviews of Off-Broadway plays, and a sexy, redheaded police reporter who wasn't sleeping with either of them as far as anybody could tell.

Lance downed two vodka-tonics in a plastic glass without ice, because they'd run out, and chatted with an author he knew named Arthur Arthur. Arthur Arthur was one of the dozen suc-cessful authors that Lance knew well enough to bullshit with at parties. Arthur Arthur, who earned $100,000 to $200,000 per book on hardcover advances, had once confessed to Lance that he despised writing, and that the whole process was utter, unre-lieved agony to him. Arthur Arthur was a more commercial writer than Lance, and took pride in the fact that he had never spent more than three months writing any of his fifty-seven books.

"You know," said Arthur Arthur reflectively, "I guess I must be the only member of our crowd who's made it really big."

Lance didn't know which part of the remark was the more surprising—that the fellow felt he had made it really big, or that the two of them were in anything approaching the same crowd.

A woman he knew named Marlene Orman caught sight of Lance and scurried over. She and her husband, Fred, had been friends of Lance and Cathy's up till a couple of years ago, when Marlene left Fred for a much younger man.

"Lance," said Marlene, "I almost didn't recognize you!"

"How are you, Marlene?"

"Well, I'm *fine*," she said grabbing his upper arm and squeezing it, while frowning into his face, "but how are *you?*"

"Fine," said Lance.

"I *heard*," said Marlene, still frowning into his face. Why was it some people stood too close to you, he wondered, and why was it always those with halitosis?

"What did you hear?" said Lance.

"About you and Cathy. I'm so sorry. You look pretty broken up—you must be taking it hard."

"You think I look broken up?" said Lance. "I thought I looked terrific."

Marlene shook her head sadly.

"Don't worry," she said. "This too shall pass. The pain gets lighter and lighter, and then, in two or three years, it will hardly hurt at all, and you can start looking around for someone else."

"Well," he said, "thanks for buoying up my spirits, Marlene."

"Look around you, Lance," she said, looking around her. "Look at the friends we used to know. What do you see?"

Lance looked around. He didn't know what he was supposed to be looking at.

"There's Ralph Aron. Do you remember what a cute couple Ralph and Rona Aron used to be? Look at what he's married to *now.*"

Lance looked at Ralph. Ralph had aged somewhat—lost crown and forehead hair, gained eye and neck wrinkles and waist flesh. Ralph was standing next to a very sexy-looking, very intense, very *young* woman who was wearing a suit and tie.

"She looks all right to *me*," said Lance.

"Ralph is forty," said Marlene. "This girl is barely *twenty-one.*"

"What's the difference how old he is if they're happy?" said Lance.

"*Happy?*" said Marlene. "That's what I mean—we thought Ralph and *Rona* were happy. We thought you and *Cathy* were happy. You probably thought Fred and *I* were happy. We all put on such a happy facade—we all invested such effort to try to convince our friends how goddamned *happy* we were—and now here we all are with different mates. Fred is here tonight too, you know."

"He is? Where?"

Marlene pointed. Lance could make out Fred standing next to a young blonde girl who had her arm familiarly around his waist. Fred, he saw, had aged as much as Ralph. Lance was secretly pleased that he looked better than they did. Fred was a fairly funny writer. He wondered how a writer as funny as Fred had managed to put up with such halitosis for all those years.

"Can you imagine him bringing that girl to a party he knew I'd be at?" said Marlene. "I could hardly believe my *eyes* when I saw him walk in that door."

"Marlene," said Lance, "didn't you leave *him?*"

"What's the *difference* who left whom?" she said. "I think it displays a certain lack of sensitivity for him to be standing there with his arms around that . . . girl. How would you feel if *Cathy* had brought somebody tonight and was standing there in plain sight of you, pawing him?"

"Speaking of Cathy," said Lance, "I guess there's a possibility she just might show up here tonight."

"You mean you haven't *seen* her?" said Marlene.

"You mean she's *here?*" said Lance, feeling his lower gastrointestinal tract suddenly drop into his boots.

"Right around the corner," said Marlene, "in the dining room. By the hors d'oeuvres. Oh, you poor *thing*, I thought you'd already *seen* her."

"Uh, no," said Lance, moving toward the bar. "Hey, listen, Marlene, it was nice running into you. I'm going to go and freshen my drink."

"I don't blame you," she said. "Liquor will ease the pain, for a little while at least."

Lance refilled his drink, knocked it down, had another, and drifted around the corner. Sure enough, there was Cathy, talking animatedly to a guy he didn't know and to Howard Leventhal. He was debating whether or not to go over to her when Howard said something to her. Cathy glanced in Lance's direction, her face got fairly flushed, and then she turned around and headed in the opposite direction.

Lance, nursing his fifth vodka-tonic, was forcing endless drinks on a plumpish but otherwise presentable-looking young woman named Joyce who wore a see-through black blouse in which nipples were clearly visible. After about seven of the Lance-forced drinks, Joyce appeared to be having a modicum of difficulty standing upright. Lance suggested that they go back to his place for a nightcap. Joyce said why not?

Lance steered Joyce into the bedroom and burrowed into the yard-high mound of coats, finally extracting both hers and his, and was weaving tipsily toward the door when a tough-looking brunette in black leather jeans and boots tapped him on the shoulder.

"You going to the East Side, chief?"

Lance had not, to the best of his recollection, ever been called "chief" before, and he was intrigued.

"I'm going as far as 48th and Second," he said.

"Terrif," said the brunette. "Mind if I share your cab?"

Lance shrugged.

"Why not?"

Lance guided Joyce into the elevator, through the lobby, and out onto the street, as the brunette gave a running critique of everybody at the party. The brunette's name was Stevie, she was a policewoman and although she had had as many drinks as Joyce, she carried it better.

The three of them got into a cab, with Lance in the middle, and Stevie began a surprisingly knowledgeable interrogation of Joyce on literary subjects as far-ranging as the influence of Gertrude Stein on the style of Ernest Hemingway and the religious symbolism in *Ulysses*. Stevie, it developed, aside from being a plainclothes police detective, also taught English to cops at John Jay College.

As Stevie interrogated Joyce and Joyce replied as best she could under the influence of seven Manhattans-in-a-plastic-cup-without-ice, Stevie surreptitiously ran her hand slowly up the inside of Lance's inner thigh, pausing millimeters short of paydirt.

Lance was wildly ambivalent. What did Stevie want—a threesome? Would Joyce want that too? The possibility of having to sexually satisfy *one* total stranger after years of nobody but Cathy had produced a certain amount of anxiety in him as it was, but now it seemed possible he was going to have to perform for *two* —a lifelong fantasy of his, but one that multiplied his anxieties geometrically.

The cab sped down Fifth Avenue. Lance suggested to Stevie that she accompany him and Joyce back to his apartment for a nightcap. To his immense disappointment and relief, Stevie declined and got out of the cab at 57th Street.

Lance was perplexed. He cursed himself for not getting Stevie's phone number. When they reached his apartment, Lance paid the cabbie and guided Joyce up the stairs to his door. The moment he closed the door behind them and triple-locked it in anticipation of not having to unlock it again till morning, Joyce announced that she was going to be sick.

Lance led her swiftly into the bathroom, and just barely managed to raise the toilet seat and point her towards the bowl before Joyce brought up all seven drinks, and remnants of her last few meals. Lance, his romantic ardor considerably dampened, held her forehead and comforted her till the last drop of bile had been retched out of her guts.

"How the hell did I manage to put away that much liquor?" Joyce moaned.

"I have a confession to make," said Lance. "I kept refilling your glass every time you weren't looking."

"But why?" she said.

"Well," he replied, embarrassed, "I wanted to get you drunk. I thought it would be easier to seduce you that way."

"*Seduce* me?" she said. "You didn't need to seduce me. I wanted to go to bed with you the minute I *saw* you."

Lance was amazed. Intellectually, he knew that women wanted sex as much as men, but years of brainwashing were hard to overcome. Emotionally, he still believed you had to trick them into it.

Joyce began having dry heaves, and Lance was persuaded to take her home. On the way out she noticed the lack of furniture for the first time. Lance dismissed her questions with the vague explanation that he was in the process of redecorating. When he put her in the cab he said he'd call her, but he knew he wouldn't. The memory of all that puking had squelched his lust for her.

The next morning he called his hosts and inquired how to get in touch with Stevie. The relentlessly polite drama critic gave Lance her number and a warning:

"Don't get too aggressive with her physically," he said. "She's a brown belt in *tae kwon do*."

Lance called Stevie and made a dinner date for the following night. They went to a charming restaurant called Café Europa that featured chicken curry baked in thick brioches, and they talked about the literary life.

"The trouble with Norman," she said, "is that he has never really lived up to the promise of *The Naked and the Dead*, you know?"

"You're familiar with all of the work that Mailer has done since *The Naked and the Dead*?" he asked.

"Familiar? I'm familiar all right, don't worry. Sometimes I wish it was only his *work* I was familiar with."

"Oh, you know Mailer *personally*, then," said Lance.

"I met him in the Village," she said. "At the Lion's Head. He was there with Jimmy and Pete."

"Jimmy and Pete . . . Breslin and Hamill, you mean?"

"Yeah. They were trying to teach Joe Torres how to throw a left hook. My *grandmother* throws a better left hook than any of those guys, Torres included."

It went like that for three hours. Stevie succeeded in dropping upwards of eighty names from the New York literary-showbiz community. Then Lance invited her back to his place for a drink. She accepted. Despite the enormous quantity of liquor he had consumed at dinner, he was not perceptibly high. His extreme nervousness at the prospect of sex with his first unfamiliar woman in eight years had neutralized the alcohol in his brain.

"What's the matter," she said, surveying his barren apartment, "you don't believe in furniture?"

"My furniture," said Lance, "was stolen by a gang of lesbians."

Lest he appear too aggressive and set himself up for painful *tae kwon do* body-blocks, Lance waited till almost three a.m. before finally making a pass at her. He was a little off his timing, but she responded hungrily to his kisses. They necked for about twenty minutes and then she looked up at him and said in a voice softer than he had heard her use all night:

"You're very tender."

"Thank you," he said, but he had missed the point.

"Sometimes," she said, even more softly, "I like a man to hurt me a little."

He wasn't sure how to react. He was initially surprised, but then figured it made sense—any woman who had that much invested in tough talk, police techniques and *tae kwon do* was probably overcompensating for a red-hot streak of masochism. She clearly wanted to be dominated.

"I'll see what I can do," he said, but he knew it wasn't going to work until he'd had time to research a few techniques in sophisticated hurting. He grabbed her by the hair and pulled her violently toward him to kiss her and almost broke his left front tooth. While unbuttoning her blouse he gave her several swift pinches along the arm, which caused her to push him away and hold him at arm's length for a closer look.

"You're new at this, aren't you?" she said.

"I've done my share of it," he said as casually as possible, "it's just that I'm a little out of practice."

Stevie stifled a yawn, noted the hour was late, and made her way to the door. Lance asked if she wanted him to put her in a cab. She smiled, bent over slightly, and patted the inside of the top of her left boot. Lance obviously didn't get it, so she pulled up her pant leg and showed him the small, stainless-steel, snub-nosed .38 caliber revolver in her boot.

20

Ernest H. Roosevelt was beginning to see how it could all work. Never mind that nothing ever had in his whole life practically. Never mind that his life so far was one bad black joke. Never mind that he was six feet five, had hands big enough to comfortably hold a basketball in each, but was so uncoordinated that he couldn't even dribble ten feet without falling down. Never mind that blacks were supposed to have natural rhythm and be dynamite dancers and that he'd never so much as learned to boogie. Never mind that blacks were supposed to be terrific in bed and he could hardly get it up at all, much less keep it up long enough to put it anywhere that mattered.

There were, for Ernest H. Roosevelt, more important things in life. Like writing.

Ernest H. Roosevelt's middle name was Hemingway. He had been named for the great novelist by his Mamma, whose only contact with Hemingway was a book in which, when the Spanish lady was screwing, it said that the earth moved. The earth had never moved for Ernest's Mamma when she screwed, but she loved the idea that it could for somebody, even a Spanish lady in a book.

Ernest's name and obvious lack of physical coordination had caused all of his teachers in school to encourage him to write. The two things often went together. Ernest had got most of Hemingway's books out of the library and read them several times each. He was disappointed by *The Green Hills of Africa*, having thought it might be about The Black Experience, but he liked the ones about bullfighting and war and fishing and hunting, and in his early attempts at writing he tried to bring together many of these elements.

The teachers had always been very encouraging. They hoped he'd be able to go to college and study writing in a university. They suggested that his writing would improve considerably if he would pay more attention to grammar and spelling, but he happened to know that professional writers had editors who corrected their grammar and spelling, so he wasn't too worried.

Other kids he knew read magazines like *Penthouse* and *Hustler*. Ernest read *Writer's Digest* and *Publishers Weekly*. He was mesmerized by reports of the kind of money authors earned on their hardcover advances. A hundred thousand dollars was not uncommon for a first novelist to make for a hardcover advance against royalties, he had read, and softcover rights frequently went for over a million dollars. Every time he read about another record advance, he took note of the publishing house and editor who had paid it, and of the agent who had made the deal. When his own book was ready, he had to know where to take it. At the moment it looked like it might be a toss-up between two agents: Lynn Nesbit at International Creative Management, and Mort Janklow of Morton L. Janklow Associates. There was only one problem.

The problem was the book itself. He didn't know what he wanted to write it about. The teachers in school had always told him to write about what he knew. All he knew about was being a lousy basketball player and an even worse dancer and a nonlover in a society where those were the three things everybody expected you to be able to do for *sure*. All he knew about was fighting roaches and rats for your food and getting stoned or drunk or hooked on bad drugs and having to rip off liquor stores and gas stations and deal drugs to earn enough to live on. Who the hell wanted to read about *that*?

There were other writers besides Hemingway that he admired. He had read several stories in *Playboy* by a dude named Lance Lerner, and Ernest had written the dude a letter addressed to the *Playboy* office in Chicago, asking for advice on how to write.

The dude had even written him back, telling him a lot of stuff about plot construction, character building, and so on, but not mentioning anything at all about the things he really needed to know, like whether to publish in hardcover first or whether to go to a combined hard-and-soft deal immediately or whether to forget about hardcover altogether and just do a straight paperback original. The one thing the dude kept emphasizing, though, was that Ernest should write about what he knew.

Well, there it was again, the same old shit—write about what you know. Maybe he'd write about ripping off a store—how you cased the joint, how you planned the ripoff, how you made your getaway, how you fenced the merchandise, and so on. He'd been doing that kind of thing ever since he was twelve. Maybe he would write about that.

While browsing one hot July evening in the B. Dalton bookstore on Fifth Avenue and 52nd Street, he came across a copy of the *Random House Dictionary* which he knew he had to have if he was going to become a professional writer. The only problem was that the mother cost a fortune and he didn't have the first nickel. What if he ripped off, not a liquor store or a gas station or a pawnshop, but a *book*store—where he could get not only the bread out of the register but the *Random House Dictionary* as *well!*

That was what he would do. And the B. Dalton on Fifth Avenue and 52nd was right in the heart of the Man's biggest high-rent area too—which meant if he got caught the media would probably give him a lot of play. All the p.r. would only help his book, which he could then finish in Riker's Island. The hardcover advance would pay his bail and his court costs, and the paperback advance would put him in fat city. If they sold it to the movies, he would arrange to play a featured role just for the exposure.

Smiling for the first time in weeks, Ernest began to make quick sketches of the floor plan and the locations of exits and registers on the back of a copy of the *Writer's Yearbook* he had just ripped off in the next aisle.

21

A publishing party in an elegant suite at the St. Regis Hotel. Butlers in tuxedos circulated with drinks and trays neatly stacked with miniature quiches, stuffed mushrooms, miniature eggrolls and rumaki.

Lance, who couldn't bear the sight of another TV dinner or frozen lasagna, was loading up on hors d'oeuvres. The butlers wore disdainful expressions as he snagged half a dozen miniature quiches and eggrolls at a crack, but he didn't care.

It was, he noted, an "A" list of invited guests. He recognized three fellow editors of Cathy's from *The New York Times Book Review*, two from *The New Yorker*, one from *The New York Review of Books*, half a dozen freelance literary critics, a dozen name authors, and a couple dozen of the top echelon of staff from the publishing house that was giving the party.

He deftly scooped seven more miniature quiches off the tray of a passing butler, then noted he was being observed with no little amusement by a stunning woman with platinum hair, absurdly high cheekbones, and a plain black gown which revealed the elegantly slim body of a high-fashion model. The woman was six feet tall.

Lance felt himself blushing furiously.

"Tapeworm?" she said with a smirk.

"Mmmmm," said Lance, nodding, chewing and swallowing three of the quiches and washing them down with a glass of champagne. "Nasty business. Have to consume at least forty pounds of food a day or I starve to death."

The woman giggled. Lance, realizing he had given a reasonably amusing retort despite his discomfort, allowed himself to approach closer. The woman met his gaze coolly with gray eyes so light in color they were almost unattractive. The little lines around the eyes and the slight slack below the chin told him she was probably no longer a high-fashion model. He figured her to be close to forty. She'd probably not look much the worse for wear at fifty-five.

"All forty pounds of it have to be in the form of hors d'oeuvres too, I imagine," she said. Her voice, he noted, was deeper than usual, and it had a slight British flavor, which was probably an affectation. Perhaps she was an actress.

"Absolutely," he replied. "The tapeworm can't handle anything but miniatures. Anything bigger, he sends it back. My name is Lance. Lance Lerner. What's yours?"

"Claire."

"Claire," he said. "Glad to meet you, Claire. You an actress?"

The woman found this a comical notion.

"No," she said, "not an actress. At least not in the sense *you* mean."

"Ah. A high-fashion model, then," he said.

She shook her head.

"An international courier," he said.

She closed her eyes and shook her head.

"Nothing that glamorous, I'm afraid," she said. "I'm just a businessman's wife."

Well, so much for that, he thought. The slight suspicion he'd had that she might be single and available was clearly not a possibility.

"What business is your husband in?" he asked, envisioning an automobile dealership that leased Rolls Royces.

"Publishing," she said and emptied the glass of champagne she was holding.

"Really?" he said. "What's his name?"

"Austin Firestone," she said. "Do you know him?"

Lance, chewing an eggroll, missed a beat and bit a hole in his inner lip.

"I . . . don't know him *personally*," he said, touching his lip experimentally with a forefinger and noting that he was bleeding slightly. "I have, however, been trying to reach him by phone for several days. Unsuccessfully, I might add."

"Really?" she said. "Why are you trying to reach him?"

"Well," said Lance, trying to decide how much he ought to tell her, then realizing he'd drunk too much champagne to apply whatever decision he might make in that area, "I wrote a novel which your husband is publishing in a few weeks, and I wanted to tell him I thought he was about to make an unsound business decision."

"Unsound? In what way?" she said.

"Well," he said, "he has allocated only five thousand dollars for the advertising and promotion of my book. Five thousand dollars is not enough to do anything. I wanted to suggest to him that either he increase the budget substantially so we'd have a chance to sell a few copies of the book, or else save the five thousand altogether, and spend it on something more apt to give him a return on his investment. Like municipal bonds."

She held his gaze for several moments.

"I think Austin would be interested in hearing your views on this subject in person," she said. "Would you like to meet him?"

"Are you kidding me? I'd *kill* to meet him," he replied.

She nodded.

"I'll arrange a dinner," she said. "Nothing fancy. Just a few couples at our apartment. I won't tell him anything about this. You'll have an opportunity to meet him in a relaxed atmosphere. Then, when you think you've got his attention, you can raise the topic yourself. I think he might be intrigued."

"God," said Lance, "would you really do that for me? I'd really appreciate it, no kidding."

She smiled at his boyish eagerness.

"I'd be glad to do that for you, Lance," she said. "Perhaps some day you'll be able to do something for *me*."

"Anything," said Lance. "You name it, you got it."

"Anything?" she said. "That's quite an offer."

"I mean it," he said, "I swear to God."

"We'll see," she said, "we'll see."

22

If there was one thing Stevie Petrocelli couldn't stand it was coming home after a night tour in the goddamn 9th precinct, with the stench of human garbage on her body, and not being able to take a long hot shower. For the past two months, every time she turned on the shower and got the temperature of the water adjusted so it wasn't either freezing or scalding and climbed into the stall, the fucking pressure dropped off to almost nothing, and then it built back up again and spurted out either thirty degrees colder or thirty degrees hotter, with the result that Stevie had on several occasions been badly burned.

She had spoken of the problem numerous times with Gladys Oliphant—Gladys the *Elephant* she called her because the woman was so big and fat—but the bitch kept saying that she was only the super and not a goddamn plumber. Stevie called the landlord and threatened to get the building cited for numerous building code violations, but the landlord advised her that she could also find herself another apartment. The tiny one-bedroom rental was nothing to look at, she knew, but the location on West 57th almost made it worth the $800 a month she had to pay for it.

She had recently changed her tactics with Gladys, figuring you could catch more flies with honey than vinegar, which was a stupid expression because as far as she knew you couldn't catch flies with vinegar at *all*. The threats hadn't gotten her any closer to having her shower fixed, so she'd started trying to be nice instead. Complimenting the Elephant on her hair (it was frizzy and red), complimenting her on her clothes (they were mostly tent-like, pastel-colored, nylon dressing gowns). Maybe the new tactics were beginning to pay off. Gladys had actually for the first time come up and taken a look at the shower, removed the head with a huge crescent wrench, and announced that what it needed was a new gizmo that controlled the mixture of hot and cold water or something. Gladys said she would go down to a plumbing supply place on Canal Street in the next day or two, get the gizmo, and come back and put it in. She thought it would be fixed by Wednesday or Thursday.

Very interesting, if true, thought Stevie. Wednesday she was working the late tour at the precinct, but Thursday she was off all day. In fact, Thursday she was planning to have dinner with crazy Lance Lerner.

There was something terribly sweet about Lance, she mused. She had picked up a copy of his last book in paperback and not liked it very much—the character delineations had been pretty shallow and the imagery not really up to snuff—but he was a good kisser, and he'd tried so earnestly to hurt her when she'd foolishly said that was what she wanted.

She had obviously given him the wrong impression by saying that. He was probably off shopping for whips and shackles, when all she'd meant was that she didn't like a man to be too soft, that she hated to feel she was tougher than the guys she went to bed with, although she almost always was. Contrary to the impression she'd given Lance, she'd never really done any S&M before, although she'd certainly fantasized about it. Still, if that's what he thought she liked, then maybe she would give it a try. He certainly didn't appear to be shocked by the idea. Which was nice. It showed he had imagination in bed. There was nothing worse than a boring bed partner.

Well, whether he brought over chains or not, she would throw him a fuck on Thursday anyway. Just to see what he was like.

23

Goose Washington was an idiot, but he was the only one of the brothers that Ernest H. Roosevelt had talked to that was willing to help him rip off the bookstore. Goose got his name from the way he was always grabbing folks between the legs, no matter who they were or what the situation. Goose didn't care if he was in church, for God's sake, if he felt like grabbing somebody.

The one thing Goose had going for him, outside of he would go along with anything you asked him, no matter how stupid, was that he always knew where to locate a piece. Goose had gotten them two pieces for the bookstore job that were as fine as any Ernest had ever seen. One of them was a .357 Smith & Wesson Highway Patrolman model, a cop gun that was so big most dudes couldn't even fire it without using both hands. The other was a little .380 Walther PPK Automatic, the gun that James Bond dude used in all the "007" movies. You were supposed to get rid of whatever piece you used after the job you got it for was finished, but Ernest was tempted to hang onto whichever one of these he could.

He and Goose had kind of moseyed through the B. Dalton bookstore a couple of times, just generally getting the feel of the floor plan. Goose thought he was crazy to want to rip off a bookstore, but Ernest said that the publishing business was going through a boom and that there would probably be a lot of bread in the register. Ernest figured that Thursday night around eight o'clock was a good time to hit the store. Goose said it was all the same to him.

Ernest gave Goose his choice of pieces, but, just as Ernest had figured, Goose could barely lift the .357 Smith & Wesson, much less fire it with one hand, so Goose chose the Walther instead. Ernest hoped he wouldn't have to shoot anybody, but if he had to he would. It wouldn't be the first time, and it kind of came with the territory.

Thursday was only three days away. He went home to take notes on what he had done so far.

24

Gladys Oliphant had never been svelte. Since grammar school she had had to endure names like Tubby, Tiny, Porky, Fats, and of course, Oliphant the Elephant, her least favorite name of all.

In point of fact, Gladys was five feet ten and weighed two hundred and forty pounds. If she lost only ninety pounds she'd be just about perfect, she felt. Not that a hundred and fifty was svelte either, but it was a weight that Gladys aspired to, a weight that Gladys had passed briefly at the age of twelve and never again seen. The truth was that Gladys *preferred* being fat to being thin. Being fat kept most men, especially the disconcertingly sexual ones, at a distance. Her father and mother and all her sisters and brothers had been fat. Fat people were thought to be jollier than skinny people. She didn't think that was true, but she knew that skinny people usually looked undernourished and depressed.

She had only gone out with fat boys in high school and college, of course. Not that she had gone out that much with boys at all. After the incident in New Mexico, she had sworn off men of all ages for several years. Particularly Indians. Not that there were that many Indians in New York who were asking her out on dates, but she really did have a thing about Indians after the incident in New Mexico, and she didn't think that anybody in his right mind could blame her.

The way it had happened was that she and Thelma, a friend of hers who lived down the street, had gone one August on a camping trip to New Mexico. They had camped three nights on the edge of a huge Indian reservation near Taos without even so much as *seeing* an Indian. And then one day, when Thelma had gone off to look at kachina dolls, Gladys went wandering in the desert, looking for cactus flowers, and who should she meet up with but four Indian braves on dirt bikes, in jeans and T-shirts, who were out of their minds on firewater.

Because it was such a hot day Gladys was wearing just short shorts and a halter top. Large folds of fat peeked through the openings of her clothing. This must have aroused the Indians, because they surrounded her and began making suggestive remarks. She was a little frightened, but tried to cover her fear with wisecracks. She even chuckled when they spoke of staking her to the ground and initiating her into the tribe. She assumed they were kidding. They were not.

Two of them wrestled her to the ground and the other two spread-eagled her on the desert floor, drove four stakes into the hot clay and tied her wrists and ankles to them. She stopped chuckling. She tried to reason with them. They tore off her shorts, her halter top, her brassiere and her panties and, after dancing around her in a modified war dance with wild war whoops for a while, they pulled down their jeans and gang-banged her.

She screamed and cried, but that only seemed to excite them, so she finally shut up and endured the indignities in silence. When they had finished raping her, they simply left her there, baking in the hot sun, and rode their dirt bikes back to the reservation.

She didn't know how many hours she lay there, staked to the ground, frying on the clay, before a kindly old Indian woman found her, cut her loose with a machete, and took her back to the reservation in a rusted-out Dodge stationwagon to treat her for shock and sunstroke.

When Thelma came back and found Gladys missing she called out the state police, and when they finally found her on the reservation they took her directly to the hospital, where she remained for several days.

The four Indians who had raped Gladys were never caught. Gladys peeled for six weeks after returning to New York.

In many ways the rape by the Indians had killed off most of Gladys's once high spirit. She'd had hopes of becoming a dancer and was not ungraceful for her size, but she gave up ballet shortly after the rape, knowing it was hopeless. She'd had some feeling she might one day do a little acting—everybody said she had a beautiful face—but there weren't a whole lot of parts for obese ingenues, and after the rape she simply stopped kidding herself. She figured some day she'd try her hand at writing. In the meantime she'd lucked into a rent-free job as superintendent of an old apartment building on West 57th Street. Her father had been a building contractor and she had gone along with him on so many jobs as a youngster that she knew the rudiments of plumbing, wiring and carpentry and was able to make most repairs on tenants' apartments without outside help, assuming she was in the mood, a fact which the landlord particularly appreciated.

Gladys's tenants were something else again. There were a number of elderly people, several foreign persons, a handful of young men living alone, and a policewoman. Most of the young men were either dancers or actors—obvious homosexuals—but one of them looked like he could go either way. He was the only man she had ever flirted with since the rape, mostly because he seemed gentle and shy and she felt he posed no threat to her. She had numerous fantasies about him, including one of making a baby with him, either in or out of wedlock—it hardly mattered to her since she wanted a baby even more than she wanted a man and, at age thirty-seven, she didn't have too many mongoloid-free years left. But all the flirting she did with the young man produced no results. She decided he was a fag after all.

The policewoman was at first the most unpleasant tenant in the building. Just because she had some problem with her shower—who *didn't* in a building this old!—she expected you to drop everything you were doing and go down to Canal Street and ransack plumbing supply houses for parts. As if she didn't have her hands full with all the other tenants' complaints, to say nothing of the assignments she had to complete each and every week for her correspondence course from the Famous Writers School.

The Famous Writers School just *happened* to consider Gladys Oliphant one of their most promising students. Or so they said. Under their tutelage she had begun a romantic novel which, they absolutely swore, was as brilliant as anything ever written by Barbara Cartland! It was only a matter of time before she would be selling her novel for a huge advance and moving to the East Side and hanging out at Elaine's with all the other famous writers.

It was very likely the prospect of her imminent success as a romantic novelist that was causing Gladys to appear less ill-humored to her tenants, and that may have been why the policewoman was acting more polite towards her. Now that she was acting so polite, perhaps Gladys would even see about fixing up that shower of hers. Besides, she'd heard that the policewoman had a few connections in the literary world, and Gladys was planning to use her as a stepping-stone in her career.

While she was in there fixing the shower, Gladys might just casually feel the policewoman out about the possibility of the two of them maybe sauntering up to Elaine's one night and getting a head start on meeting some of her future colleagues.

25

Fifty dollars a pair was a preposterous price to pay for shackles, Lance decided. If the owners of slave ships had had to buy their shackles at the Pleasure Chest there never would have been any trade to the New World.

He'd settled instead on handcuffs—four sets of them. They weren't cheap either, but they were a better bargain than the shackles. He practiced unlocking them and snapping them closed again so as not to appear a total neophyte to Stevie when he put them on her tonight. He wasn't entirely sure why he was doing all this in the first place, but he thought she expected it, and besides he figured the experience would broaden him as a writer.

He had wanted to take her to an early dinner at the Russian Tea Room since it was so close to her apartment, but she insisted on dragging him all the way down to Soho to eat in some tiny little Italian place that had just opened and was already a hangout for artists and writers. The pasta was average, but he had several White Russians, his new favorite drink, and he somehow managed to down enough of them to endure her relentless name-dropping and have a moderately good time.

About seven-thirty they left the restaurant and headed back to her apartment. He was beginning to get turned on by the prospect of putting the cuffs on her, and his anticipatory excitement was in no way diminished by the realization that he would be locking up a cop.

"I have a little surprise for you," he said as they walked into her apartment and triple-locked the door behind them.

"I know," she said. "You've got about sixteen pairs of cuffs in your pocket."

He was amazed.

"How the hell did you know that?" he said.

She shrugged.

"Lance, give me a break. You don't think a cop knows the sound that handcuffs make in someone's pocket? You don't think several pairs of cuffs would make even *more* of that sound? Let's see 'em."

He took out the four pairs of cuffs and handed them to her. She looked them over with professional detachment.

"Jay-Pees," she said. "Not a bad make. Although any perp in *my* precinct could probably get out of them in about three minutes flat."

"Show me," he said. He unlocked one pair of cuffs with the tiny key it had come with. "Hold out your wrists."

"Hey hey," she said. "Slow down there, chief."

"What do you mean?" he said.

She looked at him and cocked her head.

"You brought these over here to have a little B&D fun, am I right?"

"B&D? Oh, Bondage and Domination. Right."

"Well, take it easy. I hardly know you. What makes you think I'd let you lock me up on our second date?"

"How many dates do you usually have to have with a man before you let him lock you up?"

"Whoa, there, buster," she said. "Slow down. What makes you think I've ever done this before?"

"You mean you haven't? I thought you were an old hand at this. In fact I was looking forward to learning some pointers from you."

She chuckled and went to the kitchen and poured herself a beer.

"You want a Lowenbrau?" she called. "Hunter Thompson bought me a case."

"No thanks," he said. "I've had enough drinks for a while."

She came back into the room, sipping her beer.

"So," she said, "you want to do a little experimenting in B&D, do you?"

"Sure," he said, "why not?"

"And you actually think that I—a policewoman—would let you lock me up, do you?"

"What's the matter," he said, "don't you trust me?"

"Of course not," she said. "Why in the name of Christ would I trust you?"

"I trust *you*," he said.

"You do?"

"Sure."

"O.K.," she said, "then let *me* put the cuffs on *you*."

It was a possibility he frankly hadn't considered. But it did seem reasonable that he couldn't expect her to submit to something he was unwilling to undergo himself.

"If I let you lock *me* up, then will you let me lock *you* up?" he said.

She nodded her head. He tried to picture himself totally immobilized, totally at her mercy. He found it titillating.

"How long will you keep me locked up?" he said, beginning to get aroused.

"Not long. Ten minutes or so. The minute you get uptight I'll unlock you. I assume you'll do the same for me."

"Of course," he said, "of course. Tell me, what, uh, do you plan to do to me once you have me all locked up?"

She cackled evilly.

"We'll see," she said. "Don't worry, it won't hurt. Much."

"Are you going to, uh, have your way with me?" he said, suddenly coy.

"Why else do you think we're *doing* this?" she said.

He nodded.

"O.K.," he said. "I'll trust you, Stevie. Tell me what to do."

"First take off your clothes," she said. "If I lock you up with them on, I'm going to have to tear them apart to get them off you."

Lance smiled and began undressing. He took off his sportcoat and tie and handed them to her. She opened the closet and hung them on a hanger. He took off his boots and socks. She put the socks in the boots and the boots in the bottom of the closet.

He paused and smiled at her uncertainly. He didn't know how aroused it was permissable to be while doing this. He didn't want to find he was enjoying it too much and then have to face the fact that he might be a closet pervert.

"C'mon," she said, "we don't have all night here."

He unbuttoned his shirt, took it off and handed it to her. He unbuckled his jeans, stepped out of them and gave them to her as well. She could clearly see the shape of his erection through his jockey shorts. She raised an eyebrow at it, and hung up the shirt and pants in the closet. Then she ushered him into the tiny bedroom and pulled back the spread on the queen-size bed. The head and foot of the bed had beautiful polished brass fittings. The sheets were black satin. Stevie was evidently somebody who entertained a bit in bed.

"OK," she said, "lie down. On your back, and spread those arms and legs. Spread 'em!"

He did as he was told. She unlocked two pairs of cuffs and chained each of his wrists to the brass pipes at the head of the bed. Then, chuckling softly, she pulled off his jockey shorts, cupped his stiff member briefly in her hand and kissed the tip. Then she secured each of his ankles to the brass rails at the foot of the bed. It was a weird feeling. He was a little ashamed at being aroused. He started to giggle.

"Undt now," she said, adopting a passable German accent, "Herr Lerner, I haff you completely in mein power!"

She burst into a long, maniacal laugh.

"W-what are you g-going to do to me?" he stammered, going along with the gag.

"Vat am I goink to *do* to you?" She cackled. "Chust vait undt *see*, Herr Lerner, chust vait undt *see!*"

She went and got a feather and began tickling him all over his body. He found he was extremely ticklish and began whooping with laughter. She kept it up slightly longer than he hoped she would. Then she took some baby oil and began to give him a massage. It was exceedingly pleasant and he began to relax.

"I think I'd like a drink now, if you don't mind," he said.

"Oh, you do, do you?" she said. "And what would you like to drink, may I ask?"

"A White Russian."

"Is that so?" she said. "What makes you think I even know how to make one?"

"You can do anything," he said.

Unexpectedly pleased by this response, she went into the kitchen, mixed his drink, and came back to the bed.

"Here," she said, "tilt your head this way and I'll dribble it into your mouth."

She began dribbling, but more of it got on the black satin sheets than in his mouth. They both found the process fairly amusing.

"You know," he said, "you really used a bit too much Kahlua. Would you please make me a new one?"

She exploded with laughter.

"You certainly are a pushy prisoner," she said. But she loved his audacity and she went back into the kitchen to mix a fresh one. When she returned to the bedroom, however, her hands were empty. She grabbed her coat and headed for the door.

"Hey," he said, "where are you going?"

"To get more Kahlua," she said. "I used up practically all I had."

"Hey, listen, don't leave," he said. "Forget about the Kahlua."

"Don't worry, she said, "the liquor store is right downstairs. I won't be more than a minute."

She opened the door.

"Stevie, come back!" he yelled, but it was no use. He heard the door close behind her and he heard her key in the lock.

Well, he thought, what could possibly go wrong in the couple of minutes it would take her to return with the Kahlua?

26

Goose Washington and Ernest Hemingway Roosevelt made their way down Fifth Avenue along the edge of Central Park in a leisurely fashion. The night was warm and they were a little stoned.

Ernest fondled the .357 Smith & Wesson in his jacket pocket and tried to make mental notes of what his thoughts were as they approached the B. Dalton bookstore so that he'd be able to write about them afterwards.

"How ya feelin, bro'?" said Ernest to his friend.

"O.K., bro'," said Goose, and goosed the taller Ernest.

Ernest was the slightest bit nervous about trusting Goose with the loaded Walther, but he didn't figure he had much choice. Besides, this was hardly the first time either of them had used a piece in a holdup, and, even though none of the jobs had been bookstores, and even though none of them had been pulled outside of Harlem, it couldn't be that much different than what they were used to.

They crossed 59th Street and headed South on Fifth. Just six blocks more. Ernest ran over the layout of the store once more in his head. He had rehearsed it over and over until Goose had gotten irritated. Well, shit, what if he *was* irritated! This was important. This was going to be one of the key scenes in his novel. They couldn't fuck it up.

They crossed 53rd Street. There it was, half a block ahead.

"You ready, bro'? said Ernest.

"Ready, bro'," said Goose.

They walked into the store.

27

Gladys Oliphant was happy. She'd managed to find the part for the policewoman's shower head without much searching at all. She'd spent some extra time wandering through the shops on Canal Street, browsing among the grimy tools and fittings that had been so much a part of the pleasant years with her father. Although she didn't really see an immediate use for them, she picked up a container of epoxy putty, two cans of WD-40 and a complete forty-piece fine thread tap and die set. She loved fooling around with tools, and you never knew when you might need them.

She came home and ate a leisurely dinner watching televison, and had four or five cans of beer. She took a little nap with the TV on, and when she woke up she remembered the policewoman and her shower. While she'd been napping she thought she heard the policewoman's voice in the hallway. If she hopped up there now and fixed that shower head, perhaps the policewoman would invite her to stay for a beer.

Gladys went to her toolbox, took out an adjustable crescent wrench, picked up the shower head part and walked out of the apartment. The policewoman lived three flights up. By the time Gladys reached the right door she was slightly out of breath and puffing. She knocked on the door and waited, but there was no reply. Strange. She was fairly certain it was the policewoman's voice she had heard in the hallway. It was quite a distinctive voice.

She knocked again. Still there was no reply. Gladys's heart sank. The policewoman had probably only come back for a short time and then left again. Should she try her again tomorrow, or should she fix it now? If she came back tomorrow, she could fix the shower, then stay for a beer and discuss the literary life. On the other hand, she could fix it now, and then when she came back tomorrow the policewoman would be even happier to see her and would be even more likely to ask her to stay and chat.

All right, it was decided. Gladys put her hand into her pocket, took out her ring of keys, found the ones to the policewoman's apartment, and opened the door.

That's strange, she thought. The lights were on. The policewoman was a frugal tenant and never left more than a single light on when she wasn't home. Perhaps she was home and hadn't heard her knock?

"Hello," said Gladys. "Anybody here?"

"Stevie?" said a tentative male voice from the bedroom.

What was this? A male voice? Maybe a prowler? Gladys became very nervous. Should she leave while there was still time to call the police? She did have her heavy crescent wrench with her. Perhaps that was protection enough.

"Hello?" called Gladys once more, and crept, with wrench upraised, to the bedroom door. She peeked inside, and gasped.

She didn't know what she expected to see in the policewoman's bedroom, but if she had been asked to guess, a naked skinny man handcuffed to the bed would not have been one of the first hundred and fifty guesses she would have come up with.

28

Goose and Ernest walked into the store. Ernest nodded to Goose. Goose stationed himself at the door and Ernest ambled casually over to the main cashier's desk.

"S'cuse me, mah man," said Ernest softly to the man behind the cashier's desk, who was reading from a book entitled *Books in Print.*

The man, a white dude about fifty, bald, wearing wire-rimmed glasses and a white shirt and silk tie, looked up to see a very tall black man with a pleasant expression on his face.

"Yes, can I help you?" said the man.

"Ah'd like a copy of the *Random House Dictionary,* mah man," said Ernest amiably. "And then Ah'd like all the bread you got in that register."

The bald man didn't quite hear what Ernest had said, and then he saw the enormous pistol that Ernest had taken out of his pocket and his heart stopped beating.

Ernest looked back at Goose and Goose nodded. Goose took out the Walther and held it over his head. Ernest turned back to the dozen or so clerks and customers in the store.

"S'cuse me, folks," said Ernest in a fairly loud voice. "Ah hate to bother you, but this here is a holdup. Mah brothuh over theah has a gun, as do Ah, and we would not like to have to use them, but we will if we has to."

Everybody had looked up and stopped what they were doing. Nobody moved a muscle. Somebody whimpered. Somebody else prayed in a monotone.

"Please don't shoot anybody," said the bald man behind the cashier's desk in a polite voice. "We'll give you whatever you want, just please don't shoot anybody, all right?"

"Tha's fine with me," said Ernest cheerfully.

"What is it you want now," said the man, "the money in the register?"

"Tha's right, mah man," said Ernest. "The money in the register and the *Random House Dictionary*."

"The what?" said the man. "The *Random House Dictionary?*"

"Tha's right, mah man," said Ernest.

"Stephanie, bring this man the *Random House Dictionary*," said the clerk. "And step on it."

A young woman of about twenty, wearing horn-rimmed glasses and an exceedingly nervous expression, went to the reference book section, picked out a copy of the *Random House Dictionary* and brought it to the cashier's desk. She stared at the gun in Ernest's hand as though it had hypnotic powers.

"Thankya, sweet child," said Ernest, his heart suddenly welling up with love for the nervous white fox with the glasses, who was actually scared of *him,* of dumb old Ernest who couldn't dance or ball or dribble.

"Yo' name Stephanie, sweet child?" said Ernest to the nervous girl.

She nodded her head, unable to take her eyes off the Smith & Wesson.

"Don' be scared, Stephanie," he said. "Ah ain't gonna hurt ya."

Ernest turned back to the bald man.

"O.K., mah man, now Ah need the bread in that register and all the other registers in the store."

Ernest handed the bald man an empty El Al flight bag. The bald man nodded several times, turned around, opened the cash drawer and began putting money into the bag.

"Ah need the bread from the other registers too, mah man," said Ernest gently.

The man looked out at the rest of the store, got on the p.a. system and addressed everyone in a loud, quavery voice:

"Will cashiers at all the registers please empty their cash drawers and bring the contents here immediately?"

There was a small flurry of activity as all the cashiers emptied their cash drawers and brought the money up to the main cashier's desk and emptied it into the El Al flight bag. Ernest coolly surveyed the room, pointing his revolver this way and that, directing activity like a symphony conductor. Ernest checked Goose at the door and saw, to his irritation, that a short elderly woman was just coming through the door that Goose was blocking.

"*Excuse* me, young man," said the elderly woman, trying to push past him.

"Ma'am," said Ernest loudly, "please stop right theah, if you will. We havin' a holdup just now at the present moment, but we be through shortly."

Goose smiled sweetly at the elderly woman and then goosed her. She gave an outraged cry but didn't move.

Ernest made sure all the cash was in the flight bag, then jammed the *Random House Dictionary* in on top of it. It was a very tight fit.

"Pardon me for asking," said the bald man behind the desk, "but what do you want with the *Random House Dictionary*, if you don't mind my asking?"

"No problem, mah man," said Ernest. "Ah needs it for mah work. Ah'm a author."

"I see," said the bald man.

Ernest smiled broadly and backed away from the main cashier's desk and began edging toward the door.

"Ah thank all of you for bein' so cooperative," he said. "It was a pleasure doin' business with y'all. Ah would suggest for your own comfort and safety that you don' call the po-lice for about fahv minutes or so, or else we gonna have to shoot somebody."

He nodded to Goose, who opened the door.

"Take care now," Ernest called to the people inside the store. "Nice meetin' ya, Stephanie. And y'all have a nice day now, heah?"

Ernest and Goose moved swiftly through the door and began walking very rapidly north on Fifth Avenue. It had gone beautifully.

"Way to *go,* bro'!" said Ernest and slapped Goose's open hand.

And then they heard it:

"Stop them! Help! Police! Robbers! Stop them! Help! Police! Help!"

It was the little old lady, out on the street and screaming her lungs out.

Ernest fired one shot straight up in the air, cursed, and then both he and Goose broke into a dead run. A man on the north side of 53rd Street yelled something at them that they couldn't make out, then fired a shot in their direction.

Ernest and Goose raced uptown four blocks, then made a sharp left at the corner of 57th and Fifth, heading west on 57th Street. Pedestrians sprang out of their way like antelope, but they were now running so fast that they collided with at least five people between Fifth and Sixth Avenues.

At Sixth Avenue Goose didn't know which way to turn, so Ernest yanked him by the arm and they tore across 57th Street against the light, causing several cars to swerve to avoid them. If they could just make it two more blocks north to 59th Street, they could disappear into Central Park and they'd be home free.

29

Still chuckling to herself, Stevie walked out of her apartment building and down two doors to the liquor store. She nodded hello to the owner and pointed to the liqueurs.

"One bottle of Kahlua, please, Sol," she said.

"The large or the small?" he said.

She thought a moment. If she wasn't going to be seeing Lance much after tonight, then maybe the small would be enough. But he *was* sort of sweet—after all, he'd bought her the cuffs.

"Oh, what the hell," she said. "Gimme the large."

The man smiled, took the quart bottle of Kahlua down off the shelf and put it in a brown paper bag. Stevie gave him the exact change. Just then she heard the sounds of yelling and running outside. She went quickly to the door, just as two black men raced past her.

In scarcely more than a second her snub-nosed .38 was out of her boot and she was racing up 57th Street, shouting:

"*Freeze,* turkeys—*police!*"

30

The naked skinny man on the bed looked a lot more worried than Gladys felt. And he *was* chained to the bedstead. She didn't really seem to be in any immediate danger.

"Hi there," said the naked skinny man on the bed.

She wasn't too sure what you were supposed to say to naked skinny men handcuffed to bedsteads, so for the time being she said nothing. It was just possible that he was a sex criminal that the policewoman had apprehended, and that she had cuffed him to the bed and gone to get help. If that was the case, Gladys didn't think she ought to get too chummy with him. She continued to stand at the foot of the bed, her wrench upraised.

"Who, uh, are you?" said the naked skinny man on the bed.

He managed a forced smile. She thought it an inappropriate facial expression under the circumstances. He was behaving just like some guy trying to be polite at a bar or a party, except that they weren't *at* a bar or a party, they were in a policewoman's bedroom, and the man who had addressed her was naked and skinny and handcuffed to the bed.

Gladys appraised him thoughtfully. Aside from skinny, his body wasn't really all that disgusting to look at. And his sexual organs did seem to be in at least a mild state of arousal, which Gladys considered interesting. The penis wasn't badly shaped, she found herself thinking. Not that she was any expert in penises. She hadn't seen all that many of them, and the ones that she had seen were either the rather small and pathetic ones of the fat men she'd been to bed with, or else the rather menacing ones of the four Indians who had raped her.

No, as penises went, the one that this fellow owned was certainly not that displeasing to look at. She wondered why it seemed to be in a state of mild arousal—a "semi," she believed men called it. Perhaps the thing was in a mild state of arousal due to *her* presence in the room. The notion that she might be causing this strange man to be sexually excited made her blush.

It was ironic, she thought. The last sexual contact she had had with any man, it had been *she* who was spread-eagled and tied down and unable to move. And now the roles were reversed. Here was a naked man before her, totally helpless, totally at her mercy, and she could do anything she wanted to him, avenge herself for the Indian rapes or anything at all, and nobody would be there to stop her. She started getting excited and angry.

"Shut up!" she screamed suddenly.

The man, who had not uttered a word in the last two minutes or so, seemed startled.

"Shut up and let me think!" she said not quite as loudly. Her mind was racing, as various possible courses of action flitted through it.

She could hit him on the head with the wrench. She could scratch his eyes out. She could go and get a sharp kitchen knife and cut off that penis of his, that symbol of male aggression which had caused her so much pain and humiliation and suffering, and it would serve him right! She could always justify it afterwards as a political act.

She could also just walk over there and examine his sexual organs quite closely and in great detail in a way that she had never dared to do with any man before and would probably never have such an opportunity to do again, and when the paddy wagon or whatever the policewoman had gone to get finally arrived, she would merely say that she'd been helping to guard the prisoner, and if he told them anything she'd done before they arrived they wouldn't believe him, because it would be his word against hers and he was a criminal and she was not.

"Uh, may I be permitted to say something?" said the naked skinny man.

"No!" she shouted, suddenly enraged. "You'll speak when I ask you to speak, and not before!"

Now where the hell had *that* line come from, she wondered, shocked at the vehemence of her response. Probably from a movie she'd seen late at night on TV.

"I'm sorry," said the man.

"I didn't mean to yell," she replied. "I'm just a little . . . upset."

"So am I," he said. "Are you a friend of Stevie's?"

She turned her attention from the penis to the face.

"What?" she said.

"I said are you a friend of Stevie's?" he said pleasantly.

"In a way," she said. "I'm the super of this building."

"Ah," he said. "So *that's* why you had a key to her apartment."

"Yeah," she said. "I came up here to fix the shower head. She's been after me to do it for months."

"I see," he said. "I suppose you're wondering what I'm doing here like this."

She watched him carefully, waiting for the first hint of a trick.

"It did cross my mind to wonder that," she said.

"It's rather simple, really," he said. "Stevie and I went out to dinner together and, knowing her, uh, interest in . . . unusual sexual practices, I, uh, brought over four pairs of handcuffs as a sort of surprise . . ."

"She's interested in unusual sexual practices, you say?"

"Why, yes."

"I had no idea," said Gladys.

"Well, there's no reason why you would have," he said.

"Look, maybe you shouldn't ought to be telling me this," said Gladys.

"Why not?" said the naked skinny man. "These are very intimate circumstances we find ourselves in."

Gladys noted that the mild state of arousal which the man's penis had been in when she entered the room had considerably diminished since he'd started talking. In a way she preferred him more aroused. Perhaps that was simply the way she affected men: at first they were turned on by her, and then the more they got to know her the less turned on they were.

"What are you," she said, "a sex criminal?"

"No," said the naked skinny man, "a writer."

Gladys's ears perked up.

"A *writer*?" she said. "*I'm* a writer."

"No kidding?" he said. "Who do you write for?"

"For the Famous Writers School," she said, not without pride. "I'm writing a romantic novel under their direct supervison."

"Well," said the man, "isn't that something."

"Yeah," she said. "The one thing that always bothers me, though, is . . ." She changed her mind and shook the thought away.

"Yes?" he said. "What bothers you?"

"Never mind," she said. "You probably wouldn't be interested."

"Sure I would," he said. "In fact, I used to teach a course in writing at the New School."

"Honest?"

"Honest. What is it that bothers you?"

"Well," she said, "I'm not real sure what makes a novel, you know? I mean I'm not sure what's supposed to be *in* it."

He nodded.

"Well," he said, "there's a little catch-phrase that I learned from a writer at the *Saturday Evening Post* many years ago which might help you: 'An appealing character strives against great odds to attain a worthwhile goal.' That's pretty much the formula for all fiction, long or short."

"No kidding?"

"No kidding. Now there are three elements in that formula: the Appealing Character, the Great Odds, and the Worthwhile Goal, but if you have all those you ought to be O.K."

"I'll be damned," she said.

"Of course there are exceptions to that formula—the main character might not be appealing, or his goal might not be worthwhile in the traditional sense. Like in *The Day of the Jackal*, the main character was a professional killer and not a very likable fellow. And his goal, the assassination of de Gaulle, wasn't what you might call worthwhile. But still there were great odds, and the author had researched and paced his story so well that it didn't really matter—you still wanted the assassin, in some horrible way, to succeed and kill de Gaulle, even though you knew that he couldn't."

"Mmmmm," she said. "So who do *you* write for?"

"Me? Oh, lots of people. I'm freelance."

"Uh huh."

"I write books and magazine articles and screenplays and lots of unproduced TV pilots," he said.

"Yeah," she said, "I'll bet."

"I *do*," he said. "I swear to God."

"Mmmmhmmm," she said. "And what do you do for a *living*?"

"That's what I do for a living," he said.

"You mean to tell me you earn enough from writing to *live* on?" she said incredulously.

"Absolutely," he said.

"How much do you make a week?"

"I don't know how much it is a week, but I can tell you what I earn a year. About a hundred thousand."

She burst out laughing.

"A hundred thousand *dollars*?" she shrieked. "Get out of here!" She laughed some more.

"It's the truth," he said.

"Yeah? Tell me some of the things you've written, then."

"OK. Let's see. Have you heard of a book called *Knuckle Sandwich*?"

"Yeah . . ."

"I wrote that."

"Get out of here," she said.

"Have you heard of a book called *Fresh When Available*? Or one called *Modern Lit*? Or one called *Cut to the Chase*? Or another called *You Can't Get There from Here*?"

"Yeah . . ."

"I wrote all of those."

"Get out of here. I *read* some of those. The guy that wrote them is named . . . let me think now . . ."

"Lance Lerner?" he said.

"Yeah, that's it," she said, "Lance Lerner."

"That's me," he said, "Lance Lerner."

"Get out of here," she said a little less certainly, because now that he mentioned it he *did* look the slightest bit familiar to her. The face, that is.

"You don't believe me?" he said. "Check the ID in my wallet. It's in my inside jacket pocket, it's hanging in the closet."

"OK," she said, "I might just do that."

She went out of the bedroom and reached into the closet and found a man's sportcoat. She reached into the inside jacket pocket and took out a wallet and looked inside that and then she got the shock of her life—it really *was* Lance Lerner!

Lance Lerner, a famous author that she had personally herself seen on the *Tonight Show* with Johnny *Carson* on her very own *television* set was lying naked and stretched out and handcuffed to the bed in the very next *room!*

All at once she felt horribly embarrassed. To have been talking to a famous naked person and not even *known* it! What must he *think* of her?

The question now was, what should she do? Well, perhaps she ought to unchain him, for one thing. Although, come to think of it, had he *asked* her to do that? He had not. He was probably trying to worm his way into her confidence before doing that, but never mind. Why do it if he hadn't even asked?

Wait till she told Thelma about this! Thelma wouldn't believe her, of course. Maybe she should go and get her Polaroid Swinger and take some snaps of him so she'd have the proof, just like when you caught a big fish. Would the pictures be proof enough?

"Hey," he called from the next room, "did you find the wallet yet?"

"Uh, yeah," she said, "I found it all right."

What was she going to do? Here was one of the best-known authors in the whole country, and he was naked and completely helpless, and she could do anything she wanted with him. Anything. *Even have sexual intercourse.* Not that she *wanted* to have sexual intercourse with him. Not that she wanted to have sexual intercourse with *anybody.* Not that she particularly *disliked* the idea of having sexual intercourse. Not that she at *all* disliked the idea of having sexual intercourse with a famous author. How many women did she know who had had sexual intercourse with a famous author? None, that's how many. Would she be too embarrassed to even suggest it to him? Hell's bells, why suggest it to him? He was hardly in a position to say anything about it, one way or the other.

She walked slowly back into the bedroom. Her breathing had become shallow and rapid. Her face felt hot.

"Well," he said. "Are you satisfied now?"

"So you're Lance Lerner," she said.

"Yes," he said. "And what's *your* name?"

"Gladys," she said. "Gladys Oliphant."

"Glad to meet you, Gladys," he said. "I wonder, now that we've been properly introduced, if I might ask you a favor?"

"What's that?" she said, but she was barely listening to him now, so excited was she becoming at the prospect of having sexual intercourse with a famous author.

"Could you unlock me?"

"Hmmmmmm?" she said, and idly began unzipping her pastel pink nylon gown.

"I said would you mind unlocking me? I think Stevie left the key on the living-room coffee table."

"Mmmmm," she said.

She took the pastel pink dressing gown off her shoulders and dropped it on the floor. Blushing furiously, she walked slowly toward the bed. He had apparently guessed what she was up to, because his eyes got very big and he stopped talking.

She stepped out of her fuzzy pink slippers and faced him in her pastel pink panties and her pink lace brassiere. She was starting to sweat heavily. It stood out in large beads all over her body.

"I hope," she said shyly, "that you don't mind too much what I'm about to do, Mr. Lerner. It's a real opportunity, you see, and I'd really kick myself later if I passed it up."

He didn't reply, but when she took off her brassiere and

stepped out of her panties and sat down on the bed, caving in the mattress, she noticed that his sexual organ had become hard again, so he couldn't have been as digusted as she feared he might be.

Carefully, carefully, carefully, she stepped across his famous skinny body. She squatted over him, grasped his rigid penis and then slowly, slowly, slowly, she settled herself on top of him, keeping most of her crushing weight on her hands and knees.

If Thelma didn't believe her, it almost didn't matter anymore. She, for one, knew it was true, and that would have to be enough.

31

Stevie chased the two black guys west on 57th Street, shouting at them to stop or she'd shoot, but they didn't even slow their pace.

She started to fire a warning shot over their heads, but that was dangerous because the bullet could ricochet and kill an innocent bystander. Instead she stopped, held her breath, made sure the coast was clear, took careful aim with both hands at the one she was closest to, and fired.

The shorter guy screamed and dropped immediately to the pavement. The taller one looked back briefly and kept on running. She took careful aim at him, but now there were pedestrians in her line of fire and, as expert a marksman as she was, she didn't want to risk it. She raced after the fleeing robber, passing the one on the ground, who she quickly noted was still alive but not in danger of escaping. She scooped up his automatic, and continued running.

The taller guy reached Seventh Avenue and turned north. She figured he was trying for the park. They raced up Seventh Avenue, across 58th Street. One more block and she would lose him. She was damned if she was going to lose him—Stevie Petrocelli always got her man!

The light turned red as he reached 59th Street. He plunged into the busy thoroughfare, narrowly missing a taxicab, which swerved and hit a gray stretch limousine. Stevie followed, running hard, her hands out in front of her on her snub-nosed .38, trying for one more shot in the clear, which was all she needed to bring him down. Brakes screamed and tires screeched and more cars collided in an effort to avoid hitting the tall black man and the short white woman who was chasing him with a gun.

The tall guy had made it across 59th Street and had sprung for the high brick retaining wall which separated him from the park. It was a bad leap, she realized immediately. She was amazed that any black man that tall and that young and with legs that long had missed clearing the top of that wall, but that is exactly what happened. The robber slammed hard into the wall and toppled back onto the ground.

He howled in pain, but as she dove at him, he suddenly turned and thrust what he was carrying right into her gut. The *Random House Dictionary* knocked the wind out of her and she collapsed on top of him.

They lay there together for several seconds, gasping for breath, like sated lovers. Her snub-nosed .38 was pointed directly at his face. Neither of them could speak for fully a minute. A small crowd was cautiously pressing forward as they heard her barely audible whisper:

"You have . . . the right . . . to remain . . . silent. . . ."

32

At numerous points during his rape, Lance thought he would either suffocate or be crushed to death.

The woman on top of him was the fattest woman he had ever seen undressed. True, she did have a pretty face, but if anyone had told him that he would ever end up having sex with anybody as gross as this, much less have her be his first woman other than his wife in almost eight years, he would have told them they were out of their minds.

Still.

Still, there was something decidedly exciting about having, for once in his life, nothing whatsoever to say about a sexual experience, no way at all to feel responsibility or guilt, no need ever to worry about technique or foreplay or have to answer for the consequences. It was oddly liberating.

He was grateful that she had had the decency to help support her weight on her elbows and knees and not rest it all on top of him, and it was amazing but true that his hardened phallus was able to penetrate all those folds of flesh and actually make contact with something slippery that felt like a vagina. The pressure inside his groin kept building up and building up and finally he heard himself cry out in release. She felt it too, and it seemed to push her over the brink because she too cried out, then shouted, then screamed and shuddered and then, forgetting all about her knees and elbows and human decency, she began sinking slowly onto him, like a ship slipping below the waves.

"I love you," she sobbed, "I love you."

"Then . . . please . . . ," he gasped, "don't . . . crush me . . ."

"Oh my God," she said, redistributing her massive weight, "I'm sorry, I'm *sorry!*"

"That's . . . all right," he gasped. "I think I'm . . . OK now."

They were both silent for several moments, bathed in sweat and breathing hard.

"It was wonderful for me," she said. "Was it wonderful for you too, Mr. Lerner?"

"Wonderful," he said. "Absolutely wonderful."

At that precise moment they heard a shriek behind them. Lance couldn't see past the mountain of flesh on top of him, but Gladys turned and gave a little cry of surprise, and then Lance could see her too.

Standing in the bedroom doorway, her face bruised and her clothing torn and filthy, was Stevie.

33

"Hi there, Miss Petrocelli," said Gladys with a fishy smile.

"What in the name of Christ are you *doing!*" shouted Stevie.

"I, uh, came up here to fix your shower," said Gladys, carefully getting off Lance and standing up. "I discovered Mr. Lerner here, and, uh, we got to talking and everything, and we, uh, kind of got, uh, carried away, I guess."

"Carried away? You got carried *away?*"

"Yeah," said Gladys, swiftly scooping her bra, panties and dressing gown off the floor, "one thing kind of led to another and—"

"Get out of my house, you fat whale!" shrieked Stevie. *"Get out of my house this instant or I will shoot you for trespassing!"*

"Just going, just going," mumbled Gladys apologetically, trying to get into her dressing gown as Stevie began shoving her toward the door with both hands. Gladys turned back toward Lance and gave him a little wave. "So long, Mr. Lerner, nice meeting you. Hope to see you again."

"Out!" screamed Stevie, *"Out!"*

Doors opened in the hallway to see fat Gladys, still half naked, being shoved violently out of Stevie's apartment.

Stevie slammed the front door so hard it almost came off its hinges. She turned on Lance.

"What the hell have you been *doing!*" she yelled at him.

"What have *I* been doing?" He was incredulous. "What do you *mean* what have I been doing? I've been being *raped,* that's what I have been doing!"

"You're my *date!*" she screamed. "The minute I leave the house I come back and find you fucking my super behind my *back?*"

"Hang on there now, Stevie, for Christ's sake," said Lance. "Calm down a minute, will you?"

"Calm *down?* You screw my superintendent and then you tell me to calm *down?* Get out of here! I never want to see you again! Get out of my house!"

"How the hell can I get out of your house—you've chained me to your goddamned bed!"

She came for him and he was sure she was going to break his jaw, but then she stopped herself and merely stood there, breathing hard.

"You can order me out of here if you like," said Lance. "All you have to do is unlock these cuffs and I'll be out of here like a flash. But I'd really like to point out that I had nothing to do with this. I was chained to the fucking bed. I had absolutely nothing to say about it. I had absolutely no responsibility in this matter whatsoever, I can guarantee that."

"Oh, you had absolutely nothing to do with it, is that right?"

"That's right, absolutely none. For the first time in my life I am absolutely blameless."

"Tell me you didn't enjoy it," she said.

"I didn't enjoy it," he said.

"Did you have a stiff prick?"

He thought for a moment, and went for honesty.

"I admit that it was stiff. I did not tell it what to be. It has a mind of its own."

"Did you have an orgasm?" she said.

"Did I have an orgasm?" he said.

"Yes. An orgasm. What's the matter, don't you know?"

He swallowed hard.

"I, uh, believe that I might have had one, yes."

"You aren't sure?"

"No no, I did, I know I did. I'm sure."

"But what—you didn't enjoy it?"

"Not . . . all that much, no."

"Not all that much," she muttered.

She wheeled into the living room, tore back into the bedroom with a key and began furiously unlocking the handcuffs. In her rage she was not able to manipulate the tiny locks, and as she missed each one she cursed. Finally they were all opened and Lance withdrew his somewhat battered wrists and ankles and rubbed them hard to get the blood flowing again.

"I'd like to talk this over calmly with you," he said, "but you seem very upset."

"You're goddamned *right* I'm upset!" she yelled.

"*I* should be the one who's upset," he said, "not *you*—do you know how long you were gone?"

"I was gone just long enough to shoot one perpetrator and tackle the other and collar them both and turn them over to another cop to be booked so I could rush home and find you fucking another *woman*, that's how long!"

She began sobbing uncontrollably and pushing him out of the bedroom.

"I can see why you're so upset," he said. "Perhaps we can talk this over when you're not so upset."

She yanked open the front door and started pushing him, naked, out into the hallway.

"Hey, just a minute!" he cried. "At least give me my clothes!"

With a hysterical cry of anguish, Stevie shoved him into the hall and slammed the door. Other doors on the landing opened briefly, then closed. Lance stood there, dazed, then pounded on Stevie's door.

"Hey, open up!" he shouted. "Give me my clothes!"

"Go to hell!" she cried.

He pounded again on her door.

"Stevie, please! Open up! I need my clothes!"

He pounded some more, but it was hopeless. He looked around wildly for help. Two other doors on the landing were opened just a crack. He advanced toward them, and they closed like clams. He stood outside one and then the other and beseeched the inhabitants for articles of clothing or at least a sheet, but he was shouting at deaf ears.

It wasn't fair. In rape cases involving women victims, even the most male-chauvinist cops no longer accused the victim of enticing the rapist, or at least the situation was a lot better than it used to be. But now, when the rape victim was a man, here was a *woman* cop behaving even worse.

He started walking cautiously down the stairs, trying to figure out how he was going to get home without his clothing. It was just possible that if he waited long enough Stevie would calm down and he'd be able to go back up there and get his clothes. It was also possible that he might find Gladys's apartment and persuade *her* to lend him something to cover up with.

He crept slowly down the stairs. Several doors opened a crack as he passed by them. At least three of the elderly tenants telephoned the police. On the first floor he knocked on all the doors, figuring that Gladys had to be behind one of them, but nobody answered his knocking or his calling. It was possible that he could find something in the basement he could wear home.

Lance reached the basement door, opened it, turned on the overhead bulb and made his way down the filthy wooden steps. He wandered around the basement, past the furnace, and into the laundry room. There was a clothesline with a lot of somethings on it, but in the dim light it was hard to see what.

He crept closer. His eyes became accustomed to the gloom. What they were were nine pairs of panties, five brassieres, seven pairs of transparent pantyhose, and a pale blue half-slip. There was absolutely nothing else, either hanging up on the clothesline nor in the washers or driers, not even an old drop cloth or a laundry bag.

Was it preferable to go out on 57th Street naked or in ladies' lingerie? He didn't know. He thought it over. People would feel more threatened on 57th Street by a naked him than a transvestite him, he decided. He pulled the pastel blue half-slip off the clothesline and put it on. The he carefully made his way back to the filthy wooden steps and climbed back up to the lobby. It was lucky it was warm out.

Just as he reached the lobby door, a patrol car pulled up in front of the apartment building and two cops got out and came into the vestibule. When they saw him standing there in the pale blue half-slip, they drew their guns.

34

As a matter of fact, the cops were damned decent about the whole thing after the first few minutes.

All right, so they had a little fun frisking him and asking him what he was doing in the slip and trying to figure out where he kept his ID. All right, so they carried on a little longer than they absolutely needed to when he explained that he had been raped by a fat lady and then thrown into the hallway without his clothes by a policewoman. But he finally piqued the cops' curiosity enough that they actually knocked on Stevie's door to check out his story, rather than taking him right back to the precinct in his slip for booking, and then it all got better.

Stevie finally let the cops into her apartment, she grudgingly corroborated Lance's story, and ultimately Lance got his clothes back. And, after he had assured the cops he wasn't going to press charges against the hefty super, they slapped him on the back and left the building. Stevie still refused to speak to him, so he went home.

The following day was to be his first session of group therapy. The prospect filled him with dread. He wondered how much he would have to tell these people. He realized that withholding anything at all, no matter how painful, would hurt nobody but him. He would have to tell them everything, then. Except, of course, about being raped by Gladys and being captured by the cops while wearing a slip. And maybe one or two other tiny, insignificant things like that.

35

He felt like the new kid in class. That particular one had not been among his top ten feelings when he was a lad. There were four people in the smallish conference room, seated around a low, circular, white Formica-topped table—four, that is, besides himself and Helen Olden.

"This is Lance," said Helen. "He was in private therapy with me several years ago. His marriage just broke up, so he's come back. I've suggested that he join our group."

He was truthfully surprised that he had come at all. He and Helen had discussed it at great length during their last private session. Helen had called the group a safe place to experiment with dangerous feelings like anger and fear and—the most dangerous feeling of them all—love.

She had explained that relationships in the group were a model for all your relationships in the outside world, that however you related to people Out There is how you were going to relate to people in the group. And people in the group, unlike your friends, would tell you when you were full of shit. Friends, she said, made an unspoken bargain with you: "I'll tolerate *your* shit if you tolerate *mine*." People in the group, she said, were forbidden to do that.

Lance thought it sounded interesting, but he didn't think it would help him get Cathy back. He agreed to come, partly to humor Helen, and partly because he thought he might be able to write about it sometime.

The members of the group sat on their canvas-and-wood director's chairs and waited anxiously to see what the new member was like and which of the hoary numbers in their respective bags of tricks it might be necessary to run on him in order to neutralize the threat of his unfamiliarity.

"Lance," said Helen, "is a successful freelance writer, and he can tell you more about himself a little later on. Right now, though, I'd like each one of you to tell him your name—first name only, of course—and a little bit about yourself and what you hope to get out of the group. OK, who wants to be first? Jackie?"

Jackie, a short, stocky man with thin hair and a face that resembled the nose-glasses sold in novelty stores—thick horn-rimmed spectacles, large hooked nose, bushy moustache and furry eyebrows—raised his hand.

"OK, teacher, I'll go first," said Jackie. "My name is Jackie, I'm fifty-three years old, and I work in toilets."

"You're a plumber?" said Lance innocently.

Everybody chuckled. It had been a joke. Lance felt stupid and even more the outsider, a feeling he had worn throughout his boyhood like his older cousin's hand-me-down clothes.

"I'm what they call a stand-up comedian," said Jackie, "but I work mostly in toilets. God forbid I should get a decent room to work in, I'd probably have a heart attack altogether. That's another thing, heart attacks. I've had three mild ones so far, and the next one will probably do me in." Everybody groaned. "I'm the group's hypochondriac," said Jackie.

Arnold, a timid-looking man in a three-piece suit and round wire-rimmed glasses, turned to Lance. "The one thing we don't tolerate in here is anybody who comes on like a victim," he explained.

"Yeah?" said Jackie. "Look who's talking—Arnold, the biggest victim on the eastern seaboard."

"All right," said Helen, "you can save that for later, Jackie. Arnold, why don't you go next?"

"My name is Arnold," said Arnold. "I'm thirty-three years old, I'm a Certified Public Accountant, I'm married to a wonderful wife, I have two little daughters, I have just begun to write my first novel, and I manipulate people by pretending to be weak."

"Thank you, Arnold," said Helen. "Laura?"

Laura, an attractive but pale woman of about twenty-eight or twenty-nine with long straight hair, smiled nervously at Lance. It was reassuring to find that *they* were nervous too.

"My name is Laura," she said. "I'm thirty years old and . . . Well, actually, I'm only twenty-nine, but I look thirty, and I'll *be* thirty in just two months, so I just . . . Well, let's see. I have also started writing my first novel, but basically I'm an Avon Lady. That is, I sell Avon home-care products to suburban women in the greater metropolitan area . . . I'm not married. Recently I discovered that I'm a . . ." Laura's voice trailed off.

"Yes, Laura?" said Helen. "Go on."

Laura blushed. Lance felt himself willing to fall in love with her. Group members, as Helen had emphasized, were forbidden to see one another outside of the group. It was not inconceivable that he might wait till either he or she had achieved total mental health and left the group before claiming her. Not inconceivable, and also not likely.

"Recently," said Laura, "I discovered I'm a lesbian. That is, recently, while demonstrating some Avon products to a client, a suburban housewife in Great Neck, I allowed myself to be seduced, and—"

"Seduced, Laura?" said Helen. "I thought we agreed that—"

"All right, I set it up," said Laura. "I mean, I *was* seduced, but I *did* set it up. Or anyway, that's how it seems to the group."

"You've decided you're a lesbian just because you allowed one housewife to seduce you?" said Lance. The notion of Laura being seduced by another woman was beginning to turn him on. He suspected that this was inappropriate behavior on his part.

Laura blushed even harder.

"Well," she said, "it was, uh, more than one housewife, actually."

"How many?" said Lance, trying to make his voice as clinical as possible.

"Uh, well, actually it was seven separate occasions," said Laura.

"I see," said Lance. "Well, I'm sorry but I just don't think being seduced by even *seven* housewives makes you a lesbian."

"Thank you," said Laura. "You know, Lance, I knew I was going to like you the minute you walked into the room today."

"Thank you," said Lance.

"I think you're very kind and very sensitive, and I find you enormously attractive physically."

"*Thank* you," said Lance.

"I should also warn you that I try to buy people's love with compliments," said Laura.

"All right," said Helen. "Roger, you go next."

Roger, a handsome, thickly muscled man in his late twenties, faced Lance, smiling artificially.

"My name is Roger," said Roger. "I'm twenty-eight years old, I'm a *cum laude* graduate of the University of Illinois, where I played first-string varsity football for all four years. Today I sell insurance, chiefly health and major-medical, and I . . . Well, I'm writing a novel too, but it's not going very well, and . . . Oh yes, about two years ago I had an absurd household accident which left me crippled and . . . Well, I still have to walk with a cane, and I can't make love to my wife except to . . . I'm impotent, and it seems to be a medical problem, so there's nothing that can be done about it."

"Bullshit," said Arnold. "Four doctors so far have told you there's no medical reason why you can't get an erection."

"OK," said Roger sheepishly, "maybe I exaggerated."

Lance felt vaguely cheated. Helen was famous for having a preponderance of celebrity patients, yet none of the people here was remotely glamorous or recognizable. Of course, he'd been given only their first names—it was possible that, had they told him their surnames as well, he would discover them to be celebrity comics, celebrity CPAs, celebrity insurance men and celebrity Avon Ladies.

"Lance," said Helen, "it's your turn."

"All right," said Lance, having the distinct sensation that he was on a TV panel show. "Well, as Helen said, I'm a freelance writer. I just turned forty. My wife left me about six weeks ago, and I'm pretty broken up about that. What else? Let's see, I have a book being published September 15th, and . . ."

"Why did your wife leave you, Lance?" said Arnold.

"Well," said Lance, "I guess she felt that she had needs that I couldn't satisfy or something. She's, uh, gotten somewhat involved with the women's movement of late and . . ."

"Aren't you leaving something out, Lance?" said Helen.

"Leaving something out?" said Lance. "Oh. Yeah. That. Well, about three weeks before my fortieth birthday, y'see, I sort of decided that Cathy—my wife—was having an affair with my best friend, Les. So, uh, I—"

"What made you think that?" said Jackie. "Was she coming home with Vitalis on her collar?"

The group members chuckled tolerantly.

"How did it make you feel?" said Laura.

"Horrible," said Lance. "But I decided that all I wanted was to even the score. So I took her best friend, Margaret, to lunch, and I suggested that we go to bed, and, that was pretty much my undoing."

"You went to bed with your wife's best friend and she found you out?"

"Sort of," said Lance. Then he saw Helen raise an eyebrow at him and elected to amplify. "OK, well, it was worse than that. See, I thought she invited me over to her place to make love, but what I didn't know was that she and my wife and my best friend were planning this big surprise party for me. So I, uh, took off my clothes, and when I opened the bedroom door, the lights came on and there was everybody yelling 'Surprise.' "

"I don't mean to make light of your suffering," said Laura, suppressing a smile, "but that *is* a fairly amusing picture you just painted."

Lance nodded.

"I guess so. Maybe it's still a little too recent for me to see the humor in it, I don't know. Anyway, all I really want to do is get Cathy back."

"Have you been dating other women since Cathy left you?" said Arnold.

"Not exactly dating," said Lance.

"Have you been getting *shtupped*?" said Jackie.

"I suppose you could call it that," said Lance.

"Tell us about it," said Roger. "If you think it will help, I mean."

"Well," said Lance, "First of all, I was . . . raped by the super in the building where this policewoman I know is living."

"The super was a man or a woman?" said Laura.

"A woman, a woman," said Lance.

"How could a woman overpower you to rape you?" said Laura.

"First of all, this woman happens to weigh around two hundred and fifty pounds," said Lance. "And, second of all, I happened to have been, uh, handcuffed to the policewoman's bed."

"You know something, boychick?" said Jackie. "I think I'm going to look forward to hearing your stories more than episodes on *As the World Turns*."

36

On the third day following the publishing party where he met her, Claire Firestone phoned and invited Lance to dinner. It was to be in just eight days, on a Wednesday night at seven p.m., at her apartment on Park Avenue. Lance was tempted to ask what he should wear, but decided that was just a bit too naive a question.

"Should I bring a date?" he said.

"Oh no, I don't think so," she replied. "I'll find you a suitable dinner companion."

The night of the Firestone dinner party he began dressing an hour earlier than usual. He put on a dark blue suit, took it off, put on a pair of slacks and a sportcoat, took that off, and finally settled on a black velvet suit with a soft blue shirt and a solid black tie. He was tempted to put on his tux, but decided against it. He didn't know what you wore to impress a publisher who held novelists in low esteem, but a tux seemed to be trying just a wee bit hard.

Lance arrived at the elegant Park Avenue apartment shortly before seven p.m. He toyed with the notion of walking around the block a few times to be not quite so punctual, then said the hell with it. He gave his name to the doorman and was led into the lobby. The elevator man took him right up in an oak-paneled car with a richly upholstered leather bench in the back.

The elevator doors opened directly into the foyer of the Firestone's apartment. A maid in a black uniform ushered him into a living room that was at least fifty feet long, took his order of a glass of white wine, and left. He sat down on a long couch upholstered in gray suede.

No other guests were there yet. The Firestones were probably still dressing. He knew he should have taken a few turns around the block.

Everything in the living room was done in various shades of gray. The carpet, the couches, the chairs, even the smoked mirrors which lined the walls and ceiling and made the room look like it was big enough to house a 747. Several low gray marble coffee tables attended the couches. On the coffee tables were dozens of tiny crystal vases filled with single white flowers and tiny glass cups filled with lit gray candles.

The maid reappeared and handed him his drink, then withdrew. He was in the midst of rehearsing his first nonbusiness remarks to Firestone when Claire entered the room.

She looked fabulous. A gray silk blouse revealed the shape of her nipples, and gray silk slacks clung to her pelvis and thighs.

"Lance," she said. "How nice to see you."

"Nice to see you, too," he said, standing to greet her.

"I see you already have your drink," she said.

"Yes," he said.

The maid reappeared and looked at Claire questioningly.

"A kir royale, please, Elizabeth," she said.

"What's a kir royale?" said Lance.

"Champagne and cassis,'" she said.

"Ah," he said. "Sounds good."

The maid withdrew.

There was a moment of silence while Lance tried to think of something to talk about. He was distinctly ill at ease. His hostess seemed quite calm.

"Lovely evening out," he said at last.

"Is it?" she said.

"Yes," he said. "Warm, I mean, but perfect weather for this time of year."

"Mmmmm."

Christ, he thought, the woman is going to think I'm a fucking idiot.

"Have you been out?" he said after another pause. "Today, I mean?"

"No," she said. "Not today."

"Ah," he said, cursing himself for not having any small talk, for never in his life having had any small talk, drifting into a fast rehearsal of what he was going to say to Firestone about his book.

"Yesterday," she said.

"What?" he said, alarmed, having no idea what she was talking about.

"Yesterday," she said. "I went out yesterday. To the office."

"Oh. Yes. To the office. You, uh, work in an office, do you?"

"Yes," she said. "I have an office at the publishing house. I go in two or three days a week."

"Is that so?" he said. "How about that."

"Yes," she said. "I look at manuscripts that come in over the transom, so to speak. I'm sort of a glorified reader. It's not much of a job, really—Austin just gave it to me to keep me off the streets."

"Ah," said Lance.

The maid returned with a pinkish drink on a silver tray. Claire took it and nodded. The maid withdrew.

"So that's a kir royale," said Lance.

"Yes," she said. "Would you like to taste it?"

"Oh. Sure."

She held it out. He sipped it.

"Mmmmmm. Good," he said, handing it back, again at a loss for something to talk about.

She took a sip of her drink herself. The silence began to be oppressive, although Claire seemed to be bothered by it not at all.

Lance glanced at his watch.

"So," he said. "Who all is coming tonight?"

"Well," she said, "it's turned out smaller than planned."

"Oh?"

"Yes. One couple canceled because of illness, the other had a family emergency. It'll be just us, I'm afraid."

"Just us?" said Lance. "Just . . . you and me and . . . Mr. Firestone?"

"Just you and me," she said. "Austin was abruptly called to London this afternoon. There wasn't time to call you."

He was silent for about a minute. He stood up.

"I'm sorry," he said. "I'll come back another time."

"Not at all," she said. "Please stay."

"I do think I ought to go," he said.

"I'll be very offended if you go," she said.

Lance stood slightly off balance, torn between the momentum of continuing toward the door and coming back into the room. He didn't know what she wanted from him.

"Are you serious that nobody else is coming?" he said.

"Absolutely serious," she said.

He walked uncertainly back into the room.

"Tell me again what happened. One couple canceled because of illness, and the other had a what? A family emergency?"

"That's right."

"What kind of family emergency?" he said.

She smiled.

"What kind would you like?" she said.

"What?" he said.

"What kind would you like them to have had?" she said.

"I'm . . . not really following this," he said.

"I'm sorry," she said.

"What, uh, excuse did the couple actually give you?" he said after a short pause.

"Who?" she said. "The Benedicts?"

"Yes," he said. "The Benedicts."

"They didn't give any," she said.

"They didn't give *any?*" he said. "Then why aren't they coming?"

"I'm afraid I forgot to invite them," she said.

He looked rapidly around the room for he knew not what—a hidden TV camera or Allen Funt or something like that. Nothing and no one came to his rescue. He began perspiring freely.

"What about the other couple?" he said. "The ones who canceled because of illness. Did you forget to invite them too?"

She frowned, as though blaming her faulty memory.

"I'm afraid I did," she said.

"I see," he said.

"Good," she said. "What do you see?"

"I see that I'm in a little bit of trouble here, and I see that it could get a whole lot worse," he said. "Let me ask you something."

"Shoot."

"Was it never your intention to have anyone else to dinner tonight?"

"Never," she said.

"I see," he said. "Well, if you wanted to have dinner with me alone . . ." he looked about uncomfortably and lowered his voice, "then why didn't you simply tell me so?"

"Oh, I don't know. You might not have agreed to come. You might have been afraid that I'd make sexual advances to you and that you'd be placed in a compromising situation with the wife of the man who's publishing your book."

"Well," he said, continuing to perspire, "that possibility might have crossed my mind. Would that fear have been justified?"

"Mmmmmhmmmm," she said. She was obviously relishing his discomfort.

"Great," he said, retreating again toward the door. "Listen, Claire, it's been lovely, but I really have to leave now."

"Why?"

"Well, if I stayed I'd probably drink a whole lot of kir royales and then I might just decide that hopping into the sack with you was something other than professional suicide."

"Lance?" she called softly.

"Yes?"

"Are you rejecting me?"

"Well, that seems to be the idea, yes."

"Rejection is very aphrodisiac to me, Lance."

"Swell. Listen," he said *sotto voce*, "you mean to tell me you would actually hump another man in the apartment you share with your husband?"

"I haven't yet," she said, "but there's a first time for everything."

"What about the servants?" he whispered. "Aren't you afraid they'd notice?"

"I don't see how they could *help* but notice," she said.

"Aren't you afraid they'd talk?"

"Not at all," she said. "I'm the one who hires them, I'm the one who pays them, and I'm the one who fires them. Besides, I've got a lot more on *them* than they've got on *me*."

"Jesus," he said, "I'll just bet you have. Well, look, don't think it hasn't been stimulating."

He managed to reach the door before she spoke again.

"Lance," she said, "please don't go. I promise to be good."

He turned around. She looked contrite—chin lowered, lips pursed. Like a little girl.

"I promise I won't tease you anymore," she said.

"Was that what it was, teasing?"

"Yes."

"Why do you do that?" he said.

She shrugged.

"I don't know. Out of insecurity, I guess. I only do it with men I don't know."

"Insecurity?" he said. "Are you insecure with me?"

"A little."

"How come?"

"I don't know. Overly impressed by authors, maybe. Are you staying for dinner, then?"

"Can I really trust you?"

"Nope."

They both laughed. He went back inside.

Dinner was surprisingly nice. They ate facing each other across a glass table with the same small crystal vases with single flowers in them and with the same candles in little cups. The maid brought them an endless array of perfectly seasoned, wonderfully tasty things, most of which he didn't recognize. They drank a lot of wine.

She told him about being gawky and too tall and growing up with rich parents and horses in Virginia and then she confessed it was a lie. She had never been gawky, her parents weren't rich, there weren't any horses, and she had never been to Virginia. She had been beautiful always, with perfect bones since the age of ten, had modeled from twelve to twenty-two and fought off the boys since before the onset of puberty.

Austin had seen her picture in *Vogue* and married her within six months of meeting her when she was twenty-two. He at the time was forty-four and had already made his first few millions in the mail-order business before he switched to books—first textbooks, then trade books. He was now sixty-two, she said. He swam a mile a day wherever he was, had had three face lifts and looked sensational. She supposed he fooled around with other women, but she didn't care. He was an excellent provider, a strong protector when she needed strength, a considerate lover, and in the eighteen years they had lived together, she said, he had never bored her.

Had she had affairs while married to this seemingly model husband? She admitted that she had. Not many, but a few. But why? She didn't know. Possibly because she came in contact with a great many stimulating men and had a strong curiosity about them sexually and a strong need to control them through sex. Possibly she only did it for the excitement.

She needed excitement in her life, she said, and it was getting increasingly hard to come by. She already owned everything she'd ever dreamed of owning: a huge Park Avenue apartment, a good-size summer home in East Hampton, an apartment in London, a winter home in Acapulco, a chauffered limousine, two sports cars, a yacht, a private plane, a staff of servants. There hadn't been any children, perhaps because both of them had been self-centered, ambitious, and vain. There wasn't much to look forward to now, except old age and losing what she already had. If she took an occasional lover, she said, it was her own affair, so to speak. What she and Austin did with their own bodies on their own time was their own business.

She asked him about his separation and he told her. She didn't laugh as he thought she might. And she didn't flirt with him again. Except when he was leaving.

When he was leaving she impulsively slid her arms around his neck, kissing him sweetly on the mouth, and swiftly ran her tongue over his lips.

"I thought you promised to be good," he said, beginning to get excited in spite of himself.

"The promise only applied to dinner," she said. "Dinner's over. All bets are off."

She kissed him again and undulated her body against his. He pulled away, but not before she'd noticed his hardness.

"Tsk tsk," she said, frowning with mock disapproval.

"I think we should just be friends," he said.

"I have enough friends already," she said. "I think we should be lovers."

She grabbed him and kissed him again.

"What would your husband do if he walked in and found us like this?" he whispered.

She thought about this for a moment.

"He would probably tear your head right off your shoulders," she said.

It took him two minutes flat to make it out the door, down the elevator, and out onto the street.

37

"Yeah?" said Lance, picking up the phone.

"May I speak to Lance Lerner, please?" said a male voice with a coarse Bronx accent.

"This is he," said Lance.

"Mr. Lerner," said the voice, "this is Julius Blatt? I'm a public defender down at the Supreme Court in Manhattan?"

The caller sounded as if he wasn't sure of these facts and was checking them out with Lance.

"What can I do for you, Mr. Blatt?" said Lance.

"I have these two clients," said Blatt. "Ernest H. Roosevelt and Irving 'Goose' Washington? Their names ring a bell with you at all?"

"Roosevelt and Washington," said Lance. "Nope. Afraid not."

"They say they know you," said Blatt.

"They black kids?" said Lance.

"Yeah. They're being held for armed robberty—of the B. Dalton bookstore on Fifth Avenue. They're both writers, and one of them, Roosevelt, says he's a student of yours or something."

"A student?" said Lance. "I haven't had any students in years, Mr. Blatt."

"Well, he claims he's had some correspondence with you? Says he asked you for advice on writing, and you were generous with him and gave him lots of pointers? You sure that doesn't ring any bells?"

"I'm afraid not," said Lance. "I mean it's very likely I answered a letter he wrote me and gave him some advice. I do that quite a lot. But I can't truthfully say I remember him."

"Yeah," said Blatt. "Well, what we were hoping was that maybe you'd come down and be a character witness for him. Tell the court something about his writing, that kind of thing, you know?"

"You want me to be a character witness for a guy who robbed a B. Dalton bookstore who I never even met and can't recall exchanging letters with?" said Lance.

"You willing to do it or not?" said Blatt.

"Not," said Lance. "I'm sorry, Blatt, but it's a ridiculous request."

"OK, OK," said Blatt. "No problem. I was just asking. You have to hit all the angles on this kind of a thing. Tell me this. If we go to trial soon, would you be willing to do a human interest piece on them for the *Daily News*?"

Lance sighed.

"I don't do that kind of thing, Blatt," he said. "I mostly write novels, you know? Why don't you get somebody like a reporter at the *Daily News* to do that for you?"

"OK, OK," said Blatt. "No probem. I was just asking. As I say, you got to hit all the angles on a thing like this. Tell me this. If we could manage to start up a grass roots movement to get these boys some national publicity, would you be willing to help us out?"

"What do you mean, help you out?" said Lance.

"I don't know yet," said Blatt. "I mean if I could make them a kind of cause célèbre, you know? Like the broad that killed the guard who raped her in the slammer, you know? Or like the Chicago Seven, you know?"

"What do you mean," said Lance, "something like 'Free the Dalton Two'? That kind of thing?"

" 'Free the Dalton Two' . . ." said Blatt. "Hey, that's not too bad, you know?"

"I was kidding," said Lance. "That was not a serious suggestion."

"Why not?" said Blatt. "I kinda like it, you know? 'Free the Dalton Two.' It's kinda catchy, you know?"

"Do me a favor, Blatt."

"Sure."

"Don't use it, OK?"

"Why not? It's a great slogan."

"Just do me a favor and don't use it, OK?"

"OK, OK," said Blatt. "No problem, Mr. Lerner, no problem. But thanks."

38

The telephone rang, jarring him out of a complex and exhausting dream about moving and misplacing things, and large empty houses with windows thrown open to an impending storm and dry leaves scudding across bare living-room floors. He picked up his watch and tried to focus on the dial as the phone continued to ring. It was ten-thirty a.m., a not unreasonable hour for people to call. He picked up the phone.

"Yeah?" he said.

"Good morning, darling," she said.

"Who is this?" he said.

"Claire. How many people do you know that call you darling?"

"My mother and many gay gentlemen I know. How are you, Claire?"

"I'm wonderful. What are you doing right now?"

"Right now?" he said. "Right now I'm talking to you on the phone. I'm still in bed."

"Mmmmmmmmmmm," she said. "Why don't you put on your clothes, hop in a cab, and come over here to play?"

"No thanks," he said. "I'd rather not."

"Do you know what I'm wearing?" she said.

"How could I possibly know what you're wearing?" he said.

"I am wearing nothing," she said. "I'm all alone in a big scary bed and I want you to come over and play with me."

"I don't think so, Claire," he said. "But thanks for the offer."

"Maybe some other time?" she said.

"Yeah," he said. "Maybe so."

He hung up and had an intense fantasy about going over to the Firestone apartment and climbing into bed with Claire, as the maid served them endless kir royales. Then he got up, showered, shaved, dressed, and went through the morning mail.

There were three letters addressed to neighbors a few doors east of him, two letters addressed to somebody three blocks down, and one addressed to him correctly that had been stamped ADDRESSEE UNKNOWN, RETURN TO SENDER, which had apparently been sent back and remailed and managed to get to him despite Postal Service perversity. There was also the front half of a huge envelope which had been savagely separated from the rest of itself and from whatever it might have contained and then been crumpled up and stamped on repeatedly. He wondered if such things happened to other people as well, or if the Postal Service just had a personal vendetta against *him*.

Of the nineteen letters correctly addressed to him, five were charitable solicitations bearing photographs of grotesquely disfigured adults, children and animals; three were offerings to buy mutant grapefruit, stunted Japanese miniature trees, and foot-long penis extenders; three were entreaties to write his congressmen on behalf of whales, baby seals, rabbits being used to test cosmetics, and refugees from a country he had never even heard the name of before; two were utility bills with elaborate instructions on how to decipher the new computerized format and no explanation of why the previous three computerized formats had fallen into disfavor; one was a cheery letter from Con Edison explaining that its campaign to persuade customers to save energy had been too successful and that Con Ed had therefore applied for and won another huge rate hike to make up for lost revenues; and four were aggressive personal entreaties to claim three million dollars' worth of prizes he had already won which were waiting for him in a warehouse somewhere, feeling rejected. Lance marveled at how computers had managed to type into every other line of all five lengthy letters either his name or his address or his shirt size.

The single personal letter truly meant for him was addressed in a vaguely familiar handwriting. He tore open the envelope and took out a message scrawled hastily on lined notepaper:

> Dear Mr. Lerner:
>
> I'm sorry about the photographs. If we hadn't been high we never would have sent them. It hurt me that you hung up on me but I guess I deserved it. I really respect your writing and would someday like to discuss with you the various career opportunities open to young women in the area of journalism. I promise not to act like some dumb sex-crazed groupie.
>
> If you could spare a few minutes to see me, please call.
>
> Sincerely yours,
> Dorothy Chu

Dorothy Chu, the Chinese girl in the Polaroids! He searched the newest note for a phone number, but, like the last one, there wasn't any. He wondered if it was worth going down to Chinatown and trying to find her.

The doorbell rang. He supposed it was a messenger. He buzzed, heard the door open downstairs, then close, and footsteps come slowly upstairs. He went to the stairwell and peered down, and was totally unprepared to see Claire, in a light tan raincoat.

"Claire. I thought you were in bed."

"There didn't seem to be any point remaining there all alone," she said. "I hope I'm not interrupting anything."

"Well, frankly," he said, "I have a hell of a lot of desk work, and then I have to go out and do some errands."

She pushed him back into the apartment.

"I can't stay long," she said. "But I wanted to see you and tell you I'm sorry for last night."

"Sorry?" he said. "You didn't do anything to be sorry for."

"That's the problem," she said. "May I take off my coat?"

"Well, sure, but . . ."

She unbuttoned her coat and took it off. Except for a pair of T-strap heels, she was totally naked.

He felt suddenly dizzy and had to steady himself against the doorjamb. Her body was sensational. Small firm breasts of a twenty-five-year-old, flat stomach, small blond pubic thatch, legs that went from floor to ceiling.

"So," she said, "what do you think? Not too bad for an old lady of forty, eh?"

"Not . . . too bad, no," he said. "Look, Claire, I really don't think you should stay, I really don't."

"Now listen, Lance," she said evenly. "I am getting tired of being rejected. And so I am giving you a choice."

"Yes?"

"Either we go to bed right now, and I guarantee that Austin will never find out, or else I will go right home and call him up and tell him that you attacked me."

She was not smiling. He had no reason to believe she might be kidding.

"Well," she said, "which is it going to be?"

He sighed.

"All right, Claire," he said, "you win."

39

Lance led Claire into the bedroom. She immediately lay down on the bed, propped her head up with two pillows, and watched him with great interest as he took off his clothes.

"I love bodies like yours," she said. "Long muscles, and not an ounce of fat. That's one of the reasons I've been so persistent."

"Good," he said. He took off his jockey shorts and climbed wearily into bed.

"I've seen more enthusiasm from people going in to have root canal," she said.

"It's just that I'm used to picking my bed partners and the circumstances of bedding them myself," he said, aware that this was not an accurate description of recent experience.

"Well," she said, "then this will be a nice change for you."

He lay down beside her and began to stroke her face and neck and shoulders.

"Are you adept at cunnilingus?" she said. "I usually like to start with that."

"Veddy good, madam," he said, mimicking an obsequious waiter. "And are there any special instructions for the entrée?"

She chuckled and gently pushed his face toward her mons veneris.

He was furious with her, so furious he felt his erection wither. He feared his anger would make him impotent. His fears were well-founded, as are all fears of impotence, stage fright, and other self-fulfilling prophecies. He went to work on her pudenda with tongue and lips and teeth and fingers and a vengeance that appeared to startle her.

"Don't be upset if I don't make it," she said after a while. "I hardly ever do."

He stopped what he was doing and regarded her coolly across a smooth landscape of belly and chest.

"I don't give a good goddamn if you make it or not," he said. "I happen to like eating pussy, and whether you achieve an orgasm or not doesn't affect my pleasure one bit."

Nobody had ever reacted that way to this statement, he sensed. She had doubtlessly used her difficulty in achieving orgasm as a punitive and emasculating weapon against her husband and lovers, even at the expense of her own pleasure. Being told that it was of no concern to Lance whether she came or not removed the point of her controlling edict and must have freed her to consider whether or not she was willing to go on denying herself pleasure, because, shortly after he'd made his statement, she began to moan with pleasure.

Skillfully escalating her excitement onto higher and higher plateaus, Lance was eventually able to push her over the threshold into a deep and powerful release that left her sobbing with ambivalent gratitude. He regained his potency and injected himself into her. She dug her nails and her teeth into his flesh, but it was she, not he, who shouted. Lance hung on for dear life, trying to contain his orgasm. The pressure in his groin built up and up until he feared he would explode, and then he did, and they finished together, with her clasping his body to hers so hard he thought he'd shatter.

He lay on top of her as both of them gasped for breath. He felt spent and drained and sucked dry of every drop of fluid in his body—sperm, sweat, blood and spit. He felt he'd probably never have the strength to move again.

"How was it?" he said when he could find the strength to speak.

"Why, weren't you there?"

"I mean," he said, "how was it for *you?*"

"Nice," she said.

"Just nice?"

"*Very* nice," she said.

"Nicer than with Austin?"

She made a cry and slapped her forehead.

"Why do men always have to know if they were the best lay you ever had?" she asked. "Why can't you just be satisfied that it was very nice?"

That night he dreamed he was standing in a large hotel room that bore some resemblance to Claire's apartment and some to his own, although it wasn't an apartment and it wasn't in New York. There was no furniture in the room, not even a bed, but there was a phone and it rang. He answered it and was told by the operator that an unidentified person had called to say he would make an attempt on Lance's life sometime within the next hour.

A policeman happened to be in the room and told Lance not to worry, that he'd see to it that all exits would be covered and that no harm could befall him. Then, somehow, Claire—or was it Cathy?—was in his arms. She was frightened and he was reassuring her. They were on what appeared to be a little balcony adjoining the hotel room, and as he hugged her and reassured her he noticed that the door to the next room had slowly opened and the shadow of a large man had fallen diagonally across the floor. He knew it was the policeman and wasn't alarmed, but when he looked up he saw to his horror that it wasn't the policeman at all, it was a gorilla about eight feet tall.

The gorilla appeared to be in something of a drug-induced stupor, and it also appeared to be in flames. Lance knew, in the way that we know things in dreams, that the gorilla was wealthy, as gorillas went. Terrified, but figuring that a good offense is the best defense, and recalling from childhood that you must never show an animal your fear, Lance took a step toward the gorilla and began a low, bestial growl in his throat.

He awoke from the dream, thrashing wildly about in his bed, and growling so loudly that he was hoarse for several hours after he got up. He didn't know what the dream could have meant. He suspected he was in more trouble than he had thought. He felt that Helen would be able to explain the dream to him and, perhaps, help prevent its recurrence.

40

"Well, I talked to Lerner," said the short man in the modishly cut three-piece suit to the two depressed-looking black youths in the filthy green visiting room.

"What he say?" said Ernest H. Roosevelt.

"Well," said Julius Blatt, "he may not be able to see his way clear to testify for you in court as a character witness, but he did suggest something that I think is a hell of an idea. He suggested—"

"He ain't going to testify for me?" said Ernest. "Why not?"

"Well, I don't know exactly," said Blatt, "but he did offer to start a grass roots movement to get you some publicity and raise money to get you guys out of here."

"Publicity?" said Goose. "What the fuck we need with *publicity?"*

"Just a minute, bro'," said Ernest. "Tell me what the man suggest."

"Well," said Blatt, "he tried to sell me on the idea of starting this huge publicity campaign to get into the media with. He wants the slogan to be 'Free the Dalton Two.' I said I didn't know, I'd try it out on you before I let him go ahead with anything."

" 'Free the Dalton *Two*'?" said Goose. "What we need with *that?"*

" 'Free the Dalton Two,' " said Ernest slowly and carefully. It sounded OK. It sounded classy. It sounded like he and Goose could become some kind of something in the media with that. It sounded like maybe it could help him sell his novel.

"Tell the man yes," said Ernest. "Tell him he got my permission to put it in the works."

"You got it, my man," said Blatt, and slapped Ernest's surprised palm.

41

"Who is the gorilla in your dream?" she asked.

"I don't know," he said. "I didn't get too close to him, but from the little I saw I don't think it was a well-known one."

Helen gave him a perfunctory smile.

"Whom do you think the gorilla *represents?"* she said.

"I really don't know," he said. "I was hoping that perhaps *you* might."

She gave him one of her long-suffering looks.

"OK," he said, "maybe this is something. In the dream I had the impression that the gorilla was sort of well-to-do. A wealthy gorilla. Also he was kind of on drugs, I think. And he was in flames, although he didn't seem to be in any pain that I could see."

"A wealthy gorilla," she said. "On drugs and in flames."

"Yeah," he said.

"What does that image bring to mind?" she said.

"I don't know," he said.

"Come on, Lance. A wealthy gorilla—*stoned* and on *fire?*"

"I don't know," he said. "I sense that it must mean something very obvious, but I just can't see it. I mean I know that the subconscious mind is into a lot of symbolism and puns, but I just can't see it."

"Lance, listen to me. The gorilla is on *fire* and *stoned*. What do these two words mean to you, Lance—*fire* and *stone?*"

"I'm sorry," he said, "I'm sure it's really obvious to you, but I just can't see it."

"Are you deliberately trying to torture me?" she said.

42

As a reward for bringing her to orgasm, Claire Firestone staged a huge weekend dinner party in her East Hampton house, at which Lance was, if not the guest of honor, at least the guest she invited first.

A minor theater critic named Shipley and his wife unfortunately had been planning their own dinner party in East Hampton on that very evening for the past three weeks. The moment the Firestone party was announced, Shipley guests began phoning in cancelations due to illness at a rate that caused Ada Shipley to wonder whether Legionnaire's Disease hadn't suddenly flared up on eastern Long Island.

Truman Capote had already accepted the Firestones' invitation, as had Woody Allen, George Plimpton, Alan King, and, as a special treat, Firestone was flying Marlon Brando in by private plane.

A middle-aged literary agent named Arthur Black had a case of social frenzy so great that the very notion of attending a "B" party while in the same community an "A" party was going on without him was enough to send him into cardiac arrest. Although he had managed to wangle an invitation to the Firestones', he was nevertheless unable to come up with an acceptable excuse for canceling his invitation to the Shipleys'. On the night of the parties, Black was reduced to making his *au pair* girl telephone Ada Shipley to say that the Blacks would not be able to attend because they had a flat tire. Ada Shipley, who already knew that the Blacks had got themselves invited to the Firestones', offered the use of the Shipleys' Honda to transport the Blacks to the Firestones'.

A homosexual movie critic from the *New York Daily News* named Ralph Raitt, whose elderly mother lay dying of cirrhosis, had already canceled his invitation to the Shipleys' to be in the intensive-care ward with Mom. But when he received his invitation to the Firestones' he noted, to his mortification, that he was actually beginning to root for the old lady either to get dramatically better immediately or else die in time for him to hot-foot it out to the Firestones'. After all, he reasoned, the old gal was already in a coma and was dying anyway—what did it matter to *her* when she went?

As luck would have it, Raitt's Mom's EEG went flat only six hours before dinner time on the appointed day. Raitt did about twenty minutes of heavy soul-searching, arranged with a funeral home for a speedy cremation, and stood up for the entire three-and-a-half hour ride out to the Hamptons on the Long Island Railroad.

Raitt's social frenzy was in a league with Black's, but it was nothing new. For twelve years a rich publisher named Corman had held an annual Memorial Day party in his East Hampton house. It was one of the most prestigious parties of the year, but Corman had tired of it, and this year he'd simply decided not to have it. Most of the guests who'd been yearly invitees feared that the party was still going on, and that they had simply been dropped from the "A" list due to lack of recent professional achievement or the unwitting commission of some small social awkwardness. Ralph Raitt was the only one of these who, when asked if he'd been invited to the Corman party this year, actually went out on a limb and said yes.

Lance had not been anxious to face his little house in the East Hampton woods in the weeks since the separation. He called Cathy and asked if she was up for going out there with him now that the weather had turned hot—they never went out between November and June, and he'd had no desire to stay there without her.

Cathy declined his invitation. He said they could even have separate bedrooms if that would put less pressure on her, but the answer was still no. He was momentarily despondent, but determined not to let it throw him. He decided he could hazard a short weekend in the Cathyless cottage so long as he wouldn't have to do it alone.

He telephoned Stevie to invite her out for the weekend of the Firestone party, and although she hung up on him the first three times he called, he was finally able to keep her on the line long enough to tender the weekend invitation through the stratagem of screaming out: "MARLON BRANDO WILL BE THERE!"

When she heard why Lance was calling her, Stevie speedily forgave him for being raped by her hefty super. She got another cop to trade her two night tours, and she accepted Lance's invitation.

The Firestones' East Hampton house was a cavernous old three-story affair on the Atlantic Ocean. It featured a half-timbered front, a double-height, exposed-beam ceiling, a profusion

of little leaded-glass windows, and a swimming pool with a cement bar and bar stools imbedded in the bottom at the shallow
end.

Lance drove up to the Firestones' with Stevie in his rotting old
Porsche convertible and allowed an off-duty East Hampton cop
to direct them to a parking space. Lance took a deep breath of
sea air as they got out of the car and wondered why he had
allowed his dread of being without Cathy in their little house to
keep him in New York.

They entered the Firestone house, which was already half-
filled with people, and Stevie began recognizing celebrities and
throwing their names at Lance so swiftly it reminded him of the
old Lucky Strike tobacco auction commercial.

"There's Gay Talese," said Stevie, "and his wife, Nan. There's
Frank Perry and his wife, Barbara Goldsmith. Oh my God,
there's Hal and Judy Prince, Steve Sondheim, Jimmy Kirkwood,
Sidney Lumet, David and Leslie Newman, and George Plimpton
and his wife, Freddie."

"C'mon," said Lance, "I want to get a drink."

"Oh, Jesus," said Stevie as they passed the piano, "it's Woody
Allen, Marshall Brickman, Buck Henry, and Paul Simon."

Lance noted that several of the guests were sporting painful
sunburns. Interesting, he mused, how we emulate the skin pig-
ment of the least successful ethnic groups in the society.

Claire spotted Lance and drifted over. She looked as sensational as ever, in a simple white jersey dress that clung to her
body as though it had a self-adhesive lining. He could see not
only her nipples but her areolas in sharp relief against the material.

"Claire Firestone," said Lance, "I'd like you to meet Stevie Petrocelli. Stevie, Claire."

Stevie tore her eyes away from Woody, Marshall, Buck and
Paul just long enough to size up her hostess, who was doing the
same to her.

"Pleased to meet you, sweetheart," said Stevie to Claire, who
raised one eyebrow.

"Lance tells me you're a policewoman," said Claire, trying to
home in on her target. "That must be exciting work."

Stevie shrugged.

"It's a living," she said, her eyes professionally working the room. "Did Marlon arrive yet?"

"Oh, then you *know* him?" said Claire with a slightly bemused smile.

"I had occasion to spend a little time with Bud, as we call him, a couple of years ago," said Stevie. "Lucy Saroyan introduced us —that's Bill's daughter, you know."

"I know," said Claire sweetly. "I think we must have had to meet *all* of Marlon's friends by now."

"Didn't you just love little Wally Cox?" said Stevie. "He was the cutest thing. Bud was really destroyed by his death."

Claire glanced swiftly at Lance and rolled her eyes ceilingward.

"I'll bring *Bud* by as soon as he arrives," said Claire to Stevie, moving on. "I know you two will have a lot of catching up to do."

"Seems friendly enough," said Stevie, watching Claire greet guests. "Although she's going to need paramedical assistance getting out of that dress."

They pushed their way to the bar, as Stevie continued her recitation of recognized faces.

"There's Gilda Radner," she said, "Danny Ackroyd, John Belushi, Lorne Michaels, Jean Doumanian, Mike Nichols, Patrick and Cynthia O'Neal, and there's Jack Rollins, Woody's manager."

The bartender, a black with a missing thumb and an air of snobbism that endeared him to a number of employers guilty about their wealth and looking for punitive proxies, icily informed Lance that kir royales were too much *trouble* in a party of this size. Lance accepted white wine as a substitute. But Stevie, who hadn't even wanted a kir royale, took the bartender's remark as a personal insult and speculated aloud how far she thought she might be able to navigate the bottle of kir up the bartender's rectum.

Stevie's observation caused somebody behind them to explode with laughter. They turned around to see a man about six foot five, with close-cropped white hair fading to black at the sideburns. The man's face looked as though it had been born with a perfect tan that had never peeled nor faded in sixty-two years. He had bushy black eyebrows and cold blue eyes, and although

Lance had never met him nor even seen his picture he knew the man was Austin Firestone.

"Don't you know you're speaking to a member of a disenfranchised ethnic group?" said Firestone to Stevie with a gigantic twinkle in his eye.

"What, you mean they stopped giving out franchises to thumbless bartenders?" said Stevie.

Firestone chuckled and introduced himself. Lance, balancing resentment about the canceled tour and guilt about Claire, nonetheless found himself instinctively drawn to the tall tycoon.

"Say," said Firestone, focusing in on Lance, "aren't you the author of a book we're publishing next month?"

"That's me," said Lance, flattered that Firestone had recognized his name, but irritated that he obviously didn't remember the title of his book.

"Uh . . . *Carousing*, isn't it?" said Firestone.

"Close," said Lance, "but no cigar. It's *Gallivanting*."

Firestone snapped his fingers.

"*Gallivanting*," he said. "Damned fine book, as I recall."

"Really?" said Lance. "Then why the hell aren't you going to promote or advertise it?"

Stevie gave Lance an interested look.

"What do you mean?" said Firestone. "I thought we were."

"You call interviews on FM radio and in the Moonie newspaper a promotion campaign?" said Lance, aware that he was coming on too strong, but not knowing how to stop.

"Is that all we're doing?" asked Firestone. "What's the budget?"

"Five thousand," said Lance.

Firestone was momentarily puzzled, then he snapped his fingers again.

"*Moola*," he said.

"Pardon me?" said Lance.

"Our lead title next month—*Moola*. It's by Andrew Goodbody, the Wall Street Gnome. It's going to sell about two million copies in hardcover."

"That's a self-fulfilling prophecy if I ever heard one," said Lance. "But what does it have to do with me?"

"Look, Lerner," said Firestone, "I'm a good businessman. My

people tell me *Moola*'s going to go through the roof, so we're really doing a media blitz on it. If they thought *Carousing* was going to go through the roof, we'd be blitzing that too."

"*Gallivanting*," said Lance, "not *Carousing*. Look, you promote *Moola* like a bestseller, it'll *be* a bestseller. You don't promote *Gallivanting*, it'll go straight into the toilet all right, just like your people think—not because it's a dog, but because nobody will have even heard it was on sale. You call yourself a good businessman? Why publish *Gallivanting* at all? You're just throwing away the cost of printing and binding."

Firestone took a long reflective swallow of his drink. His eyes never left Lance's face.

"What would you consider a fair test of whether or not your book had legs?" he said at last.

"Send me out on tour as they promised me when I signed the contract," said Lance. "I'm a great promoter. See whether sales improve enough in the cities I do interviews in to warrant putting more money into the promotion budget."

"How many cities would you consider a fair test?" said Firestone.

"Ten," said Lance, then wondered if that was too high or too low.

Firestone took another long pull on his drink.

"Let me think about it," he said. "I'll tell you before the end of the evening."

Just then there was a commotion and it looked as if everyone was suddenly being sucked out of the room by a giant vacuum cleaner.

"Well," said Firestone, "it looks to me like Brando's arrived."

43

There he stood, Marlon Brando. The Marlon Brando of *On the Waterfront* and *The Wild One* and *The Men* and *Viva Zapata!* and *Julius Caesar* and *The Young Lions* and *A Streetcar Named Desire,* but mostly the Marlon Brando of *On the Waterfront.* The Marlon Brando of "Oh, Chollie, I coulda been *somebody,* I coulda been uh con*ten*duh."

Lance had seen Brando over a dozen times in *On the Waterfront* alone, and now here he was, a quarter of a century later, standing in the living room of a woman whom Lance had fornicated with, standing not six feet away. Never mind that so many years had passed and that Marlon had swallowed the Goodyear blimp. He was still Marlon, and the fifty or so people who pressed in on him, some to introduce themselves, some merely to shake his hand or stand there looking at him and just smile foolishly—even those who were celebrities themselves—were quite aware of it.

Through the folds of fatness, the old Marlon smiled back at them over the years, that same wonderful crooked little smile that had made them all fall in love with him when he was beautiful, and the smile had not changed.

To Lance's chagrin, Stevie pressed forward, caught Brando's eye and called out, "Howya doin', Bud?"

To Lance's utter astonishment, Brando said softly, "Howya doin', Stevie?" You could have knocked Lance over with a goddamn feather . . .

Celebrities and noncelebrities alike swirled around Brando like schools of fish around a whale. Brando nodded, smiled, and every now and then murmured something in the famous voice. After a while Lance got tired of the spectacle. Also he had to pee. He made his way to the bathroom.

Others had the same idea. There were two people ahead of him in line, a middle-aged man and a woman of forty. A beautiful young woman strolled up and joined the line. The woman and Lance smiled briefly at each other, acknowledging their mutual need to eliminate. He toyed with the notion of giving her his place in line and decided not to—gallantry seemed extraneous in the crapper.

When it was finally his turn to go into the bathroom he was surprised and repelled to find turds in the toilet bowl. He flushed, but they did not go down. He urinated, gave the mechanism a while to rest itself, then flushed again. They spun merrily in the whirlpool, they teased the opening of the drain, but they didn't enter.

Lance was certain that if he left now, the beautiful young woman in back of him would think the turds were his. Although he would probably never see her again, he didn't want her to remember him as somebody who left turds in toilet bowls. He waited a couple more minutes, then flushed again. Again the turds tickled the drain opening, even poking a timid snoot inside it, but then withdrew.

There was a knock at the door.

"Be right out," called Lance.

The hell with it, he thought. He put the lid down on the toilet and was about to open the door. He went back to the sink, turned on the water, then turned it off again. Bad enough to have her think he was a person who left toilets unflushed, he didn't wish to also leave the impression he didn't wash up afterwards.

Lance opened up the bathroom door. The beautiful young woman seemed irritated at how long he had taken. He flashed her a tentative smile. She pushed past him into the bathroom, began to close the door.

"Uh, listen . . ." he began.

She turned back toward him.

"Yes?" she said, her irritation now quite apparent.

"They aren't mine," he blurted.

"What?" she said.

His face broke out in prickly sweat.

"Never mind," he said, and scurried away in confusion.

He had half a dozen brief conversations with people he knew, and resented the fact that he frequently found their eyes not on him but elsewhere, working the room. He would have resented it even more if his own eyes hadn't been doing the same thing.

Austin Firestone passed him in the hallway.

"All right, Lerner," said Firestone, "I've thought it out."

"Yes?" said Lance.

"I'll give you a five-city tour. You increase sales in those cities by a substantial enough margin, maybe I'll give you a few more."

Lance nodded.

"Fair enough," he said. "How's about raising the print order?"

"How many copies in the first printing?" said Firestone.

"Fifteen thousand," said Lance.

"We'll keep it at fifteen for now," he said. "If sales start to go up after the first couple of cities, we'll order a second printing."

Firestone started to move away.

"Wait," said Lance. "Print orders are self-fulfilling prophecies too, you know. Any book with a print order as small as fifteen thousand is never going to be taken seriously by anyone—not by your salesmen, not by the jobbers, and not by the retailers either. A print order of a *hundred* thousand, though, automatically causes everyone to—"

"I *said* fifteen is enough for now," said Firestone in a voice that turned Lance's blood to permafrost, "don't push your luck, Lerner."

Firestone strode away. Lance's heart was pumping double-time. Don't push my luck, is that it? he thought. Don't push my luck? Well, I'll damn well push whatever I *want* to push, big guy, including your horny wife.

He went back to the thumbless black behind the bar and demand a kir royale.

"I regret," said the bartender in a patronizing tone, "that owing to the size of the present crowd—"

"Don't give me that crap," said Lance quietly. "You pour some champagne and some cassis into a glass *pronto,* pal, or you're going to be missing more than thumbs."

Eyes the size of golf balls, the bartender reached for the champagne bottle.

44

There was something oddly familiar about her, but he doubted that he knew her. She wore bleached jeans and a T-shirt with printed lettering on it that was so faded and cracked it was almost illegible. She had the slim figure of a girl of about seventeen or eighteen and long straight black hair and the stunningly beautiful face of an Oriental model he had once seen in *Vogue.*

"I guess I shouldn't have come," she said in a wounded tone. "I don't know why I did, except maybe I wanted to see if I had the balls."

"I'm sorry," said Lance, "but I don't believe that we—"

"Dorothy Chu," she said somewhat petulantly. "We already have a relationship: I call you on the phone and you hang up on me."

"Dorothy!" he said. "My God, come in."

She entered the apartment shyly and looked around.

"Nice place," she said. "How come you don't have any furniture?"

"My wife took it," he said.

"She leave you or what?" said Dorothy, checking out the layout.

"Well, sort of," said Lance.

"I don't blame her," said Dorothy. "You probably hung up on her once too often."

"Dorothy, listen," said Lance, "I didn't hang up on you."

"You didn't?" she said. Her petulance, no longer sure of itself, faltered.

"No," he said. "I tripped on the phone and it disconnected. I tried to get you back, but you didn't leave me your phone number."

"No kidding?" she said. Her face was breaking out in the most beautiful smile.

"I swear to God," he said. "I would have called you back if I could have. I even looked you up in the Manhattan directory, and you weren't listed."

She squealed and impulsively threw her arms around him and kissed him. It was over before he had a chance to enjoy it.

"I'm sorry," she said. "I tend to be overly impulsive at times."

"Hey, don't apologize for hugging and kissing someone," said Lance. "It was a lovely gesture."

She looked at him and smiled self-consciously, color coming into her cheeks.

"I feel kind of stupid," she said.

"How come?" said Lance.

"Because I don't know what to *do* now. I came over here because I was hurt and wanted to give you a piece of my mind, and now that that isn't appropriate anymore, I don't know what else to do. Except maybe leave."

"Oh, don't leave," said Lance. He loved how she looked and how direct and vulnerable she was. He was also trying to figure out how old she was and whether it was possible to somehow get her to hug and kiss him again without appearing to be a dirty old man.

"OK," said Dorothy.

"Sit down," said Lance.

Dorothy looked around, saw no chairs, and sat down cross-legged on the floor, in a modified lotus position. He loved the way she did that. An adult probably would have made some snide remark about the lack of furniture and made him feel bad. He sat down across from her and tried to get his legs into the same position, but it was a little painful so he didn't push it.

"I still don't know what to say," said Dorothy, blushing. "You'll have to start."

"Oh, OK. Well, let's see. What shall we talk about. Why don't you tell me about you?"

"OK, like what?"

"Well, like, what does it say on your T-shirt?"

"Oh, this?" she said. She squinted down at her chest. "It says, 'If God had not intended man to eat pussy, then why did He make it look so much like a taco?' "

They both blushed and giggled.

"Glad I asked," he said. "Well. Tell me. What made you write to me in the first place? What did you want?"

She shrugged.

"I don't know. Like I said, my friend Janie and I are sort of writer-groupies. We're both big fans of yours, and we're both writers, and, well, we just wanted to sort of meet you and get some advice from you and stuff."

"Advice? What kind of advice?"

"You know. About writing and everything. About how to crash into print. I'm really quite serious about my writing."

"I see," said Lance.

"I'm writing something now, in fact, which I sort of hoped you might take a look at and tell me if it was any good and whether it was, you know, commercial."

"What kind of thing is it?" said Lance. "A novel?"

She shook her head.

"Huh-huh. A poem."

"A poem?" said Lance.

"Not a *poem*, really, more like a trilogy."

"A trilogy?" said Lance. "About how long is it?"

She shrugged.

"I don't know exactly, I mean I haven't numbered the pages. There must be over a thousand, though."

"Ah."

"What's wrong?" said Dorothy.

"Well, I'd love to read something you wrote, but if it's a poem over a thousand pages long, I don't know if I—"

"It reads very quickly," she said.

"I'm sure it does," he said, "but I'm a little strapped for time right now. I'm about to have a novel of mine published and I have to go out on the road for several weeks and promote it. I don't really even have time to do my *own* things now—my errands and things—much less read a—"

"Hey, that's OK," she said. "I understand. I guess it was a little presumptuous of me to ask you anyway."

"Not at all," he said. "It's just that I don't really have the time right now."

"What errands do you have to do?"

"Pardon me?" he said.

"What errands and things do you have to do?"

"Why do you ask?" he said.

"I don't know. I was just thinking. I'm on vacation from school right now, and I'm kind of looking for a summer job. Maybe I could work for *you*—run your errands and straighten up your place and stuff."

Lance considered it. Many of the things he had to do were things you couldn't delegate—like going to the dentist, getting a haircut, and so on. But there *were* a great many things that could be done by someone else, provided they were intelligent. Dorothy did seem to be intelligent.

"I'm very intelligent for my age," said Dorothy, seemingly reading his thoughts.

"What *is* your age?" said Lance.

"Sweet seventeen," said Dorothy.

"And never been kissed?"

"Oh," said Dorothy, "I've been kissed, don't worry. About everywhere you could think of."

"I see," said Lance, beginning to have a lustful fantasy about her and then quickly cutting it short. Please, God, he prayed silently, don't let me ever believe it would be a good idea to have sex with this child.

"I guess maybe I shouldn't have said that," said Dorothy. "When I'm nervous I tend to babble a little."

"Oh, that's all right," said Lance. "I do the same thing myself. Why are you nervous, though?"

"I told you. You're one of my heroes. I'm really impressed with you. I think you're one of our finest writers."

"Well, that's very flattering," said Lance. "Thank you."

"You're welcome. Of course, I'm only a kid, so what do I know?"

Lance smiled wanly.

"A word of advice, Dorothy," he said. "Once you've given a compliment, leave it alone. Don't try to take it back again."

"I'm sorry," said Dorothy. "I wasn't disparaging you, I was disparaging myself."

"Why do you have to disparage either one of us?" said Lance.

"I don't know," said Dorothy. "Maybe because it makes me feel like I'm at home with my folks."

"Your folks give you a hard time at home?" said Lance.

She nodded.

"They're very traditional. Very Chinese. Do you know anything about the Chinese?"

"I'm afraid not."

"They're very conservative. Next to them Ronald Reagan is a radical. You should hear their views on sex."

"What are their views on sex?"

"I don't know. They won't discuss it with me. They've tried to prevent me from seeing men altogether."

"Have they been successful?" said Lance.

Dorothy shrugged.

"Yes and no. I mean I've been to bed with a couple of boys, but I didn't enjoy it too much. Maybe that's because of their lack of skill—do you think so?"

"Maybe," said Lance.

"I hope to God that's it," said Dorothy.

"How do you mean?" said Lance.

She looked at him carefully, as if trying to decide how much to say.

"I mean I hope it's not that I like girls better," said Dorothy.

Lance nodded, beginning to feel like a psychiatrist. He wasn't sure why she was telling him this, but he didn't think he wanted her to stop talking just now.

"What makes you think you might like girls better?" said Lance.

Dorothy shrugged again, looking down at her hands, and absentmindedly tried to form a hangnail on her left thumb.

"I don't know," said Dorothy. "It's just that sometimes when

I'm with a girl I really like, like my friend Janie, and especially if we're doing drugs, well . . . I get these feelings."

"What kind of feelings?" said Lance.

"Mixed," said Dorothy. "Sort of loving and platonic, and also sort of horny. I'm not sure I want to have horny feelings about other girls."

"It's quite normal, you know, for girls to have sexual feelings about other girls," said Lance.

"Yeah?"

"Yeah."

"It doesn't make you a lesbian?"

"Not at all."

"What does?"

"I don't know. I suppose if you have sex only with women for a long period of time, then people might say you were a lesbian."

"What if you have sex mostly with men, and then just a *little* with women? Does that make you a lesbian?"

"I don't think so. I think that makes you a bisexual."

"I don't think I'd ever really want to do it with a woman," she said. "I've had fantasies about it, I mean, but actually doing it would be really gross."

"OK," said Lance.

"Anyway, I didn't mean to talk so much about sex and lesbians. I really just wanted to come over here and meet you. And if you think you'd have enough work to keep me busy, maybe I could work for you for a while until you go out on tour."

"Do you type?" said Lance. "I'm not saying that I have all kinds of typing to do, but there might be some every so often."

"I'm a fantastic typist," said Dorothy. "I'm not bragging, I really *am*. Saying you're a fantastic typist is just stating a fact. Also I take pretty good shorthand, would you believe that?"

"That's pretty impressive," said Lance.

"Yeah. My folks insisted I learn all that stuff so when my writing career went down the tubes I could always be a secretary."

"What would I have to pay you?" said Lance.

"I don't know," said Dorothy. "Whatever you like."

"How about three dollars an hour?" said Lance.

"How about six?" said Dorothy.

"I, uh, don't really think I can afford six," said Lance.

"OK, why don't we split the difference, then, and say five?"

"Uh, Dorothy, splitting the difference between three dollars and six is not five," said Lance. "It's four and a half."

"OK, four and a half," said Dorothy. "Tell me something."

"Yes?"

"Once I start working for you and being in your apartment a lot and stuff, do you think you'll ever make a pass at me?"

"I hope to God I'm never that stupid," said Lance.

"Good," said Dorothy. "Not that I'd hate it or anything, I mean, because you really are attractive and everything, but I guess we ought to keep our relationship professional. Plus which you *are* a little old for me. Hey, what do I call you, Lance or Mr. Lerner?"

"How about Gramps?" said Lance.

45

Lance telephoned Claire to thank her for the party. It had been, he declared, a complete success. It had indeed, she said. Lance told her he felt that the five-city tour that Firestone had granted him was at least a start. Not as many cities as he had hoped for, but at least a start.

"You now have five cities," said Claire in the cadences of a game-show host. "How would you like to turn five into ten?"

"Pardon me?" said Lance.

"I said, how would you like to double the number of cities on your promotional tour?"

"Uh, I'm not sure I get your meaning," said Lance. "Are you suggesting that there is something I could do that I haven't already done which might accomplish such a thing?"

"There might," said Claire coyly.

"And would that favor be of a sexual nature?" said Lance.

"It might," said Claire.

"Let me understand something," said Lance. "Are you telling me you have the power to influence Firestone to make strictly business decisions?"

"Oh, nothing is strictly business with me, Lance," said Claire.

"In other words," said Lance, getting hot under the collar, "you have had the power all along to get me such a thing, but instead you're using it to force me to exchange sexual favors for it?"

"Whoa, boy," said Claire. "That is not what's so at *all*."

"Then what is?" said Lance.

"Here is what's so," said Claire. "I happen to be a somewhat bored woman who happens to be able to exert certain types of influences on certain people, including my husband, for certain specific things at certain specific times. Not in all areas and not at all times, but enough to be effective. *How* I do this is my business. *When* I do this is my business. It is not always easy work, I might add. It is most definitely work. And when I do work for somebody, I like to get repaid in some form, or else I feel taken advantage of. Now then, the form of repayment in your case—and in very few others, I might add—happens to be sexual. If it pleases you to do me sexual favors, Lance, I will be delighted. If not, so be it. I imagine I'll get over it somehow. But be very clear about one thing: nobody is *forcing* you to do anything at all. *You* are the one who will decide if you want to do it. Not me. *You*. You are a completely free man, lover. That's what makes you such a challenge."

Lance thought it over. What she had said was certainly straightforward. And it was not as if she were Gladys Oliphant.

"What do you want me to do?" he said.

"Have you ever made love in a moving limousine?" she asked.

A uniformed chauffeur rang his doorbell later that afternoon, and escorted Lance to the limousine. Lance thought he could detect a faint smile at the corners of the chauffeur's mouth but he couldn't be certain.

Inside the limousine Claire was waiting for him. She was wearing a long ivory-colored dressing gown. Lance got in and sat down beside her. The chauffeur closed the door behind Lance and then got into the front seat, put the car in gear and drove.

Claire smiled at Lance, then reached forward and closed the sliding glass panel that separated the front and back seats. She drew a gray curtain across the glass as well, then sank back in her seat.

"What are you drinking?" she said, indicating the bar which stood between the two richly upholstered jump seats on the floor in front of them.

"What do you have?" said Lance.

"Everything," said Claire.

"All right," said Lance smugly. "I'll have a White Russian."

Claire nodded. She opened a panel on the bar and withdrew a bottle of Kahlua and a bottle of vodka. Then she opened another panel and took out a container of cream. She took a glass from the top of the bar and mixed the drink so swiftly he was sure she must have spent time as a professional bartender.

He took the drink from her and thanked her. It tasted surprisingly good.

"Aren't you having anything?" said Lance.

"Already have," she said, indicating an empty champagne glass on the bar. "May I offer you anything else before we begin—an hors d'oeuvre? A phone call? A little TV?"

He looked at the TV over the bar and the phone to its left and tried not to act overly impressed.

"Not just now, thanks," he said.

"Maybe later?"

"Yes. Maybe later."

He drank some more of his drink. Claire reached over and began unbuttoning his shirt. He looked out the window. They were turning onto Park Avenue. Claire removed his boots and his trousers and underpants. He wondered if people outside the limousine could see in. The car was moving fairly swiftly so perhaps they couldn't.

Claire began to play with his penis. As it grew stiff, the car slowed down and stopped at a stoplight. A very proper-looking couple in their sixties stood just back from the window. Claire met their gaze, smiled sweetly at them and removed her dressing gown. Now quite naked and still smiling sweetly at the astounded couple, Claire raised herself slightly off her seat, grabbed Lance's penis and settled herself slowly down on top of it.

Lance was so embarrassed he hid behind her back. The couple, frozen in their tracks, did not move as the light turned green and the limousine surged forward.

After the first embarrassment with the couple on Park Avenue, Lance began to enjoy the outrageousness of it all. They drank, they made love, they watched *Star Trek* reruns on TV. Claire called her office and made a few other short phone calls. Lance asked her if one could make long distance calls from the limousine, and by way of response she made a longish call to a friend in Paris. While she talked, she busied her hand in his crotch.

That evening a dozen incredulous people would report to friends or family what they had witnessed that afternoon when a sleek gray stretch limousine had pulled up at a stoplight. Not one of them would be believed.

When the chauffeur finally opened the door to let Lance out at his apartment, Lance and Claire were both dressed again and it was dusk.

"Thank you for a wonderful afternoon," he said.

"Oh no," she said, "thank *you*. And congratulations."

"Congratulations?" he said.

"On your five additional cities," she said.

The following morning the telephone rang at nine-thirty, awakening him from a fitful sleep.

"Lance? Howard. Hope I didn't *wake* you?"

"You did," said Lance.

"Well, it serves you *right*. For not having to be up when I do. Guess what I pulled *off* for you—you're not going to *believe* it!"

"What did you pull off for me, Howard?"

"I put a *hell*uva lot of pressure on Firestone, and I *got it*."

"Got what, Howard?"

"Five additional *cities* on your *tour!*"

46

Hiring Dorothy had proven to be a brilliant decision. She managed to shop for groceries, take his boots to the shoemaker to be resoled, go to the health-food store to stock up on vitamins, go to the post office with parcels, and replenish his liquor cabinet in about a third the time he would have used himself.

Today he planned to have her go to the library and do some research for him, but when she arrived at his door she looked as though she'd been crying and might start again at any moment.

"Hi, Dorothy," he said. "Is anything wrong?"

She shook her head.

"I'm sorry," said Lance. "I didn't mean to pry. It's just that you looked very sad and I thought you needed to talk."

She nodded.

"I do need to talk," she said.

"What's wrong?" said Lance.

Dorothy started to cry, took out a crumpled piece of Kleenex and dabbed at her eyes.

"I'm in big trouble," she said at last.

"What kind of trouble?" said Lance.

"You remember that discussion we had? About lesbianism? Well, last night I told Janie what you said. She thought you were very wise. She's a big fan of yours, too—did I mention that?"

"Yes."

"Well anyway, we were over at my house, and we were doing some grass, and we were talking over what you and I discussed, you know? And Janie said that she was very relieved, because *she* was worried about stuff like that too. About whether she had lesbian tendencies and everything. And she said that she was relieved to hear that sometimes I felt horny towards her—like an asshole, I had told her that—because sometimes she felt horny towards *me*."

"Yeah . . . ?"

"Yeah. So I said that was nice. So she said the grass was making her feel horny towards me *now*. So I said that was nice. I mean what was I going to say? So she said she wondered what it would be like to kiss me. On the lips and everything. So I said I didn't know. So she kissed me."

"Yeah . . . ?"

"I don't mean a peck on the cheek, I mean a real kiss. On the mouth. With tongues and everything. Yecchh!"

"You didn't like it, huh?"

"Not really. Well, maybe a little bit. But it just felt so *gross,* you know? To have another girl's tongue inside your mouth? So I kind of pulled away from her and she could tell I was grossed out, and she got really hurt. She probably gets paranoid on grass like *you* do. Anyway, she starts crying and saying I'll probably never want to be her friend again and everything . . . So I went and hugged her. I mean I really *love* that girl—we've been through some real shit together and I really *love* her. As a friend, you know?"

"Yeah."

"So anyway, there I am, hugging her and consoling her, and she keeps on crying. Crying and saying how I probably find her repulsive and everything, and how she probably ruined this wonderful friendship we had. I got so sad that *I* started crying. There we were, two assholes, hugging and crying. I told her nothing could ever ruin our friendship and that I loved her. I kissed her a whole lot of times, to sort of show her how much I loved her, but definitely keeping clear of the old mouth-a-rooney, you know? But in a way that was worse than if I hadn't kissed her at all."

"Why's that?"

"Because. She saw how I was avoiding kissing her on the mouth and she ended up feeling even more repulsive than before. So, just to show her I didn't find her repulsive, I kissed her on the mouth."

"Yeah . . ."

"I stuck my tongue in there too, just to sort of make my point, you know? And . . ."

She began to cry again.

"And what?" said Lance.

"And," said Dorothy, dabbing at her eyes and nose, "I started *liking* it. I started getting really turned *on*. Janie did too. So we just stood there, kissing and getting turned on, and before I knew it we were taking our clothes off, and then there we were in bed together, *naked,* for God's sake!"

Lance could visualize the scene very clearly. It was getting him excited, which he didn't think was an appropriate reaction for him to have. He thought he ought to say something helpful or understanding, but he couldn't think of anything.

"Uh, did you each take your *own* clothes off, or did you undress each other?" he said, immediately sensing it was the wrong question.

"Each other," she said. "God, it was weird, lying in bed naked with your best friend, having sex."

"You did, uh, have sex together then, did you?" said Lance.

Dorothy nodded, then cried some more.

"Yeah," she said. "Well, sort of."

"Sort of?" said Lance.

"I mean, *she* did," said Dorothy.

"You mean she . . . ?"

"She went down on me. I felt *really* weird then, you know? To have my best friend down there licking away at my thing? I mean what kind of *people* must we be if we would have sex with our best friend? The worst part was I even *enjoyed* it! God! Now I'm a dyke for life."

Lance was having trouble speaking. The image was too powerful. He wanted to comfort her, but he didn't dare touch her for fear of giving her the wrong idea. Or the right one. Why is it, he thought, that the notion of two women together is stirring to both women and men, but the notion of two men together is unappealing to women and to heterosexual men?

"Listen, Dorothy," said Lance. "You haven't done anything wrong. You'd be surprised how many people have experimented like you and Janie and done that kind of thing."

"Have *you?*" said Dorothy through her tears.

"Sort of," said Lance.

"You went to bed with your best *friend?*" said Dorothy.

"That's right," said Lance.

"Far *out,*" said Dorothy. "I would never have thought *you'd* go to bed with another man."

"It . . . wasn't a man, exactly," said Lance. "It was my best *female* friend, but it was certainly a weird experience."

Dorothy was incensed.

"How can you even *compare* that with what I did?" she said. "How can you even speak of them in the same *breath?* I thought you were going to tell me something weird, and you tell me how you fucked a *female friend?*"

"OK," said Lance, "you want to hear *weird, I'll* tell you weird. How about this: All my adult life I've had fantasies about *nurses* —about nurses wearing translucent white *uniforms,* and being seduced by two of them while I'm a patient in the hospital and having a *threesome* with them."

"Are you *kidding* me?" said Dorothy. "You call that *weird?* That's the most boring fantasy in the world. There's not a guy in the *world* that doesn't have that fantasy."

"OK," said Lance, beginning to feel challenged, "then how's about this: I let a policewoman I know handcuff me to her bed naked while she went out to the liquor store, and while she was gone a fat woman who weighed about three hundred pounds came up to her apartment to fix her shower head and raped me."

Dorothy studied him carefully.

"Is that a fantasy or it really happened?" she said.

"It really happened."

Dorothy nodded her head.

"That's weird," she said.

"You're damn right it is," said Lance triumphantly.

"You let a policewoman handcuff you naked to her bed?"

"Damn right," said Lance.

"I think you may be a lot weirder than I am," said Dorothy.

"What?" said Lance. "Hey, c'mon now, Dorothy, what *is* this?"

"Letting a policewoman handcuff you naked to her bed?" said Dorothy. "Are you *kidding* me? That's *gross.*"

Lance felt extravagantly stupid. What in God's name had made him confess that?

"Dorothy, I was merely trying to make you feel less weird by telling you one of my own experiences," said Lance. "I was just trying to help you, and I end up feeling like a real asshole."

"I'm sorry," said Dorothy. "I know you were just trying to make me feel better. But getting handcuffed naked to a bed and being raped by a four-hundred-pound woman—*yecchh!*"

"I didn't say *four* hundred pounds, I said *three* hundred pounds, and besides—"

"OK, OK," said Dorothy. "I'm sorry I said you were gross. And I really do appreciate what you were trying to do."

"Good," said Lance. "Now then, do you feel better?"

Dorothy thought a moment, as if she were checking her mood thermometer, and then shook her head and began to cry again.

"What's wrong *now?*" said Lance, annoyed that he hadn't totally cleared up the problem.

"I haven't told you the worst part yet," said Dorothy.

"Yes you did," said Lance. "You said the worst part was that you even enjoyed it."

"That's not the worst part," said Dorothy. "That's only the *second* worst part. The worst part is that my mother walked in on us."

Dorothy began sobbing uncontrollably.

"Oh, boy," said Lance softly. He tentatively reached out to hold her and comfort her, then withdrew his hand. "What did she do?"

"She said I had dishonored the family. She kicked me out of the house!" said Dorothy, and completely fell apart.

Lance went over to her and took her in his arms. They hugged for several minutes and she continued to cry. As he feared, the close proximity of her body against his was making it difficult to concentrate on his vows to himself.

"What are you going to do?" said Lance, once Dorothy had quieted down.

"I don't know," she said. "I really don't. I guess I could go and stay at the YWCA, but that really sounds grim."

"It does," said Lance.

"Can I ask you something?" said Dorothy.

"What?" said Lance, although there was no doubt in his mind what the question was going to be, only how he would answer it.

"Can I bring my sleeping bag over here for a while and sleep on your floor until I find something more permanent?"

He thought about her question for several moments, but he finally said aloud what he had thought he would:

"Of course you can."

47

Dorothy Chu moved into Lance's apartment that very evening. She brought with her a sleeping bag, a knapsack filled with clothes, a backpack filled with various books of poetry she especially prized, the manuscript of her epic-length poetic trilogy, and a large if somewhat moth-eaten stuffed panda.

Lance decided she should spread her bedroll on the living-room floor, right where the sectional sofa had stood before the Motherloaders had removed it under Cathy's direction. It was agreed she would use the small upstairs bathroom for everything except baths or showers, when it was permissible for her to use the master bathroom off Lance's bedroom, but by appointment only. It was agreed she would roll up her sleeping bag every morning and keep her things very neat and out of sight. It was agreed that she would respect Lance's privacy and that he would respect hers and that both of them, when not in the bath or shower or their respective beds, would appear fully clothed at all times.

At first Dorothy quite scrupulously followed the ground rules that Lance had laid down. She kept her bedroll neat and out of sight during the day. She made appointments for the bath or shower hours in advance.

Then she began to get a trifle lax. One evening he walked into his bathroom to take a pee and found her in the tub. She had forgotten to make an appointment and was deeply apologetic. He asked why she hadn't at least closed the door, and she said that she couldn't stand closed doors because she was claustrophobic. She swore it would never happen again, and he forgave her, but some small damage had been done that could not be undone: he had seen her, for however short a time, naked. The sight of her lovely girlish body, nude in his tub, was one he could not eradicate from his memory, try as he might.

On another occasion he stepped into the shower, only to find that she had hung up several pairs of her bikini panties to dry there. He was irritated and noticed, to his extreme discomfort, that when he handled the still-moist garments to remove them from the shower, he found his fingers tingling.

On yet another occasion he walked into his bathroom to see her sitting on the john, her pants down at her ankles, reading. She apologized like crazy, explained that her john upstairs was stopped up and didn't flush properly, but once more the damage had been done.

The weather was extremely hot. Several times he caught her walking around the apartment in her underwear. On one particularly hot day he caught her typing in his study wearing only panties. What did she want—to drive him insane? He lectured her like a beleaguered father. She answered him like a resentful teenaged daughter. She said he was uptight about the human body, like all older men. The words stung. He searched within himself and was forced to admit that he was at least somewhat ambivalent about the human body, if not precisely uptight. To try to escape the most-ancient category in her catalogue of older men, he resolved to alter his attitudes. He tried not to scold her when she broke the rules and appeared before him less than fully clothed. He tried not to even appear upset when he got out of the shower once and found her standing at his sink, brushing her teeth. He began to get used to seeing her walk around the house with little on, if anything at all. His hands began, every so slightly, to shake.

His friend Les came over once and saw Dorothy walk through the hall in her underwear. Les raised an eyebrow. Lance explained that Dorothy was living with him temporarily, but that nothing sexual was going on between them. Les waited for the put-on to end and the truth to come out, but Lance swore it was the truth. Les finally believed him, and inquired whether he might perhaps take Dorothy to a movie one night. Lance said absolutely not. Dorothy was much too young for Les, he said. Both Lance and Les were surprised at the ferocity of Lance's edict.

Something was happening to him. It did not appear to be anything good.

One night Lance passed by the living room and heard the sound of sobbing. He peeked in and found Dorothy face down on her bedroll, crying into her pillow, clutching her panda. Lance entered the room and softly called her name. She didn't appear to hear him. He bent down and softly touched her shoulder.

"Dorothy?"

"Yeah?"

She didn't turn around. He thought she might be crying because of something he had done to her, although he couldn't imagine what. He felt horrible.

"Dorothy, what is it?" he said.

She turned over. Her eyes were very red and very wet.

"It's Janie."

"What *about* Janie?" he said.

"They got Janie," she said and began to sob again. It was like a line in a World War II movie—*They got Janie.* He imagined Janie climbing out of a foxhole and being suddenly riddled by Kraut machine-gun bullets.

"*Who* got Janie?" he said.

"My parents. They told her father what she and I were doing. They threw her out of the house."

More sobbing.

Well, he thought, at least Janie's alive. At least she wasn't going to show up in the movie's next scene in a shallow grave with her rifle plunged into it, bayonet first, her helmet dangling from the stock.

"Where will Janie live now?" asked Lance, and immediately regretted the question.

Janie Wang moved in late that night.

Janie was taller than Dorothy, larger boned, flatter faced, wider hipped, smaller breasted, more Oriental looking. She wasn't quite as beautiful as Dorothy, but she was beautiful. She, like Dorothy, had long straight black hair and wondrous cheekbones. Like Dorothy, she still slept with a stuffed animal—an incongruously blue teddy bear that looked like it had been around as long as Lance himself.

Lance made an attempt with Janie to re-establish the ground rules, but he knew it was hopeless. Their cosmetics and clothes were everywhere. Long black hairs clogged his drains. Janie appeared to have claustrophobia as severe as Dorothy's where bathrooms were concerned, so Lance was continually walking in on her on the john as well. Before long, both Janie and Dorothy passed in and out of his bathroom when he was using it as freely as when he wasn't, as freely as if it were their own. And he never saw either of them fully clothed again.

He found he didn't really mind it. It was like one happy family. Better yet, it was like the fantasies of his youth—to be invisible in the girls' dormitory. He liked the idea that they felt relaxed enough to go about the most intimate of activities in his presence without being self-conscious. They frequently hugged and kissed and caressed each other when he was in the room, though nothing more. He felt strangely honored that they were willing to share their displays of affection for each other with him.

They discussed their daily activities together at dinner and always asked his advice. The three of them went places together at night. They began to have private jokes together. They decided they were a family. Every night, at their request, Lance tucked Dorothy and Janie into their sleeping bags and told them bedtime stories of his own devising. They began to have their favorites, and made him repeat these incessantly, like small children.

They told him that they loved him and he didn't doubt it. He loved them too. His friend Les came over and saw the two of them living there with Lance and rolled his eyes. Lance swore that they were not a ménage-à-trois, but Les couldn't be convinced.

"You sonofabitch," Les chuckled enviously, shaking his head, "you crafty old sonofabitch. How the hell do you do it?"

Lance decided that Les was too obtuse to be a close friend anymore.

Often at night he would lie in his bed downstairs and listen to them up in the darkened living room, whispering and giggling. He wondered if they were having sex. He wondered if they wanted only each other. He wondered what they really thought of him. He wondered if he were jealous of the intimacy they shared with each other which excluded him. He wondered how long their present relationship would endure. He sensed that it was about to change, but he didn't know in what direction. The possibilities filled him with inexplicable anxiety.

48

Julius Blatt simply didn't understand it.

The idea was a natural. A hundred-dollar-a-plate benefit dinner organized around Lerner's slogan, "Free the Dalton Two," was only a fucking brainstorm. He already had half a dozen celebrities committed as either sponsors or speakers—celebrities a whole lot bigger than Lance Lerner, as a matter of fact—by the time he called Lerner and asked him to be a speaker at the dinner.

Blatt hadn't even been sure that Lerner was big enough to ask in the first place. The fact that he had called him at all was only a courtesy to the man who had thought up their slogan. So it was especially puzzling, *and* hurtful, to have Lerner react the way he had and to have him say the things he had. Blatt had actually thought he was doing the man a favor, and here he goes and says all these mean and hurtful things.

If, as Lerner maintained, he really hadn't wanted Blatt to use the line "Free the Dalton Two," then why had he given it to Blatt in the first place? And why would he object to their using the line anyway? Probably because Lerner was now sorry he'd given it to him for free. Money-grabbing bastard—that's all those writer bastards cared about anyway.

Well, fuck him. Blatt didn't need Lerner, and neither did Goose or Ernest. As a matter of fact, now that he thought about it, Blatt wasn't even altogether sure it hadn't been he himself who had come up with the slogan during their conversation.

49

The members of Lance's therapy group were unexpectedly tough on him. They distrusted the familial feelings which he swore he felt for Dorothy and Janie. They said he wasn't being honest with the group or with himself. They said he wanted to have a ménage-à-trois.

He told them they were full of shit. He said that maybe—*maybe* —that had been true in the beginning, but that now those feelings had evolved into something higher. He said he felt paternal feelings for the two girls, that he wanted to be their father and their older brother and their friend. He said he didn't want to be their lover.

They told him he was full of shit. He appealed to Helen, told of how he tucked Dorothy and Janie into bed every night with their stuffed animals and improvised bedtime stories. He said he'd even had a notion he would look into the legal possibilities of adopting them. Helen, too, said that he was full of shit.

The group asked Lance what he was doing for sex these days. He told them about the session in the limousine with Claire. He said that he had still not given up on Cathy. Cathy's birthday was coming up soon, he told them. He was trying to figure out whether he should buy her a present.

"Why don't you take her out to dinner on her birthday?" asked Helen.

"Oh, I don't think so," said Lance.

"Why not?" said Laura.

"Because. She'd never agree to go," said Lance.

"How do you know?" said Arnold.

"I just know," said Lance. "She's my wife. I know her."

"You know her so well that you thought she was having an affair with your best friend, but she wasn't, and you thought she would never leave you, but she did," said Arnold. "You sure know her well."

"Hear, hear," said Roger.

"Very nice, Arnold," said Helen.

"Thank you," said Arnold.

"*Touché,*" said Lance. "Look, maybe I *don't* know her as well as I think I do. Maybe I'm just afraid to call her and ask her."

"Are you afraid she'll say no," said Helen, "or are you afraid she'll say yes?"

Lance thought it over.

"Both, I guess."

"Give it a try, Lance," said Helen gently. "You might just find that whatever her response is, it's the one you want."

"And if she says no," said Jackie, "you can always go out for chinks with the teenaged dykes."

50

Lance's call caught Cathy off guard. She was almost pleasant. He asked her to dinner for her birthday and she declined, as he'd expected. But when he asked her what she planned to do instead, she couldn't come up with any alternatives that didn't sound depressing.

Lance realized her first refusal hadn't shattered him and that he was truly willing for her to do what she wanted. This realization afforded him the freedom to be looser and lighter. As their conversation continued he found himself getting back to the old him. He was peppy, confident and funny, and Cathy seemed surprised and charmed in spite of herself.

When he repeated his invitation to dinner, she accepted. He suggested the Four Seasons, the elegant East Side restaurant that had been one of their favorites. She seemed pleased by the suggestion. He asked what time she wanted him to pick her up. She said she preferred to meet him at the restaurant.

They arrived at about the same time. He saw her get out of her cab, caught a glimpse of her upper thighs as she emerged from the cramped space, and remembered what she looked like naked.

They kissed lightly and went in. He had asked that they be seated in the main room next to the marble reflecting pool and they were. She looked fabulous—even better than the terrible time he had seen her last at the Russian Tea Room. Her hair was pulled back in a way that he had never particularly liked while they were together but which he had to admit was very flattering. She wore a sleek black dress and silver jewelry that he had not given her. Where, he wondered, had it come from?

"So," he said, smiling.

"So," she said, smiling.

"You look lovely."

"Thank you."

There was a pause. They both continued to stare at each other, slightly forced smiles on their faces.

"It's good to see you again," he said.

"It's good to see you, too," she said.

"I mean that," he said.

"So do I," she said.

It was not going to go well, he thought suddenly, and cursed Helen and the group for encouraging him to bring her here. Try as he might, he could think of absolutely nothing to say to her. Their captain took drink orders and withdrew.

"It's warm," he said suddenly.

"In here?" she said, surprised, because in fact the interior of the restaurant was quite comfortably cool.

"No, outside," he said.

"Ah," she said.

"For this time of year," he said.

"You think so?" she said.

"Well, no," he said, "but I couldn't think of anything else to say."

His admission released some of the pressure and they both laughed.

"Christ, this is hard," she said. "Why should it be so hard?"

"I don't know," he said. "It's ridiculous. I mean here we are, people who know each other more intimately than anyone in the world, and we're reduced to speculation about the weather."

"I know," she said. "Well, I feel better now. How have you been, Lance? You look very well."

"I've had my ups and downs," he said. "As you know, I'm about to leave for a ten-city promotional tour for my book."

"Yes, how did you manage that?" said Cathy. "The last time we talked I think you said they'd changed their minds and weren't going to send you anywhere. Did Howard change Firestone's mind or what?"

"Well, no, not exactly. I pretty much did it myself. I talked to Firestone himself—as a businessman, not as an author—and I think it did some good."

"How did you manage to see him?" said Cathy. "I didn't think he ever talked to authors."

"Well, that's not untrue," said Lance. "But I happened to meet *Mrs.* Firestone at a party, and I told her what a hard time I was having getting to see her husband, and she set it up for me."

"Ah," said Cathy.

Talk of Claire was beginning to make him nervous. He decided to redirect the conversation elsewhere.

"So," he said, "what have you been up to?"

"Oh, lots of things," she said. "There are tons of new fall books to get through and assign, and I've been doing some of my own writing. I've started a novel."

Lance didn't know how to react at first. He thought she might be mocking him.

"Why are you looking at me that way?" she said.

"I don't know, I just thought you hated the whole process of novel writing so much."

"In *you*," she said. "Not in me."

"I see. But you want to write novels?"

"Yes."

"What made you choose the novel form?"

She shrugged.

"I want to make something of myself," she said. "I want to be acknowledged as a person in my own right, not as somebody's wife, or as somebody's editor, either. I want to be noticed. Writing is not a bad way to be noticed, I've noticed, and I seem to have some ability in that area."

Lance nodded.

"So what am I going to write?" she said. "A poem? A short story? The market for short stories died with the *Saturday Evening Post*. The market for poems never existed. I'm not interested in learning to be a journalist, I sense that writing for movies and TV is a closed shop, and writing for the theater is a worse gamble than three-card monte—you've told me that for years. So, that's why I'm writing a novel."

"What's it about?"

She smiled self-consciously.

"A woman who leaves her husband and tries to find out who she is," she said, "what else?"

"Maybe I can help you," he said.

"I don't *need* your help," she said with surprising rancor, and immediately softened. "I'm sorry, I didn't mean it to come out like that. It's just that this is something I have to do myself. To find out if I can do it by myself. To find out if I can do *anything* by myself. How can I find that out if I let you help me?"

"I see your point," he said.

"Do you?" she said.

"Yes."

"Thank you."

"How far have you gotten on the novel so far?" he said.

"Oh, not far," she said. "A chapter or so, that's about all. There's too much to do at the *Times,* and also I've been going out a lot."

He got a sudden sinking sensation in his stomach, and she must have picked up something because she quickly tried to make it sound as though she hadn't been speaking of dates.

"I've been going to lots of dinner parties, I mean," she said. "I guess people feel sorry for me or something, so they keep inviting me."

"Oh, really?" he said. "Who's invited you?"

"Oh, let's see," she said. "The Bernsteins, the Newmans, the Ramsays, the . . ."

"You know something?" he said. "Since we've been separated I don't think one of our friends has called me—for dinner or anything else."

"You aren't hurt, are you?" she said.

"Oh, no, of course not," he said. "Well, maybe a little. It's as if they felt they had to choose between us. And all of them seem to have chosen *you.*"

"Oh, come on, Lance," she said. "You don't really think that's true, do you?"

"I actually do," he said.

"Well," she said, "if it is, it's only because they probably feel that the woman of the couple needs them more than the man. That's all it is."

"I don't know," he said. "I think it's more than that. I think they're avoiding me."

"*Avoiding* you? Why?"

"I think they think that separation and divorce are a disease, and that I'm the carrier. If they're exposed to me, they could catch it and their own shaky marriages would sicken and die."

"Oh, Lance, that's ridiculous," she said. "Our friends' marriages aren't shaky. You're just projecting. Misery loves company."

"Is that so?" he said, beginning to get irritated. "You really think that we're the only ones who have troubles?"

"I *think*," she said, her voice taking on a harder edge, "that most of the couples we know do have *some* troubles, but I *don't* think that they have let them progress to the point that they are going off to have affairs with their wives' best friends in order to . . ."

The waiter returned with their drinks. They sat glaring at each other till he left. Then Cathy dropped her eyes.

"I'm sorry, Lance," she said. "I didn't mean to get so argumentative. I really wanted tonight to be nice."

"So did I," said Lance. "And it *will* be. And thank you for apologizing. It was actually my fault for bringing up the—"

"No, no," she said, "it was *my* fault."

"Oh no you don't," he said, picking up the mock fight. "It was *my* fault, you bitch."

They both laughed, clinked glasses and drank off their drinks. It had gotten off to a bad start, but it would go better now. Maybe.

They ordered dinner. Conversation at dinner went better than conversation at drinks. They had dessert and after-dinner drinks and Cathy, in a burst of warm feeling for her estranged husband, asked if he would like her to come back to their apartment for a nightcap.

Lance, envisioning her running into his two half-clothed

Chinese nymphets, replied that he would much rather see *her* apartment. Besides, he said, it would give him an opportunity to visit their furniture.

Cathy's new apartment was in a squalid building on the far West Side. He tried not to notice or comment upon the frayed carpeting or the heavy smell of cat urine in the hallways or the peeling paint on the hall walls. It was impossible to tell what color the paint had been when new.

Cathy unlocked her door and they stepped inside. It was a tiny three-room apartment. She had had it painted white and it looked a lot better inside than out, but their furniture looked like it had been crammed into the tiny living room with a shoehorn.

"Well, well," he said, trying to sound jolly, "very nice. Hello, couch. Hello, chair, Hello, other chair."

Cathy giggled. Lance walked around the cramped room, addressing every piece of furniture in turn.

"Hello, coffee table. Hello, lamp. Hello, wastebasket."

Cathy giggled a bit less enthusiastically. Lance got down on all fours.

"Hello, rug. Hello, little round rubber trays to keep the sofa legs from sinking through the carpet."

Cathy jammed a cocktail napkin in his mouth to shut him up and fixed him a drink. He drank it. They sat down on their couch and each of them had another drink. Lance put his arms around Cathy's shoulders. He was starting to feel very mellow. He leaned over and kissed her. She did not pull away. She did not melt, but she did not pull away. Did she want to make love? He couldn't tell.

They kissed some more, and she began to respond. He stroked her face and hair. They kissed some more. He lay her gently back on the couch and began kissing her face and neck and ears. He thought he heard her moan. They kissed some more. He began to unbutton her dress. They slid to the floor.

Before long, to his extreme surprise, they were making love. It had never felt so exciting while they were living together as man and wife. He felt no resentment or anger. He didn't know why and he didn't care. He was dizzy with pleasure and, apparently, so was she. She had never been so responsive since they'd first met. Just before she was ready to climax she cried out: "Go for it, lover!"

He had never heard her say such a thing. Where had she learned it? Surely not from *him*. He was shaken but decided not to spoil what was happening by bringing it up. Cathy was more loving than she had been in a very long time. They lay in each others' arms for a long while without speaking.

"Cathy?" he said at last.

"Yes, baby?"

"I love you."

"I love you too," she said.

"I'm glad I had the guts to invite you to dinner tonight," he said.

"So am I," she said. "If you promise not to say hello to every article of furniture in the bedroom, I would love you to sleep here with me tonight."

"I promise," he said.

She led him into her teeny weeny white bedroom. They fell asleep in each other's arms, in her teeny weeny bed.

The following morning they awoke and made love again. They had not made love the night before and the morning after in years.

"Cathy?" he whispered.

"Yes, darling?"

"Come back. Come back and live with me and let's continue the marriage."

She cupped his face in her hands. She stroked his cheek. She kissed him on the lips.

"Lance," she said.

"Yes, Cathy?"

"I need to live alone for a while. I really do."

"Why?"

"I just do. It's been an incredible growth experience for me. I'm going through some wonderful changes. I need to do this now. I want you to have it be all right with you."

He nodded, noting that the expression "have it be all right with you" sounded unfamiliar.

"Would you at least consent to a dating relationship with me while you're living here?" he said.

She looked at him and smiled.

"Perhaps," she said.

He smiled. She kissed him.

"This is very lovely," he said. "Being with you like this."

"It is," she said. "But I'm so hungry my stomach thinks my throat's cut. How about some eggs?"

"Perfect," he said.

Cathy got out of bed nude and pranced into the teeny weeny white kitchen.

Lance lay in bed awhile, thinking. It had gone surprisingly well, he thought. Helen and the group were right, God bless them. He felt very close to Cathy now. He was disappointed that she didn't want to come back to him yet, but he was glad she had agreed to a dating relationship. A few more dates like this and she couldn't resist returning to their home.

Which brought up an interesting question: Did he still *want* her to return to their home? He did, he decided, and he was puzzled that the question had come up at all.

He got out of bed, stretched, and looked around. On the tiny bedside table was a small lamp, a box of Kleenex, and a pile of snapshots. He idly picked up the snapshots and started leafing through them.

The first one was a close-up of Cathy in a white tennis shirt, holding a tennis racket over her shoulder. The second one was a long shot of Cathy serving. The third one was a long shot of a man in a white tennis shirt and shorts, with a floppy white tennis hat obscuring the upper part of his face. Who was this man—one of her dates?

The next one was a close-up of Cathy and the man, kissing. Lance began to get slightly dizzy and slightly nauseous, because he recognized the man that Cathy was kissing—it was *Howard!* Howard-fucking-Leventhal, his editor!

Lance couldn't believe it. Howard must have telephoned Cathy the instant he heard that they were separated, right after Lance visited Howard in his office and told him. The bastard! The opportunistic, hypocritical bastard! Lance wanted revenge. What kind of revenge could he exact on Howard? Living well is the best revenge, someone had said. A good swift chop in the Adam's apple is pretty good revenge too, he thought.

Lance walked weakly into the kitchen.

"Well, *there* you are," said Cathy brightly. "Your order is almost ready, sir—Adam and Eve on a raft with a side of down, right?"

In reply Lance merely looked at her.

"I'm afraid I found something I'm not glad I found," he said, holding out the snapshots for her to see.

She saw what he was holding and burst into tears.

"I just happened to see this pile of snapshots on the night table," he said. "So I did what anybody would do if they passed a pile of snapshots on a night table—I picked them up and looked at them."

Cathy continued to cry.

"The snapshots seem to feature my wife Cathy Lerner and a gentleman who happens to be my editor, name of Howard Leventhal."

Cathy stopped crying and blotted her eyes with a tissue.

"Oh, Lance," she said, "I feel terrible."

"*You* feel terrible?" he said. "It isn't *your* wife who's going out with Howard Leventhal."

"Lance, promise me something," said Cathy.

"What?"

"Promise me you won't tell Howard," she said.

"You mean Howard doesn't *know* he's going out with you?" said Lance.

"I mean," said Cathy, "promise me you won't tell Howard you found out we're dating. It would just *kill* him if he knew that you knew. He'd never be able to face you again."

"Oh, well, we can't have that, can we?" said Lance. "We certainly can't have old Howard not being able to face me. Tell me. What are we going to do to enable *me* to face *him*?"

"Oh, Lance, I'm so sorry," said Cathy, beginning to cry again. "Is it really going to be hard for you?"

"Cathy, what kind of a man would go out with his friend's wife?" said Lance.

Cathy looked at him closely.

"Is that a serious question?" she said. "Coming from a man who—"

"What *I* did was different," he said. "What *I* did had to to with balancing the scales, with revenge, with an-eye-for-an-eye. But what kind of an editor would go out with his author's wife?"

"What's wrong with going out with your author's wife if they're separated?"

Lance thought that one over.

"You mean outside of the fact that Howard is an opportunistic, hypocritical bastard, and that your going out with him has got to make him even more ambivalent towards me and my novel than he was already, which could seriously jeopardize the success of my book, if not my entire career? You mean outside of *that*?"

"Yes," she said. "Outside of that."

"Outside of that," he said, "there's nothing wrong with it at all."

He remembered how solicitous Howard had been about the separation. How eager he was to learn the particulars. And all the time the main thing he had on his mind was how quickly he could move in on Cathy himself. The bastard! The scummy bastard!

He tried to visualize Howard and Cathy together. Howard and Cathy *naked* together, making love. He felt sick to his stomach. So *that's* where she got her "Go for it, lover!" How *dare* Howard teach his wife such flip and intimate expressions! As if sex with Cathy were some kind of sport in a beer commercial!

He felt faint. It was an instant replay of his apparent cuckolding by Les. It was both better and worse than that, actually. Worse because this one was really true, better because . . . because why? Because he had been through all this before when he thought that Cathy was sleeping with Les. In a way he would have *preferred* it be Cathy and Les. For some strange reason, though, one of the many powerful feelings he was feeling was relief. He wondered about that.

"Cathy? Tell me something," he said.

"What?"

"Do you love him?"

"I don't think so," she said. "I don't really know."

"I see," he said. It hadn't been the answer he was expecting. "Tell me, when you're with him, do you ever talk about me?"

"*Talk* about you? No. Why would we talk about you?"

DAN GREENBURG

"I guess I just don't like the idea of the two of you talking about me, that's all. You don't ever . . . make fun of me, do you?"

"Of course not. Why would we make fun of you?"

"I don't know. Howard must have really been tickled at the thought that I was pining away for you and he was shacking up with you. He *is* shacking up with you, I assume?"

"I think that's between me and Howard," she said evenly. "But Howard has tremendous respect for you, Lance, he really does."

"Yeah, he's proven that."

"He *does*. He's really very fond of you. He's said so a number of times."

"I can just imagine."

"Well, he does. We both do. And we're not making fun of you behind your back."

"Good. Because you and I did live together for a long time, and you do know a lot of stuff about me that I'm not dying to have you tell the world."

"You're being silly, Lance."

"Maybe so. But if I growl in my sleep when I'm having a bad dream, I don't want to read about it in Liz Smith's column."

"Liz Smith wouldn't be the slightest bit interested in the fact that you growl in your sleep."

"You haven't told *Howard* that I growl in my sleep, have you?"

"Of course not," she said.

"Have you told him any of the stuff we did together, like talking in bunny voices?"

"Of course not," she said.

Her cheeks flushed and she turned away.

"Good," he said. "I'd hate it if you told him about that. Cathy?"

"Yes?" she said.

"Why Howard Leventhal of all people?"

"What do you mean?" she said.

"I mean what do you see in him?"

Her eyes glazed hard, as though they had been fired in a kiln.

"He's very nice," she said defensively.

"Yeah? Well, I just think you deserve something better than Howard Leventhal," he said, starting to put on his clothes.

"What's wrong with him?" she said.

"Well, nothing, really, I guess. I mean I guess it's not *his* fault if he's balding, paunchy and speaks in an effeminate manner . . ."

"Lance!"

"I'm sorry. I didn't mean that. I don't know why I said that. I mean Howard is really very nice, as you say. Plus which he's literate, he has a steady job with regular hours, and he's always free evenings and weekends. And after you've been with him long enough you'll hardly even *notice* he's balding, paunchy and speaks in an effeminate manner."

"I really don't think I can continue this discussion, Lance. I really don't think it's fair to Howard."

"No, I know it isn't. You're right. I promise I won't even *mention* Howard's baldness or paunchiness or his effeminate way of speaking again."

"I *mean* it Lance. I am not continuing this dis—"

"OK, OK, OK. Look, I guess I should be going, but just tell me one more thing, all right?"

"What?"

"Why did you leave that pile of snapshots on the night table for me to find?"

"Who knew you were going to go poking around through my private things?"

"Yeah, right."

"I didn't do it intentionally. I didn't know you were going to come over here and we were going to make love and you were going to spend the night."

"No, you didn't. But once I got here and we made love and you asked me to sleep over, you could have thought of it *then*."

She shrugged.

"Cathy?" he said softly.

"Yeah?"

"I think you *wanted* me to find those snapshots. Maybe not consciously, maybe subconsciously. I think you wanted me to know that you were going out with someone as good as Howard, even if he *is* balding and paunchy and speaks in an effeminate manner. I think you wanted me to know that a man I work with and respect takes you seriously as a woman."

"I . . . don't really know how to answer that," she said.

"That's OK," he said. "You don't have to."

He finished putting on his clothes.

"Well, I guess I'll be going," he said sadly.

She nodded.

"I'd just like you to know," he said, "that you didn't have to prove that to me—that men I respect take you seriously as a woman. I mean I already knew that."

"That's very sweet of you," she said.

She followed him to the door.

"I'm sorry," she said. "About the snapshots, I mean."

"So am I," he said.

"It was a wonderful birthday," she said.

"For the most part," he said.

"Do you still want to have a dating relationship?"

"I don't think it would be too hot of an idea under the circumstances," he said.

"I guess you're right."

"So long, Cathy."

"So long, Lance."

When he got downstairs to the lobby, he opened and door and, although it had done him no harm, he punched it.

51

It was necessary during the first week of September to go in and confer with Howard about the imminent promotional tour. Lance did not know how he was going to be able to do it. If he didn't do it the book would suffer. He did it.

Lance was amazed at how easy it was. He acted polite, if a bit stiff, towards Howard, and it wasn't until Howard lowered his voice and put on his sympatico frown to ask how things were between Lance and Cathy that Lance looked at the letter opener on Howard's desk and was tempted to drive it into Howard's right eyeball.

The moment passed, and Howard's right eyeball remained intact, innocent of how close it had come to being punctured.

Howard once more expressed his delight at the doubling of the number of cities on Lance's tour and once more took full credit for the improvement. Howard admitted, when Lance raised the issue, that the size of the first printing and the budget for advertising were still too small. Howard regretted that only Firestone himself, however, could change that. Lance suggested that Howard go to work on Firestone again—perhaps he would be as successful with him as he was with the tour cities.

On his way out of Howard's office, Lance passed what he now realized was the office that Claire used on those days she deigned to come to work at all. He asked the secretary at the desk outside Claire's office if Claire was in. The secretary, a blond girl with high cheekbones who could have been Claire at twenty-one, asked who she should say was calling.

"Studs Lerner," said Lance, and watched the girl pick up the intercom and announce that a Mr. Studs Lerner was outside without an appointment. The girl nodded and hung up the intercom and ushered Lance into Claire's office.

It was an extremely large office for a part-time employee. It had an industrial gray carpet, a long gray suede couch, a low marble coffee table and two large corner windows. Claire's desk was a huge antique partners desk half a football field away from the couch. She greeted him with a warm smile and a proffered hand. He took her hand and kissed it in a mock gallant gesture.

He told her of his meeting with Howard and then, because he had to tell *someone* and he wasn't due to see either Helen or the group for several more days, he told her of his date with Cathy, and of Howard's duplicity. Claire seemed both sympathetic and amused. It wasn't quite the reaction he had had in mind, but he should have known how she would react, given what he knew of her own perversity.

When he again mentioned that Howard was claiming credit for the increase in the number of tour cities, Claire laughed out loud. But she did agree with Lance that the 15,000-copy print order on his book was way too small and that the $5,000 advertising budget was absurdly tiny too.

"How would you like to double your print order and triple your ad budget?" she said.

He looked at her warily.

"What would you want in exchange for that?" he said.

"First, close the door," she said.

He went and closed the door.

"Second, climb under my desk."

"Are you serious?"

"Absolutely," she said.

"What if your secretary comes in?"

"I love to live my life on the brink, in case you hadn't noticed," she said.

"I've noticed, I've noticed," he said. "Boy, you'd sure make one dandy secretary of state."

Lance crawled under Claire's desk. He knelt between her spread thighs and raised her skirt. She wasn't wearing panties. He went to work on her. She began to squirm on her chair. And then she hit the intercom button on her desk. Lance couldn't believe it.

"Fiddle?" said Claire, her voice practically normal.

"Yes, Mrs. Firestone?" replied the tinny voice of the girl outside the door.

"Could you come in a second? And bring your steno pad."

"Yes, Mrs. Firestone."

"Are you insane?" Lance hissed up at her.

"Yes," she said. "Thank you for asking."

"I'm not going on with this," he said.

"Oh, yes you are," she said.

52

Fiddle Coleridge brushed the straight blond hair out of her eyes, picked up her steno pad and got up from her desk.

Fiddle didn't think most employers dictated letters while they were in conference, but perhaps the letters she wanted to dictate had to do with this man, Studs Lerner, whom she was in conference with. And then again, perhaps they didn't. Mrs. Firestone was a quirky and irrational employer. Not that Fiddle didn't like her. On the contrary, she was mad for her. Mrs. Firestone had told her on more than one occasion that she herself had been very much like Fiddle when she was in her twenties. Then too, Mrs. Firestone had hinted that, were Fiddle to work out at a secretarial level, perhaps one day she might be made a junior editor.

Fiddle opened the door to Mrs. Firestone's office and was surprised not to see Mr. Lerner. She looked around the room, but he was nowhere to be seen. Was there another exit from Mrs. Firestone's office? A secret panel perhaps?

"Sit down, Fiddle," said Mrs. Firestone. Her voice seemed strained, as if she were containing angry feelings. Fiddle prayed it wasn't she that Mrs. Firestone was angry at.

"Yes, ma'am," said Fiddle. She pulled up a chair, snapped open her steno pad, and waited, pencil poised, for Mrs. Firestone to begin.

"This is to Mike Fieldston, head of Promotion and Advertising," said Mrs. Firestone. "Dear Mike . . ."

Mrs. Firestone drew in her breath sharply and winced as though she were in pain.

"Mrs. Firestone . . ." said Fiddle anxiously. When she had been a girl of six, a favorite aunt had had a heart attack while reading her a bedtime story and had expired on the spot.

Mrs. Firestone appeared to recover and acted as though nothing had happened. Perhaps it had merely been gas. Fiddle decided not to mention it.

"Dear Mike," said Mrs. Firestone, "Pursuant to discussions with buyers at B. Dalton in Minneapolis, Kroch's & Brentano's in Chicago, Doubleday in New York, and the Walden chain in . . ."

Once more Mrs. Firestone caught her breath and squeezed her eyes tightly shut.

"Mrs. Firestone?" said Fiddle, now starting to become genuinely alarmed.

Mrs. Firestone, eyes still closed, continued to dictate, her phrases punctuated by little gasps. Fiddle, fearing that a beloved mentor and a junior editorship were teetering on the brink of extinction, felt her own heart begin to pound. She stared at Mrs. Firestone in mute horror, too well-bred to acknowledge the older woman's symptoms until she herself acknowledged them first, but no longer able to scribble shorthand squiggles on the lined green pad.

"Fiddle," Mrs. Firestone gasped, "are you getting this or aren't you?"

"I'm trying to, ma'am" said Fiddle, her pulse racing.

"I don't hear your . . . pencil moving," said Mrs. Firestone with difficulty.

As Fiddle stared in horror, Mrs. Firestone, eyes still squeezed shut, sank down a couple of inches in her chair. The fingers of both her mentor's hands extended, then clenched into fists. A sheet of onion-skin under Mrs. Firestone's left hand crumpled into a tiny ball.

"Mrs. Firestone," said Fiddle, "may I ask you a question of a personal nature?"

"You may . . . not," said Mrs. Firestone. "You may take . . . dictaaaaaaaaaaaaaaaaaaaaation!"

The last syllable seemed as if it would go on forever, although it probably lasted no longer than six or seven seconds, and when it was concluded Mrs. Firestone sank back in her chair and smiled the biggest smile that Fiddle had ever seen her smile. She was so still that Fiddle was certain she was dead. Her only consolation was that Mrs. Firestone had apparently died happy.

Fiddle didn't know what to do. When she was six and it had been her aunt, she had merely screamed for her Mommy. Screaming for her Mommy now would not be appropriate. She was terribly frightened. She supposed she should get up and go to her desk and call the police. She wondered, since she had been the only one present when Mrs. Firestone passed away, whether the police would want to question her. She didn't think she would be able to take it. She would crack for sure under the third degree. Perhaps they would send her to prison. Daddy's lawyers would try to get her a reduced sentence, but they were corporate tax lawyers, not criminal defense lawyers, so what could they do with a murder rap?

Fiddle got unsteadily to her feet. Her steno pad slid to the floor. Miraculously, Mrs. Firestone's eyes snapped open at the noise.

"Well, Fiddle," she said cheerily, "now then, would you read that back?"

53

Howard telephoned Lance late that night. He seemed very excited. At first Lance thought it had something to do with Cathy.

"You'll never *guess* what I pulled off for you, bubbeleh," Howard exulted, "you'll never *guess*. You want to guess?"

"You doubled my print order and tripled my ad budget," said Lance wearily.

There was a stunned silence at the other end of the line.

"How did you *guess?*" said Howard.

"I wouldn't want you to spread it around," said Lance, "but I'm psychic."

54

By September 10th the first of the reviews of *Gallivanting* began to trickle in. They were, for the most part, quite good. There was really only one reviewer who took Lance to task, a novelist named Ferdfleisch whose review, unfortunately, ran in the prestigious *New York Times Book Review.*

Ferdfleisch accused Lance of writing below his level, of descending to superficial humor, of trivializing his own seriousness for fear of being judged by harsher standards. It was probably coincidental and irrelevant that three years earlier Ferdfleisch had approached Lance for a quote for the dust jacket of Ferdfleisch's current novel and that Lance, after reading the manuscript and finding himself in philosophical disagreement with it, had to tell Ferdfleisch that he couldn't give him the quote. Only a cynic would have felt there had been any connection between Lance's failure to give the man a quote and Ferdfleisch's harsh review.

Had Cathy been aware that Lance's novel was going to be assigned to a fellow to whom Lance had declined to give a quote? In all fairness, she'd probably known no more about it than Lance himself.

In point of fact, Ferdfleisch's criticism was not wholly unfounded, for Lance preferred to put even his more serious themes in humorous form, believing that humorous material was both more valuable and more difficult to write than serious, that the only reason authors wrote serious books was that they lacked the skill or patience to write humorously, that *War and Peace* would have been a better book had it been written humorously, and that Tolstoy would have done so had he had the craft.

It was also true that Lance placed rather more credence on others' opinions of him and his work than he ought to have, and usually stood ready to re-evaluate everything in his life on the basis of the last thing screamed at him by a street-corner degenerate. Although no street-corner degenerate had succeeded in publishing a critique of Lance's novel, a reviewer in an obscure rural newspaper in South Carolina had written a review which criticized Lance for a number of things that, in fact, were not even *in* Lance's book. There was very good reason to suppose that this reviewer had not even read the book he was reviewing, but his criticism stung Lance nonetheless.

Why is it, Lance wondered, that the unfavorable reviews are generally easier to remember than the favorable ones? Possibly for the same reason that beautiful women admire men who don't value them. Was that also the reason, he wondered, that he had had such a motley string of literary agents over the years?

Lance's current agent, a man named Kronk, was currently going through a mid-life crisis which had caused him to decide that the literary life and the world of commerce were intrinsically less valuable and durable than the rural life. Kronk had bought a ranch and was breeding beefalos, although his tendency to form deep emotional relationships with the animals conflicted with his ability to send them off to market and had already cost him, by his own estimate, close to half a million dollars on the one herd.

Kronk had thus far not had much success trying to sell *Galli-vanting* as a movie. The problem, he'd told Lance, was that these days studio people in Hollywood were somewhat prejudiced against novels as a basis for a motion picture, especially those that were close to being published. They reasoned that if the novel were still available for purchase it must not be a very hot property. Studio people, Kronk said, preferred to buy options on nonfiction articles in magazines like *New York* and *Esquire* and *Texas Monthly* and develop them into plotted pictures. The fact that this technique hadn't worked since *Saturday Night Fever,* said Kronk, was no evidence to them that the process wasn't valid.

One of Kronk's chief values as an agent was his ability to collect money for work that Lance had written. Lance had grown weary of the excuses that had been given him routinely over the years in lieu of payments from book publishers, magazines, movie studios, television networks, theatrical producers and independent contractors: that although the book had sold half a million copies he had still not earned back his advance royalties; that there had been more returns than copies printed; that the publisher had a full year to render statements and another six months to pay royalties; that a check was due him but would be late because it had to be signed by the head of the accounting department who was on vacation in Tibet; that the girl who normally issued the checks had been stricken with ulcerative colitis and wouldn't be back in the office for eighteen weeks; that his check had been erroneously made out to the Philadelphia Society for the Jewish Blind and would now have to be canceled and reissued; that the check had been mailed twelve weeks ago to an address that Lance hadn't lived at since college, and so on.

The real reason that it took so long to get paid—and the *only* reason, said Kronk—was that companies made enormous interest on late payments, and that freelance writers as a group had somewhat less clout than shepherds. Since Kronk had been representing him, Lance had been able to collect most monies due him an average of three months earlier than before.

Lance telephoned Kronk to commiserate with him about the feisty review in the *Times* and to confer about the promotional tour, but Kronk's secretary said that her employer had been called away on an emergency—the breech birth of a baby beefalo.

Publication day was almost at hand. Mike Fieldston sent over by messenger an itinerary of travel details and scheduled interviews for Lance's ten-city tour.

The tour would begin on September 15th in Pittsburgh, then go on to Cleveland, Cincinnati, Chicago, Detroit, Minneapolis,

Los Angeles, San Francisco, Dallas and Houston. The trip would take two weeks. Except for a layover on the weekend in Detroit, he would be in a different city every day. He looked over the schedule and shook his head. Most days began with interviews on TV news shows at about six-thirty a.m. He was what they referred to on these programs as "color."

55

Gladys Oliphant was ecstatic.

At first, of course, she hadn't been sure. The morning nausea she'd attributed to some week-old lasagna she had eaten. The warm, flushed feeling she attributed to the weather. The sleepiness she attributed to the long hours she was now putting in every night on her novel. The increased need to urinate she attributed to her increased consumption of beer during her writing sessions.

But when her period kept failing to materialize, she finally suspected what the matter was and went to the doctor for the test. The doctor confirmed her suspicions: Gladys was pregnant!

There was not the slightest doubt in her mind who the father was: Lance Lerner was the only man who had made love to her in several years. There was not the slightest doubt in her mind what to do about the pregnancy: she had always wanted a baby, and now she was going to have one fathered by one of the most successful writers in the country. With a writer father and a writer mother, there was little doubt that the child would become a writer as well.

Gladys knew that Mr. Lerner would be as tickled by the news of his impending fatherhood as she was herself. She could hardly wait to tell him.

56

The evening of publication day, September 15th, Lance shared a bottle of Korbel champagne with Dorothy and Janie in his apartment in modest celebration. Then he packed his garment bag and his shoulder bag, gave the girls some final instructions about the apartment, the mail, and so on, kissed them both goodbye and went to the door. They followed him to the door and kissed him again, then went down the stairs with him and followed him into the street.

A cab came towards them and Lance flagged it down. It screeched to a stop and he began to get into it. Dorothy clung to him, kissed him repeatedly and whispered "I love you" in his ear. She was crying.

He was terribly moved, and embraced her.

"Please," she said, "don't die in a plane crash."

It was a somewhat unsettling request. He hadn't been planning to die in a plane crash, and yet, since the crash of the DC-10 in Chicago on May 25, 1979, with a planeload of publishing people on their way to the American Booksellers Association convention in Los Angeles, some of his old fears of flying had returned to him. Fears of the commonplace—defective aircraft, dangerous flying conditions, pilots with the level of competence of your average department-store clerk. But also fears of the unusual—

midair collisions with meteor showers or returning spacecraft or flocks of wild geese.

He distrusted every announcement made to him over the public address system, correctly assuming that the true state of affairs was being, at worst, wholly lied about or, at best, euphemized in the same manner as the routine safety announcements. When they said, "Your seat cushion may be used as a flotation device," what they really meant was, "If we crash in the ocean, your seat cushion may stay afloat for a few minutes after the plane sinks."

Lance sensed that there were things he could do to increase his chances of survival on the flights he took, but the only precaution he'd adopted thus far was to avoid DC-10s.

He got out of the cab at the American Airlines terminal and checked in for his 9:00 p.m. flight. It was just 8:30. He found, as usual, that his gate was on the other side of the airport.

He stood in line at security and wondered whether he would make the metal detector beep. Lance's peculiar problem with metal detectors was that he carried around such a heavy load of nonspecific guilt that every time he heard the metal detector beep when he walked through it he had an insane fear that this was the one trip when he had absentmindedly packed a Luger in his luggage. Didn't it occur to them that one could hijack a plane with weapons that wouldn't make a metal detector beep?

The woman ahead of him in line at the metal detector seemed exceedingly edgy. Around her neck was a Pentax in a black leather case. She turned to Lance.

"Excuse me," she said, "but will the X-rays fog my film?"

"No," said Lance, "but they *will* cause cancer and birth defects."

"Oh, no problem," said the woman, facing forward again, "just so they don't fog my film."

Lance went through the metal detector without a beep and boarded the plane to Pittsburgh. With his sixth sense he was beginning to detect the first unmistakable warnings of disaster lying somewhere ahead, but he didn't know how far ahead and he couldn't guess just what form the disaster would take when it appeared.

57

Upon boarding the plane to Pittsburgh, he was not at all surprised to find that the temperature in the cabin was approximately ninety-eight degrees Fahrenheit. Shortly after takeoff it usually dropped to a degree or two above freezing. He generally brought with him a long underwear T-shirt and a sweater to ward off frostbite, and changed clothes in one of the plane's tiny lavatories. Any time it took him more than sixty seconds, some shmuck was banging on the door, asking if he was all right in there—if you were in the john any longer than the time necessary to urinate they figured you were having a stroke or engaging in unnatural sex acts.

When the drink cart came down the aisle after takeoff, Lance obtained two Bloody Mary mixes without vodka. As soon as the stewardesses were three rows past him, Lance reached into his shoulder bag and withdrew a flask of vodka and surreptitiously poured a couple of fingers into each drink. He resented paying two-fifty apiece for vodka miniatures that cost the airline a couple of cents, but sneaking his own vodka into their Mr. and Mrs. T or Snap-E-Tom made him feel like an axe murderer.

By the time he reached Pittsburgh, he was slightly juiced. His schedule of interviews indicated that his first one was tonight, on a live radio program from midnight till two a.m. It was called *Middleman at Midnight*.

When he got out of the terminal at the Pittsburgh airport he was surprised to find it was about fifty degrees and raining. When he'd left New York it had been at least ninety. He flagged a cab, put his luggage inside, and gave the cabdriver the address of the radio station.

The cab let him off at a quarter to twelve in what looked like a deserted industrial park. As the rain slanted into his face, Lance slowly circled a series of rakishly modern buildings, unable to find either a street number or an unlocked entry door. From a public phone across the street, he dialed the radio station. It was now midnight, and he was supposed to be on the air.

After forty-five rings a grouchy male voice answered.

"Hi," said Lance, shivering in the cold, trying to speak above the whine of the wind and the splatter of rain. "This is Lance Lerner. I'm a guest on your show, *Middleman at Midnight,* but I can't seem to find the entrance to your building."

"Who'd you say this was?" said the voice.

"Lance Lerner," said Lance. "Author of *Gallivanting?* I'm supposed to be on *Middleman at Midnight.*"

"I doubt it," said the voice.

"What do you mean you doubt it?" said Lance.

"I mean," said the voice, "that *Middleman at Midnight* was never *on* this station, plus which it went off the air about six or seven months ago. I sure don't know what you're doing here now."

"I sure don't either," said Lance with disgust and hung up the phone. By the time he managed to get another cab to go to his hotel he was soaked to the bone. And his first interview the following morning was at six-fifteen a.m.

It was a great beginning.

58

When the wakeup call came it was still dark out. He knew he'd had only four hours of sleep and that getting out of bed in his condition was going to be a major accomplishment. With four hours of sleep he had the capacity to fall asleep instantly at any stage in the getting-up process. Fortunately, he had a technique:

He reached for his battered Porsche watch and squeezed it so hard the pain in his hand kept him awake long enough to sit up and swing his legs over the side of the bed. As soon as his legs were over the side of the bed he dropped to the floor and did fifty pushups. By the time he had finished the pushups, he was breathing hard enough to keep him awake till he got to the bathroom.

Once he'd washed his face and brushed his teeth, he picked up the phone again and called room service. He ordered two eggs over easy, a large grapefruit juice and coffee, and asked how long it would take to be delivered. A half hour, said the Hispanic voice at the other end of the line.

He went back into the bathroom and got into the shower, mentally reviewing all the steps in his daily process of getting ready to face the world—exercising, showering, shampooing, shaving, brushing, blow-drying, dressing, eating. With all those things to do every morning and the difficulty he experienced in merely getting out of bed, he found it a complete waste of time to be up and around for only one day before beginning the whole process all over again—if you're going to *get* up, you might as well *stay* up for at least a week at a crack.

Within sixty seconds of entering the shower he heard a violent knocking on his hotel-room door. Cursing, he stuck his head out of the shower and yelled, "Who's there?"

"*Rune* sorbis!" said a heavy Hispanic accent.

It never failed. When you asked room service how long it would take for your food to arrive they always said thirty minutes. If you waited thirty minutes before getting into the shower, they came in thirty-one. If you waited forty-five they came in forty-seven. If you jumped in the shower immediately upon ordering, they came in a minute and a half. They had an uncanny ability to know when you were naked and soaking wet. Once he'd outwitted them—he had waited forty minutes and they still hadn't come, so he turned on the shower without getting into it. Sixty seconds after he'd started the water, room service knocked on the door. The waiter had been palpably disappointed to find he was still dry.

He arrived at the TV station at six-ten a.m. An attractive young man and woman were sitting at an ersatz breakfast nook beside a window through which could be glimpsed a lovely ersatz pastoral scene. They were alternately doing news, weather and spunky repartee. Spunky repartee at that hour of the morning, Lance felt, was unnatural. He suspected they were on speed.

A relentlessly energetic young person guided him over a maze of thick serpentine cables and had him crouch down just out of camera range, waiting for a commercial break to go up onto the set.

"Our next guest," said the suspiciously spunky woman after the break, "is a man who single-handedly sailed from New York City to the Isle of Skye using only a dinghy and a sail made out of a bed sheet."

Lance looked around the studio for the man she might be describing and found that the relentlessly energetic young person was motioning for *Lance* to go up to the ersatz breakfast nook.

"Uh, I think there's been some mistake," said Lance in confusion.

"Good morning, Mr. Lerner," said the spunky young man. He extended his hand for a shaking and pulled Lance on camera.

"Good morning," said Lance, "but I think there's been a mistake here."

"I want to hear all about Mr. Lerner's voyage across the Atlantic in that *dinghy*," said the spunky woman, "but first we have to pause for one more commercial message."

The red light on the camera went out.

"Listen," said Lance, "I think there's been a mistake here."

The spunky man frowned.

"What kind of a mistake?" he said.

"About who I am," said Lance.

"Aren't you the author of *Gallivanting?*" said the spunky woman, now also frowning.

"Yes," said Lance, "but the book is a novel about a young man dating and having romantic relationships with women, and it's not about sailing across the Atlantic in a dinghy with a bed sheet for a sail."

The man and woman looked at each other, no longer spunky.

"There must have been some mix up," said the man, "but it's a little too late to do anything about it. We've got the stills set up on the easels and everything."

"Excuse me?" said Lance.

"We're a live show, Mr. Lerner," said the woman. "Our visuals were set up on easels by the art department some time ago. It's too late to change them."

"So?" said Lance.

"So," said the man, "do you think you could just be a good sport and talk about what we're prepared to talk about?"

"About voyages across the Atlantic in a dinghy?" said Lance incredulously.

"Yes."

"But I don't *know* about voyages across the Atlantic in a dinghy," said Lance.

"Ten seconds!" called the floor director.

"Can you just talk about sailing in general then?" said the woman.

"I've never sailed in my *life*," said Lance. "I get *nauseated* on the water."

"Five seconds!" called the director.

"Won't you just please do this for us, fella?" said the man with a tightly set face. "It's not a helluva lot to ask."

"Three . . . two . . . *one* . . ." said the director.

"I'll see what I can do," mumbled Lance, but he knew it was going to be a farcical experience at best.

59

Following the show in which Lance had to spend sixteen minutes making up anecdotes about seagoing voyages he'd never taken, he was scheduled to appear on a TV talk show with a large studio audience. At certain intervals in this show, the host, for no discernible reason, spun a huge wheel with numbers on its face and then made local phone calls at random and asked inane questions of whoever answered.

Lance was scheduled to be on the show after a woman who had learned to be a gourmet cook despite the fact that she had no arms, and right after a female animal trainer and her two star pupils—a tiger that could sit on its hind legs and play a concertina, and a python that could light its trainer's cigarette—and right before an eighty-year-old woman wearing jogging shorts and a T-shirt on which was emblazoned the message JOGGING FOR JESUS. The elderly jogger had made her way from Seattle as far as Pittsburgh on a coast-to-coast journey to promote the religious sect of which she was a member, and Lance rather liked her at first.

Unfortunately, the tiger shit on the floor, the python vomited up a half-digested rabbit, and the cooking demonstration of the armless gourmet went awry when the woman in her nervousness knocked a Cuisinart bowl full of béarnaise sauce off the counter with her hooks. By the time they cleaned up the tiger turds and python vomit and got the armless gourmet through her segment, they were running late.

A talent coordinator informed Lance and the elderly jogger in the Green Room that although they'd been promised two segments each, they would now only be able to do one. Lance accepted the news with equanimity. The elderly jogger was furious.

"Goddamn it," she said, "you give the cripple, the tiger and the snake two segments, you can't give the Lord only *one!*"

The talent coordinator tried to reason with her, but the octogenarian runner just got madder and madder. Eventually the Lord lost His only remaining segment, and Lance had to take it on for himself.

The next show Lance did that day was a taped radio show and he was informed that there was no telling when it would air, if ever. It was hosted by a smooth, fast-talking deejay who never got either Lance's name or the title of his book.

The next interview was on a listener-sponsored FM radio station, and the ponytailed young man who interviewed him was also his own engineer. The ponytailed man was either very new at both jobs or very inept, because he kept cutting them off the air and apologizing for it, and when they *were* on the air there was constant screeching feedback from the microphone.

"Hey, man," said the ponytailed fellow by way of explanation, "I'm so stoned I'm lucky I can do *this* good." Lance had to struggle through an hour and a half of this before the ordeal was over.

Lance's fifth show of the day was also an FM radio show, and he was pleasantly surprised to find that his female interviewer was not only literate and articulate but had also done quite a bit of research on Lance and on his writing. Maybe too much research. She asked him questions about his previous books, the answers to which he had long since forgotten. Why did people expect you to remember your own books?

His sixth interviewer of the day turned out to be a pleasant enough blind chap who, the moment they went on the air, said:

"What ever made you write such a sensationalistic, opportunistic, superficial and crassly commercial piece of trash as *Gallivanting?*"

Lance was momentarily dumbfounded. It seemed possible that the sightless interviewer was kidding, in the hostile way that people who have no sense of humor seemed to think was funny. Lance hoped that was what the man was doing. It wasn't. The man had simply decided to be vile. Since there was an hour allotted to the show, and since Lance hadn't the sense or the guts to walk off the show, the guy had a lot of time in which to be vile. Lance began to fight back and got in some good counterpunches, but when the show was over he was bathed in sweat.

"Did you really hate my book that much?" said Lance as they were leaving the studio.

"Hell, no," said the young man. "In fact, I kind of liked it."

"Then why did you attack it?" said Lance.

"Controversy makes for better broadcasting," said the fellow, flashing Lance a victory sign and a sightless wink.

Lance's seventh and eighth interviews of the day were with newspapers. Interviewer number seven was a salty woman of about fifty-five who typed with a cigarette dangling out of her mouth, *Front Page* style, raining ashes on her blouse. Interviewer number eight was a nervous young girl straight out of journalism school who took notes on a lined green pad and asked not a single question that couldn't have been answered by reading the biographical handouts which were sent to all Lance's interviewers in advance.

Between the end of his eighth interview and his evening plane to Cleveland he had about an hour and a half. As usual when he had any time left over in a tour city, he tried to visit as many bookstores as he could. Not to see whether his book was in stock —it usually wasn't—but to meet the people who actually sold the books on the floor. With the number of new titles that appeared every month in this country most books got lost in the shuffle. If the salespeople he introduced himself to liked him, then maybe they'd read his book. If they read his book, and if they liked it, maybe they'd recommend it to their customers.

After a fast look in the "Books, Retail" section of the classified directory, Lance scribbled down the addresses of six bookstores whose names he recognized. He flagged a cab and gave the driver extra money to wait while he ran into each store and introduced himself to as many salespeople as he could, buying copies of his book retail, if available, and autographing them for the salespeople who seemed the most sympatico.

The cabdriver seemed mystified by all these lightning stops in bookstores. After the fifth stop he suggested that if Lance didn't find the book he was looking for in the next store he ought to try the public library.

Lance made the plane to Cleveland by about nine minutes, but he was back in the familiar rhythms of fast-paced book promotion tours, he knew that he did it well, and he began to feel very good about himself.

The trip, he suspected, would go all right now, at least for a while. The disaster, whatever it was, was still out there somewhere, waiting for him, biding its time, but it hadn't caught up with him yet, and he had just started hitting his stride.

60

He arrived at his hotel in Cleveland and immediately ordered dinner from room service and requested a wakeup call for five-thirty a.m. He fell asleep watching TV and when the wakeup call came he was still dressed and the TV set was buzzing unpleasantly. Room service brought breakfast as he began to rub shampoo into his scalp in the shower. The nine interviews in Cleveland went no better or worse than they had in Pittsburgh, except that the weather in Cleveland was hot and humid and running around town was a bigger energy drain in the heat.

He taped a TV show along with a group of guests who, if they had anything in common other than something to plug, only the talent coordinators knew for sure. Sitting on the couches with Lance and attempting to hold a conversation were Pittsburgh Steeler quarterback Terry Bradshaw, Yiddish novelist Isaac Bashevis Singer, fast-food king Tom Carvel, Supreme Court Justice Whizzer White, dwarf Latin actor Hervé Villechaize, and the Dalai Lama. All had written books. None could find them in bookstores in the cities they'd been touring. Every time Lance started to speak, the Dalai Lama cut him off.

Cincinnati, which he got to shortly after sundown, was warmer even than Cleveland. He liked the fact that the Cincinnati airport was not in Ohio but in Kentucky—he felt it was thoroughly consistent with the other absurdities in his life.

When he got to his first TV interview of the day he found it canceled. The show felt itself in competition with his second interview of the day, the *Joe Shine Show,* and said that since Lance was already doing Shine they wanted no part of him. It was a phenomenon he had encountered in other cities so he was not surprised, although he'd heard that if the guest was famous enough the rule didn't apply. When he got to the *Joe Shine Show* the producer took him aside for a hurried conversation.

"Have you heard anything about this show?" asked the producer. Lance shook his head. "Joe tends to be a little rough on his guests," said the producer, "but it really sells books. Now, I don't want to make you nervous, but whatever you do, don't try to shake hands with Joe and don't mention cancer or wooden legs."

It wouldn't have occurred to Lance to mention cancer or wooden legs, but by the time the show began taping, he was concentrating so hard on not shaking hands and not mentioning cancer or wooden legs that he could barely speak at all.

Chicago, his home town, was the next stop after Cincinnati, and it was hotter and more humid than Cincinnati by half. It was also a better book town—possibly the best, surpassing even New York. He loved the lakefront and the architecture and the Ritz-Carlton Hotel—one of the few new hotels he'd stayed in that did not feature outside elevators and revolving penthouse restaurants, both of which made him queasy—and he even managed to squeeze in forty minutes to have lunch with his parents.

"Look how he eats," said his mother to his father, painfully watching Lance as he wolfed down a chicken salad sandwich from room service in his room. "If I had known you like chicken so much, I would have brought you a whole one."

"That's wonderful, Mom," Lance said, "but what would I do with a whole chicken on the road?"

"Maybe you'd give some to the other authors," said his mother. "Maybe you'd send a piece to Cathy. How's she doing, by the way?"

It was clear his mother was dying to know more about his separation. It was also clear that transitions were not her long suit.

"I saw Cathy for her birthday," said Lance casually.

His mother and father exchanged pregnant glances.

"*And?*" they said in unison.

"And it doesn't really look like we're going to be getting back together after all," he said. "At least for a while."

"Is it another fellow?" said his father, leaning in close so nobody in the hotel should hear.

Lance debated about how much to tell them. A little knowledge with them, he'd always found, was a dangerous thing.

"There may or may not be another fellow," said Lance, "but that's not the point. The point is that Cathy thinks she has to live alone for a while and grow some more."

"How much does she need to grow?" said his mother, "She's already five foot nine."

"I didn't mean that kind of growing, Mom," he said.

"I know, I know," said his mother sighing. "Your mother isn't as dumb as you think she is, don't worry."

After his last interview of the day in Chicago his Dad drove him around to bookstores, and he was able to squeeze in an even dozen before tearing off to O'Hare airport.

"Racing around like this is the worst possible thing for your digestion," said his mother as she kissed him goodbye at the terminal. She pressed a cold foil-wrapped package into his hand as he disengaged himself from her arms.

"What's this?" he said.

"Poison," she said. "I'm trying to feed you poison. It's just a piece of brisket for your dinner tonight, so you shouldn't have to order up a chicken salad sandwich in your room."

Although he had the thawing piece of brisket in his pocket, when they served dinner on the plane Lance decided to give airline cuisine a try. When asked his choice of entrées, the man in the seat next to him waved the stewardess away.

"Don't talk to me about airplane food," said the man to Lance, who had thus far not talked to him about anything.

"Why is that?" said Lance.

"Oh, I know," said the man, "they've upgraded the plastic dishes they used to have in Coach to real china. They've upgraded the plastic knives and forks to real stainless steel. They've even upgraded the entrée selection from one to three. But whether you order the steak, the chicken or the pasta, what you get is a lump of plastic glop suspended in amber mucilage."

"I know what you mean," said Lance.

"You do, do you?" said the man. "One time I'm sitting on an airplane, trying to eat my amber mucilage, and I notice that the guy in the seat next to mine, where you're sitting now, is vomiting quietly into his dish. The stewardess comes by, whisks it away from him and serves it to the fellow in the seat ahead of me as a hot snack."

Lance looked carefully at the man to see if he were joking, but the man continued talking.

"I once brought some airplane food home with me in a little bag and gave it to my pussycats," he said. "No *way*. They'll eat fish heads, chicken necks, spoiled meat, even their own vomit— but airplane food? *Huh*-uh. *Sorry*, Charlie. *Forget* it."

When Lance's meal arrived he sent it back. The stewardess seemed genuinely pissed.

When Lance got off the plane in Detroit he was not terribly surprised to find that Detroit was just as hot as Chicago. He took off his jacket and opened his shirt all the way to his bellybutton in the cab ride to his hotel.

As he was checking in, the clerk behind the desk noted his registration and then said:

"You have a little surprise waiting for you in your room, Mr. Lerner."

"I have?" said Lance. He didn't like surprises, especially since his fortieth birthday party. "What *kind* of a surprise?"

"I probably shouldn't tell you this," said the clerk, "but your wife checked in an hour ago. She's waiting for you in your room."

61

Lance was insanely happy. Cathy! Here in Detroit! Waiting for him in his hotel room to surprise him! But how did she know where to find him? Easy. Howard had his schedule. She had got it from Howard. She'd obviously told Howard about her birthday dinner, about Lance's discovery of the snapshots, about Lance asking her to come back to him. Howard had doubtlessly tried to dissuade her, but she'd been adamant. How could she give up Lance for a balding, paunchy man with an effeminate accent? She couldn't.

He left his bags with the bellman, and went racing around the neighborhood, looking for a florist. He found one just about to close.

"Please!" he hollered through the locked glass door, "It's an emergency! My wife has come back to me and I have to buy her flowers!"

The diminutive old man who owned the shop sold him two dozen lavender roses and Lance raced back to the hotel. Too impatient to wait for the elevator to arrive, he sprinted up six flights of stairs and stopped outside the door of his room. He took a deep breath, unlocked the door and let himself into the room.

She had drawn the drapes and gotten into bed to await his arrival. He rushed to the bed, still holding the flowers, and reached out to her with his free hand.

"Darling!" he whispered. "What a wonderful surprise!"

"I thought you'd appreciate it," she said.

It was Claire.

Claire!

Claire, not Cathy!

He staggered backwards. The roses slipped from his hands, fell to the carpet.

"Lance, what's wrong?" said Claire.

He shook his head. The sense of loss, of crushing, overpowering disappointment, almost collapsed his lungs. He backed into a desk chair and sagged into it.

"My God, what is it?" she said, getting out of bed.

She was wearing a fantastic ivory silk nightgown and she looked sensational. But she wasn't Cathy.

"I'm sorry, Claire," he said. "I guess I was . . . expecting someone else."

She lowered her eyes.

"I thought you might," she said. "I realized that after I told the clerk at the desk. But he wouldn't have let me come up here any other way, and I did want to see you."

He nodded. He could see she was hurt. He didn't want to hurt her. He liked her. He really liked her. But she wasn't Cathy.

"Maybe I should go," she said.

"No, no," he said. "Please stay. I'll be all right in a minute. It's just that I'm kind of worn out from the tour. Just give me a minute, OK?"

She came over to him, started to touch him, then pulled back. She seemed insecure for the first time since he had met her. She really *is* vulnerable, he thought. How about that? He reached out for her, caught her hands and pulled her towards him. He pressed his face to her flat belly. It was soft. And warm. And it wasn't Cathy's.

"I'm glad you came," he lied. "It was a lovely surprise."

"And it would have been lovelier if I had been Cathy," she said gently.

He sighed.

"That's not untrue," he said at last.

They ordered dinner in the room. They talked about Cathy. Unexpectedly, Claire took Cathy's side against Lance. As they talked, Claire became more and more despondent. She said she no longer liked her life. She said her marriage was a joke.

"I thought you told me your marriage was *good*," said Lance. "I thought you told me your husband was an excellent provider, a strong protector, a considerate lover, and someone who hadn't bored you once in eighteen years."

"I did tell you that," she said.

"And it isn't true?" he said.

"And it isn't true," she said. "Austin neither provides nor protects, nor does he make love to me. And the reason that he doesn't bore me is that he's never around. If he *were* around, he *still* wouldn't be around. And that *is* boring."

"Why don't you leave him?" he said.

"I can't."

"Why not?"

"Because. I've gotten too used to the lifestyle. And I'm too old now to start over with somebody else."

"At forty?"

"Yes," she said. "Besides, I doubt that anybody who'd want me now wouldn't bore me even more than Austin."

"Do I bore you?" said Lance.

She shook her head.

"Why don't I?" he said.

"I don't know, Lance. At least with you there's somebody home. You actually listen when I speak, which is quite rare. And you even seem to care about my feelings, which is positively exotic. And you're something of an innocent, so it was fun for a while to play games with you and to try and shock you."

"It *was* fun, you say?"

She nodded.

"It was. It was enormous fun to force you to make love to me in your apartment, and in the limousine, and in my office. It was even *sort* of fun surprising you here in Detroit. Until you showed up, I mean. But now it's not fun anymore."

He kissed her cheek.

"I'm sorry," he said. "If the clerk had said anything at all except that my wife was waiting in my room . . ."

"I know. Well, that's the way it goes."

She slipped out of her nightgown and began to get dressed.

"Why are you getting dressed?" he said.

"There's still one plane I can catch back to New York tonight."

"Don't go, Claire," he said.

She stopped dressing and looked at him.

"Why not?"

"I want you to stay," he said. "I want to make love to you."

"I don't understand," she said.

"I like you," he said. "I like making love to you."

He walked over to her. He took her face in his hands and kissed her tenderly on her forehead, on her nose, on her chin, on her lips. He gently took off all the clothes she'd put on.

They went to bed. Their lovemaking was much fuller than the other times. He felt that she was much more present than the other times. He felt touched. He felt that she was getting emotionally involved.

Just as she was ready to climax, the telephone rang. He didn't move to answer it. He never answered ringing telepones when he was making love. The phone continued to ring. It broke their concentration completely, but they continued just to win out over the accursed ringing. It rang twenty times. It rang thirty times. It rang forty times.

"Answer it," she said.

He shook his head.

"Please answer it," she said.

"There's nobody I want to talk to now," he said.

The phone continued to ring. Finally *she* picked it up.

"Hello?" she said.

There was silence at the other end of the line. Then a woman's voice asked if she had the right room, if this was Mr. Lerner's room.

"Yes," said Claire, "this is Mr. Lerner's room."

The voice asked who Claire was.

"This is *Mrs.* Lerner," said Claire.

There was another silence at the other end. Then the woman asked to speak to Lance. Claire handed Lance the phone.

"Lance Lerner speaking," he said into the phone.

"Lance? It's Cathy."

"Cathy!" said Lance.

"Oh my God," said Claire.

"Who was that woman who said she was Mrs. Lerner?" said Cathy. "*I'm* Mrs. Lerner."

"It . . . doesn't matter," said Lance.

"Was that Claire Firestone?" said Cathy.

Lance was astonished.

"Why would you ask me that?" he said.

"Because. Howard said Claire Firestone requested your current itinerary. Howard said he thought there might be something going on between you two. Is there, Lance? Is that who's with you?"

Lance thought Cathy might be crying.

"Cathy, what is it?" he said.

"Is that who's with you, Claire Firestone?" she said.

"What's the difference?" he said.

"Are you making love to her?"

"No," he said.

"Yes, you are," she said.

"Whatever you like," he said.

She was definitely crying. Well, the hell with her. She's fucking Howard. She deserves this, he thought. But the sound of her crying was more than he could bear.

"Cathy, what's wrong. Can I help you?"

"I need to talk to you," she said.

"Go ahead," he said. "I'm here."

"Not on the phone," she said. "When are you coming home?"

"Next Friday."

"Oh," she said.

"Do you want to see me next Friday?"

"I guess so," she said. "Call me when you get in. Call me from the airport."

"Can't you at least tell me what it's about?" he said.

"I'll tell you next Friday."

They said goodbye and he hung up the phone. Whatever it was wasn't that urgent if it could keep till next Friday. Could it be that she wanted to come back? Great. She decides to come back, she calls to tell me, and a woman answers the phone and says *she's* Mrs. Lerner. Is that why Cathy was so upset? It seemed the likeliest possibility.

"I'm sorry," said Claire. "I should never have answered your phone. It was just driving me crazy."

"Don't worry about it," he said.

He put his arm around her, but she pulled away. She got dressed without speaking and went back to New York.

He wondered how he was going to be able to wait until next Friday.

62

It was going to be harder than she thought.

Not getting the information—getting the information was the easiest part. She had gotten Lance's phone number and address right out of the Manhattan directory. She was amazed that anybody as famous as Lance was listed in the Manhattan directory. But when she called him up, some kid answered the phone and said he was out of town, promoting his new book. She had used her head and told the kid that she wanted to interview Lance and needed to know when he'd be back. And the kid said Friday night late.

If the kid hadn't told her, she would have called his publisher and got the information. So all she had to do now was go to his apartment Friday night and tell him the good news—that she, Gladys Oliphant, was going to have his baby.

All well and good. All easy as pie.

So now it was Friday night, and she had put on her sexiest Antron nylon dress, and she had gotten her hair all sprayed and gussied up, and she was shaking so badly that she had to knock down about six beers and a couple shots of rye to give her courage. She was shaking less now, but she was not quite so steady on her feet.

She telephoned Lance's apartment again and the same kid answered. She asked for Lance and was told that he wasn't expected for another hour or so. She went to his address and waited for him across the street. Telling him would be the hardest part. But then he'd know and he'd be so happy there wouldn't be anything to worry about.

63

Lance got off the plane at JFK. Although it was ten o'clock at night the air outside was like a steam room. What was August weather doing at the end of September?

He was completely exhausted. Ten cities in two weeks in all this heat, with an average of four hours' sleep each night, had taken its toll. At least the book was beginning to move. Howard had telephoned him in Los Angeles to say that all he needed to make it onto the bottom of the bestseller list was one network TV appearance. *Merv Griffin, Mike Douglas, Phil Donahue, Good Morning America,* the *Today Show* or the *Tonight Show.* Any one of them could do it. Every one of them had turned him down. Howard was going to try the *Tonight Show* again. It was a fifty-fifty shot, he said.

Lance went to a pay phone in the air terminal and called Cathy. She was relieved to hear he was back. At first she suggested he come to her apartment, but then she changed her mind. If he went directly home and she left in a little while, they could meet at their old apartment at about ten-thirty or so and save a good twenty minutes.

Lance called Dorothy and Janie at his apartment. They were overjoyed to hear from him and wanted to know all about the trip. He said he'd give them the details later—right now he needed a favor: Get lost for a couple of hours while he talked to Cathy at the apartment. They said they'd see him later.

Lance got in line for a cab, and when it was time to lift his bags into a taxi, he was so weak he almost fell over. The cabbie figured he was a wino.

Lance dragged himself up the stairs, opened the door and collapsed onto the floor of his apartment, sweating profusely and breathing hard.

After a few moments he was strong enough to stand up. He was just about to go into the bathroom to wash his face and brush his teeth when the doorbell rang. He considered a lightning fast trip to the bathroom, then said the hell with it. He buzzed her in.

He opened the door and looked down the steps and beheld, not his beautiful slim wife, but a monstrously fat woman, wet with perspiration and drunk as a skunk. It took him a moment before he realized it was Gladys Oliphant.

"Hi there, gorgeous," she said through the alcoholic vapors. "Remember me?"

"Gladys," he said without enthusiasm, "what a wonderful surprise."

"I jus' happened to be in the neighborhood," she said, "and I thought, 'why not drop by and see if old Lance is in.' "

"Well well," said Lance, "that's really nice. The thing is, though, Gladys, now is not a good time for a visit, because—"

"So that's jus' what I did—dropped by and saw if old you were in. And you were. And here I am."

Gladys had gained the topmost step and now, breathing hard, she pushed her way inside the apartment.

"Gladys, I wonder if I could ask you a tremendous favor."

"Anything," she said expansively, waving her hand and knocking over a floor lamp, "ask old Gladys anything at all. After all, we are more than friends, am I right? We have known each other carnally, as the Bible says, isn't that correct?"

"Yes, well, look, Gladys, the thing is that right now I'm expecting—"

"*You're* expecting! *I'm* expecting! That's what I came to talk to you about."

"Pardon me?" he said.

"I'm *expecting*. I'm preggers. And so are *you*. You're going to be a *father!*"

Lance was praying he hadn't heard what he was afraid he'd heard.

"Gladys, what are you *saying?*"

"Preggers. Pregnant. With child. In the family way. Gravid. Knocked up. Got a bun in the oven. And speaking of ovens, it feels like one in here. Mind if I get comfortable? Whooh!"

Gladys began taking off her clothes.

"Gladys, wait—hold on there! Please don't take off your clothes now! Please don't!"

"Why not?" she said, unbuttoning her dress. "Afraid I'll turn you on again? Afraid you won't be able to resist me?"

As fast as she unbuttoned buttons, Lance was rebuttoning them in a futile attempt to keep her clothed. Gladys pulled ahead of him and popped her enormous breasts out of their mammoth brassiere.

"Well, big boy, here they are," said Gladys, half nude and holding out her arms to him. "Why not take all of me?"

She began to sing "All of Me."

"Gladys, listen to me! Will you listen to me? I am expecting my wife here at any moment, I can't have—"

"Your *wife!*"

Gladys was outraged.

"Yes, my wife," said Lance. "She's going to be here at any moment to discuss a very crucial problem. She—"

"You never told me you had a wife!" she said. "If I knew you had a wife, would I have given myself to you? I would most certainly *not*, sir. A wife *indeed!*"

"Gladys, will you please *listen* to me!" he screamed.

That appeared to quiet her momentarily. He felt a flash of compassion for the large, seminude woman who might now be carrying his child, but there were more pressing matters at hand.

"Now listen, Gladys," he said, "I heard what you were telling me, that you're pregnant, and I'm very concerned about it. Very concerned. And I really want to discuss with you what we should do about it, I really do. But I can't do it now. Now my wife is coming. And she can't find you here without your clothes on."

"I should think *not!*" said Gladys.

"So if you would please *please* just get dressed and leave right now, I promise you on my word of honor that the moment she leaves I will call you and meet you anywhere at all to discuss this. All right? Will you do that for me?"

"I don't see why not," said Gladys, trying unsuccessfully to stuff her gigantic boobs back into her brassiere.

"Wonderful, wonderful," said Lance. "Just put your—"

The doorbell rang.

"Oh no," said Lance.

"Oh-oh," said Gladys.

"Too late," said Lance. "Oh my God!"

Lance looked wildly around for someplace to hide her. It was no mean assignment. The bedroom! He could hide her in the bedroom! The doorbell rang again.

"In here, Gladys!" he said, pushing her through the high double doors in his bedroom.

"Oh no you don't, smooth talker," said Gladys. "You're not getting *me* into your bed, no sir! That's how all this started in the *first* place!"

"Gladys, please. Just get dressed in here and wait for me. And don't make a sound, all right? Be as quiet as a mouse!"

He pulled the double doors closed behind him and went to answer the doorbell. In the bedroom Gladys had begun singing "All of Me" again. He dashed back into the bedroom, made shooshing noises and then had a brainstorm and turned on the TV.

The doorbell rang insistently. He pulled the double doors closed behind him and buzzed her in.

"Hi, Cathy!" he called down the steps. "I'm sorry it took so long —I was in the john!"

Cathy didn't say anything. By the time she got to the top of the steps he could see that she was crying. He took her in his arms and hugged her. In the bedroom, above the TV, he could still hear Gladys singing "All of Me."

"Cathy," he said, "what is it?"

"I don't know what to do," she said.

"About what?" he said.

"About Howard," she said.

"About Howard?" he said. "What *about* Howard?"

"I think he's getting tired of me," she said.

"He is?" said Lance. He didn't understand how he was supposed to feel about this extraordinary piece of news.

"He's stopped being spontaneous and romantic—just like you did—only with you it took two years, and with him about two weeks."

So here it was again, the same old complaint. You'd think she'd at least be diplomatic enough not to criticize him while asking for his help. Come to think of it, what kind of help was she asking for?

"How can I help you, Cathy?"

"You know him," she said. "And you know how a man's mind works. What can I do to keep him from getting tired of me?"

Lance had to laugh in spite of himself. It was too ridiculous— being asked to counsel his own wife in renewing his rival's flagging ardor!

"Cathy, I love you dearly, you know that," he said. "But why in the world would I want to help keep you and Howard together?"

"Because," she said. "So far I don't love him. But if he continues to reject me, I'm afraid I'll fixate on him and I won't be able to see him objectively anymore, and then who *knows?*"

Gladys's singing in the bedroom had grown louder. Lance was frantic to silence her. Cathy had begun to cry again.

"Let me get you some Kleenex," said Lance, slipping into the bedroom and swiftly closing the door behind him. To his horror he saw that Gladys, instead of getting dressed, had removed every last article of clothing and was lying on the bed completely naked.

He turned up the volume of the TV and got down on his knees.

"Please, Gladys, please," he said. "Put on your clothes and be quiet. If you do I'll promise you anything in the world!"

"Even marry me?" said Gladys with delight.

"Uh, well, maybe not that," said Lance. "But anything else."

"Awww," said Gladys. "Why wouldn't you marry me?"

"Religious differences," said Lance. "But I will promise you anything else in the whole entire world."

"Lance?" called Cathy. "What are you doing?"

"Getting you some Kleenex," Lance called back. "Be right there!"

"Would you take me to dinner at Elaine's?" said Gladys.

"Absolutely," said Lance. "You get those clothes on and be quiet like a good girl, and I'll take you to Elaine's."

Gladys squealed and clapped her hands. Lance opened the double doors a crack and slid back out of the bedroom. Cathy looked at him curiously.

"Were you out?" she said.

"No, no," he said, "I was just in the bedroom."

"I meant out of Kleenex," said Cathy.

Lance realized with disgust that he'd come out of the bedroom empty-handed.

"Oh, out in *that* sense," said Lance. "Yes I am. I definitely am. But why don't you use my handkerchief . . ."

He searched his pockets for a handkerchief.

"That's OK," she said. "I don't need one."

"Yoohoo!" called Gladys from inside the bedroom.

Lance's heart stopped. Cathy turned in the direction of the bedroom doors.

"Yoohoo, Lance!" called Gladys again. "What night?"

"I don't *believe* it," said Cathy, suddenly furious. "You have a *woman* in our bedroom! You knew I was coming over, and you still have a *woman* in there!"

"Hold on a second," said Lance. "That's just Gladys."

"*Gladys?*" Cathy snorted. "Who the hell is *Gladys?*"

"Gladys is the woman that I have come in on Fridays. To clean. She's in there now, cleaning the bedroom. Watching TV and cleaning the bedroom."

Breathing fire, Cathy whirled and threw open the bedroom doors. Gladys, still naked, lay on the bed like a beached whale.

"I can explain this!" cried Lance, as Cathy went into hysterics and headed for the front door. "This is not what it seems, I swear to God, Cathy! Won't you let me explain?"

But Cathy was already halfway down the stairs and beyond recall.

There was at least one small consolation, thought Lance as Cathy slammed the door and ran out into the night—at least I *didn't* have to explain.

64

Julius Blatt was on top of the world. His hundred-dollar-a-plate dinner to free the Dalton Two was fast becoming one of the hottest charity events of the summer.

Already Blatt had formed a coalition of a number of unlikely groups, including the Authors Guild, the NAACP, the American Booksellers Association, the Black Panthers and the United Jewish Appeal. Plans for a telethon were being formed, and Sammy Davis, Jr., had agreed to co-host with Lillian Hellman.

An editor at Firestone Publishing by the name of Howard Leventhal had called Blatt personally and made an offer on the book that Ernest was reported to be writing on the Dalton Two: $250,000 hardcover advance against royalties, and a $100,000 guaranteed advertising and promotion budget.

Blatt told Leventhal he didn't know how good a deal that was and would have to ask his old friend, Lance Lerner. Leventhal said that he, personally, was Lance Lerner's editor, and that he could guarantee that the deal was much better than that which Lance himself had on his current book.

Blatt asked why Leventhal was offering a better deal on Ernest's book than on Lerner's, and Leventhal said that it was because Lerner was a known quantity on the market and Ernest wasn't. Blatt said he'd think about it.

Then a producer at Universal called Blatt, having read in Claudia Cohen's column that Ernest had signed a book contract on the Dalton Two, and offered $300,000 for the movie rights. Blatt said he'd gotten a better offer than that already from Warner Brothers, and that very afternoon Warners called and offered $575,000. Fox came in at $625,000 and Paramount at $800,000. Universal's final offer was $902,000, with Ernest writing the first-draft screenplay and Blatt executive-producing, and Blatt took it.

65

June Wedding.

If Hiram Wedding had loved his baby daughter any less he might not have burdened her with so self-conscious a name as June Wedding. If Hiram Wedding had loved his delicate and beautiful bride any less, she might not have died in childbirth scarcely eight months after they had married.

But Hiram hadn't loved either less, and so now here he was with a motherless baby and a dead wife and, little by little, he was starting to hit the bottle and to let his grip on reality loosen up and up, till finally there would be no grip left at all.

Hiram was a longshoreman on the Brooklyn docks. His body was so solidly packed with muscle that there were no soft places on it. Luckily for him his work on the docks depended on a firm grip on many things more important than reality. He would be able to earn enough to support Baby June for several years to come.

Baby June was not, alas, a pretty baby. Her name would prove to be a cruel joke. No one would ever wish to involve her in any kind of wedding, June or otherwise. She seemed to have inherited nothing from her beautiful dead mother but her sex. Instead June got her father's squat, powerful body and blunt-featured face. Hiram, in narcissistic and paternal blindness, thought that June was the queen of Sheepshead Bay.

As Baby June grew into young girlhood, even Hiram could see that she was turning out blunt and squat instead of finely honed and delicate. He tried to compensate, buying her only the frilliest of feminine clothing. It looked ridiculous on her squat, muscular body, but not to Hiram.

Since his wife's death, Hiram had been drinking more and more. Every night after leaving the shipyard he would go home and get loaded. Through the liquorish vapors his growing daughter occasionally looked to him like his poor dead wife. He held June in his drunken arms at night and sometimes he caressed her in places where fathers were not supposed to caress their daughters. Little June sensed that it was as wrong as it was physically pleasurable, and she grew to hate him for it.

When she was thirteen, June Wedding left her father's home. She left behind all her ludicrously inappropriate feminine clothing, and took with her only denim overalls and flannel shirts. In years to come she would buy satiny underwear like the things her father had forced on her while she was growing up and wear it secretly under her denim work clothes like a furtive male transvestite.

June Wedding held a number of jobs while she was growing up that most men wouldn't have been able to endure—loading and unloading trucks, servicing and repairing heavy machinery, driving tractor trailers as soon as she was old enough to get her license. She never finished school, but she was writing a bitter yet poetic first novel and she knew things that most men and women didn't. She was an able carpenter, plumber, electrician and mason. She could tear a transmission down and put it back together again. She could fly a plane and had nearly enough hours for a commercial pilot's license, although she doubted that any airline would hire her because she was a woman.

June's face was homely and she wore her hair chopped very short. She sought out the company of tough, masculine women. She hated men, but she didn't lust for women. She had, as far as she could tell, no desire for sex of any kind. When a female coworker made a drunken pass at her, June almost tore her in half.

June stood for nothing. June stood *against* a number of things: She detested job discrimination based on sex. She detested male chauvinism of any kind. She detested male sexual aggression. Above all else, June Wedding detested rape. She read in the *New*

York Post and the *Daily News* accounts of women being raped by men which could bring her to the boiling point. She had no fear of rape herself—she was stronger than most men—but she feared for the safety of her weaker friends. When a woman she worked with at a moving company called the Motherloaders was assaulted on the Lexington Avenue subway, she organized a small group she dubbed MATE—Men Are The Enemy.

The members of MATE began to do research on rape. They photocopied newspaper stories on rape and discussed them endlessly. They took out of the public library and devoured every psychological study ever written on rape. They wrote an outline and a sample chapter for a book on rape and took it to several publishers, but they were turned down by thirty-two of them before they realized what was going on: the male pig editors had rejected their book for political reasons, and the female editors were Uncle Toms and Aunt Tessies and were scared to death to rock the boat and get in bad with their pig bosses. It was clear they would never be able to get it published. Not till after the revolution.

There were never more than four members of MATE—June and the three women at the Motherloaders whom she worked with most. They were all built short and squat and powerful like June. Like June, none of them had any sexual interest in either men or women.

Alix was the only member of MATE who had either long hair or breasts. They were not soft, feminine breasts, however. They were hard, muscular pectoralis majors, and they came from working out with weights. Alix did not need a bra.

Sandy had freckles, sandy-colored hair, heavy thighs, a nice smile, an ugly temper, and a broken nose. She had been a semi-pro boxer before joining the Motherloaders.

Wanda had a pretty face, a relatively trusting nature, and thighs as big around as Sandy's. She had the most feminine voice of the four of them and had a look of vulnerability that most men responded to. It was Wanda who'd been raped in the subway.

Two Hispanic men had caught Wanda in the sparsely populated Brooklyn Bridge station on the Lexington Avenue line. It was not late—about nine o'clock in the evening. The men seemed stoned. They began making sexual remarks to Wanda, and when she didn't respond, they took out folding knives. One held his blade against her neck, and the other pulled her pants down and raped her. There were at least a dozen and a half people in the subway station. None of them tried to help or to call for a transit policeman.

When both the men were finished raping Wanda, they threw her on the floor, called her a *puta,* and left. When the men had disappeared, some of the people in the subway station offered to help Wanda, but she refused and went into the ladies room to wash off the filth.

Wanda didn't go to the police. She could not bear the prospect of a bunch of leering men asking her accusatory questions. She went home and called her friends. Alix, Sandy and June immediately came over to her depressing furnished apartment in the East Village. They listened to the account of Wanda's degradation, they soothed her, they cursed and swore vengeance on her attackers.

For the next two weeks, they went with Wanda to the Brooklyn Bridge subway station and hung around there between the hours of eight-thirty and ten-thirty p.m., hoping to see the two Hispanic men again. They saw many Hispanic men. None of them looked to Wanda like her attackers.

On the nineteenth night, just as they were about to give up for another evening, the four women spotted a group of noisy Hispanic men at one end of the subway platform. They moved closer. There were three of them. One Wanda had never seen before, but the other two looked familiar to her.

Wanda wanted to leave. June told her to stay out of sight. Then she and Alix and Sandy strolled over to the three men and began making suggestive comments. The men responded. Joking loudly in Spanish, they drifted over to the three women and began to evaluate their sexual attributes. At a signal from June, each woman grabbed one of the men. Before the startled men knew what was happening, each found himself in a powerful hammerlock, with a straight razor pressed against his jugular vein.

June called out to Wanda to come and identify her attackers.

But when Wanda drew close to them she was certain she had never seen these men before. June, Alix and Sandy were disappointed. They had been on their quest for nineteen consecutive nights now and they were eager for a taste of blood.

June said that although they may not have been the men who raped their friend, they were ugly male chauvinist pigs. They pulled the men into a nearby ladies room and made them lie down on the floor. At June's direction, Wanda took out the scissors with which they had planned to castrate her attackers and merely cut off all the men's clothing.

When the three men were naked, the four women took turns disparaging the men's bodies, especially their genitals. Alix pulled down her jeans and sat on each of their faces. Sandy pulled down her jeans and peed on them. Then June took a can of aerosol paint and wrote slogans on the men's bodies. "RAPE IS A POLITICAL CRIME" and "MAKE WAR, NOT LOVE" are what she wrote.

66

Helen and the group were absolutely livid. What was Lance going to do about Gladys's pregnancy? Was he going to try to talk her into having an abortion? What if she refused? What if she wanted to have the baby? Was Lance willing to take responsibility for the child?

How could Lance possibly allow the situation between himself and Cathy and Howard to exist without confronting Howard about it? Didn't Lance see that all his apparent victimizations by women were actually things that he himself set up out of his repressed hostility to women and his subconscious desire to control them? Didn't Lance know that when you tried to repress your feelings in order to avoid losing control, they ended up controlling you, and that angry feelings accumulate until they explode?

Helen and the group urged Lance to have a serious talk with Gladys, and to come clean with Howard and let him know how he felt about what Howard had done. Various members of the group took turns being Gladys and Howard in a succession of psychodramas. Finally Lance agreed to confront both Gladys and Howard—more to halt the psychodramas than for any other reason. Lance telephoned Howard and made a lunch date with him for the following day. One o'clock in the Four Seasons Grill.

Howard was twenty minutes late. Lance was not surprised. With the load of ambivalence that Howard must be carting around these days, Lance was surprised that he showed up at all.

Howard did not look at all well. His thinning hair was thinning more than usual, his paunch was increasing, and his effeminate way of speaking had developed a soupçon of a stutter.

Howard observed that Lance looked unusually haggard, even for an author who'd been out touring. Howard said the book was still holding its own in sales, but that the *Tonight Show* had once again said no. Howard continued to talk, long after he had run out of things to talk about, and Lance realized he was simply trying to fill dead air because, were there to be a silence of any duration, something dreadful might pop out.

"Howard," said Lance after a while, "shut up."

Howard looked at Lance with alarm. All right, Lerner, thought Lance to himself, you've got your audience, now what are you going to do with it?

"Howard," said Lance, the anger beginning to well up inside of him, "I *know*."

Howard looked as if Lance had just pulled a gun on him.

"Y-you know w-*what*?" he said.

"Everything," said Lance. "I know everything that you've been doing with Cathy. I know you've been playing tennis with her. I know you've been romantic and spontaneous with her. I know you've been *un*romantic and *un*spontaneous with her. I know you've been fucking her brains out. I know everything. And I am vastly tempted to punch your fucking heart out, right here in the middle of the Four Seasons Grill."

Lance didn't quite know what Howard would do with this news. He certainly didn't expect Howard to do what he finally did. Howard burst into tears.

"Oh, my *God,*" Howard blubbered, wetness spilling out of his eyes and nostrils. "Oh my dear sweet G-God in *H-Heaven!*"

Lance watched Howard bawl and decided it wasn't fair. When you finally got somebody dead to rights on something as serious as cuckolding and you were entitled to do anything at all to the guy and no court would be likely to convict you, what does the guy do but burst out crying. Could you attack a man who was crying? You could not.

"I f-feel so *horrible,*" said Howard. "I f-feel like *scum!*"

"You *are* scum, Howard," said Lance.

"I f-feel like a g-gigantic bag of h-*horse manure!*" said Howard.

"You *are* a gigantic bag of horse manure, Howard," said Lance.

"I am s-so *ashamed* of myself I could d-*die!*" said Howard.

"That," said Lance, "would be a blessing."

"W-would it help at all to t-tell you I wasn't t-totally to b-*blame?*" said Howard.

"Are you going to tell me that my wife *seduced* you?" said Lance. "That would not be a fruitful direction to pursue."

"I d-don't mean to tell you *that,*" said Howard, "b-but she certainly m-met me more than *halfway.*"

"I told you that isn't a fruitful direction to pursue, Howard," said Lance, " and cut out that stuttering. If you can't speak without stuttering, *sing.*"

Howard started to say something, began to stutter, started to apologize for stuttering, stuttered on the apology, and stopped talking altogether. Lance's anger at Howard dribbled away. In its stead stood disgust and pity. Picking on Howard was like beating up a paraplegic.

"All right, Howard," said Lance, "this isn't very satisfying. Let's not talk about it anymore."

"I'm so *s-sorry*, Lance," said Howard.

"I expect you are," said Lance.

"Does that mean you f-*forgive* me?" said Howard.

"It means that I think you're too pathetic to chastise," said Lance.

"Thank you," said Howard. "You're a much better p-person than I am."

"You can say *that* again," said Lance.

67

At 4:55 p.m. on a warm day in late September, four Hispanic-American youths—Tony Garcia, Vince Lopez, Juan Rivera and Pablo Moreno—walked into the big Brentano's bookstore at Fifth Avenue and 48th Street and announced that they were conducting a holdup.

Three cashiers brought them fistfuls of currency which they dumped into a flight bag emblazoned with the insignia of Lot Polish Airlines. The most remarkable aspect of the crime was that, in lieu of fleeing, Garcia, Lopez, Rivera and Moreno hung around and chatted with the cashiers until the police arrived some forty minutes later.

When arresting officers Friedman and O'Rourke took them to the 17th Precinct to book them, the four demanded the right to call a public defender named Julius Blatt as legal counsel. In the ensuing telephone conversation between Garcia and Blatt, the following agreements were reached:

(1) The group's slogan would be "Free The Brentano's Four";

(2) Blatt would represent them for 15% of all hard- and softcover royalties, 25% of all gross income from motion picture and television rights, and 50% of all gross profits from games, toys, and T-shirts.

68

Lance felt sick about Cathy's walking in on Gladys naked in his bed. He tried to reach Cathy many times by phone, but she hung up on him every time she heard his voice.

He wrote her a six-page letter, typed single-space, but after mailing it he feared that the Postal Service was too perverse to deliver it unsabotaged, and so he hand-delivered the carbon to her building and walked upstairs and slid it under her actual door.

He tried to reach Gladys several times by phone, but failed—it was either busy or there was no answer.

He went to his therapy group and told them about the latest developments in his life. Instead of the sympathy and encouragement he was expecting, the group gave him disapproval and disgust.

"What hidden payoff do you get from feeling weak and pushed around?" said Helen.

"What are you talking about?" said Lance.

"If you act shy and nebbishy, you think people will love you more," she said. "If you act helpless, you think they'll take care of you."

"You let everybody control you," said Arnold. "You must love being victimized."

"You're crazy," said Lance. "Who have I let control me?"

"Everybody," said Arnold. "You let Dorothy and Janie move in on you. You let Gladys rape you and become pregnant by you. You let Cathy have an affair with your editor. You let Claire force you to have sex with her whenever she likes, wherever she likes, and under the most stressful and demeaning circumstances. You—"

"Now just hang on there a minute, Arnold," said Lance, beginning to get angry. "In the first place, I didn't *have* to let either Dorothy *or* Janie move in with me. I *wanted* them to move in with me. And—"

"*Sure* he wanted them to move in with him," said Jackie. "Because he wanted to *shtoop* them."

"That's not true," said Lance. "I haven't laid a glove on them and I'm not going to either."

"Bullshit," said Jackie.

"Bullshit yourself," said Lance. "You're just jealous."

"Jealous?" said Jackie. "Listen, bubie, if I wanted to have two teenybopper chink dykes sleeping on my living-room floor, I'd have them sooner than you could say 'Ho-ho-ho, Ho Chi Minh.' "

"Let's get back to what Arnold was saying, if you don't mind," said Helen. "About needing to be controlled by women."

"Yeah," said Lance, "let's get back to that. Now as far as Claire is concerned, I had sex with her under . . . exotic circumstances, but it was by choice. Nobody was *forcing* me to do anything at all. *I* was the one who decided if I wanted to do it. Not her. *Me.* I'm a completely free man—that's why she considers me such a challenge."

"A completely free man, eh?" said Roger. "Were you a completely free man when she said if you didn't have sex with her she'd tell her husband you made a pass at her?"

"Well," said Lance, "in a way, sure."

"Bullshit," said Jackie.

"Look," said Lance, "maybe the thing with Claire is a bad example. Publishing is a strange business, and sometimes you have to do some peculiar things to get your book before the public. Let's take another example. Like Cathy. I certainly didn't want Cathy to have an affair with my editor."

"You certainly did set it up, though," said Laura.

"What do you mean I set it up?" said Lance.

"You made a bare-assed pass at her best friend in front of all those people, causing her to leave you," said Arnold. "And then you informed your editor that she'd left you."

"If that's not setting it up," said Helen, "I don't know what is."

"All right," said Lance, "maybe Cathy's not the best example either. But you certainly can't say I wanted Gladys to rape me and then get pregnant because of it."

"Don't you take responsibility for your own ejaculations?" said Laura, blushing furiously.

Lance was shocked. He'd never heard Laura use a word like "ejaculations" before. Besides, he'd thought she liked him.

"Ejaculation," said Lance in a wounded tone, "is an involuntary physiological response."

"Bullshit!" said Jackie. "You mean to say you have no control over whether you come?"

"Well, sure I do," said Lance, "but—"

"How much effort did you exert to prevent yourself from coming?" said Helen.

"Well, none, really," said Lance, "but—"

"Did you try to discourage her in *any* way from having sex with you?" said Roger.

"I . . . I don't remember," said Lance.

"And you still maintain you had nothing to do with getting her pregnant?" said Arnold.

"Look," said Lance, "I was handcuffed to the *bed*. What could I have done to discourage her?"

"You could have said you didn't want to have sex with her," said Laura.

"How did you get handcuffed to the bed in the *first* place?" said Arnold. "Was the policewoman holding a gun to your head?"

"Hey," said Lance, "what's the point of all this? Are you trying to get me to say that everything that's happened to me is my fault?"

"We're trying to get you to see what part you played in each one of these situations and to take responsibility for them," said Helen. "If you can't take responsibility for what happens to you —if you can't see how the things you do contribute to what happens in your life—then you'll never be able to take charge of your life. You'll always be a victim."

So, he thought, even Helen, his own *therapist* was against him. What did *she* want? If he were at all paranoid, he'd have imagined she got them all together before he arrived and planned this. He had half a mind to not let them help him at all. Why was he paying thirty dollars a group session and fifty for private ones to be attacked like this? He could avoid all this grief and simply quit therapy. And if he really missed having people attack him, he could just go and walk the streets of New York and get it all for free.

"You know," said Helen, "I think Lance wouldn't be so eager to be controlled by women if he weren't so ambivalent about them."

"Ambivalent?" said Lance. "That's a laugh. I'm not ambivalent about women—I *love* women."

"I think you also have a lot of hostility toward them," said Laura.

"Hostility? Fuck you, Laura!" said Lance.

"You mean to tell me that when you thought Cathy was screwing Les you didn't feel hostile toward her?" said Roger.

"Well, sure," said Lance, "but that was only natural. *Anybody* would have felt hostile under those circumstances."

"But not everybody would have decided to remedy the situation by trying to fuck her best friend," said Helen. "That, to me, shows real hostility. That, to me, is like trying to assassinate somebody."

Lance thought it over.

"No," he said. "I didn't want to assassinate her. I just wanted to balance the scales, that's all."

"And what about the night you made love to her on her birthday, and then found out she was having an affair with Howard?" said Helen. "Did you want to assassinate her *then?*"

"No," he said. "Mostly I wanted to assassinate *Howard.*"

"If you can't feel the hostility," said Helen, "then you'll never be able to feel the love."

"I feel," said Lance, "all I want to feel."

"That I believe," said Helen.

69

The following afternoon Claire dropped by his apartment without warning to say hello. He was glad to see her and said so. Then Dorothy and Janie passed them on the staircase, headed for Lance's bathtub. Both girls were in their underwear, and when Claire caught sight of them her jaw dropped.

"That's, uh, Dorothy and Janie," said Lance. "They're staying here for a while till they find someplace else to live."

"I see," said Claire somewhat frostily.

"They're friends of mine," said Lance.

"I can imagine," she said.

"Look," said Lance, "there's nothing going on between us, if *that's* what you're thinking."

"I'll bet," said Claire.

He leaned in close to Claire and whispered.

"They're lovers," he said. "They have all they want in each *other* —they don't need me."

"Right," said Claire.

"You know," said Lance, "if I didn't know you better, I'd say you're jealous."

"Maybe I am," said Claire.

"Well, that's very flattering," said Lance, "but you shouldn't be."

Claire paced back and forth for several moments, thinking hard.

"All right," she said. "I *am* jealous. It's not a familiar feeling for me, so I guess I didn't recognize it at first. But that's definitely what it is. Do you know why someone gets jealous?"

"Why?"

"Because they start valuing someone too much and they begin to be afraid of losing them. They kid themselves that losing that person would be intolerable."

"I suppose you're right," said Lance.

"Oh, I'm right," said Claire, "don't worry. Anyway, I just realized I have started feeling that way about *you*."

"You have?" said Lance. "That's nice."

"Not necessarily," said Claire. "Because I can't let myself get into those kinds of situations. So to protect myself here is what I propose to you: You give up your other women, and I will see to it that you never lack for sex, love, luxuries, or influence in the publishing world."

"What are you saying?" said Lance.

"I'm saying what I want—I don't want you to have any other women but me."

Lance smiled.

"Claire, get serious, will you? What am I supposed to tell people, that I'm going steady with Austin Firestone's wife?"

"We are not amused," she said.

"Well, I think you're being silly," he said.

"I'm not being silly, I'm being serious. If you agree to give up other women, I will give you everything you ever needed. You'll be one of the most successful writers in the world."

"And if I don't?" he said. "What will you do then, ruin my career?"

"Perhaps," she said.

Rage began to well up inside of him. How dare she try to buy him like that? How dare she try to control him? How dare she threaten him? Well, the group and Helen were wrong—he was damned if he was going to be controlled.

"OK, Claire," he said. "Go and do your worst."

"That's your answer?" she said.

"That's my answer," he said. "I'm a free man. Nobody buys me, nobody controls me, and nobody threatens me. And I'm not afraid of anything you could ever do to me either."

She wheeled and charged through the door. She stopped on the stairway and looked back up at him.

"You may be under the deluded impression that your wife and Howard Leventhal are almost finished with their seamy little liaison, and that you can get her back again," she said. "If so, you're an even bigger fool than I think you are."

"What's that supposed to mean?" said Lance. "What are you talking about?"

But she had got to him and she knew it. She was down the stairs and out onto the street and into her limousine before he could stop her.

70

Claire's parting shot had really rocked him. He didn't think she was bluffing. He thought she knew of a recent development. He had to know what it was.

He telephoned Cathy repeatedly through the day and night, but she didn't even pick up the phone. He took a cab to her building, rang her doorbell, but there wasn't any answer. He stood out in the middle of the street and tried to figure out where her windows were to see if they were lit. It was impossible to tell.

Well, he thought, if I can't find out through Cathy, then I'll find out through Howard. He telephoned Howard's office.

"Mr. Leventhal is out," said his secretary. "I'll tell him you called when he returns."

"When do you think he'll return?" said Lance.

"I'm not exactly sure," she said. "Two weeks, at the very least."

"Two weeks!" said Lance.

"Yes," said the secretary. "Mr. Leventhal has finally decided to take a long-overdue vacation. But perhaps one of his assistants can help you while Mr. Leventhal is gone."

"I had no idea he was going away on vacation," said Lance. "I just saw him and he didn't mention it."

"Yes," she said, "the opportunity to get away came up quite suddenly. He grabbed it. To his credit, I might add."

"Listen," said Lance, "it is terribly urgent that I reach him. Do you know for sure that he's already left?"

"I believe he has," she said. "But if it has to do with publicity on your book, Mr. Lerner, I'm sure that Mr. Fieldston or Charlene or Judy could take care of it for you."

"It doesn't have to do with my book," said Lance. "It's a personal matter."

"I see. Well, I'm afraid you'll have to wait till his return, then."

"There's nowhere I can reach him?" said Lance.

"On a yacht? Oh my, heavens, no."

"A yacht, you say? What kind of yacht?"

"He's on the *Claire de Lune*, Mr. Firestone's yacht."

"The *Claire de* . . . ?"

A light bulb exploded inside Lance's head.

It took all of seven minutes to grab a cab and get to the Firestones' apartment building on Park Avenue. The doorman assured Lance that the Firestones had already left on holiday, but there was no mistaking the long gray limousine parked outside —he knew it intimately.

He finally lied his way past the doorman, and the elevator man took him up. The valet who answered the door said that, yes, madam was still here, but that she did not wish to receive visitors as she was just about to go off on holiday. To the extreme surprise of the valet, Lance pushed past him and ran down the hall, checking rooms until he finally found Claire.

She was just finishing packing. If she was surprised to see him she didn't let it show.

"Hello, Lance," she said pleasantly. "How nice to see you. I'm sorry I don't have time to stop and chat. If you ask Charles, however, he'll bring you a kir royale or whatever else you may wish."

"What I *wish*," said Lance, "is to know what's going on here?"

"A vacation," she said. "Austin and I suddenly felt we had to get away from it all."

"Austin and you and Howard Leventhal," said Lance.

"That's right," said Claire, "and Howard Leventhal."

"And Cathy Lerner?" said Lance.

Claire shrugged.

"I know Howard said he was bringing a playmate," she said, "I'm not sure which one."

"You arranged the whole thing," said Lance, "didn't you? You arranged the whole thing just to get me."

Claire smiled.

" 'Vengeance is mine,' saith the Lord."

She snapped her suitcase closed.

"Claire, don't do this," said Lance. "I beg you, don't do this."

Just then Firestone strode by the room and stuck his head in. At first he didn't recognize Lance and seemed puzzled at his presence. Then he remembered who he was and a dark look crossed his face.

"What the hell are *you* doing here, Lerner?" he said.

"Uh, well, I was just, uh, chatting here with Claire . . . with, uh, Mrs. Firestone, and uh . . ."

Firestone turned to Claire.

"What is Lerner doing here?" he said.

"I don't know," she said. "He seems to think he has some kind of crush on me. He seems to think he wants to sleep with me. It's all quite baffling."

Firestone turned back to Lance.

"Lerner," he said in a terrifyingly quiet voice, "I wish you to leave here *instantly*."

"Can I just say one thing before I go?" said Lance.

"*Instantly*, Lerner," said Firestone.

"Oh, fuck off, Firestone," said Lance.

Firestone walked calmly to the bureau, opened the top drawer, pulled out a blue-black .38 caliber revolver and pointed it at Lance's chest.

"Fuck you, Firestone," said Lance, but he said it very, very softly, and he was moving backwards so quickly that it was possible Firestone never heard him speak.

71

Lance waited in a taxi across the street from the Firestones' apartment building. The Firestones' valet and doorman came out and put luggage into the trunk. The Firestones came out and were helped into the limousine. The limousine took off.

"OK," said Lance, "follow that limousine."

The cabbie turned and gave Lance a pained expression.

"What are ya," he said, "a cop?"

"No," said Lance, "an author."

The cabbie nodded, as if he'd been in an equal number of car chases with both cops and authors, and put the cab in gear. The limousine headed north as far as 79th Street, then across town to the West Side. Lance still had no idea what he was going to do, but the idea of Cathy alone on a yacht for two weeks with Howard and the Firestones was more than he could bear.

The limousine pulled up in front of the 79th Street Boat Basin. The chauffeur got the Firestones' luggage out of the trunk and put it into a small motor launch. The Firestones climbed into the launch and it cast off. Lance paid the cabbie and ran down to the dock, looking for somebody who would take him out to the Firestones' yacht. He figured Cathy and Howard were probably already aboard.

Lance finally located a gnarled old gent in a yellow slicker and a battered captain's hat who agreed to row Lance out to the yacht in his boat for twenty-five dollars. Lance thought this was a little steep, but there didn't seem to be any alternative. He agreed. The gnarled gent wanted his fee in advance. Lance paid him, then understood why—the boat was a rickety old dinghy half full of water.

Sitting in water up to his shins, Lance watched the yacht anxiously for signs of Cathy as the elderly sailor rowed toward it. There were a couple of people out on deck, but the sun was in Lance's eyes and he couldn't make out who they were.

When they pulled up alongside the yacht, Lance saw that the figures on deck were Firestone and Claire.

"Permission to come aboard," said Lance, wondering if that were the correct phraseology.

"Permission denied," said Firestone.

Lance looked at the ladder on the side of the yacht, bobbing tantalizingly close. If he jumped, he could catch it easily. Well, fairly easily. He focused in on the motion of the ladder and rose to a half crouch.

"Permission *denied*," said Firestone, seeing Lance's intention.

Lance sprang and caught onto a rung of the ladder.

The gnarled sailor looked alarmed.

"Coming aboard," said Lance, starting to climb the ladder.

Firestone took his pistol out of his pocket.

"The hell you are," he said.

A shot rang out and smacked into the water a yard from the bottom rung of the ladder. The gnarled old sailor grabbed his oars and started rowing back towards shore at a speed that Lance wouldn't have thought possible.

"Hey, wait for me!" yelled Lance to the disappearing dinghy, hanging on to the ladder for dear life.

The old salt never so much as paused. When the second shot rang out, Lance let go of the ladder and dropped into the water. It was not cold at this time of the year, but Lance's swimming progress was somewhat slowed by his shirt, trousers and boots. He managed to catch up with the dinghy and haul himself over the side, only to splash down in the standing water at the bottom of the boat.

"What the hell's going on?" demanded the old coot.

"The guy on that yacht is a smuggler," said Lance. "I'm a Treasury man."

"Holy shit," said the man, "you coulda got us *killed* out there. How come you didn't call in the Coast Guard or something?"

"I thought I could take him alone," said Lance. "We T-men don't like to call in other agencies to do our dirty work."

Lance was not yet defeated. If the yacht could be boarded, he felt, Cathy could be taken off it. She'd be so impressed with the spontaneity and the romanticism of the gesture—qualities she had always complained he lacked—she would probably go along with him. Especially if he told her he was whisking her off to Paris on the Concorde or something equally romantic.

The problem was how to get past his triggerhappy publisher. He didn't think Firestone would actually have the guts to shoot him on purpose, but there were always accidents. If he were James Bond he could dress in a tuxedo, put a scuba-diving suit on over it, and swim out to the yacht during a late-night soirée. But he was not James Bond, he didn't think he could find any scuba suit to fit over his tux, and he doubted that the Firestones were planning any late night soirées before they left.

As he stood on the dock, dumping water out of his boots and wringing it out of his shirt, he saw Firestone's crew cast off and begin moving out to sea. At the rate they were moving he guessed he had at most an hour to hatch a scheme to catch up with them in some faster form of transportation before they were irretrievably lost at sea. Too bad, he thought, that he didn't have access to something like a police launch.

Come to think of it, though, maybe he did.

72

"The thing you fail to appreciate," said Stevie when he finally located her at the 9th Precinct, "is that the NYPD has better things to do with its launches than to retrieve runaway wives from yachts."

"I do appreciate that," said Lance. "I also appreciate the fact that under certain unusual circumstances, some members of the NYPD have occasionally managed to utilize various NYPD vehicles in a distinctly unofficial capacity."

"What," said Stevie, "are the unusual circumstances in this particular case?"

"That the member of the NYPD who furnishes said vehicle gets taken to such a dinner the likes of which she has never before seen," said Lance.

"And where would such a dinner be served?" said Stevie.

"Wherever the member of the NYPD who furnished the vehicle most wanted it to be served," said Lance.

"Like, for example, the Seventh Regiment Armory on Park Avenue on the night of the hundred-dollar-a-plate dinner for the Dalton Two?" said Stevie.

Lance sighed.

"Sure," he said, "like that."

"In that case," said Stevie, "we are now talking turkey."

Stevie was not able, on such short notice, to get anyone to give her access to a police launch. But when Lance suggested a police helicopter, Stevie's face brightened.

"I have this writing student at John Jay College," said Stevie. "He flew choppers in 'Nam. Now he flies them for the city."

"You think he'd be up for it?" said Lance.

"He'd be impressed to meet an author as hot as you," said Stevie. "You never know."

"The thing I can never quite get," shouted Sparky Connors over the deafening noise of the chopper, "is the structure for a nonfiction piece!"

Lance peered down at the Hudson River below him, trying to spot the Firestone yacht, and trying to make out his own shape in the shadow of the giant dragonfly drifting downstream.

"That's easy!" shouted Lance. "It's 'Tell-'Em-What-You're-Going-To-Tell-'Em,' then-'*Tell*-'Em,' then-'Tell-'Em-What-You've-Told-'Em!'"

"That's it?" shouted Sparky.

"That's *not* it!" yelled Stevie.

"It is so!" screamed Lance.

"Is not!" screamed Stevie. "The most important part is the lead!"

"What's the lead?" shouted Sparky.

"That's what they call the Five W's!" yelled Lance. "Who, What, Where, When and Why! That's part of the Tell-'Em-What-You're-Going-To-Tell-'Em."

"Oh!" shouted Sparky.

It had been close to an hour since the Firestones had cast off. Sparky had swooped low over the river every time they saw a boat that Lance thought might be the one. None of them was. Now they were out over the Atlantic, and still there was no sign of the Firestone yacht. Lance feared Firestone had pulled a fast one—doubled back and gone the other way perhaps. And then suddenly he saw it.

"There it is!" he shouted.

Stevie and Sparky looked in the direction he was pointing. Sparky brought the chopper down to hover directly overhead. There was no doubt about it—it was definitely the *Claire de Lune*. Two people were standing out on deck, gazing upwards at the helicopter. Now three. Now four. Now five. Stevie took a microphone from the instrument panel and flipped on the chopper's public address system.

"Attention!" she said, her voice booming, "This is the police! We are preparing to board your vessel!"

Sparky dropped the ladder and hovered lower, so that its bottom rung just grazed the deck of the yacht. Stevie looked at Lance.

"You want me to go down and get your wife, champ?" she shouted at Lance.

Lance looked down at the deck, which was pitching and tossing in the choppy water. Fortunately, fear of heights was not among his many neurotic afflictions.

"No!" yelled Lance, "I guess the gesture means nothing unless I do it myself!"

"You realize we can't permit you to do this, don't you?" yelled Stevie.

"I realize that!" yelled Lance.

"If you fall and break your neck or drown," shouted Sparky, "we'll say we never knew you!"

"I understand!" shouted Lance. "Well, here goes nothing!"

Lance crouched over the top rung of the ladder, still standing on the helicopter's cabin floor. Then he carefully turned around and put first one foot and then the other on the ladder, hanging on to the side of the chopper with all the strength in his hands. Sparky tried to keep the chopper hovering nearly motionless as Lance carefully descended the ladder. A brisk ocean breeze and the propwash from the helicopter's rotor sent the ladder swaying back and forth. Lance felt more exhilarated than frightened.

When he had almost reached the end of the ladder he turned around to face the people on the deck of the yacht. Firestone was closest to him, looking exceedingly piqued. If he had the pistol with him he wasn't showing it. Claire, Cathy and Howard stood a few steps back. They seemed utterly entranced.

"So, Firestone, we meet again," said Lance.

"W-what are you doing here, Lance?" said Howard.

"I have come for Cathy," said Lance. "I am taking her back to the mainland, and then we are going on the Concorde together to Paris for a romantic second honeymoon."

Nobody could come up with an appropriate response to this statement, and so nobody said anything.

"Well, Cathy?" said Lance. "Are you coming with me?"

Everybody turned to look at Cathy. This was surely what she wanted, he thought, and yet it was apparent from the expression on her face that a number of forces were tugging her in a number of conflicting directions. There was certainly rage at Lance. There was loyalty to Howard. There was intense desire to go to Paris. There was pity for Howard if she left him here. There was loyalty to her hosts. There was, conceivably, at some barely fathomable level, perhaps even *love* for Lance.

Howard, somehow sensing all of this, realizing how horrid it would be for him if his mistress consented to board a police helicopter and fly off to Paris with her estranged husband, took the only possible shot at winning—he capitulated.

"Cathy," said Howard, "I think you ought to go with Lance. You'll have a m-much better time and I'll manage fine without you, s-somehow."

Everyone on deck realized the brilliance of the move. Lance himself sensed that his own mother had never fired a more effective salvo of guilt.

"I think," said Cathy, "that my place is here with Howard."

Lance had underestimated his rival. Later he would go to pieces. Now he was desperate to save some kind of face.

"OK, Cathy," he said, "that's a noble and self-sacrificing decision."

The chopper hovered above. The deck of the yacht heaved up and down. The people on deck were in a state of suspended animation. It was still Lance's move. He smiled thinly and turned to Claire.

"How about you, Claire?" he said. "Care to fly with me to Paris?"

It was not a bad counter-move, but it was doomed to failure. There was no way that Claire could accept the offer under the circumstances.

"I think," said Claire, "that my place is here with Austin."

The time had come to leave. And still Lance lingered. He didn't know how to get out gracefully. He didn't realize that getting out gracefully was no longer an option. He looked at Howard.

"I think," said Howard, "that my p-place is here with Cathy. But th-thank you anyway."

Lance nodded, spun around, grabbed the ladder and began hauling himself up into the chopper. He was totally deflated, totally humiliated, totally demeaned.

He was definitely through with Cathy now—now and forever. He hoped he was going to be able to remember that.

73

Ever since his return from the ten-city tour Lance had been physically and emotionally depleted, and actively fighting off some gigantic physical collapse. Immediately following the fiasco with the thwarted helicopter rescue, he stopped fighting.

He went home and got into bed and had no further inclination to get up. His temples throbbed, his eyeballs ached, his throat burned, his nostrils flowed, his joints corroded and his temperature crawled up the thermometer.

He was a firm believer in the power of will to overcome disease or give in to it. He was fascinated by the placebo effect—the phenomenon which occurs when someone is told he is being given a certain medicine which is, in reality, only a sugar pill. The person's body reacts just as if it had actually been given the medicine it was told. What happens is that the body, not finding the chemicals in the bloodstream it expected to, goes ahead and manufactures them itself. If the body could do this, Lance believed, then it could either fight disease or succumb, depending on its particular emotional needs. There was little doubt in his mind that he now had an emotional need to fall ill, to get someone to take care of him.

Dorothy and Janie attended him, forced fluids down his throat, kept him warm, plied him with a ceaseless procession of medications. They checked daily with his internist by phone. They put hot compresses on his neck and cold ones on his eyes and forehead. They swabbed his flesh with alcohol. They spoon-fed him homemade chicken soup, albeit won-ton. Given how much attention we get for being sick, he thought, it's a minor miracle we are ever well.

Lance phased in and out of consciousness. He was frequently delerious and dreamed the half-mad dreams of the damned and the insane. He lost all track of time. And then, inevitably, the fever broke, the storm subsided. The attackers of his body spent themselves and withdrew.

He floated on a light, calm, peaceful plane. He was dizzy, weak, and had no desire to move. He opened his eyes and tried to see. His vision was blurred, but he could make out airy white shapes floating about him. Was this heaven or merely a hospital? He focused in on the airy white shapes and realized what they were: Dorothy and Janie. They were wearing white nylon nurses' uniforms! At first he was perplexed, and then he remembered telling Dorothy of a fantasy involving nurses. He smiled weakly up at them. He slept.

He awoke to a curious sensation. Slippery fingers kneaded his flesh. He opened his eyes. Dorothy and Janie, still in their nurses' uniforms, sat on either side of him, massaging moisturizing lotion into his skin. The bedclothes were drawn back. He was quite naked.

This had happened before, he was sure of it. On previous occasions he had barely been present to enjoy it. Today he was decidedly in attendance. As they gently and firmly manipulated his body, he began to get aroused. To his extreme embarrassment, his penis stiffened. What a cheap response to their therapeutic ministrations, he thought, but they didn't appear to be

insulted. Quite the contrary. They took it as evidence of his recovery. They were overjoyed. They hugged him. They kissed
him. They told him how worried they had been. Eventually, they
slipped out of their uniforms and lay with him under the covers.
He sensed what was happening. He knew it was illegal. He
supposed it was immoral. And he rationalized that he was too
weak to resist. Naked flesh lay against naked flesh. Soft fingers
probed nipples, hair and ticklish places. And soon they were
making love. To him and to each other. He didn't have to move,
they did it all. His feeling of exultation was so intense he knew
he was having a spiritual experience. If God appeared at the
climax and struck him dead it would have all been worth it.

But God did not appear, and he remained alive. The three of
them slept intertwined. He dreamed ecstatic dreams. They awoke
during the night and made love once more. It was less playful
this time, and deeper emotions were plumbed. When they once
more lay exhausted, they told him they were grateful. *They* were
grateful! *They!* Why? To find out they were still turned on by
men, they said.

They fell asleep in each other's arms again, but this time his
dreams were heavy with foreboding. He was in a strange long
room with a rounded ceiling. It was either a battlefield hospital
in a Quonset hut or in the inside of an airplane. Whatever it was,
he seemed to be in Holland. Through a window he could see a
windmill. Something small lay still beside him. He reached out to
touch it and found cold wetness. He opened his eyes and was
aghast—lying beside him on the hospital bed was a bloody, slimy
mess. He forced himself to inspect it and discovered it to be two
premature human fetuses joined at the back. Siamese twins.
Dead.

As he stared at the grisly sight, unable to shift his gaze, he
heard footfalls in the corridor outside his room, and then a long
shadow fell across the floor. He raised his eyes from the dead
fetuses and beheld a mammoth gorilla staring down at him,
reaching out for him. Terrified, he began to growl.

He awoke to the sound of his name being repeated over and
over again. Dorothy was holding him in her arms. Janie was
imploring him to wake up. They asked if he were all right. They

said he'd awakened them by growling. He apologized for scaring them. He tried to make a joke of it, but he knew it was nothing to joke about. He sensed it had something to do with the disaster he frequently feared was going to befall him, but now there seemed to be a difference. Not only was it coming toward him, he was meeting it halfway.

74

"What do you suppose those dead fetuses symbolized to you?" said Helen, who'd been inexplicably delighted by the dream.

"I don't know," said Lance. "What do you think?"

"What they symbolize to *me* might not be what they symbolize to *you*," said Helen. "I'd rather hear *your* associations on this."

"All right," said Lance. "Well, maybe the dead fetuses represented Dorothy and Janie somehow. Maybe the windmill and the fact that it was in Holland was a subconscious pun on the word 'dike.' "

"Sounds good to *me*," said Helen. "Tell me more."

"That's about all I can think of," said Lance.

"Then make it up," said Helen.

Lance shrugged.

"All right," he said. "The fetuses were dead because . . . well, maybe because of me. Maybe I killed them."

"Go on," said Helen.

"Do you think I killed them?" he said.

"It's not what *I* think, it's—"

"OK, OK," he said. "*I* think I killed them."

"Why do you think that?" said Helen.

"Because I had sex with them?"

"Are you asking me or telling me?"

"All right, because I had sex with them. They were . . . I don't know . . . they were too young to have sex, and so it killed them."

"What do you make of that gorilla?" said Helen.

"I don't know. Maybe he was going to kill me for what I did to the fetuses."

"Whom does the gorilla represent to you?"

"I don't know," he said.

"Make it up."

"All right. The gorilla represents . . . Daddy. Is that what you're thinking?"

"What *I'm* thinking doesn't matter. Is that what *you're* thinking?"

"Yeah. I guess so."

"So Daddy is going to kill you for having sex with Dorothy and Janie," she said.

"Yeah. Listen. Helen. Do you think I'm a monster for having sex with two teenaged girls?"

"No. Why do *you?*"

"I don't know. They're less than half my age. When they were born I was already twenty-three."

"And when you're seventy they'll be forty-seven. So what? Why do you think you're a monster? They certainly weren't innocent virgins—they're both very sensual, sexually sophisticated young women. And you didn't initiate the sex, *they* did."

"Wait a minute. Isn't that a direct contradiction to what you and the group were saying to me last time? About Gladys? About being raped?"

"Why is it a contradiction?" said Helen. "All we said was that you had to take some responsibility for having had sex with Gladys and for impregnating her. And so does *Gladys.* And you have to take some responsibility for fucking Dorothy and Janie. And so do Dorothy and Janie. Responsibility isn't *blame.* Responsibility is *responsibility.*"

"Mmmmmmm."

"The minute you take responsibility for what happens to you,"

Helen was saying, "You're in control of your life. The minute you stop, you're not."

"What if I should be flying in an airplane," said Lance, "and six wild geese fly into the engines and cause the plane to fall out of the sky? Would I have to take responsibility for that too?"

"You might not have to take responsibility for the six wild geese," said Helen. "You certainly would have to take responsibility for being on that plane, however."

75

The hundred-dollar-a-plate dinner for the Dalton Two was a huge success. The demand for tickets was so great that the event had to be moved from a good-sized dining hall on an upper story of the Seventh Regiment Armory to the much larger space on the Armory floor.

The affair was black tie. The day before the event, Blatt was able to get Ernest and Goose out on bail and into rented tuxedos that he paid for out of his own pocket. Ernest told Blatt he had written a short speech which he wanted to give at the banquet. Blatt read the speech and advised Ernest not to speak.

A dais had been set up at one end of the Armory floor. On it was the head table. Ernest and Goose sat together in the middle, flanked by Blatt on one side and the Mayor on the other.

Lance had recovered sufficiently from his illness to make good on his promise to escort Stevie to the dinner. At their table were a literary agent named Arthur Black, who confided to Lance that he had bought his tickets from a scalper for $250, and Ralph

Raitt, the homosexual movie critic from the *Daily News,* who had plaster casts on his right leg and his right arm. Raitt said he'd fallen down a flight of stairs that very day and broken his forearm and his shinbone, but he wouldn't have missed this dinner if they had had to wheel him in on a gurney.

Among the celebrities Stevie spotted at various tables on the floor were Barbara Walters, Flip Wilson, Mike Douglas, Jerry Lewis, Alan King, Jacqueline Onassis, Joe Papp, Henny Youngman, Andy Warhol, Sidney Poitier, Sidney Lumet, and Nipsy Russell. Camera crews from Channels 2, 4, 5, 7, 9 and 11 shot footage of Melvin Belli's opening remarks, of Blatt's brief introduction of Goose and Ernest, of Goose and Ernest refusing to be interviewed, and of John Denver singing a song called "Free the Dalton Two," which he had composed especially for the occasion. Stevie was in heaven.

At one point Blatt spotted Lance and tried to get him to move up to the head table. Stevie was all for it, but Lance begged off. Even attending the dinner at all, he felt, was lending the cause more of his support than he'd felt comfortable in lending.

76

Against his better judgment, Lance moved Dorothy and Janie into his bedroom, teddy bears and all. The conflicting feelings he had about such an arrangement were causing him to awake growling every two or three nights, but sleeping with them was so unbearably sweet that he was willing to risk the consequences.

Making love with two women brought up unfamiliar and tricky

feelings. The problem occurred not when the three of them were loving each other simultaneously—complex and acrobatic combinations weren't terribly hard to figure out. No, the trouble came when two of the three were active and the third was not. Grade-school children had a saying: three kids can't play together. The first time Dorothy and Janie fell into love play with each other without including him he didn't know what to do. It was exciting to watch, but it felt so lonely. He began to wonder stupid things: Do they like each other better than they like me? Can they satisfy each other better than I can because they know what feels good better than a man does?

Fortunately for him, he was secure enough to snap himself out of it. But then it came up in another combination. Although he had always had a stronger affection for Dorothy, he found himself one night concentrating on Janie. The two of them got deeper and deeper into each other until they had totally forgotten about Dorothy. At the height of their passion they reached out for Dorothy to include her and they didn't find her. They stopped and looked around. Dorothy was gone. They got up instantly and began to search for her.

They found her upstairs, lying face down on her old sleeping bag, sobbing.

"Dorothy, what's wrong?" said Lance.

Dorothy shook her head.

"What is it, baby?" said Janie, taking her in her arms.

"I just started feeling left out," said Dorothy.

They both hugged her, feeling awful.

"The other day we were all making love," said Lance, "and you and Janie seemed to forget I was there. *I* felt left out for a while too."

"I felt like the two of you had forgotten about me," said Dorothy. "I felt like I was losing both of you. To each other."

"That's crazy," said Janie, covering Dorothy's face with kisses.

"I know it's crazy," said Dorothy. "That's just how it felt. It was like I was suddenly the little girl and the two of you were my parents—like you'd both been telling me in private I was your favorite, and then I saw you together making love, and I realized I wasn't."

They all went back down to bed together. Having a romantic relationship with two other people, Lance thought, was geometrically more difficult than with one. They were going to have to try to maintain an exquisite sort of balance. He felt they had displayed adequate sensitivity this time—realizing Dorothy was gone and rushing to find her and reassure her. But he didn't know how long such a delicate thing could last.

In the morning Lance suggested that Dorothy and Janie hire a moving company and move all of their things out of their parents' apartments into his. Both girls were delighted. Dorothy said she knew the perfect company to do the job—a group of women who called themselves the Motherloaders. Lance said it was the Seven Santini Brothers or nothing. Dorothy and Janie wondered at the vehemence of his response.

77

The experience with the non-rapists in the subway station had proven oddly satisfying for June, Alix, Sandy and Wanda.

No longer confining themselves to the hunting and castrating of Wanda's rapist alone, the group now addressed itself to rapists in general and began roaming Central Park late at night, looking for them. Disguised as elderly ladies—for elderly ladies were, oddly enough, sexually attacked as frequently as younger ones —they patrolled with pinking shears. Once more they met with initial failure. They saw no rapists. They saw drunken vagrants. They saw large bands of teenaged muggers. They saw numerous old ladies, little knowing or caring that these were decoy policemen. They were once more growing restless. June toyed with the possibility of taking on a band of teenaged muggers just to relieve the monotony. They fretted that rape might be going out of style. And then, one night, success.

Shortly after midnight, they heard a woman's screams coming from deep inside a viaduct. They raced down an embankment, their hunters' blood pulsing warmly in their throats, and plunged into the viaduct. On the pavement lay a young Hispanic woman, her skirt torn half off her body, a young Hispanic man with his jeans at his knees about to thrust himself between her legs.

With shrieks of glee, June, Alix, Sandy and Wanda threw themselves at the rapist. The young Hispanic woman, hearing the shrieks of her deliverers and glimpsing their bared pinking shears, feared that worse things than rape were about to befall her and screamed the louder. Sandy and Alix pinned the amazed rapist to the ground, as June took his testicles in hand and deftly snipped them off.

The ensuing blood was more than June had counted on. Perversely, the rapist survived. His intended victim, stupefied by his spilled blood, almost did not. Paramedics, summoned by a worried MATE, swiftly transported both rapist and would-be victim to Bellevue. The young Hispanic woman was released two days after the man. June, Sandy, Alix and Wanda went to see the woman in her dreary East Harlem apartment to try to comfort her. When they told her who they were, she came at them with a machete.

The account of the castrating received scant attention in the media until MATE sent an open letter to the *New York Times*, claiming credit for the crime. In the letter the members of MATE deplored the act of rape, reviled rapists, took a healthy swipe at male chauvinists everywhere, and identified themselves as the commandos of the women's movement. So many outraged letters from feminists poured in to the paper that the *Times* featured an entire page of them. The National Organization of Women publicly dissociated itself from MATE and claimed no knowledge of its activities. The Rape Crisis Center in Cleveland said that with friends like MATE they needed no enemies.

June, Alix, Sandy and Wanda were quite hurt at the response

of their sisters in the women's movement. They stopped dressing up as old ladies and roaming Central Park. They decided to focus their energies on less militant pursuits for a while.

They decided to radicalize nurses, stewardesses, waitresses, Vegas showgirls and topless dancers. They sent a test mailing of hundreds of mimeographed letters to nurses at several city hospitals, including Bellevue, St. Vincent's, Mount Sinai, New York Hospital and Doctors Hospital. They said that for too long nurses had passively stood by and let male chauvinist doctors rape them in spirit if not in body. They said that the time had come for this to stop, that old sex roles had to be reversed, that nurses had to begin getting as much respect and as much pay as doctors, and that if the nurses weren't willing to be part of the solution then they were part of the problem. The members of MATE asked to meet with representatives of nurses' groups to assist in radicalizing them. The representatives of the nurses' groups told the members of MATE to screw themselves.

June, Alix, Sandy and Wanda were quite offended at the responses of their sisters in the nursing profession. They issued a public statement that nurses were all Uncle Toms and Aunt Tessies and deserved what they got. They turned their attention to stewardesses.

They sent a test mailing of hundreds of mimeographed letters to stewardesses at several airlines, including TWA, American, Eastern, Delta and Pan Am. They said that for too long female flight attendants had passively stood by and let male chauvinist pilots and co-pilots and navigators rape them in spirit if not in body. They said that the time had come for this to stop, that the old sex roles had to be reversed, that female flight attendants had to begin getting as much respect and as much pay as pilots and co-pilots and navigators, and that if the female flight attendants weren't part of the solution then they were part of the problem. The members of MATE asked to meet with representatives of the female flight attendants' groups to assist in radicalizing them. The representatives of the female flight attendants' groups told the members of MATE to take a flying fuck at a rolling doughnut.

June, Alix, Sandy and Wanda were quite offended at the responses of their sisters in the female flight attending profession. They issued a public statement that female flight attendants were all Uncle Toms and Aunt Tessies and deserved what they got.

But instead of turning their attention to waitresses, Vegas showgirls and topless dancers, they decided to make a stand in the commercial airline business and dramatize their political views. They decided to create a media event which would get even more attention than the castrating of the rapist. They decided to hijack a jetliner and fly it to someplace that would be politically and promotionally appropriate. After considerable research and debate, they selected as their destination a remote island in the Pacific called Mannihanni, an island which Margaret Mead had once referred to as a society where women ruled and where men were second-class citizens.

78

Lance had never been sure during his seven-year marriage to Cathy whether or not he wished to have a child with her. He was absolutely certain now that he did not wish to have a child with Gladys Oliphant. He did not know how serious she was about going through with the pregnancy. Who knew for sure if she was really pregnant?

He finally reached Gladys by phone and suggested that they get together for a talk. She was delighted and suggested that they talk at Elaine's. She was anxious to get to know some of her fellow writers, she said, and she was eager to see one of the many celebrity fistfights she had read went on there.

Lance assured her that reports of celebrity fistfights were vastly exaggerated, but said that Elaine's was not the sort of quiet spot he'd had in mind for their discussion. Although this was not untrue, what was truer yet was that Lance was not overeager to show up at a place as visible as Elaine's with a two-hundred-forty-pound date in tow. It was the sort of thing that could get around town and give him a bad reputation.

Gladys said it was Elaine's or nothing. Lance decided he couldn't afford not to discuss Gladys's pregnancy and relented. He arranged to meet her that evening at Elaine's at six-thirty. He figured they could probably drink and eat and have their discussion and be out of there before ten when the regulars started showing up. Gladys asked whether six-thirty wasn't a wee bit early, and Lance assured her that six-thirty was the choicest time at Elaine's.

Gladys was a half hour late. Lance sat down at a table and ordered a bottle of Verdicchio. When she waddled in, Lance was talking to one of the waiters. He hailed her to his table and helped her into a chair. She was wearing a flowered rayon dress and had obviously gone to a lot of trouble with her hair and makeup. Lance felt mean, small and relieved to have tricked her into coming so early.

Gladys looked around at the near-empty restaurant.

"Where *is* everybody?" she said.

"It's a slow night," said Lance. "You never know what are going to be the slow nights and what are going to be the ones when it's packed to the rafters with celebrities."

"Oh," said Gladys, her face falling about three chins. "I wish I had known beforehand. I was expecting to see a lot of famous writers."

"Well," said Lance, "that's the funny thing about this place. An evening may start out slow, like it is now, and then, suddenly, in come thirty or forty people and all at once things are happening. That's what may happen tonight."

"I doubt it," said Gladys, dubiously looking over the half dozen diners spread out across the room. "Who are those people? Are they anybody?"

Lance looked over the six people in the restaurant. Four of

them were complete strangers and two of them he'd seen before but didn't know who they were. He didn't have the heart to give her so depressing a report. He leaned in close and said out of the corner of his mouth:

"Don't look at him now, but the little guy at the table in the back is a very interesting character."

Without moving her head, Gladys slid her eyes in the direction he had indicated.

"What's his name?" she whispered.

"He goes by many names," said Lance. "You wouldn't have heard of any of them. He's a double agent for the DIA."

"The what?" she whispered.

"The Defense Intelligence Agency. He works for them and he also works for the KGB, but each of them thinks he's loyal to *them*."

"Who is he loyal to?" she whispered.

Lance shrugged.

"He himself isn't sure any longer," he said. "He's decided to write his memoirs and quit. When his book appears, he's going to have his looks altered by a plastic surgeon."

"Wow," she said. "Who else is here?"

"The rather plain-looking woman with the dishwater-blond hair two tables over?" said Lance.

Gladys slid her eyeballs in the opposite direction.

"Yeah?" she said.

"Her name is Letitia Loring," said Lance. "Big society dame. A second cousin to the Hearsts. She's an editor at Viking. She's been living with her brother for eight years."

"I don't understand," said Gladys.

Lance raised his eyebrows.

"What do you mean?" she said. "Are you saying they're . . . ?"

Lance nodded.

"They're having an . . . *affair?*" she said.

"*I* didn't say it, *you* did," said Lance.

Gladys turned around and stared at the woman.

"Ssssstt," said Lance, "don't do that. They don't think anybody knows."

"Is that her brother she's with?" said Gladys.

Lance nodded.

"They don't look very similar," she said.

"One favors the mother, one the father," said Lance. "They're brother and sister, though, don't you worry."

"Wow," said Gladys.

"Let's talk about pregnancy now," said Lance, feeling he had placated her somewhat.

Gladys looked down at the tablecloth.

"Not yet," she said.

"You want to have something to drink first?" he said.

She nodded. He poured her a glass of Verdicchio and nodded to the waiter. The waiter came over and ran down the litany of specials. Gladys wanted to order one of everything, but Lance suggested she start with the stuffed mushrooms, the *paglia e fieno*, an arugula salad and a veal chop, then see how she felt. He himself ordered only a spinach salad.

When the food came she went through it all in the time it took Lance to eat his salad.

"This is nice," she said, "but it wasn't really what I thought it would be like."

"It'll pick up," he said. "I can feel it in my bones."

He finished his last glass of wine and ordered another bottle. He was feeling guiltier and guiltier as the time passed. What would the big deal have been to come later when the regulars were here? Was he so insecure he couldn't bear to be seen with an enormous fat woman? Was he truly afraid people would think he and she were an item? Why couldn't he see past his own petty insecurities and do something generous once in a while?

"I thought I'd see Woody Allen at least," said Gladys sadly. "I thought I'd see Jackie Onassis and Norman Mailer. I thought I'd see at least one fight and Elaine would have to throw people out on the street and Ron Galella would photograph them."

"It's not like that here," said Lance. "You've heard gross exaggerations of what goes on."

The door opened and four short balding men came in. Lance recognized two of them as agents at William Morris. They were seated next to the alleged incestuous socialites.

"You see those four guys who just came in?" Lance whispered.

Gladys turned to look.

"Yeah?" she said.

"They're agents at William Morris," he said.

She seemed let down.

"Is that all?" she said.

"What do you mean 'is that all?' " he said. "These four guys happen to practically run half of Hollywood between them."

"Yeah?" she said. "Name some of their clients."

"Well," said Lance, trying to think of names she might be impressed by, "they represent Ryan O'Neal and . . . Barbra Streisand and . . ."

"Ryan O'Neal is a client of ICM," she said.

"Look," he said, "I don't know who their clients are. I just know they're big. If you don't believe me, you don't have to."

"I'm sorry," she said and put her hand over his on the table. "That wasn't polite."

Oh God, he thought, don't be nice to me.

He drank another glass of wine and once more tried to get her to talk of her pregnancy, but still she hesitated. Perhaps if she saw one legitimate celebrity she might give in and speak about the fetus she was carrying and about why she had indicated to him that she intended to have the baby.

The idea of fathering a baby was, had always been, more than he could deal with emotionally. He was attracted and he was repelled. Attracted by the notion of co-creating a little human being and watching it develop the ability to communicate and show affection and absorb learning and go on to be a little Lance in one form or another—someone to whom he could give the benefit of his forty years of greater and lesser mistakes, someone who would perhaps carry on his name and spirit after he died. Someone who . . . well, but then there were the fears.

The fear of having conceived a monster, a grotesquely disfigured baby who was either physically or mentally crippled, crippled enough to ruin the rest of his life while he brought it up and tried to pretend to be leading a normal life with it, and not crippled enough to languish and die mercifully in the hospital. The fear of having conceived a normal child and having it eat up so much of his working and leisure time that it totally transformed his life into an appendage of the child's and not his own. The fear of having conceived a child as thankless and insensitive to its parents as he often imagined he was to his own. The fear of—

"A penny for your thoughts," she said.

He realized suddenly that Gladys's hand was once more covering his and that she was gazing directly, if a bit drunkenly, into his eyes. Who besides Gladys, he thought, still used an expression like "A penny for your thoughts"? He must not have spoken for quite a while.

"I'm sorry," he said. "I was just thinking about your being pregnant. Can't we discuss it now?"

"Soon," she said. "But first I want to see what there is to see here."

He looked around. More people had drifted in. It was now nearly nine o'clock. Lance had drunk enough not to care particularly who saw him and Gladys together. The table of William Morris agents had obviously had a lot to drink. They were getting loud and boisterous. Elaine appeared, and walked over to their table and told them to keep it down. They were too scared of her to answer back while she was at the table, but when she turned her back and walked away one of them gave her the finger. She spun around, like a grade-school teacher who had convinced her students she had eyes in the back of her head, and glared at them. Not one of them could meet her gaze.

Lance told Gladys that, although he was not a regular at Elaine's, he loved the idea that there was one restaurant in New York where writers were given special treatment. He told Gladys how Elaine had kept powerful people like Henry Ford III waiting at the bar for over an hour while seating her writers. He told how Elaine allegedly shifted some of the food and bar charges off the checks of her down-and-out writers and onto the checks of wealthy socialites who wouldn't know the difference.

Gladys loved the stories as much as Lance had when they had been new to him. He encouraged her to tell him about herself. She told him about her writing, about her hopes of being the next Barbara Cartland. About her tenants in the building, about Stevie Petrocelli. About Gladys's dismal history with men, about her rape by the Indians, about what it had meant to her to have made love to somebody as famous as Lance Lerner.

Extravagant praise and large amounts of wine combined to produce a warm, runny center. He found himself feeling very mellow toward old Gladys. He ordered another bottle of Verdicchio.

Shortly after ten, three agents from ICM came into the restaurant and were given a table adjacent to the agents from William Morris. The William Morris people had got considerably louder and were now hurling innuendoes at the ICM table. Lance glared in their direction. This appeared to incense the shortest of the William Morris agents.

"Why don't you keep your eyes on your cow?" he called to Lance.

"Why don't I *what?*" said Lance, instantly furious at the insult to Gladys and simultaneously horrified that people thought she was as obese as he had feared.

"*You* heard me!" retorted the fearfully short agent. "Why don't you get a pail and a stool and *milk* her?"

Lance sprang out of his seat and grabbed the tiny man by the front of his shirt and pulled him out of his chair. All the William Morris and ICM agents stood up and pressed forward.

"Are you going to take that back," said Lance, "or am I going to have to pound you into the ground and make you even shorter?"

In reply the diminutive drunk threw a haymaker at Lance's head. Lance ducked and the punch hit the closest ICM agent in the glasses. Instantly, the ICM man punched back, and before one knew it, eight men were trading punches.

Elaine waded into the midst of the fracas and began bum's-rushing agents out of the restaurant with awesome speed. Gladys stared, slack-jawed and delighted—this was what she had *known* Elaine's was like. This was what she had come to see. Gladys was not even dismayed when, over Lance's protestations of innocence, Elaine bum's-rushed *him* out of the restaurant and Gladys had to follow him out onto the street. And Gladys was the only person who was not surprised when Ron Galella *did* appear, and snapped photographs of Elaine wielding a barstool like a lion tamer and at least one shot of Gladys with her arms around her defender.

When the evening's entertainment was at last concluded, Lance took Gladys back to her apartment. He wanted to clean up, and they had still not discussed her pregnancy, and so he accepted her invitation for a nightcap and went inside.

Once they were both settled on her couch with glasses of Kahlua, Lance again approached the topic. Unexpectedly, Gladys began weeping uncontrollably.

"Gladys," he said, "what is it?"

She continued weeping, shaking now with sobs, till he worried about her well-being.

"I l-lost it," she said at last, between sobs.

"You what?" he said. He thought he'd heard her say she lost it, but that didn't make sense.

"M-miscarriage," she blurted, "I had a m-miscarriage . . . I thought if I t-told you, you wouldn't . . . go out with me."

So she wasn't pregnant! It was a relief, to be sure, but not, somehow, the precise emotional release he would have thought it to be. He tried to comfort her, and, to his utter astonishment, he began to be rocked by waves of grief for his now dead unborn child. To his even greater astonishment, he soon found himself sobbing as earnestly as Gladys.

They clung together in attempts at mutual consolation. He experienced a rush of overpoweringly sweet feeling for this gigantic woman who had briefly borne his child. He began to kiss her and hug her and, to his further amazement, he soon found himself drunkenly undressing her and making love to her. This time he wisely chose to be on top.

79

Lance arrived home from his date with Gladys at close to five a.m. He let himself into the apartment, conscientiously trying to be as quiet as he could so as not to wake Dorothy or Janie.

He undressed outside the bedroom door, then slipped inside and made it to the bed before the light was snapped on.

There sat Dorothy and Janie, wearing their pajamas and staring at him with frigid fury.

"Where *were* you?" said Dorothy.

"We were worried *sick* about you," said Janie.

"You were?" said Lance.

It had truthfully never occurred to him that Dorothy or Janie would miss him if he stayed away all night.

"I called all the hospitals," said Dorothy.

"I called the morgue," said Janie. "We thought you had been killed by a mugger or hit by a *cab* or something."

"God, I'm sorry," said Lance. "I was out with Gladys."

"Till five a.m.?" said Dorothy.

"Hey, c'mon," said Lance, trying to jolly them a little, "you guys sound like I'm the teenager and you're my parents."

Neither one of them smiled. They were right, of course. It was typical of him that he forgot that other people had feelings too. He was not tremendously proud of himself.

"You're right," he said quietly. "I was very inconsiderate and unfeeling. I should have called you or something to let you know."

"You certainly should have," said Janie.

"I'm truly sorry. And I'll try not to have it happen again, OK?"
Eventually, somewhat grudgingly, they accepted his apology.
By the time the sun came up they were even cuddling together
again under the covers.

80

Dorothy Chu was jumping out of her skin.

Hijacking a jetliner was going to be more fun than anything
any of them had ever done before, they could see that. Every
night after they got done working at Motherloaders they would
go over to June's apartment and plot and discuss what they had
learned.

The atlases said that Mannihanni was roughly the size of Staten
Island. Its principal town was Port Pangaud on its northeastern
tip. The total population numbered scarcely more than 15,000
women—Mannihanni didn't count its men. Mannihanni had
been a French possession till 1945, when native guerrillas effi-
ciently overthrew the small cadre of French officials who ruled it.
The coup was as bloody as it was swift. The slaughtered French
officials were decapitated, dismembered and put on display in
the main square in Port Pangaud. All the guerrillas had been
women. Shortly after the coup, France—which had no interest
whatsoever in sending troops to deal with crazed guerrillas on a
worthless island—officially granted independence to Mannihanni.

The revolution had been led by a tall, handsome, fiery young
black woman named Josephine Taillevent. Shortly after the coup,
Taillevent went to the United States and studied at UCLA, apparently earning her Ph.D. in philosophy before she returned to

Mannihanni. Following her return, Dr. Taillevent—nicknamed "Mamma Doc" by her proud subjects—declared herself President-for-Life and had ruled since that time.

According to the atlases, the island's women ran the principal industries—sugar cane, rum, bananas, coconuts, coca, copra, jute, hemp and woven textiles—while the men stayed home, raised the children, and did the housework. In 1962, a huge repository of natural gas, some thirty million cubic feet of it, was discovered under the Presidential Palace in Port Pangaud. At this point, the United States, Russia, China and Japan began courting the Mannihannis, but Mamma Doc refused to recognize their diplomatic delegations because all their ambassadors were males. Males, in the opinion of Mamma Doc and her cabinet, were inferior to females and therefore unacceptable as diplomatic emissaries.

In 1969, a group of disgruntled Mannihanni househusbands stormed the Presidential Palace and tried to oust Mamma Doc. Several of the male insurgents were killed and publicly decapitated. The others escaped to Honolulu, where they were living as exiles. Since 1969, Mamma Doc had surrounded herself with a fanatically loyal group of armed female guards patterned loosely on Papa Doc Duvalier's Haitian *Tonton Macoutes*.

June, Alix, Sandy and Wanda scrutinized the location of Mannihanni on their maps. It lay south and slightly east of Honolulu. It was approximately as far west of Los Angeles as Los Angeles was from New York.

June said that hijacking the plane in Los Angeles made a helluva lot more sense than hijacking it in New York, but Alix said why should they have to pay for four tickets from New York to LA when they could just as easily hijack the damned plane out of JFK and save themselves some bread.

June said that if they hijacked it out of New York then they would have to stop somewhere around LA to refuel, which left them very vulnerable to any number of cute tricks on the part of the police, like recapturing the plane while they were refueling.

Wanda said that once they got to Mannihanni they might suggest to Mamma Doc that the four air fares they paid from New York to LA could be reimbursed to them.

They all agreed they would give notice to Motherloaders at the end of the week and then move to Los Angeles to begin planning the hijack.

81

His group ate up the latest developments in Lance's love life like miniature Reese's Peanut Butter Cups. They generally approved of his determined, if failed, attempt to take Cathy back with him on the helicopter. They heartily approved of his ending the affair with Claire in the decisive way he'd done it. They supposed they approved of his going to bed with Gladys again, since it had been his choice and since he was taking responsibility for it and not copping out by saying he had only done it because he was drunk —although that was actually the truth.

When it came to telling them about Dorothy and Janie, though, things got sticky. They all groaned and made faces when he told them how the girls had seduced him when he was weak from his illness, and although he maintained he took responsibility for it, they said he was just saying that so the group wouldn't jump on him. They were especially tough on him for staying out all night with Gladys and making Dorothy and Janie worry.

He was sorry he'd told them anything at all. It was clear they took anybody's side but his. He suspected they were jealous of his affair with the teenagers and couldn't admit it.

"I don't think you are in touch with your feelings," said Helen, "particularly your feelings about women. If you can't get in touch with the anger you feel towards them, then how are you ever going to get in touch with the love?"

"But I *am* in touch with the love," said Lance. "I'm in touch with the anger too—where it's appropriate, that is. I mean I'm sort of angry at Claire, and I'm sort of angry at Cathy, and I'm sort of—"

" '*Sort* of' isn't angry," said Laura. " '*Sort* of' isn't more than mildly annoyed. Why don't you tell us how you *really* feel?"

"How I really feel?" said Lance, beginning to get deeply annoyed. "I'll tell you how I really feel. I really feel like you are driving me *crazy*, that's how I feel."

"Who's driving you crazy?" said Laura.

"*You*, for one," said Lance.

"Who *else*?" said Helen.

"You too, goddammit!" said Lance, heating up fast.

"And who else?" said Jackie.

"*You*, you stupid cocksucker!" said Lance.

Arnold clapped his hands for joy.

"Shut up, asshole!" yelled Lance at Arnold.

"Why me?" said Jackie.

"Because not only are you an asshole," said Lance, "but you're Jewish as well, and you make non-Jews think all Jews are as big an asshole as *you* are!"

"I'm not Jewish," said Jackie. "I'm Episcopalian."

"Fuck you," said Lance.

"He's telling the truth, Lance," said Roger. "Jackie *is* Episcopalian."

"Then how come you use so many Yiddish words, asshole?" said Lance, sure they were putting him on.

"I'm a comedian," said Jackie. "You're a chef, you learn French. You're a comedian, you learn Yiddish."

"We're getting off the track here," said Helen. "I don't want to lose the wonderful feelings of anger that Lance was beginning to get to."

Lance turned to Helen.

"Is Jackie Jewish or Episcopalian?" he demanded.

"Episcopalian," she said. "But I don't want to—"

"How long has he been Episcopalian?" Lance interrupted.

"All his life," said Helen. "But I want to return to the feelings of anger you were beginning to get in touch with before—"

Lance wheeled on Jackie.

"Whatever church you worship in, Jackie," he snapped, "you're still an asshole!"

"Thanks, shmuck," said Jackie.

"Let's hear more anger," called Laura.

"Shut the fuck up with that!" said Lance. "Don't tell me how the fuck to feel!"

"Way to go!" cheered Roger.

"I said shut *up!*" shouted Lance. "Shut up, shut up, *shut up!* You are all driving me fucking bananas! I am sick and tired of you!"

"Who besides us?" said Helen

"*Everybody!* Cathy, Claire, Gladys, Dorothy, Janie—*everybody!* What the fuck do they want from me, for Christ's sake?" he shouted. *"What the fuck do women want?"*

The group was momentarily paralyzed by his outburst. Lance's face was flushed, his breathing ragged.

"Forget what *women* want—what do *you* want?" said Helen.

"I want women to *leave me the fuck alone!*" Lance screamed at the top of his lungs.

"Why?" Helen demanded.

"Because I hate their fucking guts!"

Everybody in the group broke into spontaneous applause. Lance looked at them as though they were inmates in an insane asylum.

"What the fuck is going on here?" he said, breathing hard. "I tell you I hate you and you *applaud?*"

"Sure," said Laura. "Because now we know where we stand with you, you fuck!"

"Huh?" said Lance.

"You finally trusted us enough to show us your true feelings," said Helen.

Lance frowned and shook his head, totally baffled.

"Before you never showed us the feelings you claimed to have," said Helen. "Now you did. My guess is that you were *afraid* to show us your anger before. You were afraid it would kill us, or maybe that we would kill *you* for being so angry. But you see— you didn't kill *us,* and we didn't kill *you.* We don't even hate you for it."

Lance let out a long, exasperated sigh.

"Are you still so angry?" said Helen gently.

Lance shook his head.

"I guess not," he said.

"Why not?" said Helen.

"I guess it just boiled over and went away," he said.

Helen smiled.

"And what do you feel in place of your anger?" she prodded.

Lance shrugged.

"I guess relief," he said.

"I would suggest," said Helen, "that rather than continue asking what women want, you find out where that rage you have against them comes from and discover a way to release it."

"All right," said Lance, "I'll do that. I'll change. I'll become a whole new person."

"Don't tell me you're going to change," said Helen. "Tell me what you're getting out of what you're doing now, tell me what the payoff is in what you're doing now, or else you don't have a *prayer* of changing."

82

Lance thought over what he had said in the group about hating women. At the time he had really felt he did. Now he didn't. Collectively, he liked them a whole lot better now. Individually, he disliked them more, though. The more he'd seen of women in his life, the less he understood what it was they wanted, or, for that matter, what *he* wanted from *them*. He loved women, but they were, without a doubt, one of the biggest pains in the ass that God in His infinite wisdom had ever created.

In the years before he met Cathy and began living with her, dating women was a relatively uncomplicated matter. You took a woman out to dinner, to a movie or a play or a concert, and there was never any question but that you paid all her expenses. The tacit understanding was that, in exchange for doing this you eventually earned the right to try to coax her into some sexual or presexual activity. It was always understood that women had to be coaxed because sexual activities were somewhat distasteful to them.

It took Lance nearly twenty years to find out that it had all been pretense: women liked sex just as much as men did—possibly even *more* than men. And yet they still expected to have men pay for their dinners, their shows, and so on—and, for some reason, he had gone along with it. Just before he met Cathy, Lance had had a fairly intense relationship with a young woman who designed textiles and made quite a bit more money than Lance did, yet there was never any question that he'd pick up the checks. (In truth, he probably would have felt resentful if she had, but that was another story.)

One of the things that Lance was most annoyed about was that women were always demanding to be his equal in every way, and yet they still expected him to take care of them and be their protector. That, thought Lance, was trying to eat your cake and have it too.

Like men, women had a double standard of their own. They wanted to be able to let down their hair with a man and cry on his shoulder and be vulnerable. But if a man cried on *their* shoulder, or cried on it more than, say, once every twelve years—yiccchhhh! Who could stand a man who was a sniveling crybaby!

Shortly before Lance met Cathy there was a period in which he found himself telephoning women for dinner dates for the same evening, never more than two hours in advance. They all seemed genuinely sorry they'd made other plans that night, and all of them asked for rain checks. Lance never suggested alternative dates and became more and more furious at his seeming inability to get dates for dinner. It now occurred to him: the purpose of these calls was not to get dates for dinner, the purpose was to get more reasons to be mad at women.

Because of his anger at women Lance had invested an awful lot of energy since puberty in keeping them at arm's length, starting with his mother and continuing right on through his marriage to Cathy. He hadn't been aware of doing it at a conscious level most of the time, but he had done it nonetheless. Exactly why he felt the need to do it was hard to say.

There was certainly something in what Helen had said about the fear of intimacy. The way from the onset of adolescence he had begun to squirm whenever his mother tried to hug him was not unlike the way he sometimes began to squirm when Cathy tried to hug him. There was something about being that close that sometimes simply gave him the willies.

Perhaps it *was* what Helen said it was—the incest taboo. Perhaps, he thought, we are so conditioned never to lust after Mom or Sis or anybody else we live with that , once we get married and get into a familiar homey rut with a wife, there is some ancient sensing device which detects that we are getting too chummy with a member of the family and begins to send out warnings. Perhaps that's why sex with somebody outside the home is so much more exciting as a prospect—at least until it gets familiar and chummy and homey and that person begins looking like a member of the family too.

It was likely, Lance thought, that he had, at some level of consciousness, been avoiding intimacy with Cathy and other women all his adult life. Certainly that had been one function of his workaholic writing habits. If you were continually wrapped up in your work and were staying up till all hours to do it, there was a lot less opportunity to succumb to temptation and get involved in sexual activities that had been forbidden since childhood.

But perhaps the incest taboo was not the only reason to squirm away from closeness. There was a further fear. The fear that, if you were to let a woman get close to you, really really close to you, you might get hurt. She might tire of you and leave. "You think, if somebody left you once and you survived," Helen had said to him, "that the way you survive is to get somebody to leave you."

In the love affair all little boys have with their mothers, their mothers are continually leaving them for their fathers, and usually the little boys survive. Perhaps from the time that he was a little boy and his mother continually left him for his father and he survived, he had at some level indeed figured out that the way he got to survive was to get somebody to leave him. Perhaps that was, at bottom, why he managed to get Cathy to leave him—so he could survive.

There was another thing that Helen had said to him which, at the time, he'd not been able to appreciate: "All little boys are angry at their mothers for preferring their fathers," she said. "So staying angry at all women is a way of making all women your mother." It probably also followed that making all women your mother was a dandy way to avoid growing up. He had always recognized within himself a deep-seated fear of growing up. Growing up meant taking care of yourself. Growing up meant bringing yourself closer to dying.

"I have this great fear of this *normal* thing," said John Lennon early in 1975. "I don't want to grow up, but I'm sick of *not* growing up." Lennon had been separated from Yoko Ono for about a year at this point, bouncing from bed to bed, desperately avoiding anything that resembled normalcy, and doing his best not to grow up. At the end of the year Lennon returned to Yoko Ono, announcing, "The separation didn't work out," and immersed himself in grown-up and relatively normal things.

Perhaps Lance, too, didn't want to grow up but, like John Lennon, he was sick of *not* growing up. Perhaps Lance's separation hadn't worked out any better than had John Lennon's.

Getting his rage out in the group had somehow enabled Lance to get a lot clearer about his feelings for Cathy. He knew, in fact, exactly what he wanted to do about her now.

He asked his lawyer to begin divorce proceedings. His lawyer asked him if that was what he really wanted to do. Lance said it was what he really wanted to do, and to cut the shit. Lance's lawyer gave him the name of a fellow who specialized in divorce cases. Lance went to see the fellow that very afternoon. Lance said he wanted a divorce as quickly as possible. The divorce fellow said that he appreciated Lance's feelings, but that in New

York State you had to have a cooling-off period, a year of legal separation, before you could obtain a divorce.

"Couldn't one simply go to Haiti or the Dominican Republic?" said Lance.

"One certainly could go to Haiti or the Dominican Republic," said the divorce fellow.

"And would the divorce be legal and everything?" said Lance.

"It would be legal in Haiti or the Dominican Republic," said the divorce fellow, smiling.

It seemed there was a difference between a cheap quickie divorce that might wear off and an expensive, excruciatingly long divorce that would last forever. Lance had always admired longevity in the things he bought. He told the divorce fellow to write him up an order for one of the latter.

83

Within one hour of Lance's arrival back at his apartment the doorbell rang. He buzzed, thinking it was Dorothy or Janie. He was eager to tell them of his decision.

It was not Dorothy or Janie. It was Cathy.

"Holy shit," said Lance when he saw her.

She did not look well.

"Hi, Lance," she said. "Can I come in?"

What the hell was Cathy doing here—today of all days?

"Sure," he said. "C'mon in."

She came in and looked around.

"Any unclad females about?" she asked.

Lance shook his head.

"I just got back," she said. "From the cruise."

"I see," he said. "And how did it go?"

There was a short pause.

"Not bad," she said. "Everybody enjoyed themselves."

"Good," said Lance. "I'm so pleased."

There was a longer pause.

"Shall I tell you how the cruise went *really?*" she said at last.

"I thought you already did," said Lance.

Cathy shook her head.

"It was a disaster," she said. "A nightmare. The absolute pits."

"What happened?" said Lance, secretly delighted.

"What didn't?" said Cathy. "Engine trouble. Stomach trouble. Terrible storms at sea. Horrendous *mal de mer*. We tossed more cookies out there than Famous Amos. By the third day nobody was speaking. When we landed in the Bahamas, Austin went ashore and flew to London. Claire went ashore and ran off with a beach boy. I stayed in my cabin and puked my guts out and had the runs for days on end."

"And Howard?" said Lance.

"Howard went ashore to buy native knickknacks and was mugged. He lost over three hundred dollars in cash, all his credit cards, his watch and his belt and shoes."

Lance burst out laughing.

"I'm sorry," he said, "but I don't harbor a lot of affection for old Howard."

"I don't blame you," said Cathy. "Howard probably had the worst time of all. He got into a terrible tiff with Austin on the second day. Austin called him a—what was it he called him now? —'a supercilious prig,' I think, and Howard resigned."

"Howard quit his job at the publishing house?" said Lance.

Cathy nodded.

"He said he was sick of the business anyway," she said. "He has this novel he has always wanted to write, so that's what he's going to do instead."

"How about that!" said Lance, relishing the prospect of Howard's having to put up with the same shit from *his* editor that Lance had had to put up with from Howard.

"He's not a bad guy really," said Cathy, "no matter what you think of him. Although what Austin said about him is certainly true."

" 'Supercilious prig,' you mean?" said Lance, surprised.

Cathy nodded.

"I broke up with Howard on about the third day," she said. "I'm glad I did it then."

"How do you mean?" said Lance.

"I never could have done that to him after the mugging," she said.

"That's typical," he said.

"What's probably also typical," she said, "was my not being able to go with you on the helicopter."

"How do you mean?" he said.

"It was a wonderful gesture," she said, "—romantic, spontaneous, all the things I always said I wanted from you."

"So why didn't you come with me?" said Lance. "Because you didn't have the heart to leave Howard?"

She shook her head.

"Not really," she said. "I mean, that was part of it, sure. But the main reason was that I was too angry with you. I was too angry to give you the satisfaction of letting you come out of it a hero, even if it meant losing you and losing a trip to Paris and whatever else. I just couldn't bear to see you win."

Lance shook his head.

"Whew!" he said.

"I know," she said. "That was hard for me to admit. But I've been doing a lot of thinking. And what I mostly think is that, by not going with you on that helicopter, I probably became as big an asshole as you were at that surprise party I threw for you."

"Jesus," he said.

"We're almost even," she said.

"Almost?" said Lance.

"Well, having that fat whale naked on your bed when I came over last time still puts you *slightly* ahead of me," she said.

"Cathy?"

"Yeah?"

"Did you come over here to ask if you could come back to me?" he said gently.

"No," she said. "Why would you think that?"

"I don't know," he said. "Why *did* you come over here then?"

"To talk to you. To tell you what's been happening in my life. To maybe see if you wanted to occasionally go to dinner together."

"Before you ask me that and before I answer it, I have to tell you two things."

"What? That you're having an affair with a whale?"

"Not with her, no."

"With whom, then?"

"With two bisexual teenaged Chinese girls," he said.

"No, seriously," she said.

"I *am* serious," he said.

"You're really having an affair with two bisexual teenaged girls?" she said. "I refuse to believe that."

"It's true," he said.

"And what's the other thing?" she said.

"The other thing," he said, "is that I went to see a divorce lawyer today. I filed for a legal separation."

She stared at him for several seconds. He thought he saw flashes in her eyes of anger, hurt, and several other things before the invisible shield came down.

"I can't say I blame you," she said.

"It doesn't mean that we have to get a divorce," he said. "It just means that now *I* need a while to think."

"All right," she said. "I know that I still do myself."

She got up and walked to the door.

"I'll keep in touch," he said.

"Don't take any wooden fortune cookies," she said.

84

Lance felt rotten and elated about his meeting with Cathy. He honestly didn't know anymore if he wanted to continue the marriage. He had at first thought definitely yes, then definitely no, and now he had no idea at all. She had seemed so damned nice and so damned sensible and so damned vulnerable when she came to see him. He didn't know what he wanted to do about her.

He didn't know what he wanted to do about his novel either. His ten-city tour, although it had definitely hyped sales, had not put it onto the bestseller list. And now the sales were beginning to slide again. All he had left in the way of promotion was a book-and-author luncheon with a women's club in Westchester.

He called Mike Fieldston in advertising and promotion. Fieldston said the book was doing OK, but unless it got another shot in the arm it was just going to taper off and die. There wasn't any budget for another ad or another promotional tour, he said. Lance briefly regretted having severed his relationship with Claire—perhaps by engaging in a few more dangerous and demeaning sexual acts with her he could wangle another ad or a few more cities.

"Your only hope," said Fieldston, "is if one of the national TV talk shows, like *Donahue* or the *Tonight Show,* changes its mind and decides to put you on."

"What are the chances of that happening?" said Lance.

"It'll never happen," said Fieldston.

"So what you're saying," said Lance, "is that we're giving up?"

"Hey," said Fieldston, "you sold almost twenty thousand copies —that's not so terrible."

"I didn't even make back my advance yet," said Lance.

"So big deal," said Fieldston. "You're still a relatively young guy. Maybe you'll hit it really big on your next one."

"You mean that unless I get a big publicity break like *Donahue* or the *Tonight Show* I've had it?" said Lance. "Is that what you're saying?"

"That's it," said Fieldston. "A shot on Donahue or Carson would do it. Or maybe you could arrange to get stabbed to death in Macy's window."

85

Lance was dining with approximately one hundred fifty women in the ballroom of a Holiday Inn in Westchester. He was seated at the head table, next to a little lectern with a microphone on it from which, after the luncheon, he would address the assembled women on a number of self-serving subjects pertaining to his book. A little table had been set up at the back of the ballroom. On it were stacked about eighty or ninety copies of *Gallivanting*, which would be offered for sale after Lance's talk, personally autographed by the author. It was likely that Lance would sell at least six of them.

Lance munched on gray roast beef, drank white wine and alternately made small talk with the women at his table and pondered the women in his life. The women in his life—what had they seen in him? What had they wanted from him? Cathy had, at first, wanted a husband to look up to, to protect her, to fulfill her. Then she wanted a life of her own. Claire wanted a plaything to have kinky sex with and to control better than she had been able to control her own husband, perhaps. Stevie had wanted someone to introduce her to more celebrities whose names she would be able to drop. Dorothy and Janie had wanted a successful writer to emulate, and a father figure to feel ambivalent about sexually. Gladys wanted . . . God alone knew what Gladys wanted.

What, he wondered, do the women at this luncheon want from me? Surely not a chance to purchase a personally autographed copy of my book. Surely not gray roast beef and white wine. Surely not an hour-long speech about *Gallivanting*—so what *did* they want?

"What do you want?" said Lance to the woman on his immediate right, who was looking at him as though she were about to say something.

"A little more wine," she replied and extended her empty glass.

"I mean," said Lance, filling her glass, "aside from that."

"You mean in general?" she said.

"Yes. In general. In particular. In life. What do women want?"

"An end to televised sports," she said.

Lance chuckled good-naturedly and turned to the woman on his immediate left.

"What do women want?" he said.

"Sovereignty," she said.

Lance nodded, and turned to one of the women opposite him.

"What do women want?" he said.

"Acknowledgment," she said, "and unconditional love."

"What do women want?" he said to the woman on her left.

"Money," she said.

"What do women want?" he said to the woman on *her* left.

"Romance, excitement, and security," she said.

Lance nodded, impressed.

"And what do *men* want?" he said to her.

She thought a moment.

"Glamour, sex, and mother," she said.

"Aren't romance, excitement and security the same as glamour, sex and mother?" he said.

She shook her head.

"When I say mother," she said. "I mean a *disapproving* mother. My husband has made that very clear to me, and so that is the role I have decided to play with him."

"I see," said Lance, trying to envision the woman's marriage, and turning to the slightly spinsterly lady on her left. "What do women want?"

The spinsterly lady smiled sweetly at him.

"A good fuck," she said.

86

The second-to-last job that June, Alix, Sandy and Wanda did for the Motherloaders was to move all of the furniture out of an apartment on East 48th Street. It was actually kind of a funny scene. This chick was leaving her husband an empty apartment while she took all the furniture. Lerman or Lerner, the guy's name was, and he looked so amazed he must not have known she was going to do it. Served him right, the bastard.

The chick was friendly enough to them, but a little too good looking. June liberated a small jewelry box from her top bureau drawer when they were loading the truck. She figured the chick was rich enough that she probably wouldn't even know it was gone.

When June got home, though, and looked inside, she was disappointed. Inside the little purple velvet box was not a ring or a watch or a necklace—just these two gold balls, like steel ball bearings, only gold. June didn't see what they could be good for, but she thought maybe the gold was worth something at a pawnshop. In very delicate script somebody had engraved an inscription on them. It said: "For dearest Cathy, for when I can't be there. Love from Lance."

The guy at the hockshop seemed to know what they were all right, but when he tried to tell her he got kind of flustered. He said they were called boudoir balls or Ben Wa balls, and they were from the Orient. He said what you were supposed to do with them was to put them up inside your snatch and keep them there while you walked around and did the normal things you did during the day. June at first thought he was trying to come on to her and she almost decked him, but he didn't change his story even when she grabbed him by the shirtfront and shook him a little, so she figured he was probably telling the truth. After she let him go he squinted at the balls through his little monocle and said that they were gold plated and not worth much, so June decided to hang on to them.

At home, just out of curiosity, she put the Ben Wa balls up inside her snatch like the guy had said you should. They didn't do all that much for her, to tell the truth, but they did sort of slide around in a pleasurable way, so June figured she'd keep them around and use them from time to time, when she needed an up.

June, Alix, Sandy and Wanda moved to Los Angeles. They found an apartment in El Segundo, not too far from the airport, and began planning the hijack in earnest.

Sandy located four pistols for them with no trouble at all— three .45 caliber Colt automatics and a .38 Smith & Wesson. At first they had thought they'd spend a lot of time transforming stilettos and swords and rifle barrels into metal crutches in order to get them past the metal detectors in airport security, but then Wanda remembered reading in *New York* magazine that you could get these lead foil bags for photographic film and put anything you like in them, even guns, and they wouldn't show up on the X-rays of the metal detectors, so that is when they switched to guns.

June found flights from Los Angeles to Honolulu that she liked on Braniff, TWA, Global and Pan Am. Wanda said she liked Braniff because of the great colors the planes were painted. June had read that the FAA had recently ordered Braniff to pay $1,500,000 for improper maintenance and other illegal procedures. Alix said she heard that Pan Am wasn't all that safe either. They finally settled on a Global flight to Honolulu departing Los Angeles on October 21st at 8:00 p.m., because it had a better movie than the equivalent flight on TWA.

87

The voice on the phone was not unfamiliar.

"Don't hang up, Mr. Lerner," it said, "I got a proposition I think you might go for."

"Who is this and why would I hang up on you?" said Lance.

"It's Julius Blatt, Mr. Lerner. The attorney for the Dalton Two? I'm sorry—the attorney for Ernest Roosevelt and Irving Washington."

"Yes, of course, Mr. Blatt," said Lance. "What can I do for you?"

"I know that you are not entirely pleased by our use of the slogan 'Free the Dalton Two' which you gave us, but not so displeased as to not attend the fund-raising dinner we had for them."

"Touché, Mr. Blatt," said Lance.

"What I am calling about," said Blatt, "is a matter of mutual benefit to both parties . . ."

"Go on, Mr. Blatt . . ."

"I understand that your current novel is doing good, but not so good that you would be averse to taking advantage of a good publicity break if you saw one staring you in the face."

"What is your proposition, Mr. Blatt?"

"Knowing your unhappiness with our use of the slogan which you gave us, do you think you would still appear with Goose and Ernest on a program and speak of the manner in which you conceived the campaign and the terrible injustice that you feel has befallen them?"

"What is the show you wish me to do this on, Mr. Blatt?" said Lance.

"The *Tonight Show*," said Blatt.

"Are you serious about this, Mr. Blatt?" said Lance.

"May my mother be hit by a tractor-trailer," said Blatt.

"And when would this show take place?" said Lance.

"They'll only take us as a package," said Blatt. "You, me, Goose and Ernest. They want us tomorrow. We'd have to fly out in the morning. I'll spring for the air fare."

It was, of course, exactly the promotional boost his novel needed, but to appear on national TV with the Dalton Two would be endorsing a cause that was entirely fraudulent. True, he had helped them before, but it had been inadvertent. This time it would be advertent, premeditated, and a total sellout. There were certain things a man had to avoid at all costs if he wanted to keep his self-esteem. Perhaps this wasn't one of them.

"Mr. Blatt," said Lance, "You have got yourself a panelist."

88

Lance gave Dorothy and Janie instructions about things to be done while he was gone, and then he took a cab to the airport. For some reason it did not occur to him on this particular trip to have a premonition of disaster.

Blatt and his two clients were not at the gate, and when he inquired whether they were listed as passengers on the flight he was given an envelope with his name on it.

"Mr. Lerner," said the letter inside, "I and the boys have decided to take an earlier flight so as to allow them to see something of Tinsel Town before the show. Hope this is AOK with you. See you in the Green Room." It was signed simply "Blatt."

Lance smiled a bemused smile. It was certainly AOK with him. He was not anxious to spend any more time than he had to with either The Dalton Two or their counselor.

The flight to Los Angeles was uneventful. Lance picked up his luggage and arranged to rent a Hertz car. He had plenty of time so he drove to the Beverly Hills Hotel, checked in, had himself paged at the pool and in the Polo Lounge so people would know he was there. Then he went out and hit several bookstores in the Beverly Hills area before finally heading over to Burbank to tape the show.

"Mr. Lerner," said Blatt, "may I present my clients, Ernest Roosevelt and Goose Washington."

"Mah man!" said Ernest.

"Mah man!" said Goose.

"Likewise," said Lance.

"Mr. Lerner, Goose and Ah, we very grateful for all that you done," said Ernest.

"It was nothing," said Lance truthfully.

"No," said Ernest, "we very grateful. Anything you want—Ah don't care *what*—you ask us."

"Well, thank you," said Lance. "That's very kind."

Lance was trying to be polite. It wasn't *their* fault they thought he'd expended a lot of effort on their behalf.

"So," said Blatt, "how were you planning to characterize the boys when you speak of them on the show?"

"Well," said Lance carefully, "I thought I would say that they were stunning examples of the lengths that talented ghetto youths will go to in order to find a showcase for their work."

"Sounds AOK to me," said Blatt, nodding his head approvingly. "How does it sound to *you*, boys?"

"Dy-no-*mite*, bro'!" said Ernest.

"Dy-no-*mite*, bro'!" said Goose.

"Well," said Lance during a longish pause that threatened to become awkward if not broken, "congratulations on your book deal, Ernest."

"Thanks," said Ernest.

"From what I hear," said Lance, "they gave you very good terms."

Ernest shrugged.

"Mr. Blatt say he can't get them to go no mo' than a fifty-fifty split on the paperback rights," said Ernest, raising his eyebrows.

"Well," said Lance, "Firestone hasn't done better than that for anyone else so far, either."

"Then it time," said Ernest.

"Well, you're right about that," said Lance. "As long as hardcover houses continue keeping fifty percent of their books' paperback advances, they're more in the business of selling rights than selling books—which probably explains why they don't do a better job at the retail level."

"You right," said Ernest. "That a fact."

Lance felt peculiar talking fairly sophisticated publishing jargon to a young black kid who couldn't even speak grammatically, but in a funny way he sensed that Ernest understood everything that he was saying.

"Hey, Mr. Lerner," said Blatt, "I want to ask you something."

"Please," said Lance, "call me Lance. All of you."

"OK then, Lance," said Blatt. "What would you say to a little proposition?"

"What sort of proposition?" said Lance uneasily. From Blatt's tone he could tell it would not be untainted.

"What do you say we talk after the show about maybe helping out a little on the writing of Ernest's book?"

"What sort of help did you have in mind?" said Lance.

Blatt held his palms parallel about a foot apart, then shrugged. "What about ghost-writing it for him?" said Blatt.

Lance smiled and shook his head.

"No thanks," he said. "I've got more than enough of my own writing to do."

"Think it over," said Blatt. "Don't give me an answer till later."

"All right," said Lance.

"The money is good," said Blatt. "Better than you're getting on your present book."

"I'm aware of that," said Lance dryly.

"Don't give me an answer now," said Blatt.

"OK," said Lance, "I won't."

Lance turned and saw that Goose was grinning at him idiotically. Lance grinned back. Goose goosed him.

89

"My next guests," said Johnny Carson in the awed tones he might have used to introduce Albert Einstein or Sir Winston Churchill, "are two rather unusual and gifted men. Ernest Hemingway Roosevelt and Irving Goose Washington are two young black authors from Harlem who robbed a *bookstore* to call attention to their writing—writing which they felt would otherwise go unnoticed. They were convicted of grand larceny—is that right, Ed? Were they actually *convicted*, or . . .?"

"*Indicted*," said Ed McMahon.

"I'm sorry," said Carson, "They were *indicted* for grand larceny, and through the efforts of Public Defender Julius Blatt and author Lance Lerner, they have become something of a cause célèbre in the literary and artistic community as The Dalton Two. Would you welcome, please, The Dalton Two and their defenders."

Ernest, Goose, Blatt and Lance came out, shook hands with Johnny and Ed, and then sat down. Carson seemed unsure of what tack to take with them and was apparently waiting to take his cue from them.

"Well," said Carson, "I must say you two gentlemen chose a somewhat . . . *unorthodox* method of calling attention to your work . . ."

The studio audience chuckled politely.

"If you robbed a bookstore to call attention to your writing," said Carson, "I suppose we ought to be grateful you aren't *munitions* manufacturers . . ."

A slight titter from the audience.

"Or distributors of . . . cesspools . . ."

A throatier laugh from the audience.

"Goose," said McMahon, sensing the segment was going to bomb and taking a gamble on saving it, "why do they call you Goose?"

Goose turned to McMahon, grinning idiotically, and goosed him. The audience, taken totally by surprise, exploded into relieved laughter—these men weren't intimidating militant Negroes, they were vulgar down-home guys, just like the rest of us. Carson, unexpectedly delighted, touched the knot of his tie and did seven consecutive takes for the camera, milking at least three orgasms of laughter out of the audience. It was going to be a fun segment after all.

Ernest got to say a few words about writing, Blatt got to say a few words about the courage of young people today who came from disadvantaged ethnic communities, Lance got to say how important it was for the literary community to keep getting fresh infusions of life from the Third World and somehow managed to mention the title of his book three times. But the overwhelming favorite was Goose. He didn't say a total of three words the whole segment, but whenever the camera went to him, the audience fell down laughing.

They were the last segment or Carson would have held them over. As it was, he asked them to come back. They all said that they would.

When the show was through taping, Blatt asked Lance if he could take him to dinner. Lance pleaded previous plans with a sales rep from his publishing house. Blatt said he would see Lance the following evening on the plane back to New York. He and the boys were taking the 9:00 p.m. flight on TWA—the so-called red-eye—to enable the boys to spend the whole day taking in the sights of Tinsel Town, taking the studio tour at Universal and also taking a preliminary meeting there about the screenplay of Ernest's book.

Lance said that he had already made plans to go back on the 4:00 p.m. flight on American since he had a breakfast meeting in New York the following day. Blatt seemed disappointed but said he'd catch Lance in the city.

All in all, thought Lance as he left the studio, it had gone OK, but he doubted that the segment had sold many copies of his book. Well, he rationalized, at least it had done a lot for The Dalton Two. And since he was now publicly associated with the name, perhaps it would help him obscurely in whatever subsequent publicity they got on their own.

If he hurried, he could still visit one more bookstore before dinner.

90

His dread of flying was, for some reason, stronger than usual. He got to the Los Angeles airport with plenty of time to spare, turned in his rented car to Hertz, exaggerated only slightly on his form the amount of gas remaining in the tank as shown on the gas gauge, rode the Hertz courtesy bus to the American Airlines terminal and checked in at 3:25 for his 4:00 p.m. flight to New York. He inquired once more to make sure the plane wasn't a DC-10. It was not.

Within seconds of handing over his suitcase and watching it depart on its jolly little funhouse ride on the moving rubber belt and disappear, he was informed that the 4:00 flight was being delayed. How long or why, nobody seemed to know. Airline employees always tried to make it seem that the delays were caused by things like late deliveries of hollandaise sauce for the asparagus tips, but he knew better. He visualized drunken mechanics jamming dozens of pieces of delicate machinery into a jet engine that had fallen off onto the runway, then rubber-cementing it back onto the wing.

A smiling airline employee informed him at 4:00 that the plane was now scheduled to depart at 5:24 p.m. He was angry and demanded that his luggage be returned to him so he could take another flight. It was, the employee informed him, too late for that. Why didn't he simply go into the bar and relax? If he chose an earlier flight he would only have to wait at the other end for the plane with his luggage.

He decided to wait in the bar and keep his luggage company on the plane at 5:24. He resented the pretense on the part of the airline that they had enough assurance to pinpoint the time of departure that closely. He felt it would be more honest for them to say "sixish" instead of 5:24.

As he entered the bar he was dimly aware that he might be receiving an extrasensory warning from his brain and from the collective unconscious that the flight with the baggage would crash on takeoff and that the sole purpose of the delay was to enable him to take another plane. He turned around and headed back to the gate, determined to let his luggage crash and take an earlier plane. But when he was within steps of the gate he got another extrasensory warning to ignore the previous message: it was not the flight with the *luggage* that would crash but the one he would *transfer* to, the one that departed earlier. If he did transfer onto the doomed plane at the last moment, his friends would speak of the tragic irony of his decision for years. He went back into the bar.

At 5:00 he paid for the three White Russians he had consumed, then walked to the gate. The lounge was empty. An airline employee he hadn't seen before was irritated when Lance inquired about his 5:24 flight. It was not a *5:24* flight, she said, it was a *4:00* flight, and it had departed, following a slight delay, at 4:45.

Lance was outraged. How could that have happened? He'd been told his flight was delayed till 5:24. He'd been told to wait in the bar.

The woman was not remorseful nor much impressed with his fury. It was true, she said, that the initial delay had been estimated at 5:24, but the trouble they'd had was then corrected and the new departure time had been duly announced on the p.a. system, and all of the other passengers had got on the plane and left without him. *Nobody*, she said, would have suggested that he wait in the bar, since it was common knowledge that the p.a. system could not be *heard* in the bar. If he hurried, she said, he could still probably get on the Global flight for New York which was scheduled to depart at 5:15 p.m. It was now 5:05.

Boiling with impotent rage, Lance raced away from the American departure lounge and headed down the hallway toward Global. At Global he was required to go through security once more, and although he had had no trouble at American, the metal detector at Global beeped when he went through it. The uniformed female security guard gave him a crappy little plastic box for his coins and keys and motioned for him to go through again, but when he did so it beeped again.

"I just went through security at American," he said. "It didn't beep there, even with my coins and keys."

"You've got too much metal," said the tight-lipped security woman. "Take some more off and try it again."

"But I have to catch a *plane*," he said, glancing at his watch. "It's after 5:10—my plane leaves at 5:15!"

The security guard did not appear to be alarmed.

"You should have thought of that earlier," she said, and motioned for him to go through again.

He took off his watch and put it in the plastic box and went through the metal detector again, and again it beeped.

"Take off your belt," said the security woman.

"If I take off my belt my pants will fall down," said Lance.

The security woman did not seem to be amused.

"Take off your belt," she repeated.

"And what comes next, the fillings in my teeth?" said Lance.

He took off his belt and put it in the crappy plastic box. His pants did not fall down, but the beeper beeped again when he went through it.

"Follow me," said the security woman.

"What for?" said Lance.

"We're going to have to search you."

"But I'll miss my *plane*."

The security woman unsnapped her holster. Lance sighed and followed her into a room marked "Security." It had a plain wooden table and a hard-backed chair and a metal locker. She closed the door behind them.

"Strip," she said.

"*You're* going to search me?" said Lance. "Not a *man?*"

"That's correct," she said. She took out a hard case of cigarettes, removed one, tapped the end on the box and lit it.

"I thought *men* searched men and women searched *women*," said Lance. "I mean I thought that's how it worked."

"Are you going to strip or aren't you?" said the security woman, removing her gun from its holster with elaborate casualness.

"Yes," said Lance. "Yes, I am."

He took off his jacket and tie and shirt and draped them over the back of the chair. She went through all the pockets and examined their contents. She was a plain-looking, even a homely, woman. She had doubtless been ignored or worse by most of the men in her life and she had probably deeply resented it. Here was an ideal opportunity to wreak vengeance on a proxy for the sex that had not appreciated her. He took off his boots and socks and handed them to her. She looked inside them, turned them over, found nothing.

"I'm sorry you feel you have to do this," said Lance. "You must not be a very happy person."

Her nostrils flared. She gave him a piercing look.

"Pants," she said between clenched teeth.

He unzipped his trousers and handed them to her. She went through his pockets with a vengeance. He resigned himself to having missed the second plane.

"I'm sure there are *plenty* of men who would love to go out with you," said Lance, realizing he was not pursuing a fruitful line of conversation, but unable to stop. "You seem like a nice person, and you aren't bad looking. I mean, you do have nice . . . *skin* and everything," he added, hastily scanning her for complimentable features.

"Drawers," she said.

"Pardon me?" said Lance.

"Take down your drawers."

Oh boy, he thought, I get to make up for at least six guys on this one. He pushed down his jockey shorts and handed them to her. She was staring quite frankly at his genitals.

"OK," he said, "you've searched me and you didn't find an M-16 or a hand grenade. Are you satisfied, now that I've needlessly missed my plane? Can I go now?"

"Up on the table," she said.

"What?"

"Up on the table on your knees and elbows."

"What the hell *for?*"

"I have to search your rectum."

"You're kidding me. What do you think you're going to find up there, a bazooka?"

The security woman leveled her pistol at him.

"Up on the table. Knees and elbows."

Angry and humiliated, Lance got up on the table on his knees and elbows, with his ass facing her. He was conscious of how ludicrous he looked and of how the security woman must be relishing his discomfort.

"Spread your cheeks," she said.

"Don't think this isn't going to be reported," he said. "I happen to know a few people in the Port Authority and in the Mayor's Office. You're going to regret your actions, I can promise you that."

"Spread 'em," she said and laid the cold butt of the revolver on his flank.

"You're going to be sorry you did this," he said. "You can't imagine *how* sorry."

The door opened and someone came in.

"Who the hell is that?" said a female voice, obviously referring Lance.

"Some asshole who knows people in the Mayor's Office," said the security woman.

"We're getting stacked up out there," said the visitor, "you better come and help."

"OK," said the security woman.

"Does that mean I can go?" said Lance.

The door opened. Lance turned around. The security woman and the visitor, also a security woman, were leaving. Several people outside the door, startled by the sight of a naked man on his knees and elbows on a table, were peering in at him. Lance hastily covered himself.

"You can go," said the visiting security woman. The one who had made him strip was already outside, having departed without so much as a cursory apology.

By the time Lance got dressed again it was 5:30. He was certain the Global flight had already departed, but having gone to so much trouble to gain entrance to the Global terminal he was loath to leave. He walked to the gate at a leisurely pace, and was rewarded for his peculiar brand of optimism—the 5:15 flight had boarded but had not yet left the gate. He gave his ticket to the flight attendant at the desk and scampered aboard.

91

They stood in the security area of the Global terminal and synchronized their watches. It was precisely 7:00 p.m., October 21st.

They wore khaki jumpsuits and carried small overnight bags. A lead-foil pouch containing a pistol was in each woman's overnight bag. The heavier bags they'd checked when they arrived at curbside on the Budget Rent-a-Car courtesy bus.

They had gone through every step of the plan over and over again, so there was no need to be nervous, but still they were nervous. Alix and Sandy were trying to pretend that they were calm, but June noticed that their hands were trembling. June thought Wanda looked so scared she might pee in her pants.

June herself betrayed nothing on the outside, but inside she was a wreck. She'd been up half the night with an upset stomach and a good case of the jitters. Before leaving the apartment that final time for the airport, June had gone into the bathroom with her overnight bag and closed the door and locked it securely behind her. She was going to do a few private things to give herself courage which she didn't happen to feel like sharing with the others and risk getting laughed at.

June took out a beautiful purple garter belt, a pair of purple stockings with seams up the back, a purple bra and a pair of beautiful purple panties. She had imagined it was her father and not she who had bought them for her, and that if she wore them in secret under her unfeminine jumpsuit during the hijack, in some way her father's immense physical strength would magically protect her.

She pulled off her jumpsuit and her white cotton underpants. She languidly drew on the sensuous lingerie, imagining that her father was watching her. Finally she put the jumpsuit back on, shoved the white underpants in her bag, unlocked the door and went out to join her co-conspirators.

Now, at a nod from June, the others got in line at the metal detector—first Sandy, then Alix, then Wanda, with June bringing up the rear. All four women had stopped breathing as they watched their overnight bags with the guns disappear on the moving black belt. Had *New York* magazine been right? Would the lead-foil pouches truly obscure the silhouettes of the pistols? Or would the guns be seen, whistles blown, alarms sounded, airport security police rush forward to clamp them into handcuffs and take them away to jail?

There was a silence. And then a gruff male voice behind them spoke:

"OK, girls—move it!"

June's heart stopped beating. Wanda's hands went halfway up in surrender. They all turned around to find, not the chief of security police, but a disgruntled passenger urging them to move on through the archway.

They breathed a collective sigh of relief. Sandy went through the archway. Nothing beeped. Alix went through next. No warning sounded. Wanda went through after Alix, and June stepped up to go through next. June could see their four overnight bags, neatly stacked at the end of the belt, waiting for them. It was going to work!

June stepped through the archway and the beeper beeped. A security woman walked up to her.

"Try it again," she said, handing June a blue polyurethane container.

With shaking hands, June reached into a zippered pocket, deposited keys and coins in the plastic box, went through the archway again. Again it beeped.

June looked at Sandy, Wanda and Alix. They stared back at her, afraid to move. June took off her watch and dropped it into the plastic box, then nodded to Sandy and looked in the direction of the four overnight bags. Sandy nodded, and swiftly took all four bags off the belt. June went through the arch again. Again it beeped.

"Follow me," said the security woman.

"What for?" said June, her pulse thundering in her ears.

"I'm going to have to search you."

"But we have a plane to catch. We're going to Hawaii on the 8:00 plane."

"Everybody's going *somewhere*, sister," said the security woman. "Do you have any carry-on luggage?"

"No," said June. "I checked everything at the curb."

"Good," said the security woman, guiding her gently toward a door marked SECURITY. "Less work for mother."

June followed the security woman into the room. There was a plain wooden table and a hard-backed chair and a metal locker. The security woman closed the door.

"OK, honey, strip," she said.

"Are you sure you have to do this?" said June, thinking of her purple lingerie and blushing deeply. "I'm not carrying any guns or explosives. I'm a working woman, same as yourself, going to Hawaii on vacation."

"If you strip fast enough," said the security woman not unpleasantly, "you might even make it onto that 8:00 plane with your friends."

June sighed. She unzipped her jumpsuit and peeled it down. The security woman's eyebrows went up. She whistled a wolf whistle.

"Is there some law against a woman wearing feminine under-things?" said June, her face hot with shame.

"Not at all, not at all," said the security woman. "I just didn't figure you as the type to wear stuff like that."

"Why not?" said June, but she didn't want to hear the answer.

"Let's see it, honey," said the security woman, holding out her hands.

Without looking her in the eye, June unhooked her bra and garter belt, slid down her stockings and panties, took them off and handed them to the security woman in a pile. The woman looked frankly at June's stocky body, then went through the lingerie.

"OK?" said June. "Are you satisfied now?"

The security woman took out a pocket-sized metal detector and passed it quickly over June's naked skin. When it reached her pubic area it emitted a high-pitched whine.

Oh, Jesus, thought June, the fucking Ben Wa balls!

"Up on the table, sister," said the security woman.

"Please don't do this," said June softly. "I think I know what's causing the metal detector to react, and I promise you it's not anything like a weapon or a bomb."

"Up on the *table*," said the security woman. She put down her portable metal detector and unsnapped her holster.

"Have you ever heard of something called Ben Wa balls?" said June, cursing her stupidity for needlessly jeopardizing the entire hijack operation with such moronic self-indulgence.

"Up on the table. Knees and elbows."

The security woman leveled her pistol at June.

Furious and ashamed, June got up on the table.

"Spread 'em," said the security woman.

June did as she was told. The security woman let out another whistle.

"What the hell is that gold thing in your twat?" said the security woman.

"Ben Wa balls," said June, "I just asked you if you knew what they were."

"I think I'd better get the bomb squad in here on the double," said the security woman, unsnapping her walkie-talkie from her belt.

"No, wait," said June, "*please* wait. It's not a bomb, I swear to you. It's Ben Wa balls. Boudoir balls. It's an Oriental thing. A sex thing, all right?"

"How does it work?"

"You just put these two balls inside yourself and they sort of slide around in there. It feels very . . . sexy."

"I don't know. I think maybe the bomb squad should handle this. I don't know too much about this type of thing."

"Please don't call the bomb squad. I don't want a bunch of leering, sexist pigs sticking their fingers up my pussy—do you blame me?"

The security woman sighed.

"I guess not."

"Good," said June. "We women have to stick together, that's the only chance we've got against them—if we stick together."

"Well, you're sure right about *that*," said the security woman.

"Damn right I am," said June. "We've got to stick together and fight back, even if the way we fight back sometimes looks kind of extreme."

"What do you mean extreme?" said the security woman.

"Well, like that group, MATE—Men Are The Enemy. Have you heard of them?"

"The ones that cut that rapist's balls off," said the security woman.

June nodded.

"What would you say if I told you I'm the leader of that group?" said June, aware that she was taking a chance.

The security woman looked at her oddly.

"You're the one that cut off his balls?"

June nodded, watching the security woman's face for a sign.

"Goddamn," said the security woman, breaking into a huge smile and reaching out to shake June's hand. "If it was me, I'd 've sliced off his goddamn pecker too!"

By the time June got done telling the security woman about MATE's activities—wisely deleting any mention of the impending hijack—and showing her the Ben Wa balls, it was too late to make the 8:00 flight to Hawaii. The security woman was very

apologetic and went and found a schedule of flights to Hawaii
while June was getting back into her clothes.

There were no other flights to Hawaii on Global that day, but
the security woman found one on Braniff that left at 10:00 p.m.
June was just about to voice her objections to Braniff when something else caught her eye: there was a 9:00 p.m. flight on TWA
to New York which would serve her purposes quite nicely—once
you hijacked an airplane, you could make it go in any direction
you wanted to.

She told the security woman the Braniff flight would do, then
went out and picked up her three very worried friends. They got
to the TWA gate just as the 9:00 p.m. flight to New York began
boarding.

92

Captain Eddie "Hap" Harrigan was getting madder than hell.
His Global DC-10 had been scheduled for departure from LAX
at 5:15, and now here it was 6:45 and they were no closer to
departure than they had been an hour ago.

First the goddamned aft cargo door wouldn't lock, next the
flight recorder was on the fritz, and after that somebody had
kicked over an entire cart of First Class meals and Sky Chefs were
taking their own sweet time about replacing them.

Hap pulled out his silver flask of Calvert Manhattans and took
a healthy swig, and got a disapproving eyebrow-raise from his
first officer, Bubba Bogan.

"Hey, good buddy," said Bubba, "go easy on that stuff, will ya?
We don't need any more near misses on this flight."

"Hey, good buddy," said Hap, "up your giggy with a lighted ciggy."

Hap resented Bubba's implication that the near miss with the TWA L1011 on the way into LAX had had anything to do with his drinking. Any flight that you *didn't* have a near miss, as Bubba well knew, was a dull flight, plus which if he was going to have to fly an aircraft as shitty as a DC-10, he was damned if he was going to do it sober.

The DC-10, in Hap's opinion and in the opinion of a great many pilots, was an original piece of garbage, but he was not anxious to downgrade. Stepping down from the DC-10 to a smaller aircraft required a pay cut of $1,000 to $2,000 a month. He was not *that* interested in safety.

Besides, even if the aircraft were safe, there were other things to worry about. Like this airport, for instance. The International Federation of Airline Pilots Associations had awarded LAX its Black Star rating, a rating reserved for only the most dangerous airports. How the FAA allowed operations as suicidal as those that were permitted here was beyond him—planes took off and landed at LAX in opposite directions on parallel runways. Bubba himself had called it a 200-mile-per-hour game of Chicken.

No, the only way to not let it all get to you was never to fly sober, and let the chips fall where they may. If your number was up, then your number was up, and fuck the passengers.

A stew from the Coach section poked her head into the cockpit and asked what everybody wanted for dinner. Her name was Cindy or Trudy or something, and she was always fooling around with drugs. How could you respect anybody who took drugs? He was fairly sure she was the one who had complained about the size of his wang. Miserable little slut. Small wonder she thought he had a tiny wang—if she was the stew he was thinking she was, she had a crack the size of Bryce Canyon.

93

Lance was livid. For the past hour and a half he had been sitting patiently in his seat, waiting for the Global flight to take off for New York. His baggage, he figured, was now hurtling eastward somewhere over Arizona. It would arrive several hours before him and go trundling around on the baggage carousel, unclaimed, until somebody lifted it off and quickly stripped it of valuables.

Worse yet, he realized he had inadvertently stumbled onto a DC-10, after scrupulously avoiding the jinxed wide-bodies on all but one of his last dozen flights. He wondered if it was worth the bother of getting off and taking his chances on being able to still find a 707, a 747 or an L1011 this late in the day. With his luck, the DC-10 would land safely and the plane he transferred to would collide with a Cessna and land in several counties of Kansas simultaneously.

He looked around for somebody who might be able to give him a progress report and realized he hadn't seen any flight attendants about in quite a while. He got out of his seat and moseyed over to the galley.

The curtains to the galley were drawn and he could hear hysterical female giggling coming from the other side. He didn't know if it was proper to simply pull back the curtain or if he should ask for permission first.

"Uh, excuse me," he called out, but the giggling continued with no acknowledgment of his having spoken. He didn't see why he had to seek permission to enter anyway. After all, what could they be doing behind that curtain, showering?

"Excuse me," he called again. His hand went up automatically as if to knock, but he realized the idiocy of trying to knock on a curtain and finally just pulled it open.

Two stewardesses looked up guiltily. They were both blond and young and fairly good looking in dissimilar ways. Each of them was holding a short plastic drinking straw in the vicinity of her nose. On the stainless-steel counter in front of them was an open plastic container full of white powder.

"Can I help you?" said the one nearest the curtain.

"Yeah," said Lance, eyeing the white powder, "I just wanted to know—are we almost there?"

Both stewardesses exploded with laughter. It had not been a witticism worthy of that kind of response, he knew. He figured they were stoned.

"C'mon in," said the one nearest the curtain.

He stepped into the galley and she drew the curtain closed again.

"Want some nose candy?" said the other stewardess.

"OK," he said.

The one nearest him handed him the container of white powder and the straw. He covered one nostril and breathed in deeply with the other.

"Hey," said the one farthest from him, "what's your name, *Hoover?*"

"No, Lerner," said Lance and snorted from the opposite side.

"I'm Trudy," said the far stew, "and this is Judy."

"Trudy and Judy," said Lance. "Say, you aren't twins by any chance, are you?"

Both stews looked stunned.

"That's really far out you should say that," said Trudy, "you know?"

"Oh?" said Lance.

"Yeah," said Judy. "We're both Geminis, and there's no way you could have known that."

"You're both Geminis?" said Lance. "Far out." He hated discussions like this, but was willing to see where it might take him nonetheless.

"Really," said Trudy. "I mean I'm on the cusp, but still."

"What are *you?*" said Judy.

"Jewish," said Lance.

"I mean what sign?" said Judy.

Lance was surprised, and *not* surprised, that people still spoke this way.

"I'm a Gemini too," said Lance, savoring the inevitable reaction.

Trudy and Judy looked at each other dumbfounded.

"I don't *believe* it," said Trudy.

"Three *Geminis*," said Judy. "Talk about *synchronicity!*"

"What do you have rising?" said Trudy.

"What I have rising," said Lance, "is my gorge. Why have we been sitting on the ground in this plane for the past hour and a half?"

"Hey," said Judy, "don't lay that on *us*, OK? I mean, it's not *our* fault."

"I'm not saying it is," said Lance. "I just don't understand why we're sitting here and not moving, that's all."

"Oh," said Judy. "Well, if you really want to know, I'll tell you. First the aft cargo door wouldn't lock. Then some asshole kicked over the First Class meals, and we've been waiting for replacements."

"Plus which the flight recorder wasn't working either," said Trudy. "Flight recorders come in real handy when you crash."

"*When* you crash," said Lance, "or *if?*"

"*When*," said Trudy. "It's only a matter of time."

Judy nodded.

"Flying is Russian roulette," said Judy.

Lance looked at them carefully.

"Are you serious about that," he said, "or are you joking?"

Trudy and Judy inhaled another line of cocaine each.

"It's nothing to joke about," said Judy.

"You mean flying is really as dangerous as I've always feared it was?" said Lance, not sure how eager he was to get into this discussion.

"Oh, lots worse," said Trudy.

"You mean," said Lance, "the equipment itself isn't up to snuff, or the people who operate it aren't?"

Trudy and Judy looked at each other and sighed.

"You don't really want to know this, do you?" said Judy.

"In a terrible way," said Lance, "I do. I mean I feel I ought to. Not everything, maybe, just a couple things to kind of give me the picture."

"OK," said Trudy, "where do you want to start?"

"Equipment," said Lance.

"Equipment," said Trudy. "OK, well, the equipment you're on now is a DC-10, which is a lemon if I've ever seen one. Two stews we know died on the DC-10 that went down last week in Newark."

"I'm sorry to hear that," said Lance. "I knew DC-10s were dangerous, but I don't know why."

"First of all, the pylon that attaches the engines to the wing sometimes cracks and breaks off," said Judy. "Second, the aft cargo door doesn't stay locked very well and has a habit of blowing off, which causes the cabin floor to collapse, which happens to be where the control cables are located. Third—"

"If the DC-10s are so dangerous," said Lance, "how come you fly them?"

"Shit, I don't know," said Trudy. "Both Judy and me are planning to give them up. But then, we're planning to give up smoking too, and we haven't done that either."

"The thing of it is, is that it almost doesn't matter that the other planes are safer," said Judy. "Because the peckerheads that service DC-10s are just as out-to-lunch as the dorks that service the 747s and the L1011s."

"What do mean out-to-lunch?" said Lance. "Aren't the mechanics who work on airliners certified by the FAA?"

"I've got a hot bulletin for you, sweetheart," said Judy. "Ninety per cent of the mechanics who service airliners aren't even A&Ps."

"A&Ps?"

"That's the FAA's term for qualified mechanics—it stands for 'airframe and power plant.' "

"Then there's the air traffic controllers," said Trudy, "who are about as big a bunch of booze-hounds as you'd never want to meet. And their equipment is so outdated it's a crime. Their computers that keep track of aircraft taking off and landing are always going out, and the controllers are left staring at a blank scope."

"I guess you were right," said Lance. "I guess I really didn't want to know about this stuff."

"Tell him about the fuel problem," said Judy.

"Right," said Trudy. "A DC-10 uses about $1,850 worth of kerosene every hour, so every flight—not just DC-10s—is allotted the smallest possible amount of fuel on board, especially since it *takes* fuel to *carry* fuel. Which is OK, unless you develop problems, or have to spend a while stacked up in a holding pattern, or you get diverted to another airport or something. Then you have a very good chance of flaming out and going down without fuel."

"Can't you just watch your fuel gauge and have a good alternative plan in mind or something?" said Lance.

"Sure," said Judy. "That's assuming your fuel gauge is *accurate*, of course. Fuel gauges on airliners can be off by several thousand pounds, though. And every once in a while, a plane runs out of fuel and crashes."

"I really don't want to hear anymore," said Lance, beginning to feel a little dizzy.

"You want to hear some shit about the pilot?" said Judy.

"What pilot?" said Lance. He was definitely getting dizzy, either from the coke or from the information the two stewardesses were taking such perverse delight in feeding him.

"The asshole who's about to take us into the wild blue yonder," said Trudy, "Hap-fucking-Harrigan. You want to know what keeps him going? Outside of jumping stews? Calvert pre-mixed Manhattans in a little silver flask."

"You're kidding me," said Lance. "Doesn't the FAA have some regulation about that?"

Trudy nodded.

"Federal law says that at least eight hours must elapse between consumption of any alcoholic beverage and the commencement of any flight. Go tell that to Hap Harrigan."

Lance backed unsteadily toward the curtain.

"OK," he said, "you've convinced me."

"What do you mean?" said Trudy.

"Where are you going?" said Judy.

"Off the airplane," said Lance, pulling the curtain open.

"Aww, we scared him," said Judy.

"C'mon back here," said Trudy, pulling him back into the galley and closing the curtain.

"No thanks," said Lance. "It's been lovely, but I really have to run."

"Don't go yet," said Trudy, suddenly seductive, snaking her arms around his neck.

"Why not?" said Lance.

"Because," said Trudy, giggling, and nuzzling her cheek against his, "we like you. And we want to fly with you."

"Yeah," said Judy, kissing him wetly on the lips, "if we have to go up there with old drunken Hap, we don't want to do it alone."

"You won't be alone," said Lance, beginning to get aroused. "There are about two hundred and seventy people on this junk heap to keep you company."

"We don't want *them* to keep us company," said Judy, "we want *you*."

Judy began unbuttoning her uniform.

"Have you ever made love at thirty-five thousand feet with two stewardesses?" whispered Trudy in his ear.

"Not even with one," said Lance, instantly getting an image of the three of them writhing around together on the floor of the galley as the aft cargo door blew out, the cabin floor collapsed, the pylons fell off the wings, the slats withdrew and the aircraft began to come apart.

"What's your first name?" said Judy, reaching for his belt buckle.

"Lance," said Lance, "but I'm afraid I really do have to go now."

He lurched back toward the curtain, but both Judy and Trudy hung onto him, swaying a bit unsteadily on their feet.

"If *we* go," giggled Judy, unbuckling his belt, "we're taking you with us, Lance."

Trudy unzipped his fly and stuck her hand inside his pants.

Suddenly they heard the p.a. system switch on, and a somewhat boozy male voice addressed them:

"Ladies and gennumun," said the voice, "this is your captain, uh, Captain Harrigan speaking . . . The, uh, difficulties that we were waiting to be, uh, corrected have finally . . . been corrected. So, uh, we apologize for the delay and, uh, we'll be getting underway in just a moment here. And, uh, once we're aloft, the stewardesses will be bringing us all . . . uh, bring all of *you*, that is, a complimentary cocktail with my, uh, compliments . . ."

"Oh my God," said Lance, "we're *leaving*."

"*Together*," said Trudy, locating Lance's shvantz and pulling it slowly out of his fly.

"Flight attendants, uh, prepare for . . . departure," said the voice on the p.a. system.

Judy and Trudy were giggling like crazy. Trudy had sunk to her knees in front of Lance and taken his entire organ into her mouth. As it began to expand in the hot wet cavity, all of Lance's determination to save his life by leaving the aircraft drained out of his body.

Judy picked up the p.a. system telephone off the wall and spoke into it.

"Good evening, ladies and gentlemen," said Judy, repressing a giggle. "My name is Judy Hotchkiss. I'm the First Flight Attendant on your flight today. On behalf of Captain Harrigan and the entire crew, we'd like to welcome you to Global's flight number 323 to New York . . ."

Lance leaned back weakly against the stainless-steel counter as Trudy continued to work on him.

"Please check now to make sure that your seat belt is securely fastened for takeoff . . . despite the fact that it is virtually useless and, in a forced landing, it will rupture your spleen and fracture your pelvic saddle . . ."

Trudy almost gagged with laughter, dislodging Lance from her throat. Judy temporarily forgot what came next, then plunged onward.

"Be sure that your seat back and tray table are stowed in the upright and locked position and that all carry-on items are placed under the seat in front of you . . . Although your seats are securely mounted to the floor and stressed to nine g's, nine g's is less than the minimum requirement for automobiles, so if we have a forced landing they'll probably tear loose and severely injure you . . ."

Trudy was in convulsions over that one. She reached up, grabbed Lance's hand and placed it on Judy's bosom. Lance obediently started fondling Judy's breasts as skillfully as possible under the circumstances, aware that he was participating in a fairly ludicrous tableau.

"There are eight exit doors on our DC-10," Judy continued, "although the chances of even half of them opening in the event of a forced landing are . . . kind of remote. This aircraft is equipped with floatable lower seatback cushions for your assistance in the event of a water landing. The Coast Guard considers these seat cushions unsuitable for nonswimmers and children. If you are fortunate enough to have a life vest under your seat you will find it . . . extremely difficult to locate, extract, unpack, put on and inflate."

A stewardess stuck her head in the galley.

"Jude?" she said, then saw what was happening on the floor and quickly withdrew.

"In tests we've conducted with these life vests," Judy continued, as Lance diligently kneaded her breasts, "even trained members of the crew were unable to use them properly. If this aircraft does land in water, it will float anywhere from eleven seconds to four days, assuming it doesn't break up on impact . . ."

"Ladies and gentlemen," said the p.a. system, "this is Captain Harrigan . . ."

"Since we are cargo-loaded," Judy continued gamely, "it will probably float with the nose down . . ."

"Ladies and gentlemen," said the p.a. system, "the flight attendant who is addressing you, Miss Hotchkiss, is—"

"A Coast Guard helicopter can pick up twenty people from the water," Judy continued, raising her voice over that of the captain's, "one per minute. That's in ideal conditions, of course. But the size of the group on this plane will make a recovery from the water impossible, so most of us will probably freeze to death before it arrives . . ."

"Ladies and gentlemen," said the p.a. system, "I'd like you to ignore what Miss Hotchkiss has just told you. She appears to be, uh, somewhat under the influence of, uh . . ."

"Miss *Hotchkiss,*" said Judy, interrupting him, "is under the influence of about six lines of Peruvian marching powder, which is *considerably* less debilitating than the twelve to fourteen Calvert Manhattans that the man who is *driving* this aircraft has just poured down his throat!"

Three stews ducked into the galley and tried to wrestle the phone out of Judy's hands.

"*Listen* to me, you little slut!" said the voice on the p.a. system. "You better shut that trap of yours or I'll—"

"*The man who is piloting your aircraft,*" screamed Judy, as the stews finally snatched the phone from her hands, "*has a penis the size of a cocktail frank!*"

The aircraft was returned to the gate. Judy, Trudy and Captain Harrigan were taken away to be interviewed by several people at the airline in very reasonable tones and then fired.

Lance reserved a seat on the very next flight to New York, which happened to be the 9:00 p.m. one on TWA—the notorious "red-eye." He had to hurry a bit, but he made it onto the aircraft just as the doors were about ready to close. Lance looked forward to a nice boring flight. If he had not at that point spotted Ernest, Goose and Blatt and gone to greet them, he might have noticed the four short, stocky women in the khaki jumpsuits at the back of the plane who were removing pistols from their carry-on luggage and preparing to address their fellow passengers.

94

The 9:00 p.m. TWA flight for New York took off right on time.
The passengers were all chatting loudly. June nodded to Alix,
Sandy and Wanda. They all unfastened their seat belts and stood
up. Alix, Sandy and Wanda began moving rapidly up the aisle.
June prepared to inform her fellow passengers about the life-
changing alterations she was about to make in their futures.

Two stewardesses spotted the standing passengers and shook
their heads in exasperation. They got up out of their seats and
were just about to say that the captain had not turned off the
"Fasten Seat Belts" sign, when June grabbed a public address
phone off the wall and began to speak in a loud, no-nonsense
voice.

"Your attention please," said June. *"I would like you to listen quite
carefully to what I am about to say . . ."*

Heads turned toward June at the back of the plane. A few
passengers figured she was a harmless loony and began to titter.
June held her massive revolver aloft for everyone to see. The
stewardesses halted and the tittering ceased immediately. Alix,
Sandy and Wanda continued up the aisle past the stewardesses.
They held their pistols in front of them. Several passengers gave
gasps of fear and a general panicked buzzing began.

June fired a shot into the cushion of the seat she was standing
next to. The sound of the explosion in the close quarters of the
airliner was a tremendous shock and effectively froze the buzzing.

"Good," said June. *"My next shot will go into flesh, not polyurethane. Since I finally have your attention, I would like to say a few words about what is happening. In case you haven't guessed, this is a hijack."*

A few passengers began to speak, but June pointed her pistol in their direction and they shut up. Alix, Sandy and Wanda passed through to the cabin ahead.

"As you know," June continued, *"hijacking an airliner is a federal crime, with severe penalties for the hijackers should they be apprehended. For this reason we are quite prepared to kill anybody who attempts to interfere with us. If you wish to stay alive, I suggest that you follow precisely the instructions that we give you. Are there any questions so far?"*

A woman four rows ahead of June timidly raised her hand. She was about fifty-five and had tight gray curls all over her head.

"Yes?" said June.

The woman said something in a wee, shaky voice that was hard to hear.

"Again, please?" said June.

"Are we going to Cuba?" said the woman somewhat hopefully.

"The question was, 'Are we going to Cuba?' " said June. *"No, we are not going to Cuba. Next question."*

A man raised his hand.

"Yes, pig?" said June.

The man looked as if he was about to object to the use of the word "pig" in addressing him, then he appeared to reconsider.

"Uh, can you tell us whether this hijack is motivated by political or by essentially financial motives?" said the man.

"Political," said June. *"This hijack is a political act and a media event. When we arrive at our new destination, most of the female passengers will be permitted the choice of either staying with us or leaving of their own free will."*

"Uh, what about the men?" said the man who had asked the question.

"Did I say you could ask another question, pig?" shouted June, leveling her gun at him.

"N-no," he said.

"No what, pig?" she shouted.

"No ma'am," said the man.

A woman of about sixty with white hair in a bun and granny glasses raised her hand.

"What *are* you going to do with the men?" she said.

"Any passengers of either sex whom we do not deem releasable for political reasons when we reach our destination," said June, "will be obliged to remain with us as political prisoners. Until further notice, all male pigs on this plane are political prisoners."

A young woman in a print dress with little poodles on it raised her hand.

"Can you tell us our destination, please?" she said.

"Our destination," said June, "is not something you need to know yet. You will be informed of our destination at the appropriate time."

An elderly man raised his hand. He was wearing a light tan straw hat with a jolly feather.

"Can't you at least give us a hint?" he said.

"No, pig, no hints," said June. "This is a hijack, not a game of Twenty Questions."

Some of the passengers were interested to see that even elderly men were classified as pigs. It seemed democratic, if rude.

A young woman wearing designer overalls raised her hand.

"Can you tell me where you got your jumpsuits?" she asked.

95

Lance stared at the stocky young woman in the khaki jumpsuit with a mixture of fear and relief. So this was it—what he'd been dreading for so long.

If it had been a normal hijack, he might have been able to look upon it as merely a dangerous adventure, one which he would probably be able to use in one form or another in some novel he would write in the future. But these hijackers had said they were members of MATE, the crazed women's group he told Cathy about and she'd thought he was making up. He knew he and all the rest of the men on board the plane were in serious trouble. He recalled an incident he had read about in which these same women had caught a rapist in Central Park and snipped his testicles off with pinking shears, and he shuddered.

The really strange thing about the woman who had addressed them, though, Lance thought as he stared at her, was that she seemed so familiar. In fact, all four of them had seemed familiar to him, and he couldn't say why. No photograph of them had ever appeared in the papers or on TV. He would have to think about it.

Ernest, Goose and Blatt seemed mesmerized by the proceedings. He wondered what they were thinking. He wondered what would happen to them and to him, and which of them—if any —would survive. He remembered asking Helen whether, if he were on a plane that crashed, he would have to take responsibility for the plane's crashing. He recalled her saying that if he didn't have to take responsibility for the plane's crashing, he at least had to take responsibility for being on the plane that crashed. He wondered if being on a plane that was hijacked was the same thing. He supposed it was. He tried to think what combination of elements had put him on this particular plane at this particular time, seemingly by chance. *Was* it chance that had put him here?

Well, for one thing, he was here on this plane because the plane he was on before this had stood on the runway for an hour and a half while the pilot was getting drunk and the stewardesses were getting stoned. Was that *his* fault? It was not. To be absolutely fair, however, the stewardesses were not getting stoned alone, they were getting stoned with his tacit approval and with one of them being further encouraged by his allowing her to nibble on his dork.

All right. Was it his fault he had gotten on that flight because the flight before it had left early without him? It was not.

When he thought about it, he would never have traveled to Los

DAN GREENBURG

Angeles to be on the *Tonight Show* in the first place had he not written a novel which he was currently trying to promote. And he never would have been invited to appear on the *Tonight Show* if he had not come up with that stupid slogan, "Free the Dalton Two," which he'd intended as a satiric remark. So much for satiric remarks.

Of course, if you took it a bit further, if he had not come up with that stupid slogan, Ernest, Goose and Blatt wouldn't be on this plane now either. So, in a sense, he had to take responsibility for at least four people being on this plane.

He wondered how he felt about that. It made him a little uneasy to have that much responsibility. It also made him feel kind of, well, *protective* toward Ernest, Goose and Blatt. It was not a wholly unpleasant feeling. Perhaps, if he had had so much to do with all of them getting into such a mess in the first place, he might be able to have something to do with their getting out of it as well. Strange thought.

96

Wanda had remained at the rear of the forward Coach cabin. Alix and Sandy moved into First Class. The flight attendants and passengers they encountered had all heard June's address on the p.a. system and gave the women a wide berth, especially when they spotted their guns.

Alix remained in First Class. Sandy opened the door to the cockpit and stepped inside. The captain, the co-pilot and the flight engineer turned toward her and said nothing.

"I assume you heard on the p.a. system what is going on," she said curtly. None of the three men acknowledged her question. She turned to the flight engineer.

"Show me a map of the Pacific," she said.

The flight engineer looked at the captain, then turned to his maps, riffled through them and spread one out on the table in front of him. Sandy peered down at it briefly.

"South of Hawaii and a little east is an island called Manni-hanni," she said. "That is where you are heading. I suggest you inform Air Traffic Control and begin making your turnaround immediately."

The three men continued to look at her.

"Do you have the use of your ears?" said Sandy.

"Can I say something?" said the captain in a relaxed-sounding drawl.

"What?" said Sandy.

"Why don't y'all come off this bullshit, sweetheart, and tell your galfriends to put away the guns. We'll crack open a case of champagne, we'll have a little party up here in the cockpit, and when we get to JFK we'll go back to the motel and we'll take y'all to a place that's one helluva lot better than Hawaii or Mannahanna or anything else."

Sandy regarded the captain soberly for several seconds. Encouraged by her silence, he and the co-pilot and the flight engineer broke into ingratiating, toothy grins. At length Sandy walked calmly over to the captain and stuck the barrel of her gun in his amazed mouth.

"If you don't turn this plane around immediately," she said quietly, "I am going to blow your tongue and teeth out the back of your head. If you have understood what I have just said to you, please nod your head."

Carefully, so as not to alarm the butt of the pistol or its owner, the captain nodded his head.

97

"I really needed this," said Blatt. "I really needed to get hijacked by a bunch of crazy broads with guns."

"If we do everything they tell us to," said Lance, "they may let us go once we get wherever we're going."

"Ah think we could take 'em, bro'," said Ernest. "What *you* think, Goose?"

Goose nodded.

"Ah think we *could,* bro'," he said.

"Yeah? Well, forget about it," said Lance. "Maybe you don't think they have the guts to use those guns of theirs. I'd say, judging from how they sliced that rapist's balls off, they have the guts."

"Say what?" said Ernest.

"You didn't hear about how they cut off a guy's balls who was raping some women in the park?" said Lance.

Ernest and Goose shook their heads.

"Well, they did," said Lance. "So before you get any swell ideas of trying to take them, you just think about that."

Ernest and Goose nodded their heads.

Lance decided he would think about that too.

98

By the time June took over for Sandy in the cockpit, they were nearly there. The flight had gone very smoothly. The passengers and crew seemed suitably impressed with the hijackers' seriousness and so far had complied with whatever requests had been made of them.

June had checked the flight engineer's maps and charts and was not surprised that there was virtually no data on either Port Panguad in particular or Mannihanni in general. As far as they could tell there was some sort of airfield at Port Panguad left over from World War II, but what state of repair it was in or whether the runways were long enough or smooth enough to land a jumbo jet was debatable.

The flight engineer tried several times to contact the tower at Port Panguad without much success. After trying for close to fifteen minutes, he did get some kind of response, but it was very hard to hear over the static, and it was in a language no one in the cockpit understood.

There was a heavy cloud cover over the area where Mannihanni lay according to the maps. At 20,000 feet the full moon lit the cloud cover like an Arctic snowbank. Since no other aircraft responded to their radio calls, they decided it was safe to drop below the cloud cover and make a visual check.

At 8,000 feet they entered the cloud cover and could see nothing at all. At 3,500 feet they finally got below it. There lay Mannihanni—a huge dark shape sprawled in the water like a dead animal. If there was life here it was hibernating. There were no lights.

The fuel gauges were showing very little fuel remaining. They had been burning 12,000 pounds of kerosene every hour for well over five hours and they had to find a place to land before they flamed out. If they couldn't find the airfield they might have to take their chances ditching at sea. The captain took it down to 1,000 feet. Four pairs of eyes in the cockpit raked the island for landing sites. The flight attendants had begun briefing the passengers for an emergency evacuation.

"Ladies and gentlemen," said the voice on the p.a. system, "this is First Flight Attendant Sharon Folsom speaking. At this time, all airline employees, police officers, firefighters and military personnel please identify yourselves to the flight attendants by ringing your call button. Please make sure that all eyeglasses, pens, jewelry and other sharp objects which might injure you during an emergency landing are placed in a safe area such as purse, side coat pocket, or the seat pocket in front of you. Please remove your shoes. High-heeled shoes must be removed and placed in the seat pocket in front of you. All loose items at your seat must now be safely stowed."

June saw it at the same moment as the captain: a glowing patch of ground lay just ahead—the airfield! It didn't seem very large, and the lights illuminating it were fairly weak, but at least it was better than putting her down in the ocean.

"Please make sure your seat belt is low and tight across your hips," Sharon continued. "Note the number and location of your assigned and alternate exits. If you have not already done so, please bring your seat back to the full upright position and make sure your tray table in safely stowed and locked . . ."

The captain sighed.

"OK," he said, "we're going to give it that old college try."

"I think we're going to lose an engine, old buddy," said the flight engineer.

"What's that?" said the co-pilot.

"Number three engine," said the flight engineer. "We're going to lose it."

"Why?" said the captain.

"Fuel," said the co-pilot, eyeing the gauges. "Open the cross-feeds."

"Whoops," said the flight engineer, "there she goes. Number three just flamed out, good buddy. We'd better get down there while we still can."

It was relatively cool in the air-conditioned cockpit, but June's clothing was soaked from nervous perspiration.

"OK," said the captain, squinting down at the ground. "There seems to be what looks like a field or something down there on the far side of the strip in case we're short."

"Let's do it, pal," said the co-pilot, "Before we lose the number one engine."

"Roger," said the captain. "Better tell the people."

The flight engineer picked up his microphone.

"Assume the brace position," he said over the p.a. system.

"Assume the brace position," echoed Sharon on the p.a. system. "With your seat belt still low and tight, lean forward and grab your ankles. If you are not able to grab your ankles, lean forward, cross your arms, place the palms of your hands against the seat back in front of you and press your forehead on your crossed arms."

"We're losing number one, old buddy," said the flight engineer.

"*Brace*," said Sharon on the p.a. "Keep your head down until the plane stops. *Repeat*. Stay *down* in your brace position until the aircraft comes to a complete stop. As soon as the aircraft stops, leave it *immediately*. Do not take *anything* with you during the evacuation. *Repeat*. Do not take *anything* with you during the evacuation!"

"Here goes nothing," said the captain, beginning his approach.

99

In the rear Coach cabin passengers were praying, crying, and trying to remember all the instructions they had been given.

Lance had passed through depression, anxiety and sheer terror, and had come out in a place that was oddly calm and slow and detached. It was, Lance knew, a classic form of panic, but he preferred it to the other forms he was acquainted with.

No sooner had the passengers assumed the brace position than the plane bounced onto the runway with a tremendous jolt. Lance was hurled painfully into his seat belt, squeezing the breath out of his abdomen, then thrown violently backwards and then forwards again. People were screaming loudly enough to drown out the high-pitched whine of the engines. The aircraft continued to buck violently like a maddened bronco, and then suddenly it was over. They were stopped.

"Release your seat belts and get *out!*" shouted Sharon over the p.a. system.

Passengers were still screaming, many of them unaware that they had actually landed. Some of them appeared to be injured. Many were already out of their seats and pressing forward towards the emergency exits.

"Release your seat belts and get *out!*" shouted another flight attendant on the p.a. system.

Some of the emergency doors were jammed and wouldn't open. Lance was out of his seat, trying to assist passengers who were dazed or paralyzed with fear as he headed toward the one exit he now saw they had managed to open.

"Release your seat belts and get *out!*" shouted another flight attendant on the p.a. system, and then the p.a. crackled and went dead.

Ernest, Goose, Blatt, and most of the people in Lance's immediate vicinity now appeared to be moving toward the one open exit in their cabin. FAA regulations required that all aircraft be able to be fully evacuated within ninety seconds, Lance had been told. It was hard to see how such a thing could be accomplished if all emergency exits weren't usable. He wondered how long it would be before the gas tanks exploded and the interior of the cabin became a flaming inferno.

"Jump! Jump! Jump!" shouted a flight attendant and people jumped out of the exit.

"Run! Run! Run!" shouted another flight attendant, and Lance involuntarily thought of grade-school primers starring Dick and Jane and Spot.

Dear God, prayed Lance to himself as he pushed nearer to the exit, if You're listening, and if You exist, and if You care about such things, I promise if I get out of this plane alive that I will never ever have sexual relations with fat ladies or with female executives in their offices or limousines or with kinky police-women or with teenaged girls of any ethnic derivation, and I will return to my own lawfully wedded wife and cohabit with her in harmony or do whatever in the world would please You the most.

And then Lance was at the opening of the emergency exit.

100

The crew had accomplished a minor miracle. They had managed to land a jumbo jet with two engines gone on a runway that was as full of cracks and potholes as a New York City street. The fact that the runway was scarcely half the length necessary to accomplish such a landing, and that the aircraft then traveled across three fields and stopped just short of a long, low building covered with rusting corrugated tin, which contained several drums of kerosene, made the feat even more laudatory.

Twenty-two passengers were injured in the forced landing, none of them seriously. While the passengers were still evacuating the aircraft, several four-wheel-drive vehicles jounced across the field toward it. The vehicles jolted to a stop and a number of people jumped out of them.

The people were all wearing what looked like army combat clothing: paratroopers' jumpsuits, jumpboots, berets, and—although it was quite dark out—sunglasses. They were almost all carrying automatic rifles and submachine guns. They were all black women.

The soldiers, if that's what they were, quickly herded the passengers together and began loading them onto what appeared to be old World War II military trucks. They yelled at the passengers in a language they had never heard before and prodded them with the butts of their automatic weapons until they began getting into the trucks.

June let herself be shoved into a truck. She was in a state of shock. What kind of monsters *were* these Mannihanni women, and why couldn't they recognize their sisters from America? These women were horrible. These women were—yes!—as bad as men!

"Excuse me, Miss," said Blatt to one of the soldiers, "but where are you taking us? *Donde est vous* taking us?"

The soldier looked blankly at Blatt.

"They not understan' you, bro'," said Ernest.

"I know," said Blatt. He sighed a deep sigh. "I don't know, Ernest. I don't think it looks too good for us, pal."

"Ah knows what you mean, bro'," said Ernest.

"I got to be honest with ya, Ernest," said Blatt. "I'm sorry I ever started the whole business with Free the Dalton Two. I hope you don't mind my saying that, pal."

"No, not at all, bro'," said Ernest.

101

It had taken almost two hours, but the half-dozen army trucks finally delivered them to a large building that appeared to be the reception area and waiting room of a partially constructed air terminal.

The modernistic architectural style was, Lance recognized, one that had been popular in the States about twenty-five years ago. The construction apparently had started and stopped roughly fifteen years ago. In the far half of the terminal there were plywood forms still in place, patiently waiting to be filled with poured concrete that whoever was in charge had long since decided not to pour. Framework for large plate-glass windows that would never hold glass was quietly rustling away in the warm, moist, heavy tropical air.

About a hundred and forty people—passengers and crew members—had been dumped into the terminal by the female soldiers, who now stood at parade rest, their automatic weapons slung over their shoulders, their eyes undetectable behind dark aviator-style sunglasses. Lance tried to think who these soldiers reminded him of, and then he had it—the old *Tonton Macoutes* of Haiti's Papa Doc Duvalier. Shortly before they landed, the leader of the hijackers had gotten on the p.a. system and told them they were going to an island called Mannihanni—an island, the hijacker had said with evident pride, where women ruled. Lance wondered what the hijackers thought about Mannihanni now.

The passengers and crew had been loosely segregated by sex and now huddled together on the cement floor in little groups, trying to console and reassure one another. In Lance's group were Ernest, Goose, and Blatt. They were in a state of shock, which was hardly surprising given the fact that they had been hijacked, threatened with shooting, flown five and a half hours to a strange island in the Pacific and crash-landed.

"I guess we should all be thankful we survived the landing," said Lance.

"That right, bro'," said Ernest.

"That right, bro'," said Goose.

"I hope," said Blatt, "that we're still thankful tomorrow, or whenever it is we find out what they plan to do to us."

102

They had been lying on Lance's king-size bed, watching *Casablanca* on the *Late Show,* when the newsbreak interrupted the movie.

"Authorities at the Los Angeles International Airport have just reported that a nine p.m. TWA flight to New York has been hijacked," said a black newsman with a frowning smile. "The hijackers are a militant group of women calling themselves MATE. It is not known at this time where the hijacked plane has been rerouted. Names of the passengers and crew members have not yet been released, pending notification of their families."

Dorothy and Janie looked at each other and raised their eyebrows. They did not see how this piece of news was relevant to their lives. Lance was flying to New York tonight, but he had taken a much earlier flight. They were irritated that the newsbreak had caused them to miss several critical moments of the film.

Cathy had not been watching TV that night. She'd taken a long leisurely bubblebath, then picked up a copy of Lance's first published book, which she had found, remaindered, in a bookstore that afternoon, and climbed into bed to reread it.

Cathy did not know if she wanted to get back together with Lance, but she resented the realization that, for the first time in their separation, he no longer appeared bent on their reconciliation at all costs. She had enjoyed his pursuit of her while it lasted.

She had a profound need to be pursued, to offer resistance, and to succumb. The worst part about being married was that, once you succumbed, nobody pursued you again, unless you had affairs or at least did some serious flirting and teasing.

She was surprised to see how well Lance's first book was holding up in the rereading. It had been the first thing that had attracted her to him. She had read that book and then contrived to meet its author—writing him an extravagantly literary and witty fan letter which had taken her a week to compose. He had responded almost immediately, of course, and she made him court her on the phone before she agreed to see him face to face. Not because she had any doubt that she wanted to, but because she suspected—correctly, it turned out—that he would not be interested in her if she were too available, especially after her extravagant letter.

She finally consented to see him for a drink, and refused to be picked up at her apartment because she was ashamed of the tiny fourth-floor rooms she shared with Margaret and Cheryl. They agreed to meet in the bar at Trader Vic's in the basement of the Plaza Hotel. She arrived twenty minutes late so as not to risk waiting for him alone, and he was forty minutes late, so it hadn't helped.

They ordered frivolous fruity drinks, heavy with rum, and little Polynesian tidbits on skewers. They got high. They teased and enjoyed each other. She let him take her home with him, and she let him hug and kiss her, but she did not let him put his hands inside her clothing. Eventually she said she had to go home. He tried to get her to stay over, but she refused. She was as determined as he was. He offered to escort her home. She allowed him to put her in a cab.

He called her the next day and asked her to dinner. She had already made tentative plans with another man. He talked her into breaking them. She agreed, feeling wicked. They went to a little steak house on First Avenue called Billy's. It had antique lamps and old polished wood wainscoting. They ate and drank and began to fall in love. They went back to his house to hug and kiss. She allowed herself to be talked into sleeping over, with the proviso that he promise not to try to make love to her.

He promised. He swore an oath on his mother's head. He said if he broke his word that God should strike him dead. Fortunately, he broke his word. Fortunately, God neglected to strike him dead. They made wondrous love all night, and slept briefly and started all over again. She never went back to her own apartment. She thought he was the most wonderful man in the world. She was certain that all she needed in this world was to make him happy and to be his wife. She was wrong.

Being his wife and making him happy had not paid off as advertised. She felt eclipsed by his shadow when she stood behind him in the public spotlight. She felt she was competing with his writing for his attention, and coming in second. Her job at the *Times Book Review* was not fulfilling either. There she felt eclipsed by the famous authors whose books she sent out for reviews and by the famous reviewers who reviewed them.

Outwardly, she and Lance continued to be the perfect couple. Even to each other they maintained the image of contentment. Inwardly, each felt responsible for the unrest they shared. But rather than doubt their love for each other, they began to doubt the other's love for them. They gave each other secret tests of love. Each ran the test until the other failed. The tests were designed for failure. They tried to make each other wrong. They nursed hurts and grudges. They sulked. They began to grow apart.

She began to flirt with others. Men clustered around her, wondering whether they had a chance with her. They had more of a chance than they knew. None pressed his luck and she remained faithful to her husband by default. The closest she came to adultery was agreeing to go to an afternoon movie with a married man who was a mutual friend of theirs and then necking with him in the theater like a high-school girl. It was an exciting but stupid act—anybody might have seen them. But maybe that had been the point—to be seen.

At a boozy dinner party in the Hamptons one summer she allowed herself to be led out onto the terrace by one of the male guests and kissed him hungrily with an open mouth. What neither she nor the young man on the terrace realized was that everyone at the dinner table could see precisely what she was

doing. Lance had been surprisingly understanding about the incident. She felt it was because she had given him an excuse to
cheat on her, redeemable at any time.

Lance's editor, Howard Leventhal, had pursued her harder
than anyone. It was not that she was attracted to him. It was
rather that she was attracted to his attraction to *her*. It seemed a
welcome change from Lance's lack of attention to her. Many
times she considered submitting to Howard—to get back at
Lance, if for no better reason—but she held back. Not because
of strength of character. Not necessarily because of strong moral
beliefs. Probably more because the timing had never really been
right.

She continued to resent Lance's lack of attention both in and
out of bed, and his constant expectation to be waited on. And
then Lance got caught bare-assed at his surprise birthday party.
More than shock, she felt relief. She had often toyed with the
fantasy of leaving him. Now she finally had a reason.

Howard had been a huge disappointment. She had wearied of
his lovemaking before they were more than halfway through
their first night together. If Lance had been inattentive and unspontaneous, Howard was simply inept. Lance may have been
reluctant to fondle her as long as she wanted to be fondled, but
Howard didn't quite know what it was you were supposed to
fondle. And being with Howard *outside* of bed wasn't any better.
Lance was preoccupied with his writing, but once you finally got
his attention he was fascinating and fun. It was no problem getting Howard's attention, but once you had it you wondered what
you wanted with it. Howard was a supreme bore. He had no
sense of humor, no sense of adventure, no views of anything that
could not be obtained from the *New York Times,* the *New York
Review of Books,* or the *Wall Street Journal.* The one good thing
about that God-awful cruise to the Caribbean on the Firestones'
yacht was that she finally had an excuse to get rid of Howard.

She was sad that Lance had discovered the photographs of her
and Howard together. Lance had probably been right about her
subconsciously wanting him to find them. Even Dr. Freundlich
thought so. She told Dr. Freundlich that she had been more
aroused making love with Lance while they were separated than

she had for the last six years of her marriage. It was clear that he could be spontaneous and imaginative in bed and engage in all the foreplay she could ever hope for if he only wanted to. And if sex with Lance could go on being as good as it was that night after her birthday dinner, then both of them would want to make love a lot more often than they had in the last few years.

After several sessions with Dr. Freundlich it was clear to her that she could influence how much attention Lance paid to her and how much he expected to be waited on. It was clear to her she could be as much her own person living with Lance as she had been living alone. She could listen to rock music, she could write her own novels, and she could be in the limelight as much as her own ambivalence about success would allow. In any case, whenever she felt eclipsed by Lance it was her own doing, not his.

She was chagrined to find that Lance had filed for a legal separation. She was tired of living alone. She was tired of having to make do without the luxuries his income afforded, and she no longer felt unentitled to them. She missed sharing with Lance the reports of each other's daily doings, their common outlooks on things and people, their private jokes. Cathy and Lance were, fortunately or not, a couple. And she missed him. If she really worked at it, she thought she could get him back again.

She closed the book which had drawn her to Lance originally and turned off her reading light in her tiny white bedroom and composed herself for sleep. The following morning an employee of TWA would telephone to inform her that her husband was a political prisoner on a tropical island on the other side of the globe.

103

Lance slept fitfully for a couple of hours, trying vainly to find a comfortable position on the cement floor of the air terminal. He was hot and sweaty and filthy and his muscles ached. He had taken off his boots and rolled up his shirt and stuck it under his head for a pillow, but it wasn't much help.

A couple of hours after dawn a truck pulled up outside the terminal, and several guards dumped piles of carry-on luggage from the plane into the middle of the floor. As the guards watched from behind their dark glasses and darker automatic weapons, the passengers were permitted to poke through the piles for their possessions. Lance was fortunate to find his shoulder bag, which contained toilet articles, several bottles of vitamins and other pills that Lance was sure would come in handy.

Another truck arrived with breakfast, but many of the passengers were sufficiently put off by the unfamiliar smells and tastes of the food not to consume very much of it. There was a mushy, yellowish, fruity thing which Lance thought might be a kind of melon. There were flat brownish things that looked like giant pea pods. There was something spiky that smelled disgusting and looked like a kind of sea creature. Lance nibbled on the melony thing and on one of the pods, but neither seemed to be anything you would want to put inside your actual body.

All attempts to communicate with their captors fell on deaf ears. The female soldiers either grunted or pretended not to hear. Since they were armed, nobody pressed them hard for a response.

By the time the sun came up, the temperature inside the airline terminal had risen from the eighty-five degrees it had been during the night to the upper nineties. All of the men had removed their shirts and shoes. The older ones rolled up their trouser legs. Some of the younger ones stripped down to their undershorts. Lance was interested to see that a number of the women on the other side of the terminal had done the same thing. The sight of so many women clad in underwear was the only interesting thing about his situation. He did not feel it was adequate compensation for his predicament.

Shortly after nibbling the breakfast fruits, it occurred to Lance to visit the bathroom. He got up and began making his way around the terminal, looking for the facilities. Two guards came over and asked him something he didn't understand.

"Bathroom?" he said. "Toilet? Men's room?"

They stared blankly. His intestines communicated an urgent message to him.

"*Toi*-let," he said, shaping one in the air with his hands. They continued to stare at him.

"*Rest* room," he said. "Commode? Crapper? Pissoir? *Toi*-let."

He pantomimed sitting down, pulling down his pants and straining. One of the women laughed uproariously, and turned to the other.

"Koh-ler," she said, by way of explanation.

"*Koh*-ler," he said, nodding enthusiastically, "very good! Yes! You call it *Koh*-ler? We call it *toi*-let."

"Koh-ler," said the other guard, chuckling, and made the sound of a Bronx cheer with her mouth.

"Where *is* the *Koh*-ler?" said Lance.

One of the guards inclined her head in the direction away from the entrance and indicated that Lance should follow her. He loped after her, as cramps began to clutch at his innards.

She stopped before a door. He was terribly grateful.

"*Koh*-ler," she said.

104

The day after the hijack, October 22nd, was a relatively slow news day, and so most of the print and broadcast media featured the story.

The *New York Times* focused on the political background of Mannihanni and President Taillevent. It speculated upon what Mannihanni would do with the hijackers and spoke of the United States' virtual lack of diplomatic ties to the matriarchal island. It quoted various feminist leaders denouncing the members of MATE for their irresponsibility in hijacking the jetliner and once more dissociating the women's movement from all such extremist tactics.

The New York *Daily News* published a list of the passengers and crew and featured interviews with the air traffic controller who had been the last person to speak with anyone aboard the hijacked plane. The captain of the jetliner had told him they were going to "some cockamamy island in the South Pacific," and hoped he had enough fuel to get there and a decent place to make a landing.

The *New York Post* featured exclusive and heartrending interviews with the members of the passengers' families. Because there had been no official word about the status of the landing, nobody knew if their loved ones had survived or died in a crash.

NBC pointed out that four of the passengers had been guests on the *Tonight Show* the night before the hijack, and featured an exclusive short interview with Johnny Carson, who expressed admiration for all four men, particularly Ernest and Goose, and concern for their safety.

CBS featured an interview with an FAA official who said that there was talk of putting FBI men on all international flights from now on, and when it was pointed out to him that the hijacked plane had not been an international flight he seemed annoyed.

ABC scooped everyone with an exclusive bulletin on the landing. An undisclosed source in the federal government received a report from Honolulu that the hijacked plane had landed safely at the Port Pangaud Airport in Mannihanni, that all passengers and crew members had survived, and that the four hijackers had been shot while resisting arrest. The report did not say what provisions had been made for the transportation of the survivors back to the United States.

The following day, as national attention began to shift to other stories, there was a new report from Mannihanni: An official emissary of President Taillevent issued a statement that one hijacker and twenty-two passengers and crew members had died of injuries sustained in the emergency landing at Port Pangaud. The rest were being detained at the Port Pangaud air terminal, said the statement, pending the outcome of an investigation. President Taillevent's aides were said to be trying to determine whether any of the Americans on the plane were involved in an attempt to assess the size and vulnerability of the extensive Mannihanni natural gas deposits.

A minor official in the State Department expressed bemused irritation at the notion that the United States would be at all interested in the possibility of any potential petroleum deposits on an island as small as Mannihanni. When informed of the supposed three million cubic feet of natural gas reported to have been discovered underneath the Presidential Palace in Port Pangaud, the official said that was nonsense and angrily concluded the interview.

Network switchboards were besieged with calls from frantic members of passengers' and crew members' families, trying to find out whether their loved ones had survived the crash. It was not until the third day following the hijack that a list of casualties could be obtained from the undisclosed source in Honolulu. The list numbered only twelve, not twenty-two. It was published in several papers, and the *New York Post* devoted the entire front page to the list, framed in black. In a later edition, a front-page editorial in the *Post* called for immediate military action to force Mannihanni to surrender the American hostages. This was the first time the word "hostages" had been used to describe the survivors.

The under secretary of state was interviewed on *Meet the Press* and tried to soft-pedal the situation in Mannihanni. He pointed out that neither President Taillevent nor any of her emissaries had said that any of the passengers or crew were either "hostages" or "prisoners," just that they were being temporarily detained. He called upon the news media to try to resist escalation of a potentially delicate diplomatic situation in an attempt to stimulate newspaper sales and television viewership.

Lance's novel, *Gallivanting*, finally made it onto the *New York Times* bestseller list. There was a run on bookstores, on map stores and on public libraries for information on Mannihanni. There was a run on anthropologists to appear on radio and TV talk shows and discuss the matriarchal society on Mannihanni. Mannihanni gags began to appear in the monologues of stand-up comedians in little clubs across the country. Johnny Carson had the restraint to resist making jokes about Mannihanni or Mamma Doc for the first week of captivity.

To Cathy Lerner the hijack was not remotely amusing. From the moment TWA notified her that Lance was aboard the hijacked plane she went into a mild state of shock. She refused to believe at first that Lance had actually been on the plane at all. She telephoned the apartment and spoke with Dorothy and Janie, who were also terribly distraught. When they heard news of the hijack it never occurred to them to worry about Lance, since he had telephoned them the night before and said he was taking a 4:00 p.m. flight back to New York. When he hadn't arrived that night they began to worry. When TWA phoned the following morning, they realized Lance must have somehow decided to take a later plane and been unlucky enough to pick the one that was hijacked.

Until the list of casualties was printed and Lance's name was not found among them, Cathy had convinced herself that Lance was dead and that this was God's punishment for her affair with Howard Leventhal. After the list was published, Cathy felt reprieved—God was giving her a second chance. She didn't know how long Lance and the other passengers and crew members were likely to be held captive. She knew that she, Cathy Lerner, was not going to allow what happened to the hostages in Iran to happen to her husband. She did not know what it would take to get him back. She knew only that getting him back had suddenly become the thing in the world that she wanted most.

Cathy kept the television on constantly, frantically switching back and forth between the channels for the latest bulletins on the situation in Mannihanni. When the news wasn't on, she telephoned the network switchboards and, when the switchboards could no longer handle the volume of calls about the hostages, she telephoned every hour the special number that ABC had set up with recorded updates on the situation.

Cathy also called the offices of her senator, congressman, and the Manhattan borough president. Nobody she spoke to in local government was able to tell her even as much as she had learned from the news on television and from the special ABC recorded bulletins. She was intensely patriotic but had come to hate the government. She thought it was scandalous that the U.S. Treasury was allowed to print up money without additional gold backup, thereby devaluing everybody's money and making inflation worse. She thought the U.S. Treasury should be arrested as counterfeiters. Still, the government ought to be able to do *something* to get the hostages released—step in and do it by force, if necessary. Surely the United States armed forces weren't afraid of whatever military defense could be mounted on the tiny tropical island of black women. And yet . . .

And yet, maybe they were. Before Vietnam Cathy had always taken for granted the fact that the United States was so powerful that nobody could stand up to her militarily. After Vietnam, and after Iran, she no longer knew. It was just possible that a bunch of black women on an island in the South Pacific was enough to scare the military leaders of a nation that had apparently lost its nerve. When she was a little girl in grammar school, the toughest boy in her class inexplicably had been beaten in a schoolyard fight by a somewhat smaller student. From that day on the tough kid shied away from fights, and even the littlest kid in class delighted in taking swipes at the former tough guy, knowing he had lost his nerve and would never fight back.

Well, the joint chiefs of staff might have lost their nerve, but not Cathy Lerner. And if the military was chicken to take on the Mannihannis, then there was always the private sector. TWA was a gigantic corporation, larger than many nations. Surely *they* would be quite anxious to resolve the situation in Mannihanni, if only to effect the return of their jetliner, which must be worth millions upon millions of dollars.

As an editor she'd been trained to get information. There were a number of time-consuming stratagems she could employ, and then there were certain people, like Claire Firestone, who were useful red-tape cutters. She went to see Claire Firestone.

Claire was surprisingly pleasant to her, considering how horrible the cruise had been and how nobody who had been aboard appeared to want to have anything to do with anyone else who'd been. Claire said that she wasn't sure what they could do themselves, but seemed willing to at least find out what efforts were being made by the government and by the private sector to have the hostages returned.

Claire took Cathy to meet with a vice-president at the airline named Boynton. Boynton was a large florid-faced man of about fifty, who seemed simultaneously glad and nervous to see Claire. Cathy assumed Claire had had an affair with the fellow.

"Terrible situation in Mannihanni," said Boynton, "simply terrible. I hope they get those poor people out of there faster than they did the hostages in Teheran."

"What's being done, Arthur?" said Claire.

"Precious little, I'm afraid," said Boynton, sneaking a covert peek at Claire's legs, which were crossed at the knee and visible to at least mid-thigh.

"Does the airline plan to do anything if the government doesn't act quickly enough?" said Cathy.

"The airline?" said Boynton, regarding Cathy warily.

"I don't think the airline is really as eager as you might think it would be to get its airplane back, Cathy," Claire said.

"Why not?" said Cathy.

"The aircraft on this airline are insured," Claire explained. "The insurance more than covers every crash—which is, for example, why the airlines are not as interested in air safety as you or I."

"Now, Claire," said Boynton, taking out his handkerchief again, "that is not fair and you know it."

"The hell it isn't," said Claire. "What incentive do you have to improve your safety record if it doesn't cost you anything when you lose a plane?"

"What about the insurance company?" said Cathy. "Maybe *they'd* be interested in mounting some kind of effort to get the airplane back."

Claire shook her head.

"The insurance company doesn't care either," she said. "They're tickled pink to collect their premiums, invest them, raise their rates, then pay out a relatively small settlement with inflated dollars whenever a plane is lost."

"Now, Claire," said Boynton, forcing an unimpressive chuckle, "this young lady may not know you as well as I, and she may actually think you're *serious.*"

"You're goddamned *right* I'm serious," said Claire. "These insurance companies are so rich, Cathy, they don't even *wince* picking up a 747 or a DC-10. Forty or fifty million dollars over three or four years is chopped *liver* to these guys."

"Claire, please," said Boynton.

"Most airlines," said Claire, "could double or triple the number of planes they lose without any problem at all."

"I hope you don't believe all this, Mrs. Lerner," said Boynton with a strained smile.

"*Believe it,* Cathy," said Claire. "A few years ago National Airlines crashed one of its 727s into Escambia Bay in Florida. National made an after-tax profit from the crash of $1,500,000 because of excess insurance coverage on the aircraft. That amounted to eighteen cents a share on their stock. Ten days after the crash, National issued a press release which said that this

356   DAN GREENBURG

profit came from 'the recent involuntary conversion of a 727 aircraft.' "

"Is this really true, Claire?" said Cathy.

"Ask *him*," said Claire. "He knows the case very well."

Cathy turned to Boynton, who was rapidly patting his forehead and cheeks with his still-folded handkerchief.

"Did that really happen, Mr. Boynton?" said Cathy.

"I don't know," said Boynton. "I'm not familiar with the case."

"He worked at National when it happened," said Claire.

Cathy regarded Boynton for a moment, then nodded and stood up.

"Well, Claire," she said, "I don't think we're going to get a lot of really gutsy support from old Boynton here."

105

Although the meeting at TWA had made Cathy angry and despondent, Claire seemed relatively unaffected. It had been, said Claire, exactly the response she'd expected.

They walked north on Fifth Avenue, discussing the meeting and scanning department-store windows. Cathy asked if Claire knew anyone in government who might be able to help, and Claire didn't respond. At first Cathy thought Claire hadn't heard the question, but then she could see that Claire was thinking. From the way that Claire looked while she was thinking, Cathy felt it was not so much a matter of running a list of former lovers through Claire's mental computer to see if any of them were in government so much as running a list of former lovers in *government* to see which might be effective and willing to help.

"All right," said Claire, validating Cathy's suspicions, "there are two. One is a congressman, the other is CIA."

Cathy was impressed. What would it be like to go to bed with a congressman, to have an affair with someone in the CIA? All she could summon were images from old James Bond movies. What would it be like to permit yourself to hop into bed with any man you wanted to? What price, if any, was being exacted upon Claire for such promiscuity? Was it the obviously wretched state of Claire's marriage to Austin? If so, there was no justice—until she'd left Lance, Cathy hadn't hopped into bed with *anyone,* and *her* marriage was just as wretched as Claire's.

"May I ask you something very personal?" said Cathy.

"What?" said Claire.

"Are these men—Boynton, and the congressman and the CIA man—all people you've . . . been intimate with?"

Claire did not respond.

"Why do you ask that?" said Claire after several moments.

"I don't know," said Cathy. "I'm sorry. I know it's none of my business. Please forgive me."

"I'm not offended by your question," said Claire, "just interested why you would ask it."

"I don't know," said Cathy, blushing furiously. "It just seemed to me that you're more . . . at ease with your sexuality than I am, and I wondered how . . ."

"You wondered how . . . ?"

". . . it felt," said Cathy.

"I see," said Claire.

"I'm really sorry I asked," said Cathy. "I really had no right to be so presumptuous."

"I *told* you I wasn't offended," said Claire, "so stop apologizing. The answer is yes—Boynton and the congressman and the CIA man are all people I've been intimate with. And how it feels to be at ease with one's sexuality I couldn't tell you."

Cathy regarded Claire quizzically.

"You're saying you're *not* at ease sexually?" said Cathy.

"To do something frequently is not necessarily evidence that you're at *ease* with it," said Claire.

"I guess you're right," said Cathy. "It could just as easily be evidence of the *opposite*. Tell me, do you at least . . . enjoy sex? I'm sorry, you don't have to answer that if you don't want to."

"I don't mind answering it," said Claire, "but if you're going to continue asking me presumptuous and intimate questions, at least stop pretending that they just slipped out and you don't really want to know the answers."

Cathy smiled a slow smile.

"OK," she said. "I'll stop pretending."

"Good," said Claire.

They crossed the street and Claire stopped to look at something in one of the Mark Cross windows.

"Do I at least enjoy sex . . ." said Claire, seemingly more intent on evaluating the leather object in the window than rating her level of sexual enjoyment. "Well, that's a complex question. I enjoy many *aspects* of sex, but the most pleasurable ones are not necessarily those centered in my erogenous zones."

"What do you mean?" said Cathy, realizing she knew.

Claire again allowed several moments to elapse before replying, then turned to face Cathy.

"The reason that I'm taking so long to reply to your question," said Claire, "is not that I'm trying to figure out the answers. It's that I'm trying to figure out how candid I want to be with you."

"If you're wondering whether you can *trust* me," said Cathy, "all I can tell you is that I have no reason to betray you."

"Well, maybe you do and maybe you don't," said Claire. "But don't worry, I don't trust anybody anyway."

"Well," said Cathy, snorting with laughter, "I guess that settles *that*."

"Not necessarily," said Claire. "Just because I don't *trust* you doesn't mean I can't be *candid* with you. I could tell you things that don't cost me very much. Or I could tell you things that wouldn't do me much harm if I were candid about them. Or I could tell you things which would do *you* more damage than *me* if you revealed them."

Cathy chuckled with unexpected amusement. There was something about this woman's outrageousness that tickled her.

"Are you this guarded with your friends?" said Cathy.

"I don't have any friends," said Claire. "I have acquaintances,

I have people I use, I have people who use me. I don't have friends."

"I feel sorry for you," said Cathy.

Claire nodded.

"I feel sorry for myself," she said. "Maybe that's why I'm talking like this. I don't know. Maybe it's because it's time I tried to *have* a friendship."

"With me?" said Cathy.

"Maybe," said Claire. "I had an opportunity to observe you quite a lot on that horrible cruise. And I liked what I saw."

"What did you see?" said Cathy. "Besides a miserable lady tossing her cookies, I mean?"

"I saw a woman who was fairly decent and straightforward as women go," said Claire. "I don't know many women who are either decent or straightforward. Most of them would just as soon stab you in the back as look at you."

Cathy nodded.

"I'm not sure that I'm not one of those myself," said Claire. "I just thought I'd warn you."

"All right," said Cathy. "I'll take my chances. I'm a big girl."

They passed a black beggar with a seeing-eye dog. He had a sign strapped to his chest which said THANK GOD YOU CAN SEE. Cathy took a handful of change out of her purse and dropped it into the blind man's cup. He nodded at her as she passed.

"People like that make me feel so guilty," said Cathy.

"Why?" said Claire. "Just because you're so much more fortunate than they are?"

"No, because I always find myself wishing something dreadful would happen to them so I wouldn't have to look at them."

Claire laughed. They continued north on Fifth Avenue. They passed vendors selling hot chestnuts, mixed nuts, pretzels, hot dogs, orange juice, pencil drawings of animals, umbrellas, handbags, costume jewelry. They passed musicians playing trombones, violins, flutes, guitars, steel drums, with their hats and instrument cases open before them on the pavement and sprinkled with small change.

"I remember when Fifth Avenue used to be an elegant boulevard," said Cathy. "Now it's a combination minstrel show and flea market."

Claire chortled.

"Are you usually this crotchety," said Claire, "or are you just trying to get in my good graces?"

"I'm not changing how I feel," said Cathy, "just how much I express."

Claire nodded.

"Look, Cathy, I don't know if we can be friends, but I do want to clear the air about something."

"All right."

"How do you feel about the fact that you called your husband at a hotel in Detroit and I answered the phone?"

Cathy stopped to drop a few more coins in the cup of a blind man in ragged clothing who was sitting on the street, stroking a large black and white rabbit. She wasn't sure what part the animal played in the man's life, unless it was a seeing-eye rabbit.

"I don't love it," said Cathy, "but I figure I deserved it. I mean Lance and I were already separated at the time, and I *was* having an affair with his editor. I don't see how I could really be too convincing in the role of the wronged wife."

"Yes," said Claire, "but how do you feel about *being* with me, knowing I've slept with your husband?"

"That depends," said Cathy.

"On what?"

"On whether or not you're planning to sleep with him in the future," said Cathy. "Assuming there *is* a future," she added quickly.

"You want him back, don't you?" said Claire. Cathy nodded. "I mean you want to live with him again, don't you?"

Cathy nodded again.

"You haven't answered my question," she said.

"I know," said Claire. "Well, I'm *not* planning to sleep with him in the future. Although, to be brutally frank about it, I suspect that is more his decision than it is mine."

"Do you . . . love him?" said Cathy.

"I don't think I love *anybody*," said Claire. "I do find Lance terribly attractive and fun to talk to and to be with and to . . . manipulate. I was able to manipulate him for a while, and then he realized he didn't have to allow it. When I saw he wasn't letting me manipulate him anymore, I got really angry. But I also started respecting him a lot more than before."

"How were you manipulating Lance?" said Cathy.

"It's not important," said Claire. "I tend to manipulate everybody, especially men. It's always amazing how easy men are to manipulate."

"Because they're weak or stupid or what?" said Cathy.

"Because they want to be manipulated," said Claire.

"Yeah, you're right," said Cathy. "Having a woman manipulate them reminds them of their mommies. And if they're being manipulated they don't have to take responsibility for their actions."

"You sound like you've been talking to a shrink or two."

"I've been going to a shrink ever since my separation. It's one of the smartest things I've ever done," said Cathy.

Claire made a face.

"What do you need with a shrink?" she said. "You're not crazy."

"That's where you're wrong," said Cathy. "We're *all* crazy. But people who go to shrinks tend to screw up their lives a little less than people who don't."

"My life isn't screwed up," said Claire. "My life is great."

"You're full of shit," said Cathy smiling. "Your life is so great you don't trust anybody, you don't have any friends, you feel you have to manipulate men into having sex with you, and when I asked if you at least *enjoy* the sex, the most you could say was that you enjoy certain *aspects* of it."

Claire sighed.

"OK," she said, "*touché*. You know, what I most enjoy about sex is the excitement of seduction. Of being the seducer."

"Why do you think that is?" said Cathy.

"It's about the only way I can feel in control," said Claire.

They passed by Tiffany's and both women paused to look at the contents of the windows.

"Control comes in a whole lot of different forms," said Cathy. "Sometimes it's hard to know who's controlling whom."

"I know," said Claire.

"Why do you think you have to feel in control all the time?" said Cathy. "Is that the only way you think you can survive?"

"Could be," said Claire.

"To control everybody you come in contact with all the time?" said Cathy.

"Every single second," said Claire.

"Are you controlling me now?" said Cathy.

"I guess I must be," said Claire, "by definition."

"It doesn't seem like you are," said Cathy. "It seems like you're being really candid and vulnerable."

"That could just show how insidious and sneaky I am at controlling you," said Claire.

"Yeah," said Cathy. "Or it could show you're so vulnerable that you try to convince people you're manipulating them even when you're being completely honest."

"It could show that," said Claire.

"You're a strong woman," said Cathy. "You don't have to manipulate people in order to survive."

"Perhaps," said Claire.

"I'm not as strong as you are," said Cathy. "And when I finally assert myself and do something I should have done for myself a long time before, I feel so guilty I can hardly enjoy it."

They passed a man in dark glasses, sitting on the pavement, holding a cup. Cathy reached into her purse and dropped the last of her coins in his cup.

"Hey," he said, "what are you doing?"

"What?" said Cathy, confused.

The man stood up and poured the coins out of his cup and handed them back to her.

"I'm not a beggar," said the man.

"I'm so sorry," said Cathy, "I saw the dark glasses and the cup, and I—"

"I'm a guy on a coffee break on a sunny day," said the man. "Gimme a break, for God's sake, will ya?"

Claire burst into laughter. Cathy babbled apologies. The man walked away, muttering.

106

Lance was aware of his fellow passengers to only a limited degree. Blatt had withdrawn into a deep despondency and spoke very little. Ernest and Goose chattered to each other and tried to flirt with the guards. As inept as Goose must have been with the women in the States, the Mannihannis appeared to be amused by him. Goose entertained the guards with headstands, cartwheels, and grotesque faces. Two or three guards would stand together, watching him and giggling. They appeared to be more than a little intrigued by a clumsily designed tattoo Goose had on his right bicep. In homage to Muhammad Ali, or perhaps to Goose himself, it said "THE GREATEST."

Ernest and Goose were of the opinion that the only way out of their predicament was through a romantic liaison with the guards, and to this end they were ceaseless in their attempts to endear themselves. On the fourth day of captivity, Goose finally succeeded.

He had been doing mock obeisance to them, touching his head to the floor, kissing the toes of their combat boots, and then, on an impulse, he began kissing his way right up the leg of the guard who was closest to him. When his kissing neared her crotch, she became alarmed. She seized his head in both her hands and began to scream at him in her native tongue.

The passengers who had been watching Goose's clowning held their breaths to see what she'd do next. Several guards clustered around her and began a heated argument. At length the guard who held Goose's head between her hands asked him a question.

Goose grinned idiotically at her and didn't answer. Once again the guard asked him her question. It was impossible to guess what she was asking, but nonetheless Goose decided to agree. He nodded his head and smiled. The guard turned toward her colleagues and conferred briefly with them.

Lance tried to make out what they were saying, but could understand nothing. The language at times sounded almost French, but there were no recognizable French words. It also sounded a little Spanish and a little Indian and a little African. The one sound Lance heard repeated was a name: Monte.

Monte? Monte *what?* Monte *who?* Monte Cristo? Monte Carlo? Monty Python? Monty Clift? Monte Hall? Monte Rock? The guard turned back to Goose and asked him another question containing the name Monte. Once more Goose grinned idiotically and nodded his head. This appeared to please the guard, for she stroked his face. She then motioned for Goose to follow, and led him out of the terminal. Just before he went through the front door, he turned back and waved to Ernest, Blatt and Lance, and then he disappeared.

Ernest turned to Blatt and Lance and gave them an I-told-you-so look.

"Well," said Ernest, "it look like mah man has made the grade."

"Maybe," said Lance.

"Maybe?" said Ernest. "What you mean, 'maybe,' Mr. Lerner?"

"I mean," said Lance, "I want to hear what he tells us about his experience before I draw any conclusions about whether or not he made the grade."

Lance took the edge of his thumbnail and carefully etched a graffito in the soft plaster of the wall. "Free Lance Lerner," it said.

He liked the look of that. He felt it worked on several levels. As an exhortation to his captors. As a professional title. As a memo to his restrictive super-ego. He thought he might one day have it set in type and hung above his desk. Assuming, of course, that he would one day be able to *return* to his desk.

The only other such sign on the wall of his study in New York was one which he had appropriated from a *New Yorker* cartoon shortly after he became a full-time freelancer. The cartoon was of a kid in a very progressive kindergarten asking his teacher, "Do we *have* to do what we want to do?" He had had the caption set in Old English type and framed. He sat staring at it for hours on end when the sense of too much freedom in his new professional capacity threatened to overwhelm him. DO WE HAVE TO DO WHAT WE WANT TO DO? For a long time it had had the power for Lance of a Zen koan.

On the way back from the men's room to the floor space he shared with Ernest, Goose and Blatt, Lance passed the four hijackers. The leader looked up at him, frowned, and snapped her fingers.

"Shit!" she said.

"What is it?" said Lance.

"I just realized where I know you from."

"Where?" said Lance.

"Did you live in an apartment in the East Forties in Manhattan?" she said. "Forty-eighth Street?"

"Yes . . . ?"

"And your old lady walked out on you and took all the furniture?"

"Yes . . . ?"

"Shit!" she said. "We're the ones who moved her!"

"You're a *Motherloader?*" said Lance.

"Yeah."

"I'll be goddamned!" said Lance. "I *thought* you looked familiar!"

"Yeah," she said. "Small fucking world, huh?"

"You're not kidding," said Lance.

They smiled and shook their heads in bafflement, a sudden bond of kinship formed between them.

"Yeah," she said, "Alix, Sandy and Wanda were the other three on the job that day—we were a team. Small fucking world."

"Jesus," said Lance. "And you're the same group that castrated that guy in the park? The rapist?"

"Yeah."

"How about that," said Lance. "Listen, I hope you don't mind my asking, but how did you go from moving my wife's furniture to castrating rapists to hijacking airplanes?"

June shrugged.

"How does anybody do anything?" she said. "You do something that doesn't particularly interest you for a while, and then one day something better comes along."

When Goose did not reappear that night, Ernest took it as a very good sign—Goose was spending the night in bed with at least one of the guards, and possibly even more than one. And however rustic the guards' accommodations might be, they had to be luxurious compared to the floor of the terminal.

When Goose did not reappear the following day, Ernest said it must mean that he had managed to please the guards enough to make them want to keep him with them. Ernest himself now began to play up to the guards, but he was too self-conscious to clown around the way that Goose had, and so he was not successful. The guards did not smile when he tried to speak to them, and soon he stopped trying.

There seemed to be fewer people lying about on the terminal floor than when they first arrived. It was impossible to say if this was actually so, but that was Lance's impression. He wondered what had happened to the others, if indeed anything had happened to them at all. He wondered if they had charmed their way into other guards' beds, or had merely died of dysentery. He felt it was time for him to try to improve his situation.

On his next trip to the men's room, he indicated to the guard that he wished to communicate a request.

"*I,*" he said, pointing to himself, "wish to *speak* to someone."

The guard looked blank.

"*I,*" he repeated, pointing to himself, "*speak.*" He pantomimed exaggerated processes of speaking, yelling, declaiming, shaping billowing clouds of verbiage from his mouth. "I . . . *speak,*" he repeated.

"I . . . *speek,*" parroted the guard.

"Good," said Lance, nodding enthusiastically. He knew she hadn't understood, but at least she appeared to be willing to listen to him.

"*I,*" he said, "*go* speak." He pantomimed exaggerated walking and then speaking.

The guard looked confused. Well, thought Lance, confusion is a slightly higher state than blankness. Next comes noncomprehension, and from then on it's all uphill.

"*I,*" he said, "go speak to *boss. Your* boss. Do you have a *boss?*"

"*Boss,*" said the guard, clearly having no idea what the term connoted.

"*Boss,*" he said, trying to think of a way to act out the concept. He mimed an angry employer shaking his fist, yelling, pointing, pounding his desk. He mimed a scared employee smiling nervously upwards, cringing behind his upraised arms, warding off blows. By the time Lance thought of saluting, the charade had been going on for ten minutes. The guard's face immediately registered comprehension.

"*Boss,*" she replied excitedly, and returned the salute.

"*Wonderful,*" said Lance, "*very* good. I don't know why I didn't think of that sooner. Here I am, trying to convey the concept of boss by enacting a melodrama in an office, when a simple salute would have . . ."

"*Boss!*" said the guard again, whipping off another smart salute.

"*I,*" said Lance, "go *speak* . . . to *boss.*" He mimed going, speaking, and saluting. The guard was beginning to put it together.

"*I,*" she said, pointing to Lance. "*Speak,*" she said, miming his speaking motions. "*Boss,*" she concluded, whipping off another crisp salute.

"*Yes!*" said Lance delightedly. "*Yes!* Very *good!*"

The guard appeared to think this over, then arrived at a decision. She grabbed him by the upper arm and began to pull.

"*Speak boss,*" she said. Lance could have kissed her.

107

The guard led Lance to an American jeep. It was painted black and had a somewhat familiar-looking insignia on its doors and hood. Lance didn't at first know where he had seen it before, and then he remembered—it was a gigantic blowup of the symbols the guards wore around their necks. He assumed the symbol to be either religious or political or both.

The guard motioned for Lance to climb into the jeep. He did. She climbed in the other side.

"What's that?" he asked, pointing to the symbol around her neck.

She looked at him uncomprehendingly.

"*That,*" he said, and pointed directly at the symbol.

She pulled in her chin and peered down at it with crossed eyes. She looked back up at him and pointed to the symbol, obviously surprised that he didn't know what it was.

"*Monte,*" she said.

"*Monte?*" he said. There it was again, the name he'd heard in their conversation about Goose. Whoever this Monte fellow was, he was pretty popular to be on the jeeps and around the necks of the soldiers. The guard said something with the name Monte in it, but realized he wouldn't understand. She smiled and shook her head, then started the engine and took off across the bumpy terrain.

Once they left the airfield, the terrain grew greener and hillier. To Lance's right was, he guessed, the Pacific. It seemed utterly calm, and the glare bouncing off it was too painful to look at. To Lance's left were low hills choked with palm trees and vines.

The road they were traveling on was a two-lane dirt road, but it appeared to be the major thoroughfare along the ocean. They passed a number of native women on the road, driving oxen and cows and pigs. The only motorized vehicles they passed were army trucks with the same symbol of Monte on their sides.

After about thirty minutes of driving, they entered a populous area. Dozens of corrugated-tin huts, adobe huts, and huts made of what looked like blocks of dung. A primitive gas station with one rusting pump. A handful of tiny stores with corrugated-tin roofs and open stalls. A couple of open-air bars, with large bottles of cheap rum standing on a table, and groups of native women sitting on stools, drinking and conversing. Lance had traveled in Mexico, Guatemala, and many islands in the Caribbean, but he could not recall seeing housing and living conditions as poor as these.

They stopped at a military checkpoint, manned by two female guards with the same uniforms as those who guarded the terminal, except that these wore white patent-leather Sam Browne belts and holsters. The guards at the checkpoint had slung submachine guns and the pistols in their patent-leather holsters were automatics. The driver of Lance's jeep spoke with them briefly. The guards peered in at Lance, then let him pass.

Once past the checkpoint, the road got flatter and better tended. The bushes on both sides of the road were dotted with red and purple flowers. Lance didn't know their names. Up ahead was some kind of castle. They went through another checkpoint, and then Lance could see the castle clearly. It was enormous. It was made of huge stones, and it appeared to be several stories high. It had high conical turrets, with flags sporting the symbol of Monte, and it was surrounded by a moat.

The jeep stopped at a third and final checkpoint, and then clattered across the wide drawbridge. They entered a beautiful courtyard. Parked at the far end of the courtyard were two army trucks and three Mercedes-Benzes. One of the Mercedes-Benzes was a white stretch limousine. Four little flags with the Monte symbol flew from the corners of the limousine.

He pointed to the limousine.

"Boss?" he said.

The guard nodded and rolled her eyes.

"Mamma Doc," she said.

"Mamma Doc—then the scuttlebutt on the terminal floor had been accurate. Mamma Doc Taillevent—President-for-Life—was the power here. Was this the Boss he was being taken to see?

The guard parked the jeep and motioned for Lance to get out. He stepped carefully to the ground, wobbling slightly, and steadied himself by leaning against the side of the jeep. The guard got out and motioned for him to follow. Several female soldiers stopped to stare at Lance as they made their way to the castle entrance. Lance realized that he hadn't seen a single native man on Mannihanni since his arrival. He wondered where they were.

They entered the main doors, went through yet another checkpoint, and then turned down a passageway lined with rock. It was much darker inside and about thirty degrees cooler. Lance followed the guard into a large office. Behind a desk sat a receptionist, also in uniform, typing with two fingers on an old upright typewriter.

The guard said something to the receptionist. They both looked at Lance, and then they spoke some more. The guard motioned for Lance to sit down on a worn wooden bench, then waved goodbye to him and left. Lance was sorry to see her go. Although they hadn't communicated more than three or four words, he felt that she was his first friend on Mannihanni. He wondered whom it was she'd brought him to see. He sensed that it would not be Mamma Doc.

After he had waited for perhaps an hour, two more guards appeared, and walked up to him without smiling. They motioned for him to get up. He followed them into a large dark room with a desk and three chairs. One of the chairs was made out of steel. It had been painted over several times, and was fairly dirty. Next to the steel chair was a large rectangular metal box with numerous dials and switches. Lance figured it was a shortwave radio.

The guards motioned for Lance to sit down in the steel chair. As soon as he did so, they swiftly bound his wrists to the arms of the chair with leather thongs.

"Hey," said Lance, "what's going on here?"

One of the guards bent down and tried to tie Lance's ankles to the chair, but he moved his legs out of her reach. The second guard brought the muzzle of her submachine gun up to Lance's jaw and he let his ankles drop back down again. The first guard bound his ankles to the chair legs with leather thongs.

Lance was beginning to get really nervous. What had he gotten himself into by asking to see the boss? Who was this boss who was going to see him, and why was it necessary to have one's wrists and ankles tied to a chair when one saw this boss? Lance began to get very nostalgic about his old home on the cement floor of the stinking terminal and wished that he was back there.

The first guard stood up, ripped open Lance's shirt, and unbuckled his belt.

"Uh, listen" said Lance, "I changed my mind, I *thought* I wanted to see the boss, but it turns out I didn't want to after all. It turns out I completely forgot an appointment I had made in the terminal to see—"

The second guard unzipped Lance's fly and yanked at Lance's trousers. He felt a sudden spasm in his bowels.

"Please," said Lance, forcing a pained smile, "I really do have to leave now."

The second guard yanked again, and pulled Lance's trousers down below his knees. In a perfect world, he thought, he would have had clean underwear. In a perfect world he would probably also not be tied to a steel chair in a castle on a strange island in the Pacific, having his trousers yanked below his knees. He had spent the ten years before his marriage trying to yank down the pants of women, and ever since his separation it seemed that every woman he met was trying to retaliate in kind.

When the guard yanked down his undershorts as well, Lance got even more nervous than he was already, but not nearly as nervous as he got as soon as he saw what they were up to. What they were up to was attaching wires to terminals on the shortwave radio and bringing them over to where Lance was sitting.

Please, God, he prayed, let them be hooking me up to the shortwave radio to hear a stereo concert from Prague while I'm waiting to talk to the boss and not what I think they're doing.

The guards attached wires to Lance's wrists and ankles by means of perforated rubber straps with metal terminals on them.

One thing now was certain—they were not hooking him up to a shortwave radio to hear a stereo concert from Prague. Please, God, he prayed, let them be hooking me up to an electrocardiograph machine as part of an exhaustive physical examination.

The guards attached more electrodes—to his chest, his right ear, his right nostril, and his penis. It was looking less and less like an electrocardiograph hookup every second. Finally the guards finished their hookups and withdrew.

Lance had seen *Midnight Express,* he had read countless stomach-churning charitable solicitations from Amnesty International, and he could no longer pretend that what was going to happen to him was anything other than what he dreaded most: he was going to be tortured.

Even when Lance was a small boy growing up during the Second World War and heard stories of how soldiers were tortured by the Japs and the Germans, he never understood how anybody could endure it. He himself had never fostered any illusions about whether he could endure torture. He would admit to the Mannihannis whatever they wanted him to admit to—it didn't matter what.

"Just tell me what you want me to admit to," he said aloud, although the room was empty. "I'll swear I've done it."

108

Lance had been sitting, strapped to the steel chair and wired to the machine, for about ten minutes when he heard somebody enter the room behind him and close the door. The somebody walked slowly and heavily to the desk.

The somebody was a very tall, very husky black woman in a black uniform, a black Fidel Castro hat and dark glasses. She was smoking an enormous cigar. She looked carefully at Lance, as if trying to figure out what he was doing there, and then sat down heavily in the chair behind the desk.

Lance waited, with pounding heart, for something to happen, but the woman continued to stare at him and smoke the cigar and say nothing.

Lance cleared his throat.

"Uh, I'd like to go to the toilet, if I may," said Lance, aware that the person behind the desk probably could understand him no better than the guards at the terminal.

There was no reaction from the large person behind the desk.

"*Koh*-ler," said Lance carefully. "I . . . wish . . . *Koh*-ler."

The person behind the desk erupted in laughter. Lance was startled. The person behind the desk seemed to find Lance's request the height of wit.

"Hew don't have to say *Koh*-ler," said the person. "Hi understand 'twalette.' "

"Good," said Lance, genuinely heartened, having enormous faith in his ability to communicate verbally, provided one spoke his language.

"Hi em General Maxime," said the person behind the desk.

"Ah," said Lance, impressed at the rank. "How do you do, General Maxime. I am Lance Lerner. I'd shake hands, but I'm afraid they've tied my wrists to this chair for some reason."

The General did not apparently find this humorous. She did not reply.

"I wonder, General, if I might go to the toilet just now? I have a severely upset stomach, and I really have to visit the toilet."

"Hew may not veeseet the twalette," said the General. "Hew are a prisoner."

"A prisoner," said Lance. "Yes. I know that. But why, General? Why am I a prisoner? What have I done wrong?"

The General smoked silently for a while before replying.

"Hew deed not come here because hew were hijacked," said the General.

"I didn't?" said Lance. "Then why did I come?"

"Hew weesh to spy on our natural gaz supply," said the General. "Hew theenk les Etats Unis can capture thees natural gaz from Mannihanni, but hew are wrong."

She leaned over to what looked like an intercom on her desk and pushed a lever. Instantly, searing pain sped through Lance's body and he realized the torture had begun. He bit down hard on his lower lip to keep from screaming, and the pain eventually stopped.

He was amazed. He hadn't screamed. He hadn't made a sound at all.

"I am not a spy," he said, and tensed.

The General hit the switch again. Once more searing pain shot through his body, once more Lance bit down on his lower lip, once more it stopped, and once more he had not cried out.

"I am not a spy," he said again. "I'm an author."

Suddenly he felt courageous. He had withstood two electric shocks and he hadn't crumbled as he was always certain he would. Maybe he wasn't the coward he had always feared he was.

"Hew are what?" said the General.

"I'm an author," said Lance. "I write books."

"Books?" said the General. "Wheech books?"

"Novels," said Lance. "*Knuckle Sandwich, Fresh When Available, Modern Lit, Cut to the Chase, You Can't Get There from Here*—those are all the titles of novels I've written. *Gallivanting* is the latest one."

"*Gallivanting?*" said the General.

"Yes," said Lance. "Why, have you heard of it?"

The General grew suddenly livid and smashed down on the lever on the box on her desk. Once more the fiery pain attacked his body. Lance bit through his lower lip and blood ran warmly down his chin, but once again, miraculously, he had survived and not made a sound.

"Hew deed *not* write *Gallivanting!*" said the General. "Hi know thees to be a *fact!*"

"How would you . . . know such a thing?" said Lance.

He was beginning to lose consciousness now, but he didn't care. If he was going to die, at least he could die content that he hadn't been a coward after all.

"How Hi would *know* such a theeng?" thundered the General.

"How Hi would know such a theeng ees that I hev seen who wrote *Gallivanting* on the *Tonight Show!* And *hew* are not *heem!*"

"I am . . . Lance Lerner . . ." he said, now barely able to speak. "I am . . . the person you saw on . . . the *Tonight Show* . . ."

The General lurched out of her chair and came over to where Lance was sitting. She aimed her desk light at Lance's face, and held up his chin.

"Hew do not look like heem," said the General less certainly.

"I don't . . . look like him because . . . when you saw me on the . . . *Tonight Show* . . . I had shaved and . . . showered and . . . was dressed . . . differently . . ." Lance mumbled.

The General lifted Lance's chin a bit higher.

"Now that hew mention eet," said the General, "Hi theenk there *ees* a slight resemblance."

"Good . . ." mumbled Lance, genuinely pleased that he was able to look at all like himself, even now.

"So," said the General, "hew are the author of *Gallivanting*. Tell me sometheeng."

He was sinking in black fur. It was a lovely feeling. But somebody had asked him a question. It would be possible to answer it before he left. It would be impolite not to.

"What . . . can I . . . tell you . . . ?" whispered Lance.

"What ees Jawnny Carson really like?" said the General.

109

Lance awoke between cool sheets in a clean bed.

He was back in New York, he knew it. The whole nightmare in Mannihanni had been just that—a nightmare, and now he was awake and back in the land of the living.

He opened his eyes.

"Hew slept?" said a familiar voice.

He was not back in New York. The nightmare was still on. The person who had spoken was seated opposite his bed in a big wicker rocking chair, smoking a cigar.

At least he was alive.

He was still weak, his wrists and ankles and nostril and ear and chest and penis hurt where the electric shocks had been administered, but at least he was still alive. Not only was he alive, but somebody had given him a bath, a shave, possibly even washed his hair, and dressed him in what felt like cotton pajamas. Who had done this and why?

"Hi owe you an apologize," said the General. "Hi have checked your story and hew are who hew say. Hew are famous auteur. Hew are not a spy."

"No kidding," said Lance weakly. He wondered why they were mutually exclusive—why you couldn't be a famous auteur *and* a spy—but wisely he did not raise this philosophical point.

"None of us is a spy," said Lance, "and I suggest that we all be released and allowed to return to our homes in America."

The General continued puffing her cigar.

"Ees not my job to decide thees," she said between puffs. "Ees job of our President-for-Life, Madame Taillevent."

"Well then," said Lance, "I would appreciate having an opportunity to speak to her about this."

"Madame Taillevent ees very busy woman," said the General. "But porhops she weel find time for the friend of Jawnny Carson."

Two more days passed before Lance was able to arrange an audience with Mamma Doc. On the evening of the third day, a guard appeared in his room carrying an old black wool tuxedo on a hanger, reeking of mothballs. She handed it to him as if he was supposed to know what to do with it.

"What's this for?" he said.

The guard merely extended the tuxedo to him.

"Thank you," he said, taking it from her, "but what is this *for?*"

"Mamma Doc," said the guard.

Lance brightened.

There was a white wing-collar shirt and a white bow tie. The jacket sleeves and trousers were four inches too short, and the body of the jacket was far too roomy, but there didn't appear to be time to visit a tailor. Lance wasn't able to tie much of a bow in his tie, and no shoes had arrived with the rest of the clothing. He was forced to follow the guard down the hall barefoot. Considering all that had happened to him thus far, it did not seem to be a noteworthy detail.

After a long walk down many stone corridors, Lance was ushered into a baronial dining room. At the end of a table that was easily twenty feet long and set with white linen, china, and gold flatware, sat Mamma Doc. She was much as Lance had imagined —tall, husky, black and female. Her hair, unexpectedly, was white, and she was dressed in a white silk variation of the General's modified army uniform, but without the hat or the cigar.

The guard saluted her and motioned to Lance. Lance bowed. The guard withdrew. Nobody had yet said a word. Lance prayed she spoke English.

"Hello," said Lance, enunciating clearly. "My name is Lance Lerner."

"We are Madame Taillevent," said Mamma Doc. "Please to be seated."

Mamma Doc motioned Lance to a chair at the other end of the table. He sat down. He realized that he was to dine with Mamma Doc—certainly a great honor, and one that would doubtlessly not have been conferred upon him were it not for his intimate friendship with Johnny Carson.

"Well," said Lance, "this is an unexpected pleasure, Madame Taillevent. I mean I had no idea that we would be dining together."

Mamma Doc gave him the briefest of smiles and inclined her head.

"Eet ees not often that we are able to dine weeth a fameuse auteur."

A guard appeared with a bottle of champagne and filled the gigantic crystal goblet in front of Lance's plate. Mamma Doc, he noted, had a filled glass already.

"Well," said Lance, raising his glass to Mamma Doc, "I, uh . . ." He suddenly found himself unable to think of a toast suitable to a female president who used the royal "we." In fact, the only toast that came to mind was one that he'd seen Bogart use in the movies. "Here's looking at *you*, kid," he said to her at last.

Mamma Doc appeared to find the toast acceptable. Either she was a Bogart fan or else she assumed it was a traditional American toast to royalty.

"Heer's looking at *hew*, keed," she intoned solemnly.

They drank. It was surprisingly good champagne.

The champagne was a little *too* good—before he knew it he had drained the glass. The moment he put it down a guard appeared from nowhere and swiftly filled it up again.

"So, Meestair Lerner," she said, "how hew theenk of Manni-hanni so far?"

Lance smiled uncomfortably, then opted for politeness.

"I, uh, like it fairly well," he said. "What I've seen so far, I mean."

"Yais?" she said. "Hew like fairly well the grinding poverty of the peasants?"

"Uh, heh heh, well, now that you mention it, I *don't*," he said, somewhat unnerved. "I was just being polite, as a matter of fact."

"Not to be polite, Meestair Lerner," she said. "We een Manni-hanni are not polite. Politeness ees a luxury we cannot to afford."

"Well then," said Lance, "to be brutally candid, Madame President, I was *shocked* at the living conditions of the peasants that I saw on the way to your palace. Especially in contrast to the way you yourself live—your champagne, your crystal glasses, your gold flatware, your Mercedes limousine."

"How we leev een the Palace," she said, "ees not so much for our own plaisir as for the peasants. The peasants demand that their leader leev een splendor—eet geev them dignity."

"Dignity?" said Lance. "What kind of dignity can they have if you live in splendor and they live in rusting corrugated shacks?"

"Hew do not understand our ways, Meestair Lerner," she said. "Eef we were a reech country like les Etats Unis, then all our peoples could to have the champagne, the crystal glasses, the gold flatware, the limousine. Seence we are not, they weesh for *us* to have eet at least."

"I find that hard to believe," said Lance. "I'm sorry, but you did ask me to be frank."

"We do weesh hew to be frank, Meestair Lerner," she said. "We weel tell hew, then, that we deed at first, followeeng the revolution, leev een the corrugated-teen shacks as the peasants. But the peasants tell us, '*No*, Madame la Présidente, *no*, Mamma Doc—eef hew leev as we do, then the leaders of the beeg countries like les Etats Unis weel not respect us."

"Then why don't you do something to improve the quality of their lives?" said Lance.

"We do," she said. "Every Sunday we go ride een the limousine and veeseet weeth the peoples. We tell them of the advances we making een the government. We throw to them the gold coins."

Lance sighed.

"Look," he said, "what you do with your own people is your business, I guess. What you do with mine upsets me a lot more. Why are you holding us prisoner?"

"We do not hold hew preesoner, Mistair Lerner," said Mamma Doc.

"No?" said Lance. "You mean we're free to leave?"

"Yais, of course," said Mamma Doc. "Only we must to determine first why hew come here."

"Look," said Lance, "the General says you think we're spies, that we're interested in your natural gas deposits. We never even *heard* of any natural gas deposits before we arrived here. We never even heard of *Mannihanni* before we arrived here."

"You no like the General?"

"That would be a gross understatement."

"You no like her because she ees woman or because she ees Negro?"

"I no like her because she tortured me when I was first brought to the castle."

Mamma Doc appeared truly shocked.

"No! The General do thees to *hew*?" said Mamma Doc. "Eet ees not possible!"

"I thought she did it at your behest," said Lance.

"No!" said Mamma Doc vehemently. "Not our behest! The General tortures only at behest of the *General*. The General ees vicious, weecked, *evil* person!"

"Then why do you allow her to continue in such a position of power?" said Lance.

"Why?" said Mamma Doc. "We *tell* hew why. Mamma Doc ees good—the peoples all loving Mamma Doc, yais? But the General ees evil—the peoples all hating the General. So eef sometheeng unfortunate have to be done that the peoples weel hate, we have the General do eet, and the peoples not hating Mamma Doc."

Lance nodded. He supposed Mamma Doc was right. Two guards brought several platters of food to the table. One of the dishes appeared to be some kind of meat. Another appeared to be fish, and a third was neither meat nor fish, though probably not fowl either. Smaller platters contained varieties of mashed fruit and what looked like seaweed.

"Ees not like your food een les Etats Unis," said Mamma Doc. "Ees not like your McDonald's homboorgers."

"It's certainly not," said Lance.

Mamma Doc seemed vastly amused.

"Een les Etats Unis," she said, "we have experience the same deefeeculty weeth the food as you do in Mannihanni."

"You were in the United States?" said Lance.

Mamma Doc nodded.

"Shortly followeeng the revolution against the accursed French," she said. "We deed not have the education. A world leader must to have the education. So I go to les Etats Unis for the education."

"Where did you study?" said Lance.

"UCLA," said Mamma Doc. "We study Heestory, Pheelosophy, Engleesh, French . . ."

"I would have thought you already *knew* French," said Lance.

"We *deed*," said Mamma Doc. "We take French because we theenk maybe we can *ace* eet."

Lance chuckled. There was something fairly ingratiating about this woman, he thought. Ingratiating and oddly familiar.

"How did you pay for the tuition?" said Lance.

"The people of Mannihanni geev me scholarsheep," said Mamma Doc.

"And what degree did you attain there?" said Lance. "A Ph.D.?"

"No no," said Mamma Doc. "We go only one semester. Then we feel we serve better the people of Mannihanni in Port Pangaud than een West Los Angeles."

"If you only went to school one semester," said Lance, "then why do they call you *Dr.* Taillevent and Mamma *Doc?*"

"Ah," she said, "that ees because we receive the Doctor of Deeveeneety degree from the Universalist Chorch. By mail."

"I see," said Lance.

"No," said Mamma Doc, "we deed not weesh to stay more than one semester een les Etats Unis. Your country ees, forgeev me, not to my taste."

"Why not?" said Lance.

"For many reason," said Mamma Doc. "The McDonald's homboorgers, the poleeteecal seetuation, the pollution of the atmospheres, the commercialism of everytheeng. But most of all, ees too unpleasant for me to be een society wheech ees not separateest."

"Which is *not* separatist?" said Lance, incredulous. "You mean you'd like blacks and whites to be *segregated?*"

She shook her head impatiently.

"Not black and white," she said, "man and *woman.*"

Lance laughed.

"So that's why I haven't seen any men so far in Mannihanni," he said. "Where do they live?"

"The men of Mannihanni," said Mamma Doc, "they are not a problem weeth us. They know their place."

"And what is that?" said Lance.

"The usual," said Mamma Doc. "The work of the house. The procreation. The care of the small babies. The work wheech does not tax the mind—that ees what they like the best."

As they continued to chat, Lance noticed with utter astonishment that a hairy black spider the size of a soup bowl had suddenly dropped onto the tablecloth from above and was now ambling in a leisurely fashion toward the food. He watched it, frozen with fascination, not daring to breathe for fear that it would be attracted to him.

If Mamma Doc saw the spider she was giving no indication.

When it was two feet from her plate, Mamma Doc soundlessly raised her fist above her head and brought it swiftly down on the spider. Lance heard a sickening splat. The spider's legs twitched and curled into a ball.

Lance turned away, certain he was going to vomit. When he glanced back at Mamma Doc he noted that she had covered the spider's remains with a large cloth napkin and had already resumed eating her dinner. These people are barbarians, he reasoned, why should I be surprised?

"Meestair Lerner," chided Mamma Doc, "Hew do not eat your deener."

"I'm, uh, not too hungry tonight, thanks," said Lance.

"Do hew grieve for the spider?" she said.

"No," he said, "I scarcely knew him."

Mamma Doc laughed.

"Hew have a droll manner to express yourself," she said.

"Death brings out my antic side," he said.

"Do hew appear often on the *Tonight Show?*" she said.

"Not that often," he said. "Once every few years."

"What ees he like?"

"Johnny Carson?"

"Yais."

"He's a good guy. Smart, smooth, handles himself nicely. I don't really know him that well, if you want to know the truth."

"Last night he say your book ees on the bestseller leest."

"No kidding?" said Lance. "Did he happen to say what number it was?"

"Eight," said Mamma Doc.

"Far fucking out," said Lance. "Well, next time a young author asks me how to publicize his novel, I'll know what to advise: get hijacked."

"Hew are quite eentelligent for a man," she said.

"Thanks a lot," he said.

"Do hew have the fortune to be married?" she said.

"Sort of," said Lance.

"Please?"

"Well, yes, I'm married," said Lance, "but my wife and I no longer live together."

"Ah," said Mamma Doc. "And does thees condeetion deestress hew?"

"It did at one time," said Lance. "A great deal."

"Not at present?" said Mamma Doc.

"Not that much," said Lance.

"We een Mannihanni could to use a man of your eentelligence."

"Oh?" said Lance. "In what way?"

"The men of Mannihanni have leetle eentelligence," she said. "They adding nothing to the bloodlines when they breed. A man weeth your eentelligence would add much to the bloodlines."

"I see," said Lance.

"Porhops hew would to conseeder to stay een Mannihanni when the others leave," said Mamma Doc.

"And become a stud horse?" said Lance.

"That and other theengs," she said.

"What kind of other things?" said Lance.

The notion of staying in Mannihanni for any purpose at all, even as a court stud, was not enthralling.

"We have the weesh," she said, "to write a book."

"Stop the presses!" said Lance. "Tear out the front page!"

"Please?"

"I'm sorry," said Lance. "I was being impolite. I know a great many people who are writing books."

"Ah," she said. "But thees book *we* weesh to write weel be our autobiography. Porhops hew would weesh to help us."

"Hey, listen," said Lance, "I really appreciate the offer—I'm really knocked out by the offer and all—I mean I'm really honored that you would even ask me. But I'm afraid that it just isn't the kind of thing I like to do."

Mamma Doc nodded slowly.

"Een les Etats Unis hew have the expression 'every man have hees price,' no?"

"Yes," said Lance. "But I'm afraid that there isn't anything you could offer me that would change my mind."

Mamma Doc took a last bite of food, chewed it slowly, swallowed.

"What eef we say to hew, 'Meestair Lerner, eef hew stay een

Mannihanni to help us to write our book, then we letting every-body else go home'?"

"I thought you said that you were going to let all of my people go anyway," said Lance. "I thought that's what you said a few minutes ago."

"What we say," said Mamma Doc, "ees that we weel eenvesti-gate eef all the peoples on the airoplane come heer because they are forced, or eef they weesh to spy. *Then* we letting them go."

"And now you're saying that you'll release them only if I stay and help you write your autobiography?" said Lance.

Mamma Doc nodded.

"Hew are not required to geev us answer tonight," said Mamma Doc. "Hew may cogitate about thees for a while."

"All right," said Lance.

The guards began clearing dishes.

"Hew weesh a brondy, Meestair Lerner?" said Mamma Doc.

"Oh, no thanks," said Lance.

"Hew weesh to come to our bed now and make sex?" said Mamma Doc.

"Uh, not tonight, thanks," said Lance, trying to suppress his shock at her question.

"Hew theenk we are too old for hew?" she said.

"Old?" said Lance. "Oh *no*, Madame Taillevent. Not too old at *all*. I *love* older women."

"How old hew theenk we are?" said Mamma Doc.

"How old?" said Lance, stalling for time. He had absolutely no idea how to play this. He figured she was around seventy-five.

"How old?" said Mamma Doc.

"Oh. Well, uh, I'd say, about . . . forty-nine?"

Mamma Doc let out a shriek of laughter which startled him.

"Hew theenk we are *forty-nine?*" she cried, helpless with mirth.

"You aren't?" said Lance.

"We are seexty-seex," said Mamma Doc.

"Sixty-*six*," said Lance, playing up the surprise angle. "You're *kidding* me! I don't *believe* you? Sixty-*six!* That simply isn't *pos-sible!*"

Mamma Doc beamed with satisfaction.

"How many years have *hew*, Meestair Lerner?" said Mamma Doc.

"Me?" said Lance. "I'm forty."

"Forty," said Mamma Doc. "Forty ees not too old for me. I have made sex weeth boys of only twelve."

"Is that so?" said Lance. "When you were how old?"

"Not how *old*," said Mamma Doc, "but what *time?*"

"Excuse me?" said Lance.

"We make sex weeth a twelve-year-old boy only thees morning."

"Ah," said Lance.

"Hew find thees unusual?" said Mamma Doc. "That we take a boy thees age for sex?"

"Well," said Lance, "I guess it *does* sort of surprise me. I mean I guess I'm always surprised to find out what a woman wants."

"What a woman wants?" said Mamma Doc. "A woman wants energy."

"Energy?"

"Energy from the act of making sex," said Mamma Doc. "We store it up. It geev us strength. That ees why we ordered to make sex by our god."

"Your *god* orders you to have sex?" said Lance.

Mamma Doc nodded.

"Monte," she said.

"Why does Monte order you to have sex?" said Lance.

"Eet make Monte hoppy eef we make sex," said Mamma Doc. "The act of making sex geev strength to us, then we geeving strength to Monte. Hew certain hew don't weesh to come weeth us now to bed and make sex?"

"Uh, well, not tonight, I'm afraid," said Lance.

"Hew weesh rain check?" said Mamma Doc.

"Yeah," said Lance. "I'll take a rain check."

A guard appeared to escort Lance back to his room. Mamma Doc extended her hand to Lance. He didn't know whether he was expected to shake it or kiss it. Playing it safe, he did both.

"Please to theenk about whether hew weesh to help us weeth our book," said Mamma Doc. "Please to take all of the time that hew require. Only give us your decision sometimes tomorrow."

It wasn't fair. Why should the fate of all the passengers hang on whether Lance was willing to sacrifice himself by remaining in

Mannihanni? Most of them he'd never even met. Would they sacrifice themselves for *him*? On the other hand, how was he going to feel if their imprisonment lasted months or even years —knowing all the time that he could have saved them? How was he going to feel as the elderly and sickly passengers began to die, knowing that he could have spared their lives by giving up his freedom?

What if he *did* stay in Mannihanni? Would it be any better than death? What kind of life would he have here? He would certainly be given exceptional treatment—wonderful living quarters, champagne, perhaps his own limousine. He would evidently be given an endless supply of Mannihanni women to impregnate, and would watch as dozens—possibly even hundreds or thousands—of his children were born and grew to maturity. The notion of having that many children was momentarily intriguing, but then he remembered that in Mannihanni it was the men who raised the children and his fantasy dissolved.

If he stayed in Mannihanni, he would be forced to become Mamma Doc's lover. The huge, sixty-six-year-old black woman was not exactly his ideal mate. On the other hand, how many more years would she even *want* to have sex? Probably well into her late nineties, with his luck.

Needless to say, he would never again see anyone he loved back in America. Never see Cathy. Never see his folks. Never see Dorothy or Janie or Stevie or Claire or any of the others. How could he face that? The notion of a future in which he would never know anyone but Mannihannis plunged him into despondency.

Lying in his bed, Lance debated the decision that Mamma Doc had asked him to make by the following day. He fell asleep debating.

110

Maybe it was because they'd been frisked and the guards knew they no longer had weapons. Maybe it was because they were women and the guards therefore considered them either weaker than men or simply less hostile. Whatever the reason, on one of the nights when June, Alix, Sandy and Wanda were escorted to the women's room, their armed attendant made the mistake of propping her automatic rifle against the wall and relieving herself alongside her captives.

No sooner had the guard squatted over one of the holes in the floor than June knocked her cold with a karate chop. Alix bolted the door from the inside. Sandy boosted herself up to the window ledge, smashed out the glass, crawled through the empty frame and dropped to the ground outside. Wanda and Alix went next. Just as June was about to boost herself up onto the ledge, somebody outside tried the door, found it locked, and began to pound on it. June jumped for the ledge, missed her handhold and slid back into the room just as the door burst inwards.

The guard who had kicked down the door fell forward with the momentum and temporarily lost her balance. Within the next second all these things occurred: the guard regained her balance, June saw that it was too late to jump for the ledge again because she would be shot in the back, the guard registered her unconscious compatriot on the floor and June as the probable attacker. June saw that she was too far away from the guard to use karate on her. Within the following two seconds these things occurred:

June's right hand went inside her jumpsuit to her crotch. The guard's submachine gun was raised into position. June's thumb and first two fingers of her right hand entered her vagina and found the first of two Ben Wa balls. The guard clicked off the safety and began to squeeze the trigger. June's right hand came out of her pants, snapped back over her right shoulder, and hurled the gold-plated ball with all her might at the guard's forehead.

The submachine gun chattered, but the bullets thunked harmlessly into the wall, because the owner of the finger which had pulled the trigger was in the process of falling onto the floor unconscious. June leaped for the ledge, and this time she made it. She crawled through the window and dropped to the ground. The four women were already across the field and into a corrugated-tin shed before the searchlights went on and the yelling started.

111

Lance awoke, drenched in his own sweat. He got up, washed, put on his tuxedo, and buzzed for a guard. When his door was unlocked and the guard appeared, he said simply: "Mamma Doc." The guard evidently understood what he wanted, for she immediately nodded and disappeared.

Within twenty minutes the guard had reappeared and led him through the dark, damp stone corridors of the castle to see Mamma Doc.

Mamma Doc sat in a bed that must have been twice king-size,

dressed in white satin pajamas, watching a game show on television. The guard brought Lance into the room, bowed to Mamma Doc, and withdrew.

"Good morning, Madame Taillevent," said Lance.

"Good morning, Meestair Lerner," she said. She inclined her head toward the television set. "You know thees program, *Fomeely Feud?*"

"Uh, sure," said Lance. "How are you able to get American TV shows on Mannihanni?"

"Eet arrive on the satellite," she said, then grimaced. "Thees show ees excellent exomple of the decadence of les Etats Unis."

"Why is that?" said Lance.

"What do they compete to know—answers to questions one find een the Encyclopedia Britannica or the Koran or the Judeo-Chreestian Bible? No. They compete to know answers to questions wheech most numbers of peoples geev when asked. The highest aspiration een les Etats Unis ees to *be* like everybody else and to *theenk* like everybody else."

"Well, that's certainly true of *some* people in the United States, but I don't think it's fair to say that *everybody* in the country feels that way," said Lance.

"Yais?" said Mamma Doc. "Porhops hew tell us now hew not part of the attacking of our girls that happens yesterday een the night!"

"*What* attacking of girls happened last night?" said Lance.

"Hew standing there and saying hew not *know?*" shrieked Mamma Doc. "Weeth your name on one of the weapons of the *attacking?*"

"I have absolutely no idea of what you are *talking* about," said Lance. "I *swear* to you!"

"Tell me, Meestair Lerner," she said, "your Christian name is wheech?"

"Lance," said Lance.

"Lance," she repeated, withdrawing something small from the pocket of her gown and holding it out to him so he could get a close look at it.

It was a small gold ball. It was . . . Lance couldn't believe what it was she was showing him—one of the two Ben Wa balls he had given Cathy years ago in New York! And now, for some reason that God alone could grasp, here it was, on the other side of the world, in the hand of the dictator of an obscure South Sea island!

"I . . . have absolutely no idea what that is doing here," said Lance incredulously.

"So!" said Mamma Doc. "Hew confess that hew *know* thees object!"

"I confess that I know it," said Lance, "but I—"

"Hew confess that hew throw thees object een the head of one of our girls yesterday een the night een the lavatory of the women?" said Mamma Doc.

"Absolutely not!" said Lance. "How could I have been in the lavatory of the women last night? I was here in the palace, locked up in my room, asleep."

Mamma Doc pondered this a moment. It was undeniably true that Lance had been in the palace the night before and locked up in his room.

"Very well," she said, "we weeling to believe hew not responsible. But unteel we finding out who *ees* responsible, we keep your peoples here."

"That's really ironic," said Lance.

"Why ees ironic?"

"Because," said Lance carefully, "I came here this morning to make you a counter-offer on the writing of your autobiography in exchange for the release of my people."

Mamma Doc looked at him for several moments before replying.

"Your mind ees eenteresting to me, Meestair Lerner," she said. "Porhops we shall ask Monte what we are to do weeth your people."

Lance was tempted to suggest that if she refused to let his people go, Mamma Doc could expect locusts, floods, and the slaying of her firstborn, but he thought better of it and restrained himself.

"Perhaps we could ask Monte together," is what he said instead.

Mamma Doc's eyebrows raised themselves, seemingly independently of their owner's intent.

"Hew weesh to take part een ceremony to honor Monte?" she said.

"Yes," he said. "I would consider it a great honor."

"Ees great *great* honor," she said, "but we weesh to be certain thees ees what hew truly weesh to do."

Lance sensed this might well be the tipoff to back down, but he somehow felt that going through with it would win him many more points than he'd lost with the Ben Wa ball.

"Taking part in a ceremony to honor Monte is what I truly wish to do," said Lance.

"Een thees case," said Mamma Doc, "we cannot to refuse hew such an honor."

"Thank you," said Lance.

"Porhops hew weesh now to have the further honor to breeng hyour meelk-white body to our bed to make sex weeth us?"

"Oh, not just now, thanks."

"Porhops hew weesh another rain check?"

"Yes, a rain check would be better."

"Eet amuse us to pretend we geeving you thees choice."

"I beg your pardon?"

"We know anytime we weesh hew to come to our bed and make sex weeth us, we have but to send for hew and hew weel do what we weesh."

"I will?"

"Yais. Because hew so attrocted to us and because hew weesh to keep hyour penis and hyour balls attached een the place wheech they now attached."

Lance was speechless. Mamma Doc smiled a smug smile and returned to her televised game show.

112

By the time Lance was returned to his room and locked in to eat his lunch, he was trembling with anger. Mamma Doc's insinuations that he belonged to her, that he was sexually on call whenever she wanted at peril of castration, filled him with rage and fear. More rage than fear. Did she honestly think she could force him to service her sexually whenever she wanted? On the other hand, did he honestly think she *couldn't?* What kind of a man would he be if he acquiesced to such an arrangement? On the other hand, what kind of a man would he be if she had his gonads amputated? It was a paradox—the only way to keep his balls intact was to pretend he didn't have any, the only way to show he had balls was to lose them.

What would his group say now—that he was letting himself be victimized again? That once more he was willing to let a woman control him sexually? That what Mamma Doc wanted was a grotesque parody of what he felt all women wanted? That the feelings engendered in him by Mamma Doc's pronouncements were merely an exaggeration of the feelings he sometimes had about the sexual demands made upon him by his own wife?

Maybe it wasn't so farfetched after all. Maybe the anger toward women he had apparently been feeling all his life stemmed from fear. Fear of women. Fear of sex with women. Fear of what sex with women led to—commitment and permanence. Commitment and permanence, in his mind, led to having children, to having grandchildren, to growing old, to dying, to death.

When Lance was about eight, his parents took him to a resort in the Indiana Sand Dunes called Duneside Inn. One night, shortly after they'd put him to bed, he began to think about such matters as how far out did outer space go, where did it end and, more important, what lay beyond the end? Then, perhaps logically, he began to think about death. For the first time in his life he realized that when he died that would be the end of him.

He got nauseated and claustrophobic and felt he couldn't breathe. It seemed he was falling slowly upwards into a black infinity. He called out tearfully for his Dad to come and explain away his fears, to make it all right as he always had before. But for the first time in his life his Dad wasn't able to make it all right. He told little Lance that we lived on through our children, that we lived on through our work, but that we didn't really know what happened after death, if anything at all.

Lance found no solace in his father's words. He couldn't bear the thought that he would die someday, that he would cease to exist for the rest of time. Did others know they were going to die? If they did, then how could they just go about their lives as if nothing were wrong, as if they were going to live forever? He wanted to run up to people on the street and ask them if they knew they were all going to die and what they planned to do about it.

Eventually he calmed down. He pretended to himself that everything was all right, that everything was still the same, that nothing had changed, but he knew better. He never overcame his fear of death, he just repressed it to some subconscious level where he didn't have to deal with it. The same level at which he probably truly believed that having sex with women put you on a cosmic conveyor belt that led inevitably to death. If you could avoid sex with women, then maybe you could avoid getting on that conveyor belt and somehow manage to avoid death. If that was how he had it pegged subconsciously, then it was certainly useful to harbor anger at women. Harboring anger at women was an effective barrier against being intimate and sexual with them.

He sat down at the table and began picking at his lunch. There was a meatlike dish which looked like what he had been served at dinner with Mamma Doc—*carpus* she had called it, he seemed to recall. There was also a fishy thing again, and seaweed, and several things that looked like mashed fruit, and something that looked like squid or octopus with two big eyes staring up at him from the plate.

He took a large piece of seaweed and covered the creature with the two big eyes and took experimental bites out of the fish. Possibly it had not been refrigerated very well, because it tasted less than fresh. He took little bites of the mashed fruits but found them rather bitter. He cut off a piece of the meatlike *carpus* and began to chew it. It didn't taste quite as sickly sweet as it had at dinner with Mamma Doc. He swallowed the piece he was chewing and put another, somewhat larger piece in his mouth.

The larger piece was a mistake. It was just too chewy and tough. He took it out of his mouth and put it on the side of his plate. It looked like leather. He peered closely at it. It *was* leather. It even had lettering on it. He couldn't quite make out what it said because of the brown sauce on it. He wiped off the brown sauce and picked it up and held it close to his eyes. The letters were E . . . A . . . T. Eat? Was this some kind of a gag? Why would they serve him, along with his lunch, a small piece of leather encouraging him to eat?

He wiped at the small piece of leather and looked closely at the word EAT. There was something about the lettering that looked faintly familiar. Where had he seen it before? How *could* he have seen it before? The letters were a poor imitation of the lettering in the Superman logo. Where was the last place he had seen lettering like that?

An image flickered through his consciousness, no longer-lasting than a subliminal image in a television commercial. He knew better than to chase it. The best thing to do when you were trying to summon a forgotten word was to just let it go, relax, and let it come back of its own accord. He closed his eyes and relaxed. The image came flickering back briefly, and then was gone again, but this time he had had enough time to read it. What it said was THE GREATEST.

THE GREATEST—the Muhammad Ali tattoo he'd seen on Goose's skin! That was it, he was certain of it now. The EAT was taken right out of the middle of the tattoo! The Mannihannis had cooked Goose's goose and served it to him. He had just eaten human flesh!

Lance got up from the table so violently that he upset the tray. He had just chewed and swallowed part of a fellow named Goose Washington, a person he had known and spoken with and even appeared with on the *Tonight Show*.

He lay down on the bed. He had to make sense of this extraordinary piece of information immediately, because it related very directly and very immediately, he sensed, to his own well-being.

The last time he had seen Goose was in the airline terminal, flirting with the guards. One guard in particular had been the focus of Goose's attention. It had seemed that she was interested in Goose sexually. She had discussed Goose's behavior with her fellow guards. She had asked Goose something, and he, having no idea what it was, had nodded agreement. The question the guard had asked of her colleagues and of Goose had the name Monte in it, Lance was almost positive of that. And then the guards had taken Goose out of the terminal, presumably to fuck, and that was the last anybody had ever seen of Goose again. Till now, that is.

Had Goose unwittingly volunteered to participate in a religious ceremony honoring Monte—the same kind that Lance himself had recently committed himself to with Mamma Doc? And was the standard consequence of the Monte ceremony that the volunteer was killed, cooked and eaten? When Lance had still been in the terminal it had seemed to him that there were slightly fewer passengers than when they had first arrived. Were the Mannihannis simply cannibals who were keeping them like cattle to be slaughtered for food?

Perhaps Lance was wrong. Perhaps the piece of meat was not part of Goose's tattoo at all. Perhaps it really *was* a piece of leather with the word EAT on it which Mamma Doc had slipped into his lunch as a prank. He devoutly prayed that this was the case. He devoutly prayed that the Monte ceremony was simply a pagan religious ceremony and that nothing more occurred in it than that a group of people got together, did some drumming and dancing and chanting, and then Monte was pleased enough to grant them good health or great wealth or whatever it was they wanted, and that was that.

Surely that was the extent of the Monte ceremony. Surely there was nothing more sinister about it than that. And yet. And yet, the Mannihannis were a violent people. And they had at least in part modeled themselves on the Haitians, who were also black, descended from Africans, and former subjects of the French. They had even appropriated the uniforms of the Haitian *Tonton Macoutes,* and the nomenclature of the Haitian presidency— Mamma Doc Taillevent, President-for-Life. Didn't it therefore follow that the Mannihanni religion might be patterned after voodoo, with the same sort of bloody sacrifice to the gods as a requisite part of every ceremony? If the Haitians butchered pigeons, chickens, pigs and sheep in *their* ceremonies, wasn't it possible the Mannihannis butchered men in *theirs?* Many primitive tribes ate the brave animals they hunted to absorb their strength or courage—wasn't it possible the Mannihannis ate men they sacrificed in their ceremonies for the same reason? Wasn't it possible that when a Mannihanni woman said she wanted to have sex with you and eat you, that she wasn't merely using a figure of speech?

This is insane, thought Lance, I am going insane here. I am being swept up in paranoid fantasies and convincing myself that these people are cannibals and that I am about to be slaughtered and eaten, and the only evidence I have is a little piece of leather with the word EAT on it. There has to be a saner and more conventional explanation to all of this. There has to be. Perhaps if I just lie here and try to relax and not think about the food all over the floor and the creature with the two big eyes and the little piece of leather with the word EAT on it, the truth will come to me.

Lance lay across his bed, staring up at the Monte symbol on the wall, trying to decide what was paranoia and what was real. The answer lay in Monte. The Monte symbol was doubtlessly an abstraction of something, but what? It looked like a peace symbol that had sprouted legs, sticklike legs. Or arms. Or claws. Claws like a crab or a lobster. Claws like some kind of hideous insect. Like some hideous, carnivorous, grasping, preying . . . mantis.

Praying mantis. That's what the damned thing looked like—a praying mantis! Mantis pronounced with a French accent was ... MONTE! The praying mantis, whose chief claim to fame is that, when it has finished mating, the female bites the male's head off!

Lance buzzed for a guard, his chest pounding.

113

Mamma Doc looked up from the TV as the guard led Lance back into her bedroom.

"So," she said with a raucous laugh, "do hew return to tempt us weeth sexual favors, Meestair Lerner?"

"No," said Lance carefully, "I return to ask you a question: What happens in the Monte ceremony?"

"Please?"

"What happens in the Monte ceremony?"

"Releegious copulation."

"Religious copulation and ... death?"

"Yais, of course, death. Copulation and death they are always close. Een hyour language sometime the sexual climax ees called 'the leetle death,' no?"

"Yes, but that isn't intended as a literal—"

"Thees ees what sex ees *about*—death. You have sex and then you have death. Death and tronsfiguration."

"In the Monte ceremony, *whose* death and *whose* transfiguration are we talking about?"

"The male who ees offer heemself to the High Priestess een

releegious copulation. And the tronsfiguration of hees body eento sometheeng holy and perfect, wheech ees then come eento the body of the High Priestess where eet and the High Priestess and Monte Herself become one. Eet ees exqueeseet to die and sojourn weeth Monte."

"Yes, I'm sure it is. Tell me, how . . . I mean, by what means does the male who has offered himself to the High Priestess in religious copulation . . . achieve death?"

"Ees very sweeft," she said somewhat defensively. "Ees almost weethout pain."

"What is the means?" said Lance.

She seemed hesitant to answer.

"Is it by . . . beheading?" said Lance.

"Thees happen to be the very humane death," said Mamma Doc. "We don't expect somebody he come from les Etats Unis to appreciate the Monte ceremony."

"It's barbaric," said Lance.

"Hew calling our releegion barbaric?"

"Barbaric and totally immoral."

"Hew are releegious bigot, Meestair Lerner! We under the eempression een hyour country releegious bigotry has been out-lawed!"

Mamma Doc seemed a little unsettled. She reached toward the bedside table, opened an ornately carved wooden box, extracted a cigar, bit off the head and lit it up. Beside the carved box was something that Lance hadn't noticed on his previous visit this morning—a wig stand. On it was a black wig. The General and Mamma Doc were one!

"You're cannibals, too," said Lance quietly, "aren't you?"

"Please?" said Mamma Doc.

"You're cannibals," said Lance. "You eat human flesh."

Mamma Doc raised her eyebrows.

"Yais, of *course* we eating human flesh. Ees very *tasty*, human flesh. Ees a great *delicacy*, human flesh. *Hew* have been eating human flesh as well, Meestair Lerner, seence the day hew arrive here."

Lance closed his eyes. There seemed little point in passing out now. Everything seemed so surreal. Surreal and more lethargic than real life, like a movie which has lapsed into slow motion. He felt a definite need to leave Mannihanni rather rapidly, before anyone processed him as a candidate for a transfiguration or a smorgasbord.

"This morning," said Lance, "I mentioned an alternative proposal to the one you offered me regarding your autobiography. I would now like to outline that proposal."

Mamma Doc gave him an interested look.

"I am not willing to ghostwrite your autobiography," said Lance. "I *am* willing to *write* your *biography*. If it's written in my voice rather than yours, the complimentary things in it will be more believable. But I will not write the book unless you agree to let me include some critical things about you as well. And I will not write the book unless all of the hostages are released by sundown tonight, and unless I am among them."

Mamma Doc erupted in maniacal laughter.

"Thees ees no proposal," said Mamma Doc, "these ees *boolsheet!* Hew leaving Mannihanni tonight, we never seeing hew or the biography again! What hew theenk we are, Meestair Lerner, a bimbo?"

"I do not think you are a bimbo, Madame Taillevent," said Lance, letting his gaze stray to the box of cigars and the wig stand. "On the contrary, I know that only a bimbo would believe that any author in the world, no matter how successful, could make a deal on a book as important as this without spending considerable time meeting with editors in New York, querying them about their marketing and promotional capabilities, and ensuring that the book would be guaranteed an enormous amount of attention—attention that makes the difference between a book that sinks without a ripple, like thousands of books that come out every year, and a book that hits it so big that its author and its subject are asked to appear on the *Phil Donahue Show* and the *Mike Douglas Show* and the *Merv Griffin Show* and the *Tonight Show*."

He paused to let his words sink in, watching Mamma Doc's face intently for a reaction. She drew in a cheekful of smoke, held it briefly, then expelled it into the air. She thoughtfully shaped the ash in an empty bowl which had probably recently held delicacies, like parts of hapless fellow hostages.

"Tell us, Meestair Lerner," she said after a while, her eyes still on the ash of the cigar, "what make hew theenk Jawnny Carson weesh to put the President-for-Life of Mannihanni on hees show?"

"What makes me think that? First of all, you'd be a great talk-show guest. Second, Johnny does tend to put on whatever guests I ask him to whenever I'm on the show, although I must admit he usually doesn't bring them out of the Green Room till the very last segment."

Mamma Doc expelled another cloud of cigar smoke and appeared to be searching the swirl for guidance. After perhaps two minutes of silence she spoke again:

"Eef hew make heem guarantee us two segments, Meestair Lerner, hew have a deal."

114

Lance was unable to get the hostages released by sundown that day. But within forty-eight hours of making his verbal agreement with Mamma Doc, he was able to reach Kronk by radiophone at the beefalo ranch. Kronk offered the Taillevent biography to the six largest hardcover publishers in New York on a bidding basis, and a combined hardcover-softcover deal was struck for an advance of $775,000, the money to be divided equally between Lance and Mamma Doc. A cable outlining the terms of the deal arrived at the Presidential Palace just as the first of the three military C-130 cargo planes touched down on the ancient Port Pangaud landing strip.

Lance was the final person to board the last of the three cargo planes, and Mamma Doc herself accompanied him to the aircraft.

"Een the words of the accursed French, Meestair Lerner, *au revoir*," said Mamma Doc, clasping his hand.

"*Au revoir*, Madame Taillevent," said Lance, squeezing her hand in return and finding she was unwilling to relinquish his.

"Please, Meestair Lerner," she said. "Not to judge the releegious customs of theese country by hyour own. And please not to hate so much the General for what she does to hew when hew arrive. We shall puneesh her severely for thees atrocity."

"OK," said Lance, not quite sure how that was going to work.

As Lance turned towards the plane, Mamma Doc suddenly threw her arms around him and squeezed him so tightly he could scarcely breathe.

"Eef we not see hew again, hew break an old woman's heart," she whispered hoarsely into his ear, and planted a wet kiss on his lips.

The media were waiting for them in Honolulu with minicams and flowered leis. The freed hostages, when they learned that Lance had been the instrument of their deliverance, were adulatory. All three networks carried footage of Lance being hugged and kissed by scores of grateful men and women. The Royal Hawaiian Hotel insisted upon giving all the former hostages who didn't need to be confined to the military hospital at Pearl Harbor free room and board for three days on Waikiki Beach. Don Ho personally serenaded them with "Tiny Bubbles," and "Lovely Hula Hands." So many funny rum drinks with flowers in them were pressed upon Lance by grateful former hostages that he was stricken with a hangover worse than all the sickness he'd endured on Mannihanni.

After three days the media got bored and went back to hotter stories, and the former hostages began trickling home to the mainland. Lance telephoned Cathy and was surprised how clearly he could hear her voice. She must have been terribly self-conscious talking to him, though, because she went on at some length about matters that he'd ceased caring about during his incarceration in Mannihanni—about how bills he'd been unable to pay in his absence had caused his major-medical policy to lapse and his telephone and gas and electricity to be turned off, and so on. Lance supposed he would begin to care about such things again once he returned to a phoneless and gasless and electricityless apartment, but for now he was more concerned about what Cathy *wasn't* saying than what she was. She had avoided any talk of their relationship, except to say that her separation papers had come in the mail and that she had torn them up.

He supposed that meant she wanted to come back to him. He *wanted* her to come back to him, but he worried that the woman he'd loved for so many years had changed so much he wouldn't respond to her in the same way anymore.

He had so many wonderful moments with Cathy mounted in his mental album. Like the time he'd said "Ready when *you* are, CB," and she'd thought that CB stood for Cute Bunny. Like the time her robe fell open and she caught a glimpse of her sensational body in the mirror and gasped with surprised delight. Like the dinner party where she led him to discover she was wearing the garter belt and stockings he'd previously been unable to convince her to wear.

Lance fervently prayed that Cathy hadn't changed too much.

The flight in the cargo plane from Port Pangaud to Honolulu hadn't bothered Lance at all, but when his commercial jet took off from Honolulu, Lance began to get the shakes. At first he thought it was an enduring symptom of the hangover, but then he realized it was a recurrence of his old fear of flying. When the plane landed at Los Angeles to refuel, Lance got off, took a cab to the railroad station and bought a Pullman ticket to New York.

He'd expected the four-day train ride to be boring, but it wasn't. He reviewed more happy moments with Cathy in his mental album. He watched the often spectacular scenery roll by. He loved the sound of the wheels on the rails. He imagined he was Cary Grant in *North by Northwest,* then realized that what he'd endured in Mannihanni was no less harrowing than what Cary Grant had gone through on Mt. Rushmore. The train pulled into Grand Central Station slightly before four a.m. He walked outside and marveled at the city he'd accepted with little more than irritation for so many years. He took a cab to his apartment and gave the amazed driver a tip larger than the fare.

115

Cathy's life had taken a gratifying turn. She'd sold three chapters of her novel and an outline of the rest to Claire for fifty thousand and an unprecedented sixty-forty split on the softcover rights.

Dr. Freundlich was very impressed when Cathy told him the news in their weekly session, and even more impressed when she announced she was quitting her unfulfilling job at the *Book Review*. But when she told him her other news—that she was pregnant—he waited noncommittally till she indicated how she viewed this development herself.

How Cathy viewed her pregnancy was with great perplexity. Part of her confusion was that for the first time in her life she thought she didn't want an abortion, that she might be ready for motherhood, but she was not interested in raising the child by herself and she already knew the depth of Lance's own anxieties regarding children. The idea of raising a child with Lance appealed to her, but she doubted that he'd go for it, even under the best of circumstances. Under the best of circumstances she would have been clear whether the baby was fathered by Lance and not by Howard.

Well, the only thing to do was to try the idea out on Lance and see how he reacted. And at dinner at Lutece, with all that great expensive French food and after a couple bottles of French champagne, would be an ideal time to spring it on him.

116

Lance got to the restaurant promptly at eight. Cathy was already seated, having arrived early. An unopened bottle of Dom Perignon was in an ice bucket at her side. Each of them was so preoccupied with conflicting feelings of longing, dread, remorse, resentment, love, and terror at the meeting that at first they didn't even recognize each other. Then they did and embraced shyly and awkwardly.

Lance thought Cathy looked very beautiful and very elegant in her new blue blazer and tan slacks, but oddly strained and unfamiliar. My God, he thought, we were once so close we could complete each other's thoughts and never needed to speak in whole sentences. Now here we are, virtual strangers who don't recognize each other in a restaurant and who embrace like polite acquaintances. One of the great hazards of growth, he thought, is that you risk leaving someone you love behind. They had both grown enormously since their separation, but perhaps not on parallel paths. He'd been fairly sure before that they could still make it as a couple. Now he didn't know.

"Hello," he said, extending his hand. "My name is Lance."

"Glad to meet you," she said. "My name is Cathy. I've heard a lot about you."

"All of it good, I trust?"

"Not really," she said, but she was smiling.

They finished off the first bottle of champagne in just under ten minutes. The alcohol helped unfreeze some of their words.

Lance told Cathy about the ordeal in Mannihanni. She seemed very sympathetic. Cathy told Lance about her novel. He was delighted for her. It was beginning to flow now. They were beginning to remember who each other was.

They were well into their second bottle of champagne when Cathy said she had more news. Lance looked at her expectantly, a smile on his face.

"I'm pregnant," she said.

The smile took on a slightly glazed patina.

"Well," said Lance, "I don't suppose that's as big a problem as it might appear to be."

"I'm not entirely sure whether it's yours or Howard's," she said.

The smile crumbled and fell to the table.

"I'll pay for the abortion," said Lance, "no matter *whose* kid it is."

"I don't think you understand," said Cathy, beginning to cry. "I'm thinking of *having* this child. And even if I wasn't, I certainly don't need *you* to pay for my abortion. I have more than enough money to do *that* now. But I don't want to *have* another abortion —I don't think I could face it. And I resent the callous and dismissive answer you gave me—'I'll pay for the abortion.' What a fast sexist response that was. I really thought you were past that kind of reaction by now."

The captain approached, smiling, bearing menus. He heard the tone of Cathy's voice and swiftly withdrew.

"Look," said Lance, "I won't deny that I or any other man is sexist or that we have treated women in a less than wonderful manner. I myself happen to have recently gotten in touch with my own bewilderment and anger at women, which I didn't even know I had. But just springing this on me now without warning, is, well . . ."

"Yes . . . ?"

"Well, *you* know my feelings about kids, Cathy, my fears of producing abnormal children and about the responsibility of bringing somebody into the world that I'm going to have to . . . It's like opening up Pandora's box, for God's sake."

"So? Go ahead and open it. What do you think you'll find in there?"

Lance considered this. He had, as a matter of fact, been forced to deal with a lot of these kinds of thoughts when he was a prisoner in Mannihanni, and they hadn't done him in then. There was no reason why they should now. He drank off his glass of champagne, poured himself another, and opened up Pandora's box.

He took a long hard look inside, expecting horrible slimy things to slither out, the terror of the unimagined, the gaping black maw of the unconfronted, but to his extreme surprise the horrible things had left. They'd already been imagined, confronted and flushed in the expurgations of feeling resulting from Gladys's short-lived pregnancy and from the deep soul-searching that had been forced on him in Mannihanni by torture from the General, threats of castration from Mamma Doc, the prospect of his own death by beheading in the Monte ceremony, and from the ghastly realization that he'd been eating human flesh. No, there was nothing much left in Pandora's box but a few rather tired and pedestrian worries, the kind that most people have every day. And if having sex with women and conceiving kids and committing yourself to a relationship put you on a conveyor belt that ended in death, then it was also true that *not* doing all those things still put you on the same conveyor belt.

"You know what?" said Lance. "I'm not as scared as I thought I'd be."

Since the frightening negative thoughts were under control, he was now free to consider the positive ones—as he had when Gladys had admitted she'd miscarried. And the notion of a junior version of himself, of whatever sex, growing in the womb of his wife, was rather appealing to him—assuming it *was* a junior version of himself and not of Howard Leventhal.

"You're serious?" said Cathy, amazed. "You're really not scared?"

"No. Not if it's really *my* kid."

"I don't really think it's Howard's," she said. "I think it happened that night you took me to dinner on my birthday, because I wasn't using anything that night or the next morning either, and Howard always uses condoms—those silly multi-colored ones with the big—"

"I'm not interested in Howard's taste in prophylactic fashion," said Lance cutting her short. "But if you believe the kid is really mine, I think I'd like to help you bring it up."

Cathy looked at him in astonishment.

"Are you seriously saying you want this child?" she said, her eyes once more filling with tears.

"Yes," said Lance, his own eyes beginning to moisten.

They stood up and embraced across the table. The captain, who had hoped the lowering of voices indicated it was safe to return with menus, once more withdrew.

"You know what?" said Cathy.

"What?"

"I love you."

It was going to be all right.

117

"You're pregnant, Mrs. Oliphant."

"*Miss* Oliphant," said Gladys.

The doctor raised his eyebrows.

"Oh, it's all right," she said, "it's a wanted child. My boyfriend and I have been trying to have this child for months. He'll be so glad to hear we finally managed to do it."

She had apparently conceived again the night Lance took her to Elaine's. To prevent the embarrassment of another false alarm, she wouldn't tell him this time till just before the baby was due.

"Your *boyfriend*," said the doctor uneasily, "must be a very unusual person."

"Oh, he sure is," said Gladys. "He's a famous author. You've probably heard of him. His name is Lance Lerner."

"The author of *Gallivanting*?" said the doctor.

"That's the one," said Gladys.

Epilogue

"Excuse me," said the tall young black man in the three-piece blue suit, the white shirt open at the neck, and the loosened rep tie. "Attention . . . May I have your attention, please? . . . Hello? Hi. I know it's a little crowded in here, but I'd like to beg your indulgence for just a few moments here, if I might.

"As most of you know, we are celebrating tonight the fiftieth birthday of our good friend, Lance Lerner. I didn't get a chance to meet all of you yet, but, as most of you know, my name is Ernie Roosevelt, and Lance and I go back a long way. I hope your champagne glasses are full, because I would like to propose a toast. To Lance Lerner—my mentor, my friend, the godfather of my son, the man who is responsible for my marriage, my literary career, my new career in politics and, well, just about everything else in my life, including my life itself. May the second fifty, Lance, be as wonderful and as productive and as inspiring as the last. *L'chayim!*"

The more than two hundred guests jammed into Lance's living room raised their glasses in salute and drank.

Lance nodded and smiled back at them and felt his eyes fill up. Time was accelerating now at a rate he found alarming. When he was a little boy each day had seemed interminable, each weekend a holiday to be celebrated, the return of winter unimaginable. He remembered late afternoons in summer, with the distant cry of swallows and grackles, afternoons which seemed as though they would go right on until the middle of the night. He recalled long Sunday afternoons in winter with the light coming into his parents' apartment at an angle that now filled him with inexplicable sadness. As a child nothing passed fast enough to suit him. Time was something to be slogged through with difficulty and great resistance, like trying to run through waist-deep water. He had thought he would never get out of grammar school. High school seemed exotic and grownup and highly unlikely.

But then it began to go a little faster. Grammar school *did* end, high school was more than likely, and then, wonder of wonders, he was even a college man. Time was speeding up. Like a rocket at Cape Canaveral, starting out so slowly you felt it was never going to even clear the launching pad, but then beginning to move a little faster, faster, faster yet, until it shot into the sky and disappeared.

His life had started speeding up in the same manner. Years which had previously contained as many as twenty-two months each when he was a kid contained scarcely more than eight by the time he was forty, while the years nowadays contained no more than five months each. There was barely enough time to dig your summer clothes out of the closet before it was time to put them away again. He watched his hair turn gray, the skin beneath his eyes and chin go slack and wrinkled, even saw his slim and always-firm buttocks begin to droop a bit. How many years did he have left? Thirty? Twenty-five? He had spent his thirties and forties trying to preserve the status quo, only to find that there had never *been* a status quo, that things had always been in flux and the illusion of stability in his life had been precisely that—an illusion. It had been a hard, exciting football game, and now he was in the third period and to his consternation found that the clock had been kept running even during time-outs, even at half-time.

Could it really have been ten years since he had been caught bare-assed at the surprise party Cathy had thrown for him, since he had tried so hard to get her back and stumbled into affairs with Stevie and Claire and Dorothy and Janie and Gladys and all the rest? Could it really have been ten years since his plane was hijacked and he'd nearly lost his life in Mannihanni? Ten years ago he had been consumed with the question of what it was that women wanted. He had ultimately concluded that women wanted what they'd *said* they wanted—romance, excitement, security, sovereignty, acknowledgment, unconditional love, money, a good fuck—everything, in short, that men wanted too.

God, it was overwhelming, all that had happened to him and to all whom he had known in the past ten years. *Gallivanting*, of course, had been at the top of the bestseller lists for over a year, and the movie they'd made of it had done surprisingly well before it began appearing on late-night TV. The book he had written about his experience in Mannihanni, *I Remember Mamma Doc*, had replaced *Gallivanting* on the lists, and the movie of that had been not much of a hit, but then they'd made it into a TV sitcom and that was still in syndication.

His marriage to Cathy had resumed after his return to New York and for the most part was better than it had ever been before. He supposed part of it was that Cathy now had an identity beyond that of Mrs. Lance Lerner. Her writing had matured. Novels had not proven to be her ideal form of expression—trenchant literary criticism had. Cathy, writing under her maiden name, had become one of the most trenchant of literary critics in New York and had a column that was nationally syndicated.

Several months after Lance returned from Mannihanni, he and Cathy had a baby. A boy. They named him Michael. And despite all of Lance's fears, the baby was completely normal. And beautiful. And Lance loved him very much, and felt that the energy which had begun ever so slightly to drain out of him now had a place to be collected. Michael was eight years old. One of his closest companions was named Lanny. Lanny was the love child, as his mother described it, of America's favorite new romantic novelist, Gladys Oliphant, and a mysterious stranger. Although Lanny was quite a bit plumper than Michael, people marveled at how alike they looked. Almost like brothers, some said.

Lanny and Michael played a lot with Ernie and Dorothy's boy, Goose. Ernie had had to adapt his written experiences with the Dalton Two to include the incarceration in Mannihanni, but the book was an even bigger hit than *I Remember Mamma Doc*. Ernie's attempts after that to write a novel or anything else didn't work out, but Lance had insisted that Ernie go to college and get an education, and that *did* work out. Ernie had moved himself and

Dorothy and little Goose to an apartment on the same block as
Lance's and, at Lance's urging, finally campaigned for and won a
seat in Manhattan's 18th Congressional District, the so-called Silk
Stocking District.

Ernie and Dorothy were still somewhat friendly with Janie,
although neither of them much cared for her lover Tamago, an
overbearing Japanese woman who owned a sushi bar on East
48th Street. Janie and Tamago were considering adopting an
orphan from the war in Peru.

The members of MATE were captured by Mamma Doc's
guards and given the choice of enlisting in the army or being
beheaded. They chose the former.

It was largely through Lance's influence on Mamma Doc that
Mannihanni had evolved into a modern nation—selling natural
gas to the U.S., bringing heavy industry to Port Pangaud, dis-
couraging cannabalism, and, just this year, finally giving its men
the vote. Lance sometimes wondered whether that hadn't been
Mamma's plan all along.

Claire divorced Austin shortly after their traumatic cruise with
Howard and Cathy. Austin sold Firestone Publishing to Insurance International, Incorporated, which first kicked him upstairs
and then kicked him out entirely, forbidding him to use his own
name again in business. Austin had publicly stated that he was
thrilled to be rid of the publishing business, never having understood it anyway. Austin professed not to care when I.I.I. hired
Claire as chief operating officer of Firestone Publishing.

Lance, Ernie, and all the alumni of the Mannihanni saga who'd
written books about their experience had been represented by
Julius Blatt, who gave up being a public defender to become one
of the hottest literary and show-business agents in the industry.
After a year at William Morris he was hired by Creative Artists as
a full partner, but had left only this year to become the head of
Universal Studios. He was here tonight, wearing a silk shirt open
to the navel and about a pound of gold chains around his neck.

Stevie had gotten into trouble with her superiors in the NYPD
for appropriating the helicopter for Lance's abortive kidnap of
Cathy and quit her job in a cold fury. Shortly afterwards, she
opened a place in the Village which was a combination restau-

rant, bar and karate school. It was still fairly successful and you could always find a dozen or more celebrities present in the late hours, but it wasn't quite Elaine's. Stevie had supplied all of the booze and most of the food for Lance's party tonight, but Lance thought she was less happy as a restaurateur than she'd been as a cop.

After Lance dropped him as a protégé, Les found another older mentor, had an affair with the man's wife, but was never found out.

Margaret and Cathy never renewed their friendship. Margaret got married two more times, but neither union lasted more than six months. Margaret's friends told her it was the man's fault in both cases.

Lance heard that Howard, his editor on *Gallivanting,* had become a novelist, and was tickled to learn that Howard's first effort sold fewer than a hundred copies because his editor allowed the book to go totally without advertising or promotion. Lance heard rumors that Howard had entered into a ménage-à-trois with a fifty-five-year-old woman and her husband, but hadn't believed it. Tonight Howard had shown up with a white-haired couple in their sixties who were always touching him, and Lance decided to believe the rumor.

Not far away from Lance stood his Mom and Dad, who were chatting enthusiastically with Helen. Lance's Mom had published three books of recipes and become a local celebrity in Chicago. Lance had stopped going to Helen for therapy when the baby was born, feeling he had finally graduated. And a year after that, Helen dropped the rest of her patients to become the host of an evening talk show on PBS. Helen, to her credit, had as guests on her show every member of Lance's group who'd published a novel, and often co-hosted with Jackie until he hit it big in Vegas and was no longer interested in educational TV.

Ernie drifted over to Lance and put his arm around him.

"Well," said Ernie, "how does it feel?"

"To be fifty?" said Lance. "Exactly the way it feels to be forty. At least physically. Hey, Ernie, am I imagining it or are you a little preoccupied tonight?"

Ernie looked at Lance and then sighed.

"It shows, does it?" he said.

"What is it, Ernie?"

Ernie sighed again, then steered Lance over to a less-populous corner of the room, and lowered his voice.

"I feel a trifle foolish even talking about this," said Ernie, "but I really need to verbalize it to someone."

Lance took a sip of his champagne.

"I want to preface what I'm going to say," said Ernie, "by saying that Dorothy and I have a good marriage, a really good marriage, Lance. And I don't at all begrudge her the fact that she was once, well, homoerotic. Dorothy tells me that that phase of her life is completely over, and I believe her. And yet . . . ."

"And yet?" said Lance and took another sip of his champagne.

"And yet," said Ernie, "I have lately come to the inescapable conclusion that Dorothy is having an affair with our *au pair* girl and, frankly, I feel that that state of affairs has upset the balance of our relationship. You know, Sigmund Freud, the father of psychoanalysis, put it so well when he asked, 'What do women want?' "

Ernie was now looking oddly at Lance, doubtlessly due to the fact that, while Ernie had been speaking his last sentence, Lance had choked and coughed out a spray of champagne.

"Are you all right?" said Ernie.

Lance caught his breath, wiped his mouth and nodded.

"Ernie old man," said Lance, putting his arm around his friend's shoulders, "I want you to listen very carefully to the story I am about to tell you. And I hope that you can profit from my own experience. . . ."